Testament Book 1

'Gods and Monsters'

Anthony Browndog

This is a work of fiction. Unless otherwise indicated, all the names, characters, businesses, places, events and incidents in this book are either the product of the author's imagination or used in a fictitious manner. Any resemblance to actual persons, living or dead, or actual events is purely coincidental.

Copyright © 2022 Anthony Browndog

All rights reserved.

ISBN: 9798402346697

For Jo

(Mrs Browndog)

♥

ACKNOWLEDGMENTS

Thanks to my dear friends whose names and in a few cases (positive) personality traits I may have used as reference. Any negative traits are purely coincidental and not based on reality, in this universe or any other. *Note all the usual legal wording and disclaimers.*

The real brothers of the sleeping sword are far from hopeless losers and do not smell.

Thanks also to Sally, my wonderful sister who has proof-read and corrected my poor spelling and my utterly random punctuation.

X

Chapter 1

Autonomous Accumulations

It was polite Britannic weather. It was the sort of weather that made conversation without committing itself. Neither sun nor rain, nor lack of either, intrusive enough to bother anyone too much.

A light breeze was gently rustling the trees, not cooling anyone particularly but then neither was the sun warming them uncomfortably or causing much in the way of photosynthesis in the plants and trees of the street below. Most of them, by now, had lost their leaves and for late December the weather was benign, unusual but not without precedent.

Through the laminated glass of the twenty seventh floor of Autonomous Accumulations, the weather was decidedly different. It was astounding that an entire geosphere of conflicting weather cycles, fighting each other on their perimeters and generating energy beyond anyone's comprehension at their cores, could produce such a light touch on the earth as it did in Londinium that day and yet; one man could generate such a storm in a room. It put the weather to shame.

The Chairman of Autonomous Accumulations had one of his headaches. Alongside tolerating his splitting skull, he also chaired a business that ran the country through capital ownership and influence. They ran government through the consultants they provided to desperate ministers, and the taps on the shoulder and backhanders, that slipped between the sights of the parliamentary commissions. They had a sprawling control on national monopolies and a portfolio of businesses and property that they had, over time, bought from the government in deals to provide services. Over years, the contracts went their way and the profits purchased the stone and concrete that the system of national government and governance sat within. A similar approach was taken with other national services; health, transport, crime, intelligence. They had the expertise, the resources, the ground it all stood on and they made the decisions that suited them. Their government was a patsy who sucked up to the electorate on their behalf. Not officially, of course, that would get in the way of their reputation, a reputation carefully contrived to be everywhere, but nowhere. Not lacking substance, far from it, but everyone saw Autonomous Accumulations, and no one knew what they did. As with Government services, so it was with the media. Autonomous Accumulations decided what the media thought and what the opposition media wrote, they ran the institutions that shaped the national identity like a new religion. It was an Empire, not a business and the Chairman was emperor of it all. The Chairman and his Executive were playing the odds against the odds and oddly winning. Life was short and empires only had a finite timeline, but while they were on the right side of both they were extracting as much collateral from the damage they caused and continuing to profit immensely. It was once said that the Chairman's soul was a painting in an attic made with egg tempera and exotic minerals and the rats were eating their way through it bite by bite. The rodents were being slowly poisoned and passing precious coloured stones at the same time.

Autonomous Accumulations made a profit, an enormous profit from their portfolio. They were venture capitalists mostly, operating an umbrella company that had no fear of the rain and it would take one hell of a storm to even notice the wet. Their corporation, whilst small at its head office, was a sprawling behemoth of ownership and repressed silent partnerships. All the time Autonomous Accumulations made a bigger profit, bought a little more capital and took a little more stock from the oblivious nation of shopkeepers.

The executive sat around a large obsidian desk, a block of cut and polished volcanic glass that dominated the room. It was a surface which reflected the veneered ebony and African blackwood wall panels and gave the room a sense of layered darkness. The boardroom was not an unnecessarily large room, it was big enough, but it wasn't the proportions of the room that cowered anyone entering it. Unlike a medieval cathedral that had been built to awe the faithful and intimidate those non-believers by its size and scale and opulence, this room had been built with gravity at its very centre. It was a dark star of a room, super dense matter in a small space. Your chest would tighten as you entered, it was black on black on black, reflected layers toying with the low winter light as it came in through the tinted windows and reflecting it obliquely, in a mixture of angles and shadows. It was not a dark room in itself, there was light enough, but somehow the way it absorbed and refracted photons, toyed with your mind and peripheral vision and put you at the edge of discomfort. It was a reminder that light could be both particles and waves, as it split and divided and delivered them back to the vanishing point of your senses.

A roar of rage and there it was. The temper, the storm, the explosion; the headache now more frequently experienced, that tipped the balance. The seven executives sat at the black glass desk and scenting blood, swivelled eyes and tilted necks and cocked their heads just a little.

"What the hell do you mean you stupid little girl? I don't pay you to tell me NO. Get the hell out of my building. Someone, deal with that little piece now."

'Pay' was more a turn of phrase. Martine was an intern and did not get paid at all. She was ushered out of the room by one of the middle aged, balding, grey suited ghosts that seemed to hover on the edge of every decision. In every room there were spectral figures present to facilitate the play-out of uncomfortable situations, without ever displaying any real depth of being.

It mumbled. The sounds were almost as indistinct as the being. When the door closed behind them and they were out of earshot of the boardroom it said, "Mmmm might I remind you young lady, that you signed a non-disclosure agreement and you, well, you will not get paid if any of this conversation leaves the ah... building. You signed the contract, its enforceable by law. Incidentally, we mostly own the law at a corporate level. Well, we influence it significantly, don't we?" It was a rhetorical question.

"You don't pay me," Martine replied, slowly collecting her thoughts.

"It doesn't matter; the agreement allows for that contractual exception. Paragraph 87. Collect your belongings and leave now. We do not need people who cannot give us the answers we want."

"The answers you want, what about facts?" Martine, now that shock was becoming anger, spat out.

"Hmm…" the grey thing said. "It's not within my remit to comment on that. Were you still employed we could escalate the issues you raise. However, well… currently you are exiting the organisation. We are releasing you so we shall not be wasting our resources any further on this conversation. Thank you for your service and ahem, goodbye"

And that was it.

Martine collected her things, a handbag which would be searched by security as she was escorted out of the office and again as she exited the building. Also a light coat and her comfortable shoes that she did not now have time to change into, though she desperately wanted to. The cramped heels that she had been advised to wear when speaking to the Chairman were pinching her feet and she could feel a blister forming between her third and fourth toe.

The anger was growing but she could see no release for it. The lumpy grey shadow walking next to her, far too close to her, was just an empty grey suit and it would be like screaming into a void shouting at it. Not him. Grey, neither black nor white not even damn blue! She had never even seen a blue suit in the offices. The executives were dressed in black, the drones in pale grey. Layers of management in between were shaded light to dark depending on a complex and undocumented set of social conventions that developed over time and between roles. It was a hierarchy that was not contractual nor discussed nor designated, it just happened to be that way. It was remarkable to think that an organisation so powerful, so influential, so despicable and divisive could be portrayed in a colour palette so restricted. Even the glass of the building was tinted so the sky looked almost permanently grey. The clouds were off white and the sun, when it shone through the windows, was dulled by the architecture of Autonomous Accumulations.

Martine could not believe it. She had been doing some work recently for the Chairman, some paperwork on personal files, some of his business interests that he didn't want discussed in an open office and she had been the only member of the executive finance team with the right skills. As she was familiar to him and everyone else was terrified of him, she had been asked to go and deliver his tea to the executive floor. She had not been able to find his favourite tea and had used her judgement instead.

The storm in the room was about a teacup. The irony would hit Martine later but not now. As she left, the glass doors closing behind her, she looked back at the building and bit her lip and swore she would get revenge. She had picked up a few old dry bones in her few months in the company of monsters, in the personal files of the Chairman, and revolutions started with small seeds of descent.

The grey creatures fell back into their routines on the twenty seventh floor, shuffling people around like papers would have been shuffled before the paperless office. Shuffling peoples hollowed out souls around, in what was now a soulless office.

Back in the boardroom the drama of the tea subsided, coincidently as the pulsing headache faded and conversation returned to a more mundane discussion about the imminent possibility of a terrorist attack threatening their commercial interests.

"The threat that has been identified, we should alert the government sir." Number Four commented, smiling at the prospect. Number Four enjoyed the excitement of impending disaster, it was his hunter instinct, he thought. The moment when the elephant is in your sights and it smells you on the breeze and it slowly turns and you know it's going to charge, you can see it in its eyes and feel it in the air. Time slows down and you are standing there, locked in the moment, gun to tusk and squeezing gently at first, feeling the bite of the trigger engage. It cannot be too soon, because without the fear of your imminent death impaled on long ivory teeth, there was no fun in the hunt. The thought ran briefly through his mind. He didn't even know if that was how you hunted an elephant, but there the elephant was, on the table and everyone else was ignoring it and his mind had wandered. It had been a long day and it wasn't yet over.

"It doesn't matter," the Chairman replied. "I have seen the report and it makes no commercial sense to interfere. The police will find out and involve themselves, let them because the money flows back to us anyway. The bridge needs upgrading to increase traffic throughput and frankly, the heritage organisations will be all over it like rats on a rotting old hag. If it's damaged, we'll bring our plans forward to upgrade it, in fact," he smiled as he thought of an angle so beautiful and so obtuse, it was almost acute. "If people are killed in the process, it would be quite convenient all round? We need that bunch of road warrior idiots to lose some public support. Get someone in to design a plaque, we'll stick a plaque on the new bridge commemorating the lives so tragically lost in the terror attack."

"How many lost lives shall we put on it?" Number Five smirked. He was the newest to the table and had only been promoted recently. He was gift to the organisation; good school, good family, bad egg. He had the full educational benefits of one of the biggest bank accounts in the country. He had been excused from both his school and his family for immoral behaviour that was so undiscussed publicly, it was a legend, although no one really knew was it was he had done. It undoubtably involved sex and drugs and money and guns. The former was part and parcel of the best upper class education money could buy, the latter two home life. Papa had interests in both and over a number of generations had become one of the most successful military resource supply chain magnates in the world and the family's wealth was measured equally in lucre and firepower. Number Five had been employed initially as a junior sales executive and had increased sales as much by weakening opposition as by positive and proactive selling, the results though were undeniably successful. He was still young enough to be keen, but also, thought the Chairman, a caged animal and as likely to bite the head off his master. Always give him someone else to bite he thought, keep that one well fed.

"You'd better not guess the number of casualties but do some market research and get a good design ready for the mourners. If there are no dead, we'll at least have it ready for the next accident," the Chairman answered. "That's the beauty of owning the roads, there are always accidents to create drama and where there is drama there is publicity and where there is publicity the money follows, manage it well."

"Sir." Number Fives quick volunteering upset Number Four and it was evident in his eyes, though he smiled. The rest of the directors watched the power play as it burnt bright for a moment, then fizzled out.

"Now" the Chairman rose from his desk and wandered to the window and looked at the sky as it continued to do nothing much. He glanced down at the insects below, then he looked out at the five-lane road disappearing into the distance. He turned back and smiled, "Is there anything else or are we done?"

The rhetorical question was answered with nods and the Chairman stood and took a step towards the door.

*

Martine started to cry as she walked down the road, the realisation hitting her, that the corporation that she thought she could trust had abused her dreadfully. The relationship over the ten months and three days she had worked there had been controlling, coercive and abusive. She had been manipulated, she saw that now and couldn't understand why she was blind to it previously. She had wanted a job, so she loved the organisation because it gave her one. She was proud to be part of what was the most influential corporation in the country. By its own promotion Automated Accumulations was the country and yet the job was unpaid. It was an offer for the future, a possibility, potential. She had been described as potential by her professor, 'Potential leader of the future, an ambitious young lady who is driven by hard work and strong principals of fairness and equality, who will succeed in everything she does because she refuses to tolerate any other alternative.' She had worked hard, she had a first in political science, accountancy and economics, which had cost her four years of her life. When she was not studying, she was working; to pay to learn, to live and to eat. No, on reflection it was not living. She barely lived, she just survived for those four years because she was too busy. She grabbed meals in the moments between lectures, study and work. Work; cleaning work, shop work, bar work. Martine had appeared as an extra in three films after seeing an advert and applying out of curiosity. After the first film she found out that it was good money for a lot of sitting around, where she could read and complete her coursework. She had appeared as a waitress in a seedy bar (as she had in her real life), as a dead body (as she so frequently felt in her real life) and once as a scientist who was evaporated by a shape changing lizard with laser breath, in a children's television program, (which was how she felt now). How life so often imitates art.

At so many points she was juggling the three jobs, negotiating shifts and desperately completing her coursework to get to where she was now. Or where she was yesterday, she felt she was nowhere now and she couldn't see tomorrow. It was like the end of a love affair and suddenly she could see it as it was, a toxic relationship. She had been groomed, used and discarded by a corporation that had five pages of documentation about how it valued equality, fairness and diversity. Autonomous Accumulations had procedures for everything and could be audited to show that every member of the organisation had signed their acceptance. They could demonstrate that everyone knew how to behave to each other and yet between the lines of those words, there was a lot of empty space. When you read the process, the procedures, the documentation which were the DNA of the corporation's outward appearance; it was lycanthropic and could change. It could change into the vulpine NDA that was also signed annually to say that, well... you were in the jaws of a wolf in sheep's clothing. A slathering wolf, in a very expensive woollen coat.

Martine had been recommended for the job by her university lecturer. Each year the corporation took the brightest and the best from a handful of universities as graduate intakes. It worked well as a principal, desperately bright and financially desperate young people, who were ambitious and who had barely seen the world, were recruited. Young people who still had endless energy and capacity to give, who could be flattered, manipulated and like Zimbardo's classic prison experiment, could be filtered and trained to rule the pack. Many would not become leaders, some would fall along the wayside, but mostly it was a good opportunity to add some extra canine teeth to the packs ravenous appetite and sharpen all of those teeth in the process. Even the less aggressive could be relied upon as future critical mass. Martine was not a wolf, she was bright, the brightest in her class. She was ambitious, she wanted to be successful and to be loved, she knew that as well but she was mostly just nice. Not incorruptible, no one was, but certainly the organisation could not easily turn her into what they wanted. She would chide people for their snide comments, find more reasonable ways to complete work, comment on the ridiculousness of legacy tasks. She was bipartisan in her dealings with her colleagues, she thought competition was just that; a fun way to succeed. She saw the value in success but did not agree it should be measured solely in profit and loss, she suggested improvements and smiled all the time. Her work was completed diligently and frequently before everyone else. She did not take coffee breaks, she did not come to work with hangovers, she frequently started early, stayed late and asked for more things to do. Martine defended her colleagues when they failed to deliver and helped them when they struggled. She was so utterly reasonable and indefensibly nice that she was despised and distrusted by everyone she worked with. Which was one of the reasons that she was fed to the Chairman when the tea that had run out and had not been replaced, was demanded. She was fed like a sacrificial lamb to the twenty-seventh floor.

As Martine slowly walked down the road, she thought deeply as the tears flowed. Partly it was having to tell her parents she had been dismissed and she would worry about how they would feel, but equally the world suddenly looked a far bigger and far more threatening place, she wanted a hug. A simple thing, a hug. Apart from her parents who lived in a small village one hundred and eighty-three miles away in the west of Albion, there was no one she knew who could do that and she felt very lonely. Now, without work or purpose she realised she did not even have any friends she could speak to and the tears flowed and flowed and in the process, smudged her makeup. She knew that and she knew her hair had reacted to events by throwing itself into a state of chaos. Her blister was screaming blue murder at her from her shoes and she didn't care, she just walked.

It was thirty-eight minutes into her walk when Martines life took its second big sidestep of the day. A blue saloon car with a dent already in its offside wing turned left into Presbyterian Close. The driver was not concentrating on the road, as he was momentarily distracted by an advertisement promising a cure for male disfunction with a picture of a large chested nurse bending over a hospital bed with a rather suggestively sized thermometer. It was unclear if this was the cure or motivation for a cure, but Julek "Jude" Drazkowski's mind was elsewhere. At twenty-six years old, it was likely that elsewhere was the nurse and equally likely he was in no need of being cured. He drove into the dark-haired girl who already looked like she had been in an accident. Her eye makeup was streaming down her face, her hair was in a mess and she was also not concentrating on where she was going. She crossed the road without looking or stopping. Jude braked instinctively and he felt, rather than heard the collision. He didn't brake however, before she had looked up and stared briefly into his face, frozen; then on impact with the front of the car, folded in slow motion over the bonnet, banging the side of her head hard and leaving a remarkably realistic impression of shock in the metal. She left a black streak of eyeliner and some tears on the blue paintwork before rolling off, rather inelegantly twisting and hitting the other side of her face on the ground. Jude jumped out of the car convinced he had killed her and he was only assured further that he had, when he reached the front of the car and saw her lying on her side, crumpled and to his mind, bent in an unnatural shape. Her face was streaked with black and tears and as he looked closer, her head lolled over to the right and he looked in horror at the mess of blood and grit and face. Jude looked around for help, there was no one, Presbyterian close kept itself to itself, except where that advertisement was concerned. The residents had a standing complaint to the local councillor on the positioning of the sign. The complaint was made quite reasonably, after three car crashes and two collisions involving bicycles in the four months that it had been put up. A broader observation was that the nurse seemed to be in the wrong job, it would appear that there was less male disfunction on the corner of Presbyterian Close and a far greater need for accident and emergency.

Jude knelt down next to her and did the only thing he could think of, he took her hand. She squeezed and he realised she was not dead, though his first thought that this was some sort of automatic muscle response or rigor mortis. It wasn't and she opened her eyes and reached out with her other arm which was luckily not broken or twisted unnaturally and he reached back and they hugged each other, Jude mainly in relief that he was not a murderer and Martine, because she just wanted a hug. A car accident was a small price to pay for real human connection at this time and they both cried into each other's shoulders, for completely different reasons and for about five minutes.

Martine was the first to say something. "Thank you."

Jude was thrown, totally thrown and confused! "I am sorry!?" It could have been a question or a statement

'No really, thank you, I needed that so much."

"To be run over?"

"A hug."

"But I killed you? I mean I thought I killed you."

"I didn't die."

He noticed her breath on his neck, "But you should of?"

"I think that is known as adding insult to injury and I think it is should *have*, not should *of*"

"I am so sorry."

"For the crash?"

"For the insult and my grammar." He looked at her, adding as a very misjudged afterthought "You look a mess." After an awkward silence he added "Oops no, I didn't mean that, I meant the crash, everything. I am sorry about everything and your face, it's hurt."

When she heard that, Martine started to feel her face again and it did hurt. It was sore and throbbing and her head ached and her arm felt weak and she saw her knuckles were grazed. She thought she actually liked the confused young man who tried to kill her but she suddenly felt faint. Under the blood and grit and tears and mascara and the immense weight of the world which was slowly coming back to her; along with pain in every part of her body, she turned very pale and whispered, "I feel sick... dizzy… I need to lie down." Jude gently put his arm around her and took her weight. As all her strength left her, he helped her into the blue saloon car with the dent in the offside wing and the imprint of shock on the bonnet. Still shaking but fighting the shakes as hard as he could, by breathing deeply and not blinking and focussing his mind on where he was going and humming Gloria Gaynor's 'I Will Survive', followed by the Bee Gee's 'Staying Alive' and to the most awkward disco themed mercy mission ever contrived, he drove her to the local hospital.

Chapter 2

Christopher Sunday

Christopher Sunday first woke up in Sir Peregrine Matthews Hospital on the fourth of April, he was then immediately sedated.

This was a reasonable precaution considering the facts, he had been in a vegetative state for the first eight years of his incarceration.

Christopher was an anomaly for so many reasons. He had been brought to St Matthews hospital and treated under what was then the National Health Service.

He had been admitted with severe head injuries and estimated to be around twelve years old. No one had seen the accident, no one had witnessed it or claimed him and no one cared. Well, that was not strictly true. Lots of people did care when the young boy had been discovered in a street in Londinium, injured so badly that it was inevitable he would die. When expert hospital consultants made a statement to say that he was being put on a ventilator only to allow his family to come forward and say goodbye, there was an outpouring of public grief and condemnation by every keyboard consultant in the country. They demanded his living corpse should be preserved and maintained, the sanctity of life, for gods' sake. The fact that there was no measurable brain activity did not mean he was dead. There was a precedent for this internet diagnosis of sentience without any noticeable brain activity. It was every keyboard consultant in the country, demanding his corpse should be preserved.

It was painful for everyone to accept that, in this case, the voice of the internet had been right.

Christopher's family never did come forward and so the internet did again. Lawyers appointed by the charitable trust set up by strangers desperate to preserve this mysterious life from nowhere, earned and spent significant money managing the waterfall of donations that came pouring in to stop Christopher fulfilling his potential as worm food. It frustrated the hospital management who were stuck with this anomaly, neither alive nor dead. That was modern life and the funding softened the blow somewhat.

During 'the grand plan', St Matthews Hospital was changed from a trust to a business and it was renamed Sir Peregrine Matthews Hospital, after the business consultant who had identified the benefits of running healthcare for profit. He had also developed the Healthcare Lottery as a promotional opportunity and a way of generating additional income and adding some life-death excitement into the process. 'Everyone's a winner,'' he had said and somebody always was. For every death and recovery, for every child born or limb lost; a complex set of scores, multipliers and formulas were created for every healthcare provider in Britannia. These had primarily been to measure the hospitals against each other and relative to a standard set of agreed metrics. They would then use this scoreboard to track performance and profit and to ensure that the margins squeezed out of lives could be appended with pound signs.

Peregrine Matthews, subsequently Baron Matthews of Cock-le-Mouthe, squeezed out extra income, by awarding prizes based on predictions and it allowed everyone the opportunity to dice with death from the comfort of their sofa and win a fortune as well. It was a masterstroke which had made stars of the Doctors and created a tiered medical care system. This was ok, because it was easily justifiable to tell failing healthcare professionals that they were responsible for the income of their hospitals and government and its advisors could focus on policy and not politics.

Christopher, anomalous to the end did not stay in his vegetative state. What was announced publicly was that he was in a coma for eighteen years. What was observed by the hospital was no less than a miracle. His brain was thought to have been damaged in an accident from a fall from a building nearby, but it would have had to have been at a velocity that confused the police. He would have had to have been thrown downward, to have hit the ground at the speed necessary to inflict his injuries. His fatally injured brain seemed to re-assemble itself. It was almost as though the majority of it liquified and over a period of years, reconstructed itself around a small undamaged core. That was how it was explained in simple terms, but the activity tracked by monitors, medical consultants, universities, cryptozoologists, pseudoscientists, mediums and out and out fruitcakes was explained in words, numbers, exasperation, feelings of otherworldliness, and a knowing wink. Perhaps it was the government (or at least Autonomous Accumulations) that had lost him from a laboratory. It was an example of neuroplasticity that had never before been witnessed.

Christopher Sunday captivated everyone; he was a star and no one could switch him off because of it. No one knew what his real name was and as he had been found on a Sunday, a religious day, he had been named by the hospital pastor. It fitted then and it fitted now.

What was even more remarkable, was whilst initially his muscles wasted and his body did not develop from that of a twelve-year-old, after six years on a ventilator being pumped full of liquid nutrients via intravenous and nasogastric tubes, his body started to produce body hair and increased musculature and he continued to develop from boy to a man.

Fascinated by this process, Doctors ensured that physiotherapists were assigned to exercise him daily. They would move his arms and his legs, twisting and moving him in his bed and stimulating his muscles with mild electrolysis. His body responded both to the movement and to an increase in carefully calibrated nourishment that he was provided via tubes and injections. Christopher Sunday's body thrived though his mind was somewhere else, ebbing and flowing it seemed like a tide of electronic pulses and bursts of colour on the screens. He was checked and monitored and tracked with MRI, fMRI, ARI, MEG and EEG and a number of other abbreviated bits of electronic magic, which might just as well be spells and incantations. None of the machines did anything constructive but watched, counted and measured as Christopher Sunday slowly came back to life. His hair was kept trimmed to shoulder length and he was allowed a short beard, which it was felt was easier to maintain.

After twelve years in a coma, his neuroimaging results started showing bizarre signals. What initially looked like random electrical signals flashing backwards, forwards and throughout his brain, started to form what appeared to be a complex pattern. The Doctors could not understand it.

It was a junior IT technician who happened to be updating software on the computer workstation next to where two senior Doctors were discussing their recent observations, that suggested it looked like a cold reboot to him and that Christopher was defragging himself.

The junior IT technician was immediately put on a disciplinary for making inappropriate comments about a valued patient.

*

Ernesto Golding, Consultant Neurologist was talking on the telephone, "I know, we will allow him to wake up on the morning of the twenty-fifth, I know what I have promised you." It would be in time for the Christmas Jackpot, where the healthcare lottery would provide the annual 'biggie', the prize between Christmas and New Year on the twenty-seventh and also in time to feed into the end of year statistics, which would be collated and presented to the public on the first of January. Whilst Christopher's contrived arrival would not significantly influence the lottery results; Golding was more than aware that a triple rollover, the end of year special, a surprise recovery and a storming last quarter would amount to quite a show from the hospital. It would be a publicity coup for *Sir Peregrine's*, when their most famous patient would miraculously come back to life on Christmas Day. There would be signs of life before that of course and a *"will he or won't he"* moment of national anxiety to generate some tension, but when Christopher Sunday came back to life, there would be fun, excitement and it would also add lifesaving drama to the hospitals end of year score. On January the first the Sir Peregrine Matthews Hospital would be in the headlines yet again and at the top of the headlines, because of his star quality; Ernesto Golding, Consultant Neurologist, who was also thinking about his performance bonus. He could remember a time when Doctors pay was just very good. Now Doctors at the peak of their career could compete with footballers and rock stars, not just for remuneration, but for girlfriends and fast cars and gossip and scandal and glamour and the front pages of newspapers and fame. He smiled and looked at his fingernails, I should get them polished he thought, they are looking dull and that will not photograph well. It's all about the detail, that's what the camera picks up.

*

Number Five pressed the button on his desk, disconnecting the call at the other end of the line and pressed another button, which made a trill ringing noise as it rang through to its recipient. "All organised sir, there will be a Christmas miracle. I am making some more calls but I think we can create a nativity scene that the media will enjoy. Who do you want to cover it?"

"Everyone," came the reply. "Everyone. The good, the bad and the ugly. Just get the drama out of the way quickly, the business needs that and then I can make Christopher Sunday an offer he cannot refuse." The voice at the other end of the phone had a very specific motivation. He really needed Christopher Sunday.

*

Two hundred yards down the long corridor, off to the left after the vending machine but before the sign to the toilets, the waiting room for the accident and emergency department was almost empty. Except for Jude, who looked sullen and worried.

Martine had been seen quite quickly but the bruising to her head and face was already showing. Her right eye was bloodshot and though she had recovered a little from her faintness in the car, she had been sick in the hospital carpark. Jude was concerned.

It wasn't necessary to worry. Behind the door a nurse had cleaned up the gravel from her cheek, washing out the grit and the dirt with saline solution squirted from a bag and lightly scrubbed with successive sterile pads. Martine clenched her teeth in pain and sobbed quietly to herself. It hurt. She had a clean pad taped to her face to protect the grazed skin, but it was not badly injured. Her hands had also been cleaned and examined along with the bump on her head. It was sore and painful, messy looking but not serious. The Nurse was just shining a light in her eyes as she told her that she was lucky that her injuries were *painful but superficial*. "Take some over the counter painkillers and do not go to work for a few days." *Ha!* thought Martine.

Back outside Jude was reorganising his wallet. He had taken everything out twice and was trying different combinations of cards in the pockets, considering what would be optimum efficiency. Probably, optimum efficiency would not include an old healthcare lottery ticket and a shop receipt for cat food, however, he ordered the cards alphabetically, by purpose, by colour and when the door opened and Martine walked out, he jumped up excitedly and threw the whole lot inefficiently on the floor. It took him a moment to collect them back up again as he half talked, half concentrated, looked embarrassed and also tried to pretend he was in control of a situation. He was so ridiculously out of control of a situation that was so ridiculously unimportant that Martine just laughed.

"I am sorry." Again.

"What for this time?" Martine smiled at him prostrate on the floor with wallet in one hand and a bunch of plastic cards, a receipt and a lottery ticket in the other. She found it painful to smile.

"I don't know." He smiled back sheepishly.

"For requiring me to have reconstructive surgery on my face?" Straitlaced and looking him right in the eyes.

"Oh my god, I am sorry" Jude replied dropping all of his cards and the old lottery ticket again. He managed to hold onto the cat food receipt.

Martine laughed uncomfortably and told him he was an idiot and she pointed to his cards on the floor and suggested he "Pick them up, and by the way, I am fine; it's just grazes and bumps and nothing serious. I'll be ok in a few days, I am just a bit sore. Please could you take me home? I don't live far away." She looked at his blank face and the hand holding the receipt in the air expectantly. She plucked it from his hand and read it. "Cat food, you have a cat?"

"Of course, of course" Jude replied, a question behind and then "Yes, a cat" and he was relieved again that he was not a murderer and the nice girl who currently looked like an extra from a horror film, was not dead. "My name is Jude. By the way, I know you are called Martine, I heard you tell the nurse when we came in."

"Well, hi Jude, It's good to know the name of the worst murderer in the world"

He looked back at her confused. He was struggling to keep up with the conversation.

"You didn't murder me very well, did you?" she helped him.

"Oh! No. I didn't," realising now that she was teasing him again. "I am quite glad I didn't."

"So am I" replied Martine, smiling broadly, and adding "Ow!" as the smile stretched the grazed skin on her face. "I'll tell you where to go. By the way, I like cats."

And out they went, minus Jude's driving licence which stayed where it landed under the chair until it was picked up forty-five minutes later by the receptionist as she walked around and tidied up the chairs and magazines. The receptionist should have posted it back to DVLA, to the

address on the card itself or sent it to lost property, but she put it behind the screen on the reception counter, assuming incorrectly, that someone would be back to collect it soon.

Chapter 3

Gen. Collecting

Jude woke up promptly the following day. He had only slept for an hour because he had spent most of the night staring at the ceiling and thinking about Martine. He liked her, he liked her a lot and he could not shake the thought that he had almost killed her.

He thought she liked him and he had gone into her flat and had met flaky Kate, the neighbour from the flat above who had just been going out. He didn't know why but it made him feel more involved in Martine's life, meeting her neighbour. Why meeting a neighbour was more involved than running her over he didn't know, but he was tired, so his thoughts were muddled. Kate had looked with horror at Martine, who by that time really did look like she had walked out of a zombie film. It would have been somewhere near the end of the flick and after she had been partially disassembled by a weapon wielding lorry driver. Flaky Kate didn't know why she thought of a lorry driver, it certainly was not the rather awkward but pleasant looking young man that made her think that. *No*, she thought, the idea now having a life of its own, *the zombie killer did not resemble Jude in any way shape or form* and she promptly forgot about Martine and started thinking about zombies and lorry drivers and pottered off down the road in a world of her own fantasy. She walked about fifteen steps before stopping and turning and asking, "Oh… are you ok hun?"

"I am fine Kate. I was run over earlier"

Jude looked more awkward than ever.

"Oh bad. And good news. Can you sue?" she thought creatively.

Jude had not even considered this.

"Maybe, said Martine, I am just asking my friend Jude for advice, he is a lawyer you know. She turned and whispered to Jude; "I call her flaky Kate, it's probably obvious why.

Jude, in his head, breathed again. His lungs were still frozen and he almost choked when he tried to say "Oh," in reply.

But that was yesterday evening and it was now tomorrow morning, or today, as it would seem and he wasn't a lawyer. As he bolted down the last of his coffee and charged out of the door, slamming it shut and instantly regretting the damage he may have caused to the crumbling wood of the doorframe, he wondered what his assignment today would be.

Jude's official job description was 'Trainee Inspector, waste re-engineering, department of health sciences.'

However, his management line did not report into the minister of health but the home secretary. Whilst heavily layered behind every other possible and plausible department name, he had one of the dullest jobs in the national security services. Colloquially, he was referred to by other members of the department as a *junior gen-collector*. It was a role which, outside the department, he had to describe as vaguely as he could. "As a Civil Servant, I work with waste disposal as a junior inspector", and then, if he valued his salary and his freedom, he would then talk about something else. He was not just NDA'd up to his ears but had also had to sign the official secrets act. Jude's job, which even now he did not understand how he got, nor had worked how to *not* do it, was to collect DNA. DNA that could be validated, analysed, sequenced and be added to the government's DNA database of every citizen in Britannia. It was an ongoing secret project to collect and catalogue the DNA for the whole population of Britannia.

There were a number of reasons for this project. The primary reason had been to distract the cabinet from one of the prime ministers many indiscretions. It was an act of populism that, had he been allowed to keep talking, would have split the government's most powerful from left to right and pulled out the centre. It was nothing so salacious as an affair but public support for the POTUS in waiting, a very wealthy American industrialist who had traced his family back through eight generations to a small town in Britannia and had suggested a merger of Interests, when he was in power, of the two great Anglo-Saxon nations of the world.

"It could not just be a vote winner but a new world order." He'd suggested that a *United States of Greater Britannia*, ruled from Washingtonia and with Buckingham Palace moved brick by brick to a site opposite the Jefferson Memorial in Potomac Park, could rule the western world.

Whilst the Prime Minister of (the still just about greatish, by general consensus) Britannia thought the idea stank like his old rugger socks, it had occurred to him that his tenure was limited in time and scale and the opportunity to roll the yankee fool and become king of the world, had legs aplenty. Acknowledging this on Question Time had been a mistake. Finishing his thoughts with *'Whaam Baam thank you Ma'am'* had immediately caused the government to be sued, both by the estate of the late Pop Star, whose words had been used and who wanted to distance themselves from the politician. Also, from *Grrrlstorm*, a prominent protest and lobbying group who argued quite credibly that *whamming and baamming* women was an appalling abuse. Grrrlstorm demanded an immediate retraction and a general election. The cabinet had to take sides and as a distraction the Prime Minister brought in consultants to do a full policy review. The consultancy, a company owned by Autonomous Accumulations, the government's partners of choice, had produced a top-secret report. It demonstrated that 'knowledge being power', a DNA database of every human resource in the country could cut crime, benefit health, shape the future of the country and it also had the opportunity to generate a large number of associated business concepts that would benefit the nation to the sum of many billions. As long as nobody found out.

The report made clear, that the resources of Britannia voted for the government to make difficult and sometimes discrete decisions on their behalf. These good people would not vote for a Prime Minister who would abuse that trust and, therefore, it was logically and quite reasonably an acceptably dark project, for everyone's benefit and a mandate that was well within the law. Although the law may need 'tweaking a little.'

Everyone got behind this killer of an idea once the Prime

Minister had gone on record retracting everything and apologising to the Pop fans, who he then accused of provoking Grrrlstorm by veneration of such outdated and inappropriate lyrics, adding that there was nothing he liked more than women and Grrrlstorm particularly.

A united cabinet was back in business. The Prime minister shook off another scandal, with a resounding "Huzzaar!" and Jude somehow got a job in a sprawling national organisation that desperately needed to recruit people who would do anything and say nothing and that went through people's dustbins, collecting and cataloguing DNA.

Jude's job was slightly more structured than going through people's dustbins collecting and cataloguing DNA, but Jude was not convinced it was that much more structured.

He switched on his EWP and waited for a few moments whilst it fizzed and burped and pinged in his hand, as he walked briskly down the street. Jude watched as it threw up an error message `MEMORY ERROR t1171653 PRESS OK TO CONTINUE`, a notification that he has *347 messages to archive, did he want to do this now? NO* and it crashed. He held down the power button, counted from one to "blinkin' heck, every time" and waited for the whole process to complete again. It was as much part of his routine as ignoring breakfast.

When his EWP eventually switched on: fizz, burp, ping, OK, NO... then FINALLY!!! He clicked on the blue icon for *schedule* and noted that he had two jobs today. The first; quite close to the office, which was convenient and the second further away, but still relatively close to the waste lab. He should complete both by four o'clock and be able to get home early.

As he rounded the corner to the office; he looked at the dark grey brutalist concrete structure that was the local department of civil inspections. It said nothing on the door, it did not even have a number. There was something fascinating about the way an ugly block of concrete and mirrored glass could sit so incongruously in a residential area. People were so embarrassed and revolted by its ugliness that they turned away and avoided the monstrosity to the point where they even stopped noticing it. Jude, ever the pragmatist, was pleased that it was only a ten-minute walk from where he lived, so he overlooked the fact that it was ugly.

He walked in through the sliding glass doors.

"Morning Jude."

"Hello Jude." Dave and other Dave, the security guards.

"Badge check. We are just checking we know who is entering the building." said Dave in the clipped manner of someone who thought he should have been a soldier.

"Never know when someone might be… err… minded to steal a badge" added other Dave in the manner of someone who had been a soldier and wished he'd been a policeman.

"But you know me, you just said Hello Jude?" said Jude.

"Orders." Dave said, "Badge now please sir"

Sir!?! thought Jude. Followed immediately by *idiots*. But he said "Of course. Here you are" and he handed over his badge.

"OK, it says 'Mr Julek Drazkowski' Dave".

"Facematch?" other Dave.

"Check, Dave"

"Ok Mr Drazkowski, you can proceed to the security doors"

"Thank you" Jude added graciously, his eyes staring at the ceiling in despair.

"No worries Jude." Said other Dave. "Gotta' be sure. You know, especially as, well… you know."

Jude didn't know so he left that comment hanging in the air and walked over to the card reader. He put his card on the electronic pad, waited for the long BEEEEP, then looked into the camera, where his iris was scanned. After another short BEEP! the glass doors slid open.

He walked in through the doors and as the panels closed behind him, took the fourteen steps to his office. Every day he counted the steps. He had once done it in twelve steps and it had worried him for hours that he had grown but this was resolved the next day and he adjusted his gait to ensure it always took fourteen steps. It was a small office and only had three staff based out of it. Jude rarely saw them as their schedules infrequently crossed over and they typically covered different shifts. Jude preferred that.

He slumped down on his chair and looked at the mess of

forms on his desk, shuffled a little of it to the side and decided that he needed immediate sustenance to deal with the chaos of paperwork. He stood up, walked over to the coffee machine, clicked a few selection buttons, waited for the machine to click, whirr, steam and pour the drink into its cardboard cup. He grabbed the coffee from the plastic holder and then went to the store cupboard. There he picked up a new sterile polyethene suit, nitrile gloves and mask and went back to his desk. It still looked a mess, so he ignored it and looked at his EWP again.

'Subject1: Male, 47. Name: Gerald Edward Baker. Status: Single. No23 Presbyterian Close.'

Oh, he thought, *there again! Back to the scene of the crime* and Martine flashed through his mind again.

He read the comments section. 'Comments: NGS, NBD, NCR, NVT' (*NGS*-No Government Service, has not worked for any public server sector service, where regular drug testing ensured that DNA was well recorded, *NBD*- No Blood Donor, had never donated, *NCR*- No Crime Record. *NVT*- No Voluntary Test). In short, he had, like a surprisingly small number of people whose DNA profile now needed scraping, like chewing gum from the paving stones of their lives, by a sprawling administrative process, missed every opportunity to voluntarily give up one of the few things that was his and his alone. His DNA. By the end of the day, he would have had it taken from him and recorded for posterity, crime control, border management, or perhaps money, who knew? But, Gerald Edward Baker was complicit in the process by being part of a democracy that allowed his government to make difficult decisions on his behalf.

It was a democratic process where his vote, or rather the vote of the twenty-three percent that could be bothered to waste their time voting, had voted for a government who were mandated to make difficult and sometime secretive decisions on their citizens behalf. Ninety-seven percent of the electorate hated the government which included twenty percent that had voted for them.

Ironically, nobody voted for democracy, you had to fight for it and when the fight was won you got what you then voted for, from a shortlist of very little. In the current case, this was a rat pit of vipers, sharks, clowns and alcoholics. It was an unpleasant circus all round and a circus you voted for, because you wouldn't pay to watch it, but voting was still free. Voting was free if you could afford the bus fare to the ballot box or could be bothered. Most people fell into one category or another so twenty-three percent nailed it for the next four years.

Jude didn't believe half the politico-spin that he was told by his manager about the moral imperative to complete this vital role, but he did need to pay his rent, so he did as he was told.

He caught up with the waste disposal engineers on the corner of Presbyterian Close and thought briefly again of Martine, it was only yesterday and he was both sad and glad there was no more permanent reminder of his meeting on the ground where they had met.

Jude liked the '*Waste Recycling, Upcycling and Disposal Engineers.*' They were happy. They had fun while they worked and he didn't even mind that they made fun of him.

"Julie, ya knob'ed, still calling us disposal engineers? We're blinkin' binmen" shouted one of the crew before they all burst into song, a surprising well harmonised version of *'Hey Jude'*, by the Beatles. They sang as they danced and skipped down the road picking up bags and boxes and slinging and singing the contents into the compartments of their truck, which trundled along by the side with far more flashing lights that seemed necessary. The combination of flashing lights and dance and song was like some strange and ramshackle mobile disco, with a slight lingering after-smell.

"Which one are you inspecting today, Julie?"

"Number twenty-three," Jude replied as he walked up the road to sticker the recycling boxes and bags at number twenty-three Presbyterian Close, with barcodes spat out by his EWP.

The waste disposal engineers caught up with him, removed the bags and boxes and replaced them with new containers and Jude posted a standard note through the door. It advised Gerald Edward Baker that his *recycling boxes were being replaced as they had shown signs of excessive wear,* because, *the Waste Engineering Service wanted to ensure its customers had the most efficient means to collect and recycle their waste.* It thanked him for being a *conscientious citizen.*

That evening when he returned from work, Gerald Edward Baker, 47, saw his brand-new recycling boxes and was pleased but also rather confused. Next doors ripped bag and one wheeled bin had not been replaced. But in the grander scheme of things, Gerald Edward Baker, 47; had new bins, so all was good with the world. He went inside, took off his grey suit jacket, made himself a cup of tea and sat down to have a quiet night of loneliness and existential despair.

The collected boxes were put into a special compartment on the van where they would be delivered to a small laboratory attached to the back of Jude's concrete carbuncle. The waste disposal engineers thought that the inspections were randomised checks of bin contents for statistical purposes, which they partly were.

Jude checked his EWP for the next address, the final collection of the day, which if he could complete before half past ten, meant that he would be on schedule for an early finish.

'Subject1: Female, 28. Name: Maryam (NONAME) White. Status: (UNKNOWN). 2a High Road. Comments: Subject NGS, NBD, NCR, NVT.'

Pretty bog standard, thought Jude, *except it's probably a flat.* He hated flats, it was always a fight to identify the correct bins.

He checked the map and decided that he would be better catching the bus. He removed the polyethene suit, gloves and mask put them in his backpack and headed to the bus stop. He watched the electric double decker glide to the bus-stop. He took a moment to read the banner advert on the side of the bus. 'Automated Accumulations – Engineering a better life for everyone.'

The logo ubiquitous for the Britannia's highest profile corporation, was two black italicised letter A's on a coloured background. It occurred to Jude that he had no idea what they were advertising, it didn't say and nor was it ever obvious. Automated Accumulations was, however, a brand that wanted to remain both discrete and in everyone's consciousness and it was succeeding at both.

The bus arrived and it was a short trip to High Road. Conveniently, there was a bus stop fairly close to his destination. Jude got off the bus, pulled his protective clothing from his bag, decided that actually he only needed his gloves so stuffed the polyethene and mask back into his bag and put the gloves on. He walked the last kilometre to Flat 2a and was relieved to see that the bins were obviously labelled and outside the door to 2a, which was distinctly separate to flat 2. He had beaten the bin men, so he printed off four sticky bar codes and was just sticking the third on the box for food waste, when a voice said "Hi."

What Jude heard was tinkling bells, he turned to look at the voice and he stared.

"Can I help? You are putting stickers on my recycling."

Jude opened his mouth but couldn't quite find the words. It was like looking at someone who could only be described in sounds and smells and colours and music. Maryam White, who was also dressed almost exclusively in white, shone in the street.

Jude shut his mouth and thought he had said something. He hadn't.

Maryam laughed, throwing her head back and her long dark brown hair seemed to move in slow motion in an arc through the air. She reached out and touched his arm, "Are you ok?" the touch tingled and then suddenly and almost involuntarily, his body spasmed and it was like an electric shock that went all the way through him, it reached earth and discharged and the moment was gone and he took a step backwards. As he did he almost tripped over the cardboard waste but found his senses at the same time. "I am Jude" he just about got out, then took a deep breath. "I inspect waste."

"Thank you Jude, it's a noble job, we should know what we are throwing out shouldn't we?" From anyone else, that could have sounded patronising, but Jude didn't feel patronised.

"Erm… yes" he muttered, "Here" and he passed her the letter that he was expecting to put through her letterbox. He pulled his hand back quickly when she took the piece of paper.

"Thank you Jude, its lovely to meet you, see you soon", Maryam White said, which again, sounded to Jude like music when she said it.

He looked at her again, she was perhaps the most beautiful person he had ever seen, exquisite. He didn't know the reason why and he didn't want to but there was something very unpleasantly wrong with touching Maryam White. He could look at her and listen to her and in fact smell her, as her perfume lingered in the air; forever, but he was sure that he would never want to touch her again. It was like a little part of him died and it was frightening. He turned and hurried back down the road just as the recycling lorry arrived.

"Julie... Julie... Julie... What number Jude the dude?"

"2a" Jude shouted back to a reprise of *"hey Jude"* which faded out as he got closer to the bus stop.

He was strangely tired by the time he got back to the office. Dave and Dave looked at him suspiciously but didn't mess around with the card rigamarole and so he grabbed a coffee, a bar of chocolate and a bag of crisps from the vending machine and wandered through to the lab.

Collection was the easier part of the job. Once the bags and boxes were delivered, he had to go through them. He sighed as he sat in the open area of the lab, ate his crisps, drank his coffee and thought about the two girls he had met. One looked like she had been involved in a car accident, which she had – he had made sure of that by running her over. The other looked like music, or light, or something so stunningly intangible that he could barely remember what she looked like but she still lingered on the periphery of his memory, fluctuating in and out of it like fluorescence. The first, Martine, was warm and had hugged him and that was despite him running her over and the second, Maryam, had touched his arm and he felt he had lost a few seconds of his life. He was intrigued by Maryam but he really liked Martine and he wondered what she looked like without a bandage, bruising, a slightly swollen head, hair all over the place, a bloodshot eye and a pained expression on what he could see of her face. One eye looked almost normal, it twinkled and he was pleased that he had left just a little bit of her intact.

But back to work, he shook off the thoughts, put on his protective gear and typed the code on the keypad to go into the secure area.

He laid out a polyethene sheet on the stainless-steel table and started with the general waste. It was a pretty unpleasant job but he was used to it. He needed ten samples and would trawl through the rubbish, sorting out anything that could contain body fluids; like tissues, sanitary products, used plasters, bandages or condoms. Then anything that could contain tissue samples; typically, used razors were perfect (there were always used razors) but also toothbrushes, nail files, dental floss, hair or, he almost gagged when he remembered finding a toe in someone's rubbish once. It had a yellow painted nail. He had flagged that for more urgent investigation but never did find out what happened and who the toe actually belonged to. He had thought, as he really could not shake off that memory, that it was very badly painted and wondered if it had been cut off by the owner in disgust. Finally, food waste, which was a lower category but anything that had a bite mark was good, he would always look out for apples which were high on the approved list of sources.

All of these items were bagged, given a squirt of ONCONAA937, a liquid which he was told preserved and amplified any residual human DNA. Or something like that, he had switched off during the lecture because he had a hangover and he didn't need to know why he did what he did as it made little moral sense, let alone practical sense.

The bags were zip-locked, barcoded, double bagged, barcoded, boxed, barcoded and put in a refrigerator where they would be collected by a security van each day.

Everything was taken off to a more sophisticated laboratory somewhere and that would be the last Jude heard of his work. Occasionally he got a recall and was sent out to the same address because the collected materials were not of sufficient quality, or more likely came from too many sources to be validated as the subject.

He drew up the corners of the polyethene sheet, pulled the pile of detritus together, dumped the contents all in a single large orange bag, which would also be bar coded and collected for (presumably) destruction and after scrubbing the table down with disinfectant and apart from some paperwork, that was his day complete. It was three thirty-seven. He might just finish by quarter past four.

*

Martine meanwhile, was eating chocolate and ice-cream, watching nonsense on the internet and in-between, stalking Jude on social media. Even in a state of mild distress, she had clocked his full name on a bank card in the hospital and filed it for reference in a part of her brain that had not been aching. It wasn't difficult, he talked a lot to the world about everything except his work, which was nice. She began to get to know him a little better and whilst this research was an odd and very modern way of developing a friendship, it was three days until Christmas Day and Martine was on her own. She had expected to be working and had told her parents she could not visit this year. They had consequently booked a holiday abroad and would have already left, so there was no changing that plan.

Martine was bruised, miserable and alone. She picked up her phone and rang it. "Hey Jude."

"*La. la. la. Lalalala...* erm sorry." Jude sang. He'd used that so often it sort of rolled off the tongue.

Martine laughed; her face hurt but she laughed anyway. "Fancy a pizza tonight?"

Chapter 4

Christmas Day

It was Christmas Eve, the weather was still blowing nothing and still shining a little. The temperature was above average unless you were from Britannia, in which case it was hotting up like you would not believe. In the headlines, at least.

Outside Sir Peregrine Matthews Hospital, Ernesto Golding (*MBE, perhaps soon* he thought?) was making a press announcement.

"Ladies and Gentlemen, thank you all for attending and for your interest. Yes, yes as the news has somehow got out (*leaked conveniently*, he thought smugly) we now need to update you with the current status to avoid any unhealthy speculation. The nation (*well the internet, the online nation of cranks, crazies and bleeding hearts*) has saved Christopher Sunday, named after the day he was admitted, Sunday fourth April, eighteen years ago. Ladies and Gentlemen, Christopher has been showing signs of consciousness. Christopher is being closely monitored and we are of the opinion, that he is likely to re-enter our world. Christopher, after eighteen years away from us, is being reborn. Under a star like the most famous of stories." Golding left that hanging like a decoration, rather proud of himself for the Christmas allusion, despite it being a contrivance. As he spoke, he looked up to the star on the Christmas tree that stood just outside and to the left of the main doors of Sir P's. Christopher had been awake but sedated now for two weeks, nominally to monitor his vital signs, practically for the Christmas miracle and a revenue promotion, which would lead to a new year miracle for Golding. Though Christopher's destiny lay beyond the hospital, Golding knew they needed him to be awake to choose the path that had already been chosen for him. He well knew that plans were already made for Christopher once the furore died down. A life had been carefully planned for him and he'd choose it because it was made the most attractive.

The crowd started calling out questions. The press at the front were already running their headlines. **'The Christmas Miracle.' 'Back from the Dead.' 'Goldings Goldmine.'** The last was a speculative piece on how much money would be generated from the remarkable timing of Christopher's *rebirth* and which was the only accurate article written about the miracle. The news was all mostly ignored by a baying public who wanted a new media sensation, photographs in the press and an interview with the star of the show, Christopher Sunday. In a bizarre display of post cynical anti-cynicism, the public railed against the "Goldmine" headline as not being in the spirit of Christmas and not something anyone wanted in their holiday downtime, or any time.

There were more shouted questions, Golding smiled for the cameras as they flashed, his teeth caught the light and he flexed his hands because he wanted his manicured nails on record and he also thought that drawing attention to his hands made it look like he had been busy.

In the private room where Christopher was asleep, a nurse carefully changed his drip, checked his catheter and primed a syringe with a reduced dose of sedative. She checked her watch briefly and adjusted the cannula so she could inject the 'medicine' which was serving Christopher with no medical advantage, except to assist him in being the most perfectly timed statistic.

"There you go love." The nurse said and as she turned away she did not see his eyes briefly open, flicker at the light and close again. Neither did she see his lips move as they tried to say, "thank you," though the sound, like everything else for as long as he could remember, was only in his head. Although he had a voice, it had been so long since it had been expressed as air, forced through vibrating tissue, that his body didn't direct the air over his vocal chords and no sound was produced.

Christopher could remember, but not much. Not much at all, but he could remember. Words, sounds, smells, feelings, taste, touch, pain. All from a very long time ago but enough to start to structure his thoughts.

What he knew though, was that he had spent years in a void. It was an empty place where he could remember time passing as though he was floating through a corridor of darkness. Darkness, where there was movement through time but perpetual sensory deprivation. He could reflect on that missing time as time spent nowhere in nothingness, existing but not living or feeling or thinking. Then a point in the darkness opened, it had appeared as a pulsing light and it had cast shadows that gave texture to the absoluteness of the void. He could not see the light but he felt and sensed it. It was a warm flicker that gave him hope. Little by little, further bright dots came out like stars in the hemispheres of his mind and he was living in a night sky. The darkness was replaced by colour and movement and the universe played out inside him as lightness. Motion coalesced into ideas and the harmonics of songs and a primordial orchestra of sound enveloped him. It sped up and light was now rushing in around him and carrying him and cushioning him and the sounds were not songs that he could remember, or even describe to himself, but it was the music that described existence. Notes were whispering dreams; in the clouds of light he was bringing together in his mind. The clouds became images and the images became substance and he started to feel the blood in his veins pulsing around his body. He sensed, he didn't feel, the extremities of it all and that was all, because he could not move and he could not know of anything outside. He was again part of the universe but trapped in the metaverse of his mind. Everything else was beyond his reach but he knew he was there and he knew he was alive.

After this, all he had was his thoughts and he thought for a long, long time. He had few points of reference, some memories, not many but he could structure his thoughts. He felt he could communicate but he sensed everything was on the outside, on the outside of something and he did not know what. He remembered walls of light and people, he could see them, was this what he looked like? He could sense changes, responses to his thoughts. Sometimes he created dark sounds and flashing colours and other times tranquil music and ambient feelings.

I think, he thought, I must exist? But where am I? And time passed. A lot of time.

Golding strutted down the corridor, a senior nurse to his left and a junior doctor to his right, behind him the hospitals press officer, the chief accountant, commercial manager and a service manager.

"The publicity, we'll increase our market share after this" said the commercial manager, to everyone and no one.

"If enough people get sick" replied Golding, "Let's not lose sight of that."

"But the point is, that after the grand plan, it's all elegantly scalable" commented the chief accountant. "We don't need to worry about health, well we do obviously; at a personal level, but financially it pays for itself. In fact, the sicker our clients are, as long as they are stable the more revenue and the better the margin. The only thing I cannot squeeze any GP out of is the dead, but if you can keep them alive for long enough, we can cover our costs at least."

"Clients," muttered Nurse Ball to herself. She had seen it all, but she still thought that patients were patients and people, not clients.

They got to Christopher's room and Golding pushed the door open and walked in. He wandered over, pulled the blinds, looked out briefly and was disappointed that there were no cameras. He let the blinds crack shut again and next wandered over to the LCD screen at the end of Christopher's bed. He put his thumb on the sensor which unlocked the screen and he scanned through several charts. "Hmm" he said to no one, perhaps it was dramatic effect.

He then walked over to Christopher. He looked at him for a moment and for reasons he did not fully understand, he gently lifted his eyelid. Christopher's eye rolled down and looked at him, the eye dilated and Goldman stared at him for a moment. "Were bringing you out Christopher, we are bringing you out. You do not know what you have missed," he said and let the eyelid drop. He went back to the screen at the end of the bed, which was still unlocked, he typed in some comments and looked at everyone else. "Tomorrow, he said, definitely tomorrow."

*

Martine was on the phone to Jude. They had spoken every day since Jude had almost killed her and it was obvious to both of them and neither of them, that something was happening. They liked each other so much, that neither wanted to risk casting a shadow over the moments they spent and talked together. So they slowly got to know each other, a conversation at a time. Nervousness and anticipation were the chaperones that maintained a level of modesty in their fledgling relationship.

"So, what are you doing tomorrow?" Martine asked, almost assuming that Jude would have plans.

"Oh, nothing" Jude replied.

"But it's Christmas?"

"I know, but my mother is in Caledonia and as I was working today, I can't visit. She sent me a present, so I'll just probably just open it have lunch and watch TV. What are you doing?"

OMG, thought Martine *please, please, please, ask…*

"Same"

"Oh!" Said Jude, "You are not seeing your parents?"

"No." She replied and tried to think how she might make herself appear even more lonely. "They have abandoned me" (*Nooo! overdone*) "I mean, well they haven't. I was expecting to be working, but with well, you know."

She had told Jude about her Internship, "I haven't been abandoned, but because they were not expecting me to visit they have gone abroad on holiday so I am on my own…" She left it, just open enough.

OMG, thought Jude *shall I ask? but what if she'd rather be alone?*

I don't want to be alone you idiot, Martine was thinking. *Ask… Ask… go on…*

If she wants to see me, she'll ask, thought Jude.

There was an awkward silence, then Jude, braver than he'd been for a long time, said; "Well if you would like to…" But that was as far as he got.

"YESS" interrupted Martine, then a cough before slightly calmer "I'd love to come round for Christmas lunch."

"Brilliant" said Jude excitedly but also conscious that he now had to prepare Christmas lunch.

"Erm, is a curry OK, I can do a turkey curry? and I'll do some czerwona kapusta" my mum's recipe. It works surprising well with curry. Well according to my mum it works well with everything. You can preserve it if you like, you can take some home with you, I'll put it in a plastic pot, you can have it as a side dish or a condiment, or cold with a salad, it freezes well." Jude suddenly realised that he was so nervous about everything, he was speaking nonsense.

"Cool." Martine replied, "what's czerwona kapusta?"

"It's great" said Jude, no longer thinking about what he was saying but what he had just said about preserves a moment ago and how embarrassed he was with that. Then he realised that he'd answered automatically and didn't even know what the question was.

"Cool" replied Martine again, still none the wiser, "I'll bring a pudding."

And as she said that, a car horn honked in the street outside and whilst it wasn't the peel of bells that either of them would have liked, it did at least distract Jude from one hundred and one things to do with red cabbage and that was most definitely for the best.

Chapter 5

Jerusalem House

Jerusalem House festered from the ground up, it rotted from the top down, it was grossly unpleasant from the middle out. It was a mid-century concrete three story block of flats that sagged vulgarly in the middle, dribbled from its extremities, leaked unpleasant fluids from parts that would not be mentioned in polite society and was surrounded by the debris of a sad night in. It had no personal respect. Jerusalem House was like a lonely old man, whose wife had left him long ago and who existed self destructively with little self-worth, health or hope. Its state of repair (lack thereof) and that it was even still standing, was beyond most people's comprehension. The concrete was rotten to the hard-core and the hard core was barely hard enough to take its own weight. Jerusalem House managed to be self-destructive without expending much, if any, effort. Bits flaked off like the shedding of scales and were replaced by clumps of algae and moss that had made poor life choices. Physicists could have used it as the perfect example of entropy if only they could understand how; despite gravity working its damnedest against it, it still stood. It was a two fingered salute to engineering and architecture and the rats who milled around in the basement were embarrassed by the fact and hoped nobody knew that they lived there.

The Brothers of the Sleeping Sword; Brother Matthew, Brother Simon and Brother Garry sat around a table, in flat 13b.

They were holy warriors united in their zeal, although Brother Simon and Brother Matthew were very disappointed that Brother Garry did not have a more appropriate name for a holy warrior. There was no disciple called Garry as far as anyone knew, it was a recurring bone of contention.

"But", Brother Garry had argued, "I have two 'r's, not one", which was a weak argument, but it was a point of fact.

"Whaa, two arse?" inquired an only half listening, only half-sized Brother Simon.

"That's not appropriate language for the work of the lord." Brother Mathew had interrupted and so the bickering had continued until the subject had been exhausted. Eventually, they had all agreed by mutual concession that perhaps there might have been a disciple called Garry with two r's but in ancient Aramaic it probably sounded more like Peter or Paul or Mark. Or, equally as likely, it was an ancient Aramaic middle name. There were after all, lots of disciples and the chances of one of them having Garry, Gary or a variation thereof in their name was likely, if not certain.

The brothers were an order of self-ordained secret warrior monks. Delusional, socially inadequate, and not what anyone would call fully formed adults, despite all being in their fourth decade and far hairier than their maturity levels would have anyone believe. They had been doing the Lords work rather ineffectively, in flat 13b for some years. It had initially been a thought experiment after an intense three-week game of *'dungeons and dragons'* that had been played without sleep, little food and some inappropriate medication. A thought experiment that went desperately wrong because it turned into an epiphany as they crossed through the doors of perception and sanitation. Or, it could have been perception and sanity? It was difficult to tell which, due to the smell. For the first few of those years they had only been holy warriors. Encouragement by every female that they had come into contact with and had tried to persuade to join their crusade, had helped them decide to follow a life of monastic celibacy. Their chosen path was as warrior monks. Somehow, giving in to the ordination of fate had made their circumstances feel even more of a calling than of abject failure.

'The Lord's work', was the prophetic words of the second coming, contained and described in William Blakes 1804 Pop Classic.

'And was the Holy Lamb of God,

On Albion's pleasant pastures seen?'

Not yet but they were damn sure it was on the horizon. Or rather and more appropriately, would be damned if it wasn't. It was Christmas and they were certain that Christopher Sunday was the Holy Lamb in question. The news said so and how would Seraphs expect to make their news known in the modern age, except via the internet and the news channels. Everyone was setting fire to things these days, there were riots in the streets so one would take a burning bush seriously. They were slightly concerned (and quite reasonably so) that the Holy Lamb of God was going to be well and truly roasted, but with their help he could build a new Jerusalem among the dark satanic mills. The first act in creating their new Jerusalem, would have to be rescuing the new Messiah.

Jerusalem House would make a Dark Satanic Mill look like a boutique holiday in the Coteswolds by comparison, but the Brothers of the Sleeping Sword knew hardship and felt better for it, philosophically at least. In practical terms they wished the flat was not so damp.

"There needs to be three wise men Brother Matthew" Brother Garry offered up.

The offering which had been thrown out there rather speculatively, was taken up by Brother Simon. "Our work is to find them?"

"Boys" interrupted Brother Matthew, "Brothers, I *have* found them."

"Where?" harmonising together accidently, in that way that sometimes happens when you breathe and speak and don't quite choke but manage to squeak your words out. This happened almost in unison. It could have been a heavenly choir creating a rather special moment or a group of Jazz musicians, if it wasn't discordant, out of time and in a mixed pitch. The response from Brothers Garry and Simon, was at least synchronised in as much as they used the same word. Beyond that they were very unlike a small group of angels or a Jazz trio; they were unmusical, badly dressed and numbering only two.

"…are they?" Brother Simon managed to spit out the rest of the sentence.

Followed by "How?" from Brother Garry, totally spoiling

the moment of oneness and synchronicity

"Us" said Brother Matthew.

"Arse?" Said brother Simon, mis-hearing again – it frequently happened. "I thought we agreed that language was unbiblical?"

"No, Us, Us, US! It's divine. It's part of the prophesy, well it's written between the lines, sort of implied and suggested in the text. Well, not so much suggested as left for the gaps to be filled in by only those that know. Those of us with a line to the Lord, those few of us with insight. It's us, think of it. There are three wise men and we know the name of the one, the new Messiah, the second coming, we have seen the sign and the symbols. The man who will save the world. We are the only ones wise to this moment of salvation and we can prevent damnation."

"Three wise men?" Still not quite getting it, Brother Garry asked and then; "Shouldn't we be kings?" "Or Magi?"

"Well, we are wise" said Brother Simon, lifting a hot cup of tea to his mouth and then immediately "Ow! stuckt… whoops, I swore, sorry amen" as he burnt his tongue and spat the tea out over his trousers, leaving a warm damp patch on his lap. "But I can do that trick with the cards where you pick one and I tell you what it is and then…"

"Last time you tried to do that trick, I picked the ace of spades and you refused to guess it because it was bad luck," argued brother Garry.

"Ah, yes, but at least I knew which card it was, that was

bad luck."

"But you could have said any card was bad luck."

"Ok, but why would I say any card was bad luck when only the ace of spades is bad luck?"

"it's actually not bad luck."

"It is."

"It's not."

"Why?"

"Oh, oh, right, well you could say THAT about any card!"

"But I wouldn't, because..." Brother Garry sat back in his chair, with an air of the wise man and Magi who was just about to nail the argument. He breathed deeply and flexed his fingers together, hoping for a slight dramatic cracking sound but none came, so he let the silence fill the space for just a little bit more but the pregnant pause gestated for just slightly too long and before Brother Garry's moment of intellectual glory showered down from the celestial heavens of his mind, Brother Matthew interrupted.

"You are the worst and actually, while I am at it, you are also the shortest Magi." and to Brother Garry, "And you, well, you are an um? You are an. Onanist."

"He is." agreed the worst and shortest Magi", who was also already on his mobile phone looking up onanist and instantly regretting the picture search.

And that was that.

*

In St Peregrines, Goldman looked at the time on his watch. Less than twenty-four hours until Christopher would make a dramatic re-emergence, which would be a media sensation. A cherry on his statistical Christmas cake. More fame, more unfettered glory, adulation and wealth and all because the money men had created a market that did not previously exist. Talk about selling sand to the Arabs and snow to Eskimos. They were selling life to the living, death to the dying and carving off a percentage from both.

*

Number Five was also looking at his watch with broadly similar thoughts. He was sitting with his third whiskey in 'Diemos', a private members club in James Street, behind Marquis Square. It was a blackened brick building with a white porticoed doorway. It was not especially big as it did not have an especially big patronage. It was identifiable only by a small brass plaque above a bell to the left side of the green front door that had an engraved picture of a man's face in clouds and lines radiating outwards from his mouth. It was as you might see in the clouds of an ancient sea map. The club was unknown to anyone uninvited to join, which was almost everybody.

Number Five was rolling the smoky, salty whiskey around his mouth, enjoying the sensation and sensuous taste as the chilled drink warmed in his mouth, changed texture and released different oils and flavours. He looked up, the chancellor was walking back over, having interrupted their conversation to take a call. He swallowed the liquor and smiled.

"You are back. And?"

"It's done."

The room still felt like it had the lingering cigar smoke from so many of its previous generations of patrons and perhaps a hint of opium as well, though there was no smoking in the main member's bar now. It was not dirty, but the subdued lighting and the dark rich claret red of the velvet seating, along with faded brass fittings, opaque and sick glass in the low light and the oxidising silver on the mirrored walls, allowed the faded grandeur to leak back out into the room. The old cigar smoke would never leave the warp and weft of the rug on the floor, nor the pile in the velvet furnishings, the smells just hung there, mellowed and matured, like the flavours of the whiskey. The pungent smells from a million previously held private conversations, would occasionally be disturbed and particulates would resettle, after reminding you that this was an old club that did not change much or at all. It held a million secrets in the fabric of its existence and they would move around the room, from time to time, but never leave. You should move slowly, because you did not want to disturb them too much, for fear that you would carry them with you and be tainted by association.

Another dirty secret was hidden in the peaty salty smoke and ethyl alcohol that Number Five breathed out. It soaked into the matter of the room as it had been drawn out of the barrel it had matured in.

"Thank you, it's a pleasure doing business with you." Number Five said, moving only his head at a slight angle when he spoke.

"Don't get over yourself" replied the chancellor, "it's business doing business with you." He looked Number Five in the eyes, which were darker than the ancient, aged, mahogany furniture of the room.

"Ha ha, yes, but still thank you. It is business yes, but that is what we do."

The chancellor did not respond, he stood up, nodded his head, looked around to see if anyone was looking, though what difference it would make was anyone's guess and he walked towards the door. He stopped for a moment and breathed deeply and he did not enjoy what he breathed in. It was two hundred years of pollution of the soul. It was dirty, it was wrong and it was corrupt but it was, he had to accept, business.

*

The Chairman of Automated Accumulations was drinking tea and playing chess with himself, he lived in a glass and concrete bunker in the sky, a penthouse apartment in the centre of the city, he could see for miles and miles and he could see everything. He would win the game but he hated the fact that in doing so, he also had to lose. He reminded himself that feeling the inevitable anger would take the sweetness off the win.

He looked at the board and thought through the next 14 moves:

White Queen to f5, Black Rook to e6.

White Pawn to h4. Black Pawn takes h4

White Queen to g4, Black King to f8

White Queen takes Pawn h4. Black King to e7

White Knight to f4, Black Rook to a6

White knight to d5, Check

Black King to d8

White Queen to h7, Black Knight to e5…

He paused and looked again at the board. "Interesting" he said to no one in particular. He reached over and picked up both the Black Knight and the White Queen. Looking at the Queen in his right hand he rolled the ivory piece over, examining it carefully and caressing the carved hardened dentine with his thumb before lifting it up to his mouth and kissing it gently. As he did, he could feel the pain start in the centre of his head, creeping out initially like tendrils, toxic fibres caressing and probing his brain, then the pulsing agony which would come and go for several hours. It would recede eventually, the medicine controlled it, but just not yet perfectly. It was a painful distraction he had to fight. Another day and he could relax in the knowledge that he would keep the pain under control, perhaps a little longer more and it would be gone forever. Hopefully. He fought it, pushed it down refused to tolerate it, but it was eating at his temper. "What will you do?" and he grimaced through the pain as he squeezed the little white female like she was a gag that he was biting on as a distraction. Then, the release, "You little bitch," and he threw the piece onto the board, where it sent Pawns, Rooks, Bishops and Knights flying. The pain, now in remission until the next wave, allowed him an exhausted moment of thought. He considered the Black Knight in his other hand and put it down on the table, off the board, where some of the other pieces had fallen.

The Black Knight was alone, surrounded by the dead.

Chapter 6

Pigs

Christmas Morning, Ian Piggot-Smith (pronounced Smythe) had welcomed the day with a small glass of sherry. "Just the one!" he had joked to his wife Katie (never Kate, but occasionally Katherine), before he poured himself another and sat down.

"Oh" Katie had said, just as he slumped in the armchair. "We are out of milk, would you mind dear?"

"Damnit to Hell woman, I have just sat down!"

"Well, the exercise will do you good, the golfing doesn't, that is supposed to be exercise but you drink more calories in the bar afterwards than you burn on the course every week."

"It is exercise dear, it's very good exercise. It's only a couple of glasses of '*Châteauneuf-du-Pape*' and red wine is good for you, a glass a day keeps the Doctor away. Isn't that how the rhyme went?"

"No, it wasn't and even if it was, you have had about four by the end of most days."

"Oh for Goodness sake dear, your average Gaul spills more than that before breakfast and they have a quarter of the heart disease of Britannia. In fact, with my Mediterranean diet I am probably going to live to be one hundred."

"Mediterranean diet?"

"Yes dear, if you remember we had a takeaway from Dionysus last night and went out to Pizza-Pizza two days before that, I could only be more Mediterranean if I owned a donkey and beat it with a stick twice a day"

He smiled smugly to himself at his joke, then added, "But I'll get some cow juice, do you need anything else while I am at the, er… Asian retailers?" He was proud of his revised description for the little shop on the corner which he had found perfectly described it without offending anyone too much.

He had never understood everyone's offence at his previous description. *"It's only a word, it describes where they are from. It's only offensive if you mean it offensively. Abi-wotsit probably doesn't pay any tax anyway but at least he is hard working, so we'll keep him for a while yet eh? ha-ha."*

"I'll be back shortly," he called out, as he pulled the front door closed behind him and trotted to the shops, a slight skip in his walk brought on by a couple of Christmas morning sherries.

The corner shop was owned by Mr Abeygunawardena who was from Sri Lanka. His tax returns were filed religiously and on time every year and he took every penny that he earnt from Ian Piggot-Smith as poor compensation from the boorish man who, on most visits, joked about how much better the Britannic were than 'all those Asian fellas' at cricket.

"We taught them cricket, you know. Mind you I can't ride an elephant so you have got me on that one." Piggot-Smith would add with a friendly wink.

"Aha, Happy Christmas Mr Abi-Wotsit! I know you probably don't celebrate it but it's a great day in Britannia and you're almost a Brit now, you have been here long enough. Well, you will be a fine Brit when you master the over arm bowl, Eh? How are you? Need some milk, can you pop back and get it, I'll just look at the whiskey selection while you sort that out, there's a good chap."

Mr Abeygunawardena was struggling to be a good chap at that particular moment. He would rather have been upstairs with his wife and children watching cartoons on Christmas morning, than down here serving this idiot that he would like to crack in the face with an over arm bowl. Despite all of this he smiled. "Of course, of course. Happy Christmas Mr Piggot-SMITH." He had been corrected a number of times previously but pretended he could not pronounce Smythe. It was a small but amusing victory, every time.

"Smythe" Piggot-Smith beamed generously, but you call me what you want. I am a man of the world, I don't offend easily, unlike some. You probably don't have the same sounds in Hindu or Urdi or hoodia," then he festively added "or hohohodii," adding idiocy to insult and injury.

"Right then, twenty pence is it? Assume we are negotiating. I went to Bombay once, it was Bombay then, no idea why you needed to change the name. Always good to barter with the natives. Hah, only joking, here's a pound, keep the change."

But Mr Abeygunawardena was not going to keep the change, he counted out the coins carefully and put them in the charity box to the left of the till. "Repellent idiot" he muttered under his breath as Piggot-Smith initially left the shop.

The door was just closing behind him, when "Oh," he remembered, poking his head back in. "Let's have a Healthcare Lottery ticket, triple rollover you know and the Christmas special draw. Don't really need the money, self-made man you know, but I could have a bit of fun with a touch of that magic. What you think?" and he walked back up to the counter, not really caring what anyone thought and dropped a five-pound note on the desk. He was given a ticket, the numbers randomly generated and he took the pound change, which he looked over both back and front suspiciously, before putting it in his pocket. "Cheerio then Mr Abi-wotsit, hope you are nice and busy today. Hard work and lots of play, you know. It's good to be busy" and off he went back to his home, to do nothing but eat, drink and complain about everything.

"Repellent idiot" said Mr Abeygunawardena again and he left the shop by a door next to the stockroom at the back to go upstairs and join his family for their own Christmas celebrations.

*

Jude was nervous, he had been cooking all morning and mostly had made a mess. It was quarter to Martine arriving and he felt that the flat should be tidy and the table should be set. The table was clean and he found a white sheet which at a push, resembled a tablecloth once it was folded in half and he had a wine bottle with a candle in it. The music was playing from his television and from the speakers the bells were ringing out for Christmas Day, but he felt like a scumbag and a maggot, because whilst the curry was cooking quite nicely, its spattering had pebble-dashed his wall with orangey yellow curry sauce. The rice was overcooked and the room smelt of vinegar. He was also wondering whether czerwona kapusta really would go well with curry. Oh, and the prosecco was not chilled. The side issue of not having seen his cat, Copernicus, for 24 hours was hovering on the periphery, but Copernicus had a cat flap and did whatever he wanted, he was fed by at least three other people in the street so that was fine. He was more concerned that the cat would pop in and at least say hello to Martine.

He had made a nice little starter, a tapenade on toast (crusts trimmed) from a jar of mixed olives. The little black fruits were arguably past their best but they were not mouldy, so with capers, garlic and a splash of oil they would be fine and then *oh hell, the rice*. It had almost set solid in the sieve. He boiled the kettle full of water to run through it to try and remove some of the starch and… he looked at the saucepan full of red cabbage? If he put it all on a plate it would actually dwarf everything else. There was enough for about twenty people. It was a lovely colour though, red was very Christmassy as long as it didn't get on the sheet... tablecloth *(who was he kidding, it was a sheet!)* He wondered if he could get away with the cabbage as both a starter, it would be nice with the tapenade if it was cooled, and as a main course side. His mother would have done that, he was absolutely sure she would have done that, his mother would have added cream and served it as a desert as well. In fact, he had once been given it blended with yogurt and bananas as a breakfast smoothy experiment. He wondered whether actually it wasn't that it was such a flexible dish, but that there was always so much of it that his mother had just developed creative ways to use it up.

Jude opened the fridge, grabbed a cool (not quite cold, although it should be by now) lager, popped the top and drank it straight from the bottle. At least Martine was bringing a desert so it wouldn't be a full three courses of cabbage.

He just had time to pour the boiled water from the kettle over the rice and was relieved that it ran in a translucent gelled liquid from the bottom of the sieve, rather than be absorbed further. He also managed to put two mis-matching wine glasses on the table before the doorbell rang. He took a deep breath and went to open the door.

"Hi!" Martine smiled, then looked at him "Jude, you are covered in curry, it's all over your face?"

"Sorry!" Jude said, staying on script. He noticed that the bruising on her face had gone down a lot, though there was still an unusual purplish hue. She was a lot more beautiful than he had thought before, looking less like a car crash.

"I have got some ice-cream and a Christmas pudding"

"Great, come in." He was thinking about the best car

crash ever.

Martine walked in through the door. It was a relatively small flat, like hers, the ground floor of a split house but much smaller than the flat she had been bought by her parents, it also only had one bedroom where she had an additional single. She walked straight into a short corridor with a door off to the right, she glanced at it.

"That's the bedroom" Jude blushed as he said it but Martine didn't notice. "The next door is the bathroom, the loo is in there," he added, as though it wasn't obvious that a bathroom contained a toilet. He wondered why he said it. The short corridor opened out into a bigger room which Martine was surprised was quite tastefully decorated in a pale blue with white cornicing. It was a living/dining room with a kitchenette through an arch at the back. She could see a small courtyard outside. The room had a large television and along with a game station, there were a jumble of books. There were some comics piled up on the floor and a single poster on the wall. The robot from Metropolis, Fritz Lang's classic film.

"Maria?" Martine commented looking at the poster. Jude looked up.

"Close, 'Maschinenmensch,' just *the Robot*, she is never referred to by name in the film but she is known as 'Futura' in the book"

"Oh, you are a Sci-Fi geek then?" she smiled, knowing she was teasing the ever-vulnerable Jude.

"Sorry" Jude replied on cue. Martine sniggered. He added, "I do like Science-Fiction"

She continued to scan the room, the set table was cute. Amateur but cute. It put her in mind of an enthusiastic child trying to replicate a dinner party held by their parents with an assortment of what was available in the house. Mismatched but lovely. Full of love actually. She surprised herself with that thought and shook it off. They were friends at the moment.

Martine then wandered through to the kitchen where the battle of Ypres had coincided with the final charge on the fields of Waterloo in another alternative universe. There were no dead soldiers (well one rather beaten about and exhausted Prussian maybe) but there was red liquid (*cabbage water,* she hoped) on the floor, air-burst curry on the walls and rice shrapnel stuck to the side of the saucepan and drying off from the latent heat. There were more knives than seemed necessary to slice up a cabbage and they were discarded across the work surface of the small kitchen and there was a smell of... what was it? bleach and vinegar... or chlorine gas? She leant over the battle-weary Jude and opened the window. He thanked her and said that everything was just about ready and she could sit down. She did.

Remarkably, despite the adjoining warzone, Christmas lunch fell beautifully into place.

Jude served the starter, an olive tapenade, which despite slightly anticipating the surprise to come, was served with a small (chilled) serving of czerwona kapusta, and of which the spiced and subtly sweet/sour flavour worked wonderfully to offset the olive spread. The colour was great on the plate too, far nicer than it worked on the kitchen floor where it resembled a massacre.

Jude and Martine lost themselves in conversation, talking about themselves and their families, they opened the prosecco and Jude served the main course. Turkey curry, a slightly smaller portion of rice than you might expect, which had recovered mostly from being boiled to oblivion and a plate of czerwona kapusta which was served on a tray in the centre of the table because there was not a large enough serving plate. It was perhaps the first time that Martine had been served red cabbage as the centrepiece of a Christmas dinner, with a side of curry and rice but in the right proportions, lunch was delicious and conversation rambled on endlessly. They were happily in their own world until interrupted by a ringing phone. Jude looked up.

"Oh god" he said out loud, "that will be my mum."

He tentatively picked up the phone and pressed the answer button, Martine watched and she broadly understood the conversation from the squirming and uncomfortable look on Jude's face as he spoke.

"Hi Mum. Happy Christmas... I know... no I didn't open my present last night... no, I saved it... no I haven't opened it yet... because I have been busy... cooking... er... no. Yes. A friend. She is... um... [PAUSE] ok... She is called Martine"

He then handed a confused Martine the phone, accidently

turning the volume up as he did, his dexterity had been afflicted by the dangerous cocktail of both wine and mothers. "She wants to say Happy Christmas."

It was all going so well. Sadly, for Jude, his clumsiness with the volume meant he heard every word.

"Happy Christmas Martine, are you having fun, of course you are, he is such a lovely boy, sensitive though. He likes his films, silly spaceships mostly. He should have opened his present last night, don't tell him it's a jumper, it's going to get cold you know, the weather. What has he cooked? I hope he has done some czerwona kapusta, it's also nice with cream. I made some here, too much. Actually, you can never make too much. It freezes well. If you have containers, you can have it for lunch every day. So how long have you been..." She paused, for slightly too long, it wasn't to think of what she was going to say next, more to have the gap filled for her. Jude's mother always knew what to say next, mostly just after she said it, but Martine decided not to say anything, thinking that in law and in mothers-in-law (*whoa, where did mother-in-law come from!?*) the right to silence, was the best option on almost every occasion. "Friends" Jude's mother added, rather too succinctly. It was more a of a challenge that demanded to be corrected. Then, not waiting for a response, she added "oh do look after him. Has he shaved today? He should shave even though its only wispy, he is very good looking when he shaves, he has his grandfather's jawline, has he shown you photos? His grandfather had medals, he flew spitfires in the war. He is a hero, so is Judek in his own little way, do be nice to him. Happy Christmas. Lovely to speak to you, pass me back."

Confused and slightly shellshocked, Martine handed the phone back to Jude. Who, blushing and slumping into the chair said a weak and insipid "hi."

"Oh!! Judek darling, she is a lovely girl, congratulations, I do hope you are taking sensible precautions, you cannot be too careful, I want to be a grandmother but not so soon."

Jude looked up, mortified. His face initially the colour of the cabbage, slowly drained to a pallor just slightly whiter than the rice. "Got. To. Go. Mum." He hung up and dropped his phone on the floor.

"Oh. My. God. Mum. No. Sorry. God. No. Mean. Said." he managed to try and say, but the words started to lose cohesion, comprehension and even the will to be heard.

Inwardly finding it hysterical but also blushing and deciding that discretion, being the better part of valour, she should not comment on the call but change the subject rapidly; Martine said, "Er, she is a character isn't she? your mum... I like her (*in a land where 'like' is a synonym for 'fear'* she thought). Anyway, I got you a present, well us really. It's not very exciting. A lottery ticket, it's a triple rollover and I thought we'd split the winnings. Well, if we win."

Jude just sat in shock, Martine wondered whether she should call an ambulance. He looked like he was in a catatonic state and it was only half past three, there was still more fun to be had, but she wasn't sure Jude was up to fun. "Um, ice cream and Christmas pudding?"

"Later. Walk. Air. Fresh. Pudding. Not."

Martine understood, she was a little flushed by the conversation as well and decided fresh air was the best thing for everyone.

"Let's go and see what's happening at the St Ps, the news crews are getting aggie, that Christopher guy who's been in a coma is coming round and its all over everything. That and all the trouble in the city. Everyone is getting so angry and over excited about everything".

"Sorry".

"Ok" Martine acknowledged and she blew out the candle, hauled Jude up by the shoulder of his shirt and dragged him towards the door, flipping the living room light off as they went.

*

The news crews were most definitely getting aggie, as were the crowd. It was hard to believe there might be so many people gathered outside a hospital on Christmas afternoon, but there were. You might cynically think that there were an awful lot of people who had decided that the washing up was best left to someone else and it was an easier option to take the dog, kids, parents, self, out for a walk and abandon the house. The mild weather made it easier to hang around a hospital carpark wondering if someone was going to live or die.

A robin in a nearby tree looked on with mixture of agitation and pent-up aggression. His flushed red chest and little bird brain deciding whether to take the lot of them on or not, as they stood around interrupting the peace, aggravating the worms and probably treading on fallen seeds. "DAMN MONKEYS" he tweeted to no one in particular as he psyched himself up for a fight.

"Oi, what's going on, where is Goldman?" a news reporter shouted out, "when do we hear something?"

The crowd of mainly single adults with either dogs and children or airs of loneliness, surged forward a little at the rallying cry of the news hound, but settled back when no reply came.

Jude and Martine were almost both recovered from the most awkward of job interviews. It was a job which nobody knew existed but was still in the planning stages. They mooched around the corner and looked at the chaos. Both wondered why so many people would hang out here on Christmas Day, neither questioned why they were also there.

Someone caught Jude's eye, "Oh, look. Maryam White." he pointed at the crowd.

"Who?" replied Martine.

Shock! Jude had just thought out loud, "Oh, no one a client, from work." He looked away just as Martine saw her.

"Oh." Martine saw Maryam. She was speechless.

Maryam White had just seen Jude looking at her and had turned towards him, as she took a step forward the crowd moved. She created a bow wave as people took both an unconscious step backwards and also a deep breath as she passed. Male and female alike were transfixed. No one noticed that the dogs dropped their ears and scurried behind their owners when she went past them.

"Hi, Jude the bin inspector" Maryam White called out, waving. "What a surprise to see you again so soon. How are the bins, inspected any good ones recently?" She said it with genuine enthusiasm and in a lilting melody. It was remarkable, everything she said sounded both naive and genuine. Everyone who heard her speak would swear that everything she said was accompanied by bells.

"Bins?" Martine said, still unable to take her eyes off the girl walking towards her... *her Jude!* "Client?"

"Um, yes." Jude replied, "my job, it's like a civil service job I am a, a sort of rubbish inspector" pause. "Junior, it's quite scientific. Mostly" he added as an afterthought.

"She's beautiful." Martine said, she couldn't help herself.

"Is she?" Jude lied and hated himself for saying it. It was the most unconvincing thing he thought he had ever said. That, and saying his job was mostly scientific, which was equally as unconvincing. He hoped Martine realised that he inspected rubbish, not that he was rubbish at inspecting or, oh no, which was worse? *Oh what a day,* he thought, smiling awkwardly as Maryam stopped next to them.

"Hi. Again." Jude simpered "This is my…"

"GIRLFRIEND." Martine interrupted, defensively and perhaps a little passive aggressively.

"umm yeah... er girl. Yes" Jude confirmed, vaguely.

"Hi" Maryam turned to Martine and held out a hand.

"Girlfriend" Martine said again, not so defensively this time. She even wondered whether she was addressing Maryam and not talking about herself. She reached out but just before they shook, a rather cantankerous robin flew down from the tree and swooped past Martine's face. It startled her out of her trancelike state, it landed on Maryam's shoulder briefly before threatening both Jude and Martine with the foulest language a particularly angry robin could summon up when looking for a fight. Twit...twit...twit tweet, it screamed at them.

"Hey, little man. Chill out." Maryam said shaking her shoulder and the robin flew off, looking for some more aggro, elsewhere. "Birds like me you know, it's an odd thing. Dogs and cats don't" she said "It's a shame." Then, "Nice to see you again Jude, be happy. Bye Jude's girlfriend, you are lovely, it's no wonder he loves you," around she turned and floated away.

"Wow" was all Martine could manage to say. "That was weird!"

Jude was blushing again, so much so that he was at risk of permanent damage to the capillaries in his cheeks. Neither Jude nor Martine fully processed that moment and they could barely remember the conversation when they spoke about it later.

They remembered some nice music that they couldn't quite place.

Chapter 7

Christopher

The crowds were pensive. This included Jude and Martine but no longer Maryam, who seemed to have just evaporated back into the ether. News was expected and the reality was that the excitement now was about the expectation of news, not whatever the news would be. The media and its sponsors had created and sold a story that nobody needed but everybody was buying.

Inside the hospital, doctors put on their jackets, nurses brushed down their uniforms and various body fluids were mopped up from where they were spilt. All of this was done with a sense of urgency not seen since the *New Plan* was passed into law and the commercialisation of the ex-National Health Service propped up the dying, fiddled the statistics and boosted the pay of the top earners, while ensuring that the lower earners had no route of complaint. The government were no longer their masters, the accountants were, accountants incidentally from one of Autonomous Accumulations partner agencies.

"Jolly good job" the Prime Minister had said, "we spend far too much time arguing with national servicers about national services, we just need them to get on with it, "boff, boff, boff." It's the right thing to manage them out of our management structure if we can manage it" and manage they did. The New Plan created the stats that drove the funding and fed into the Healthcare Lottery that created the drama that allowed the service to run like football leagues, buying in and selling off players and stars. Agencies moved in like locusts to feed on the fresh new shoots of the *New Plan*. Big pharma got excited. When big pharma got excited, the happy pills were distributed freely and everyone ended up with a smile on their face. The government especially did and the accountants did and the shareholders did and that was ok, because if you want to prioritise happiness, then the theory that you make the top tier happy and let happiness flow downwards like a waterfall, was a principal so sound that logically, it had to work.

"Happiness" the Prime Minister said, "is the only valuable currency in this world and it's a commodity we can distribute like water." A consultant, introduced to the Prime Minister by Number Two had pointedly advised, "It's not measurable, but it is quantifiable. Its food, drink, television, pills. It's cheap people in expensive clothes and expensive people in no clothes at all. All you have to do is allow everybody else to find their own happiness and share it out. It's the promise you cannot fail to deliver against. If people don't lap it up and drown themselves in it, then blame the press, blame the poor, blame the opposition and blame everyone. You can take a horse to water but if it doesn't drink, damn it, damn it, damn them all..." The damning speech never made it to the lectern.

*

Christopher's eyes opened just a fraction, almost a response to the possibility of seeing, he didn't think that he could control them. He could hear voices, he recognised the sounds but they sounded muffled. He wanted to move, but he could not.

His medication had been removed, his pipes in and pipes out had been taken out. The bed had been remade and he had been given a haircut. The hospitals publicity manager had suggested light make up to "add a little joi d'vive to his expression," but someone somewhere showed some restraint. He was waking up from the dead, not yet skipping through fields of wildflowers. Tracking his progress through winter into spring, might bring that opportunity and, "we'd need to see some transition from this point to then, so hold that thought about the make-up."

There was a flash, followed by another three fast flashes. Christopher sensed a mixture of light and shadows, movement and sound in the room.

Round the bed stood the wise and the wonderful. Goldman, Mr. Consultant, the two most photogenic nurses that could be trolleyed in at short notice, one of which was due to go off shift to catch up with her family Christmas and the other was supposed to be doing ward rounds. But publicity, they were told, was more important than either of those activities even on Christmas Day, in fact especially on Christmas Day. The sick could wait for their medicine and "wouldn't your children rather see you online than at home? Of course they would. Your moment of celebrity Nurse... Nurse... Nurse?" "Nightingale! What a unique coincidence we can make a follow up story on that when this one has run its course."

"Everyone please, tighten up we all need to get in shot."

The Police Commissionaire was on site already to check

that the crowds were not getting out of hand. He had decided that checking security personally in the building was a sensible step that also would allow him to join the photo opportunity. The Chancellor was there, a slippery fellow he was, but he managed to louche in between the two nurses, with a smile like a snake doing an impersonation of a crocodile. It was necessary for politics to represent the great and the good and then, celebrity!

A chance admission yesterday was Tucker, the West Country Sheep Man who had been on a publicity stunt in a nearby television studio. He had been brought in on Christmas Eve with a twisted testicle, but was telling people he was being monitored for, "well you know" a knowing nod and "I would rather not say the words."

"Well, you know" was clearly less embarrassing than being kicked in the "you know whats" by a two hundred kilogram fighting sheep, thought Britannia's foremost promotor of sheep wrestling. The news companies would speculate wildly and Tucker would be described in the celebrity columns in the following days as Albion's bravest ram, confronting "you know what" with stoicism. This pleased him greatly, as all publicity was good publicity except a kick in the wotsits on primetime. St Peregrines needed a celebrity in the mix and it turned out to be a Shepherd of sorts, on Christmas Day. With the re-birth of the previously comatose Christopher Sunday, Tucker was a shoo-in that you could not have planned for. It was a gift from the gods. Hallelujah.

In a corridor in the next building, three holy warriors, probably the most hopeless holy warriors in the history of the world, were shuffling around in green scrubs and facemasks and trying to look at least, like the most hopeless medical staff in medical history.

"Brothers, we need a wheelchair"

"I need chocolate, I feel faint."

"I need a moment", Brother Simon added, "these scrubs are so long, it looks like I am wearing a dress. Why didn't you get a smaller one?" He said, rolling up the sleeves and trying to tuck some of the green fabric into his belt.

"A dress, Brother? No. You are wearing holy robes, chosen by the lord, it is your... destiny" Brother Matthew responded knowingly, and he looked up just a little to see if a light shone down. It did, a spotlight reflected off his balding head.

"Nope, looks like a dress." Said Brother Garry.

"Brother Simon, is the chariot of fire awaiting us, is it fuelled and ready for our calling?"

"It stinks of petrol" moaned Brother Garry "when you told him to fill it full of petrol, he filled it all right, petrol tank and inside it as well, it totally stinks of petrol."

"I only filled the petrol tank, its full. It's just fumes, they permeate." Said Brother Simon confidently.

"Permeate?" Brother Garry, now he'd got himself worked up, argued, "…and while we are talking about the deathtrap of fire, I don't understand why our order, would drive an Italian car. We are building a green and pleasant land in

Albion, not the holy Roman Empire. It's not right, it should be a Britannic car, like a Rover, that's also a bit more warrior-like"

"Or a Saab" threw in Brother Matthew. I mean, I know it's not technically Britannic, but there were Vikings when the Lord first alighted on our shores and the quality of the engineering is fantastic and Vikings are warriors so it makes sense, er and runes are Celtic. I think."

"Alighted on our shores!" Brother Garry looked at Brother Matthew with a mix of incredulity and annoyance, "Why are you speaking like a Sunday School teacher. We are warrior monks, it involves fighting not talking like an old lady. The Templars wouldn't have said something stupid like that."

"They would probably have spoken Gaulish," Brother Simon called out, slightly muffled by his mask but, pretty unhelpfully given the way the carefully coordinated plan to liberate Christopher Sunday was rapidly un-coordinating.

"Oh, yeah. Ok, they might have said something stupid like that then," conceded Brother Garry and he huffed off, ahead of the other two. He was wishing that he really did have a bow of burning gold, rather than a slight headache bought on by petrol fumes and annoying people.

The Warriors of the Sleeping Sword, made their ramshackle way down the corridor of the hospital, not really knowing where they were going, but generally following the noise and excitement and hoping a wheelchair or some transport might materialise.

"Ah, Brothers... lo, ahead of us." Brother Matthew

pointed, quite magnificently he thought. It had the air of mystery about it.

"Lo, ahead of us" mumbled Brother Garry, "what's he talking about now? Idiot."

"There's a little old lady in a wheelchair" Brother Simon answered.

"Be she provided by the lord to fulfil our quest!" Brother Matthew voiced to an audience that did not exist.

"Be she?" He has gone from "Shakespeare to Jolly Jack Tar." Brother Garry made the side comment to Brother Simon. "At least we are treating this seriously and not as a melodrama masterclass."

Brother Simon looked sheepish and decided not to comment, he just nodded without looking at his compatriot. He did think the overall plan needed a little "dramatic effect" and he had taken some steps, but his idea was to keep it subtle. When it all was added to the great tome and recorded for posterity, his little touch to the proceedings would be more emphasis than anything too overblown.

"Madam" Brother Matthew walked up to the little old lady.

"Hello dear." She replied.

"The Lord hath provided, stand and you shall walk,"

"Oh, it's Christmas Day and they were just going to take me down to see my family, apparently nobody is allowed up on this floor because of him."

"She knows" Brother Matthew said with a feigned air of conceit.

"She probably reads the news, stupid." Brother Garry muttered and he barged in front. "We need that wheelchair, can you get out now".

"Oh, I can, I can't walk far though, I have gangrene in my foot, do want to see it?"

"No, get out of the chair, sit there" Brother Garry pointed to two chairs that had been placed outside a nearby door."

"It smells you know, it makes it very painful to walk."

"Good" Brother Garry responded without listening and he shuffled the gangrenous old dear across the corridor to a chair in a not so holy manner. "Sit there, Happy Christmas, someone will take your order soon."

"Oh, thank you dear, you are a little bit like my son, he has a bushy beard and not very much hair, and you have friendly eyes like him."

Brother Garry was a little bit annoyed by that last comment, he thought he had the fierce stone-cold eyes of a religious zealot that would not let anyone or anything stand in the way of his mission. "Yeah, well someone will be along soon." he said sulkily and stomped back to the others.

"Right, Brothers, follow me." Brother Matthew, nominally back in charge, carried on along the corridor. He was pushing the wheelchair in front of him and trailing one sulky and one sheepish (but also secretly excited by the little surprise he had prepared) religious zealot behind him.

Outside, excitement had given way to pandemonium. There were now sirens, police and the fire service had turned up. People were being moved back from the building to allow the professional services access.

"What's going on?" Shouted the press, "When are we getting a statement?" the noise was building to a crescendo.

The police parked their cars in the most obtuse way possible as if to make a point. Officers subverted the Christmas spirit by shouting orders to people who were never going to listen. Children cried, dogs barked.

Jude and Martine decided to cross back to the other side of the road and look on the chaos and… from a safe distance… the smoke?! rising from the other side of the building.

"It's all kicking off." Jude said, watching a fire engine try and navigate its way through the crowd, trying to avoid the need to add an ambulance to the parade of emergency vehicles in attendance.

"Mmm, Happy Christmas," added Martine, more as a general comment than directed at anyone.

Back inside the hospital, the Brothers, on their mission from God, were rather surprised to see a crowd of suits, uniforms, cameras and microphones charge across a corridor and disappear into a room on the left. Immediately afterwards, they heard the fast click of cameras added to the noise as the journalists photographed something. Brother Matthew wandered on and had a quick glance at the rabble peering out of a window overlooking a carpark, then glanced back at the door that they had all just exited. A light flashed, illuminating the moment (a camera flash from the corridor) but it did illuminate the moment as well as their destiny. Christopher Sunday lay in the bed, static but on his own. Whatever had distracted everyone previously in the room with him, had left him on his own, perhaps only briefly, but for long enough.

"Oh wonder." said Brother Matthew out loud.

"Oh wonderful." added Brother Garry, recognising a lucky break that didn't involve gangrene and old ladies.

"I wonder what they are looking at?" said the sheepish monk "Oh well, let's get on with it."

Christopher Sunday was lifted gently out of the bed, put in a wheelchair and draped in a sheet, he had a surgical mask put over his face and a medical hat put on his head. Surreptitiously, he was wheeled out of the room, under the noses of everyone who was looking, pointing and camera flashing something in the car park below.

Exit from the hospital was straightforward for the wheelchair and its kidnapping doctor monks. There was only one incident. They passed a couple of blue suits, one containing a beady eyed weaselly man and the other a bulldog, who barked; "Sunday, Christopher Sunday" at them.

Brother Garry pointed up the corridor. "That way, third on the right."

"Good, clear the floor now." The weaselly one responded.

"That's what we are doing" Brother Simon answered, and they picked up the pace.

Christopher Sunday, eyes now open frantically looked from side to side, still not able to focus, but with the drugs wearing off he was starting to get some sense of self. His arms and legs were tingling, he didn't think he could move, but there was sensation. He had spent eighteen years in darkness, the light, was not quite what he expected.

Down the corridor, lift, ramp, corner, corridor and carpark. The boys were there at the door, "behold the Chariot of Fire" announced Brother Simon, pride coming just before a fall… "oh"

"Oh is an understatement, what have you done?" said Brother Garry.

"   ." added Brother Matthew, dumbstruck.

"Erm, it might have been the incense"

"Incense? No sense."

"Well" Brother Simon was mounting a hopeless defence. "I am not saying there actually was a smell of petrol in the car, there might have been a slight odour, but... but more importantly, I thought the smell of incense might have leant a little 'j'nai se quoi' to the moment. You know, like in church. So I left a little stick burning in the ash tray, so you know, when we got back."

"Yer ner say what?" said Brother Garry.

"It was only little and also I had the cassette all ready to play the Hallelujah Chorus…" Brother Simon added, hopefully.

Brother Matthew looked at the spray of water, the fireman, the flashing cameras. There were police, children, dogs crowds, nurses, doctors pushing patients out as they moved people away and evacuated the hospital wing. In the centre of it all in the hospital carpark, in a transformative moment like the proverbial bush, the Chariot of Fire had gone from the allegorical to the literal and was now a chariot on fire. Well, less chariot and more a roaring inferno of rubber and plastic and metal and Italian engineering. It was creating the distraction that nobody wanted.

"Oh. Clouds unfold," Brother Matthew whispered to himself, "Oh clouds unfold."

Chapter 8

Midi5

Tuesday the twenty-seventh of December, Jude had to go back to work. It was a ridiculous situation, the waste collections had been suspended for the Christmas period and until New Years Day. He had no work to do but he had to attend the office. *At least,* he thought, *I can do a short day.* He thought about the mess of paperwork on his desk and wondered if he genuinely could have a short day.

Jude had enjoyed a lovely Christmas and surprised himself. He wondered whether he should have got drunk and made a move. He was glad he didn't. He didn't move well, drunk he would have looked like an idiot and actually, he wasn't sure that making a move was the right thing to do. He felt Martine deserved a little more respect than *a move*, especially a bad drunken one. Honestly? He was waiting for divine intervention and hoping it would happen soon. He hadn't realised that a relationship could be built on a road accident and he was hoping like hell that it actually could. He had a relationship with Martine, but it wasn't… well it wasn't, not yet. *But almost*, he thought, just that bolt from the blue, that thing that happens. It needed to happen. *God something needs to happen* he thought.

Jude reflected on the excitement at the hospital, he wasn't quite sure what he witnessed. Chaos, a fire, most of the emergency services. Doctors were evacuating patients from the wing near the carpark and he chuckled at the memory of three hysterical doctors, still masked and running a poor guy in a wheelchair up the road. Perhaps they were worried about smoke inhalation, they were certainly doing their best to get away from the hospital.

Then, my god the news! Christopher Sunday, coma victim/medical marvel wakes up on Christmas Day and is immediately kidnapped. No one has seen what has happened and it was thought an unregistered Fiat Uno was burnt in the car park to cause a distraction and Tucker the West Country Sheep man, was at the hospital with a possible cancer diagnosis, which caused excitement in the business news. Rumours of a buyout of Sheepwrestling.com became a possibility and rumours of three quarters of a billion, including merchandising and global licensing. Australian and New Zealand press had gone mad and both thought they had what it took to win a global championship, if the infrastructure could be set up. Tucker's sore balls had never felt bigger, but that wasn't reported in the news, that was a secret Tucker kept well concealed.

It all happened, Jude had enjoyed a lovely meal, walk, drink and conversation into the night with Martine. She had left at midnight in a taxi because she had a train booked in the morning to visit her cousins and uncle and aunt and maybe her other aunt if she was in the country.

And his mother, oh god. His mother. Oh well, mothers!

But now it was work, he had to go back and tidy his desk. He almost didn't switch on his EWP but he decided he had to because that was the routine. He waited for a few moments whilst it fizzed and burped and pinged in his hand, threw up an error message MEMORY ERROR t1171653

PRESS OK TO CONTINUE, the notification that he has 382 messages to archive, did he want to do this now? NO and it crashed so he ran through the whole damn cycle again. Fizz, burp, ping, OK, NO.. then FINALLY!!! He clicked on the blue icon for his schedule and was surprised to see a note telling him he had a meeting at 09:00. He never had meetings. He once had a meeting with his manager for an annual appraisal. It was the most excruciating twenty seven minutes of his life. It was more awkward than a Christmas call with his mother. Jude and his manager had agreed never to do that again and next time they would just email his results out. It was never going to be quite as collaborative as the HR documentation pretended and in truth, his manager neither knew nor cared what he did as long as he did it. Whatever it was?

The meeting had started with... "Yes, err well done Mr Drazkowski. Your performance is commensurate with your grade and at least comparable with your peers and you met the criteria and well, yes congratulations on an excellently adequate year. You should be very pleased with an er… adequate grading, it means you are performing to a standard, that we er… well, we definitely appreciate." It got no better. By the end of the meeting, Jude had no idea how he performed, relative to his job grade, his peers or himself. His manager's technique for looking like he was engaged, without having to make a personal connection, was to look at Jude's right eyebrow as he spoke. He was almost looking Jude in the eyes but not quite. Jude didn't know this but he sensed it and he left the room feeling a little queasy. It didn't help that he was, not once, referred to by his first name.

But this meeting would not be an appraisal, it was also a

month earlier than the appraisal dates, which always happened a month late, in February.

Jude arrived at work and was met at the door by Dave and Dave. "Come with me." said Dave, officiously.

Unusually, Jude was escorted through the gate, he was swiped through by other Dave. No one asked to see his card and he didn't even use it to open the gate. Dave and Dave were having the best day of their lives, it was a Christmas present from the organisation, the chance to represent the government on a secret mission. Well, if '*secret mission, should you choose to accept it'* was to escort a member of staff through an electronic door to a meeting room in a highly conspiratorial manner.

Other Dave, many years later, would tell his grandchildren of this order and swear them to silence, whilst looking around nervously. Dave, many years later had forgotten most things, except how to put cheap vodka into a half pint glass. Such was the divisive nature of these mysterious circumstances.

Jude was urged into an office, it was an office that was usually kept locked and it was quite small. He looked at the two faces in the room and his heart dropped, he didn't know why. They both turned to Dave. Dave looked expectantly for a medal or commendation or at least a tacit acknowledgement for his service.

"OUT. DOOR. NOW." Growled the larger face.

"sit down now" sneered the smaller face.

Jude, nervously, desperately confused and now rather frightened, squeezed between what felt like a gorilla and a rattlesnake, to a chair on the window side of the room. It was a high window allowing light in through slightly opened blinds but it had no view out. Jude scanned the small bland magnolia room. Drawing pins on an empty pinboard, a metal filing cabinet and an empty wastepaper bin. The table had been pushed to the side, it had some paperwork on which he glanced nervously at. He was sitting on the only chair in the room which had been centrally positioned against the back wall.

"HOW NICE MEETING YOU JUDEK. DRAZKOWSKI." The gorilla said, growled or perhaps threatened. Jude had never before been threatened so explicitly by intonation only. His name had just been weaponised. Nice trick if you can pull it off, but it helped if you were six four, twenty two stone (ish) and squeezed so dangerously tightly into a suit, that you should be embarrassed by it. The monster in front of Jude was clearly not embarrassed. Jude briefly worried that saying his name in full, could be the straw that broke the camel's back and it would split a seam in the gorilla's monkey suit.

That thought was quickly dismissed by the rattlesnake who said. "yessss very nice to finally meet you judek k k" The rattlesnake managed the sentence without capitals and punctuation and had a strange glottal clicking noise as he finished his words, over emphasising the repetition of the hard consonant. Alongside the sibilance in his speech, this created a terrifyingly intimidating interviewer.

Jude still had no idea what this was all about but had

already decided that of the two matching blue suits, he was more freaked out by the slithery good cop and would probably prefer to be dismembered by King Kong cop, given a choice.

"Are you policemen?" he asked, nervously.

"no" hissed rattlesnake.

"WORSE." Gorilla was more guttural than phonetic, difficult to describe in normal communication terms.

"Oh" said Jude and he shuffled awkwardly on his chair.

"my name is gun mr' said Mr Gun. "thisss is mr savage"

"SAVAGE." Emphasised Savage, who made it clear that the 'Mr' was an unnecessary title and got in the way of imparting a simple idea.

"Oh" said Jude and he shuffled awkwardly on his chair again.

"have you heard of midi5 mr judek drazkowski"

"No" said Jude and he shuffled awkwardly on his chair for a third time.

"GOOD," Said Savage. Savagely as it happened.

"nooo you won't have because you were not authorised to" said Gun. It did go through Judes mind that Gun and Savage were suggesting something with their names, but someone should tell Mr Gun that his name didn't quite fit his personality. Mr Savage, however, fully fulfilled his obligations in that department.

"WE ARE FROM MIDI5" said Savage. Softening his tone slightly, to just pure terrifying.

"What's MIDI5?" asked Jude. Registering the use of 'were,' not 'are,' in Gun's comment. Adrenalin was causing his mind to race a little now, he was shuffling less and contemplating the stress responses fright, flight, freeze and considering whether freak-out should be added to the 'f' list and promoted to the top of it.

"luckily you have now been authorised"

"How?" asked Jude.

"MANAGER."

"Oh, does he know about MIDI5?" Impressed that his manager might know anything at all.

"NO. NOT AUTHORISED."

Confused, Jude asked again.. "What, er who is, er.. are MIDI5?"

"weee" hissed the snaking Gun, are an investigative arm of the ministry of disinformation" [pause] "we are an external agency employed and engaged to investigate transgressions" [pause] "we do things that the police do not dooo" [pause] "we ask the questions the police doo not ask"

"WE FIX THE PROBLEMS THE AUTHORITIES CANNOT FIX."

"wee have a level of disconnect"

"OF PLAUSABLE DENIABILITY."

"of opportunity"

"TO INVESTIGATE AND ENFORCE THE MINISTRIES ACTIVITIES WITHOUT THE OVERSIGHT AND INTERUPTION OF LAW."

"wee could make you disappear mr drazkowski"

"WE DON'T EXIST YOU SEE. WE ARE UNNACOUNTABLE. GOOD EH? WE CAN DO WHAT WE WANT."

"Disappear!? What murder me?"

"IT WOULD BE POLITICAL EXPEDIENCE, WOULDN'T IT MR GUN?"

"yesss it would definitely be politically expedient mister savage" [pause] "so mr drazkowski some questions'"

"The ministry of disinformation?" Jude was barely keeping up.

"the ministry of disinformation exists to protect the information in the ministry isnt it obvious mr drazkowski we manage that by minimising and maximising the matrix of media distributed and leaked" [pause] "by implementing a system of valves"

"Valves?"

"valves" [pause] "mr savage is a valve are you not mr savage"

"CORRECT MR GUN. I MANAGE THE FLOW OF INFORMATION FOR THE MINISTRY BY

POSITIONING MYSELF CROSS STREAM AND RESTRICTING AND DIVERTING UNTIL THE FLOW DIMINISHES. WOULD YOU LIKE TO BE A DIMINISHED FLOW MR DRAZKOWSKI?"

"No" said Jude adding, "Sir" for good measure. Jude was struggling to understand what the hell was going on. "Sir," he said again to the person who wasn't standing between Mr Gun and Mr Savage, which he felt was safer than looking at either of them. "what have I done?

"WELL MR DRAZKOWSKI, THAT IS WHAT WE WANT TO KNOW"

"Nothing?" said Jude hopefully.

"lets hope soo mr drazkowski so tell us"

"What?"

"EVERYTHING, ALL OF IT."

"I don't know where to start."

"THE BEGINNING."

"shall I give you a clue judek"

'Judek' was a development, "Yes please Sir."

"you have a new friend a female friend"

"Martine?" Said Jude.

"NO."

"Oh" said Jude, he wasn't sure that he had any other

friends.

"write that down mr savage"

Jude was unsure that Savage could write, it seemed a stretch, then he noticed him holding a pen and wondered whether the pen would buckle with the stress of the activity. The pen managed to hold it together, although no one would be able to read Savage's writing.

"MS WHITE."

"Maryam?".

"first names mr savage first names"

Savage went to write something down, changed his mind and cracked his knuckles instead. Jude couldn't quite understand how it echoed in a room so small, with no reflective surfaces and with any airspace in-between absorbed by a man monster and his slippery friend. Savages knuckle cracking managed to rebound from the walls menacingly and sound in translation like *you're screwed Jude*.

"you were seen with ms white on twenty-fifth December afternoon is that usual behaviour for your clients mr drazkowski" A barbed question. Jude was very aware that whilst he might not understand the full extent and implications of his job, it was secret. He was signed up to secrecy and he knew he did not inspect dustbins for the waste management services and he shouldn't talk to his 'clients'.

"PERSONAL RELATIONSHIP." Savage said out loud and as he started to press the pen down to (presumably) write the same, it popped audibly, folded in half and a small piece of plastic ricocheted across the room. Jude followed it with his eyes, tempted to be helpful and pick it up for Mr Savage, then reconsidering.

"no records to be kept now mr savage nothing recorded" then Gun added, "my my what might be said that may not get out of this room"

Jude was slightly intrigued that the only apparent method of recording this conversation with the snake man was by a secretarial gorilla who wanted to destroy the pen more than he wanted to destroy Jude. It didn't fully sit with his vision of the secret security services, even if the secret security services in question were so secret that even the government did not even know about them. Apparently.

A red faced Mr Savage reached over to the table, dumped the bits of broken pen and brought the sheaf of papers back over. He waved them dramatically as he said "TELL US ABOUT MARYAM (NONAME) WHITE. STATUS: (UNKNOWN). 2A, HIGH ROAD. NGS, NBD, NCR, NVT." So Jude, given the little choice he felt he had, did. He did not feel he incriminated himself, though he had made contact with her on his collection and communicated on Christmas Day. He told them about everything except the weird shock he got when she touched his arm and the fact that she seemed intangible and that any description of her was better expressed as sensations.

"AND THE SAMPLES YOU COLLECTED SON?"

Son, thought Jude, *are we bonding*? "Oh, the usual. I bagged them, I can't remember what it was now, some hair I think a razor, the usual sorts of stuff. It was all bagged correctly."

"and, how were those samples treated mr drazkowski think carefully what did you uuuse"

"They were double bagged, given a squirt of ONCON, erm ONCONAA937," he added, but as he watched Mr Savage look upwards to the stars beyond the ceiling, he realised it was probably not necessary to explain.

"AND THAT'S ALL?".

"Yes sir."

"THEN HOW DO YOU EXPLAIN THESE?" and Savage pulled some photographs from the paperwork and held them in front of Jude.

The first was a confusing picture, a plastic bag, clearly, but with a mass of something gelatinous inside. The colour picture was not fantastic quality but it looked like a mass of yellow bubbles, surrounding a purplish lump and liquid, perhaps a greyish oily liquid. It looked pretty revolting. The second picture was a little more distinct, again the polyethene bag and this one obviously contained a cheap blue disposable razor, but where the head of the razor should be, again a smear of oily grey liquid, some red/purple lumps of something and yellow fatty bubbles. There were also white fibres protruding from this mess. It was again, neither distinct nor explainable, or nice to look at.

"What are they?" asked Jude.

"YOU TELL US SON, WHAT DOES IT SAY ON THE BAG?".

Jude could make out the number, he read it out loud.

"IT'S THE SAMPLES FROM MARYAM (NONAME) WHITE, SON. WHAT DID YOU DO TO THEM?".

"Nothing said Jude, just the normal?".

"then what do you think young judek has happened here"

Jude did not know. In fact, at this point he did not care. He did think that he might escape being a diminished flow as the questions were getting less aggressive. He was beginning to feel like Gun and Savage might just need him alive for long enough, at least to tell the story.

The interview was suddenly interrupted by a loud BANG from outside the room. Nobody inside knew that Dave and Dave were having a marital moment. Both had let Gun and Savage in without challenge. Both had read between the lines of the explanation that they were here on official business, *they should have been warned and they should be escorted to a private office*. Savage's aggression was quite persuasive, it would have been like stopping a train. Dave had treated them with such embarrassing deference that he had offered them coffee on arrival and other Dave had swiped them through, without even asking to see any identification. Both the Daves had been proud of their behaviour at the time. Both had subsequently realised after the event, that the fine line they trod between enacting government business and enacting government business, had been somewhat compromised. It had been trod rough shod with cringing servility and perhaps, just perhaps, they might now, just might want to see some credentials.

The bang had been other Dave making his authority known, or at least trying to suggest it by slamming a door in a manner befitting his status.

Gun and Savage looked at each other, stood up and left the room. A bang was a bang in anyone's book and banging needed investigating. Jude was left in the room, though he noticed uncomfortably the door clicked shut and double click locked behind him. He was alone with a table, some drawing pins, an empty filing cabinet and some paperwork which might just tell him what was going on.

He didn't know how long he had, so he moved quickly over to the folder. Moving the photos away, he had after all seen them, he looked at the papers. The Top Sheet was just a label, similar to his, it just said: `Subject: Female, 28-32? Name Maryam (NONAME) White. Status: (UNKNOWN). ADDRESS: 2a, High Road. Comments: Subject NGS, NBD, NCR, NVT`. And in ballpoint pen, scribbled on top. 'Investigate. Judek Drazkowski????? FRIEND????'. He turned over the sheet.

The next page made him take a deep breath.

>>>>>>>>>>>>>>>>>>>>>>>>>>>>>>>>>>>>>

AUTHORISATION LEVEL: 1 (High - Governmental)

SECURITY LEVEL: Secret (High)

SUBJECT: WHITE, M. [F].

GENCHECK: Positive.

PHENOTYPIC TRAIT: New, 9+

TRANSGRESSION: None reported.

THREAT LEVEL: Low, NCD

RISK LEVEL: Low. No identified family.

ACTION: Investigate & incarcerate, force approved.

TERMINATION ORDER: Report in.

COMMENTS:

Known contacts.1, Judek Drazkowski, Gov't employee. 2 known meetings, relationship unknown? Investigate. If required raise section 4.

AGENTS ASSIGNED: Gun/Savage

AA19874300.1

>>>>>>>>>>>>>>>>>>>>>>>>>>>>>>>>>>>>>>

A few words jumped out; *incarcerate, force approved, termination order, section 4*. Quite a few words, in fact an unhealthy proportion of them. They jumped out just a little too far. They jumped into Jude's head and rattled around like broken cogs in a gearbox, they damaged the finely tuned engineering of his mind, they crunched when the thoughts should roll and they caused a blockage when ideas should flow. Jude put the paperwork back and sat down with a very deep breath and a slightly tight chest.

By the time Gun and Savage returned, Jude was slumped in his seat. Colour had drained from his face, he had no fight, there would be flight and fright, but now he was caught in a brief moment of abject depression.

Christmas, an exciting fun Christmas that started with him running over his new best friend and maybe, hopefully more? A Christmas caught in the media chaos of a hospital's rising star, of fires and mothers and curries and cabbage. Of beautiful creatures... and he stopped just for a second with that thought. A broken gear tooth dropped into the sump of his cranial cavity and loosened the wheels and the gears started moving again so he repeated himself, beautiful creatures... Maryam White seemed barely human and the paperwork seemed to confirm that.

> *GENCHECK: Positive.*
>
> *PHENOTYPIC TRAIT: New Variant, 9+*
>
> *TRANSGRESSION: None reported.*

'None reported' whatever it was? it was unfair.

ACTION: Investigate & incarcerate, force approved.

TERMINATION ORDER: Report in.

What the hell did that mean! Fight, flight and fiddle the damn Termination Order! Jude smiled and his cheeks flushed as the blood flowed back to them and he thought, *damn your NDAs, damn the official secrets act, damn you all and your section four whatever that is.*

The gorilla cocked his head slightly. "YOU OK?"

Jude was unsure whether that was a degree of compassion or just curiosity, but he sat up a little and replied, "Yes Sir." Because Jude was OK. He really was ok, he had just had a moment of clarity.

"GOOD, WE DONE, MR GUN?"

"i think we are mr savage I think we are" [pause] "are we not young judek k k" and the rattlesnake click was there. "will we see you again I hope nottt" which was another veiled threat, not rhetoric and a shiver went down Jude's spine, but the die was now cast

Jude noticed that, as they left the building a fawning Dave asked Gun and Savage if they would like a coffee, "for the journey Mr err?" No answer. Other Dave opened the doors for them "Nice to meet you Mr um?" No response.

Jude was glad they were gone, he had things to do.

Chapter 9

And did those feet

Jerusalem House was slumped in a dirty, grumpy architectural post Christmas hangover. Jerusalem House had eaten too much, drunk too much and it had bits of food debris down its front and on the floor where it had crashed unconscious.

One of Jerusalem House's most fascinating features, unless you lived there, was its ability to inhabit the equal and opposite reaction to every positive moment. The sun shone, Jerusalem House managed to be in the shade. Snow turned to dirty slush on touching it. Rain somehow soaked into it, to come out later as damp, when and where you least expected it. Christmas happiness was exhibited as chaos and excess and suspended in that state until the christian, western and highly commercialised first world recovered from the festival season by getting fit, tidying up and planning a summer vacation. Jerusalem house followed Christmas excess with hair of the dog. Dark matted dog hair. On sofas, in drains and in unexpected clumps when you poked around in the corners.

It was Jerusalem House's uncanny ability to be overlooked, out of embarrassment, queasiness or moral indignity, that made it the perfect place to stash a recovering and very confused Messiah (alleged). A second coming that was actually struggling to come to, at all. Despite the best attempts of his devoted rescuers, kidnappers, disciples or village idiots, depending on the subjectivity of your view, Christopher was not moving. He was at least breathing. The self-appointed holy order got away with this grand conspiracy because everybody looked in the opposite direction, instinctively.

In the opposite direction to Jerusalem House was a long-abandoned rusting and rotting garage forecourt. It was full of bindweed and buddleia, decorated with crisp packets, tin cans and dog faeces, it was still a better view than Jerusalem House. People could at least speculate on what it once was, or might be again. The garage forecourt at least, had potential.

Even the police did not consider Jerusalem House and its residents as suspicious, that would involve considering them at all and nobody wanted to do that. Especially the police. It was easier to program the cameras to press criminal charges and heavily fine jaywalkers, fly-tippers, shoplifters, people committing acts of indecency in public, parkour on public property and double parkers on double yellows. Crime that made a net profit were the crimes to focus resources on. Occasionally you had to throw it all at a murder, but mostly murder hunts were publicity stunts and viewed by the police service as loss leaders. "Until such time as a full DNA database, integrated with a criminal justice system, made all crime fighting proactive, not reactive." The Commissionaire had once said, after a little coercion from the Chief Constable. How prophetic.

"How pathetic?" Brother Simon poked Christopher in the arm. There was no response.

"You could have killed him," said Brother Garry.

"He is the lamb of god" said brother Simon, as though it was relevant "and anyway, I put him in the recovery position"

"Lying flat out with a pillow under his neck is not the recovery position and if he wasn't the son of god… well another one, the other one died and rose again." He thought about the logic of this and paused momentarily but ploughed on because Paton would have done the same "…he would have died."

"And risen again." Argued Brother Simon, indignant that his medical supervision needed to be supervised.

"Again, again?" Said Brother Matthew thoughtfully.

"No, just again, he has been reborn, not risen. You are complicating the prophesy, its simple".

"Well he is alive, I just saw him move". Said Brother Simon.

"Well duuhhh! He *is* the son of God. Technically, another one".

Christopher Sunday had moved. Since absconding (let us allow history to judge the motives of his disciples) he had slept. Solidly, deeply and naturally, as the chemicals, drugs and fluids that had been pumped in to sedate and control him for a number of months passed through and passed out of his system. He moved again and just gently, blinked his eyes. The light was still too much. He had opened his eyes in hospital or had them opened for him as part of his checks, but that was under sedation, now his brain was trying to process the light. He blinked again and looked around the dingy living room. He did not realise at this point that he had been laid out on a large, worn, slightly unhygienic sofa and had a sheet, two blankets and a green parka coat put on top of him. It was winter and though the weather was untypically mild, Jerusalem house had its own microclimate, which was always worse than the weather outside. It also had its own flora and fauna and should have been interesting to scientists. Any intelligent scientist, however, would rather investigate stinking, rotting, tropical swamps with a disproportionate number of leaches, insects, alligators, viruses, bacteria and the chance of long-lost headhunting tribesmen eating their brains, than look too closely at Jerusalem house.

"I… am..." The first words Christopher Sunday had said in eighteen years quietly, huskily, creakily like a light breeze blowing the dust of generations from an opened door of a long derelict house. He said again, "I am…"

"There," said Brother Simon, interrupting the first words spoken by the scientific miracle and would be second son of god, "I told you I didn't kill him."

"Shhh you idiot." Brother Matthew was quietly and calmly, but fast, approaching a moment of transcendence. It could turn out to be wind, but it still had the sensation of religious ecstasy.

"Who?" Said Christopher.

"Right" said Brother Garry, who had been born for leadership and favoured a direct approach. "You are called Christopher Sunday, you have just been reborn from an eighteen-year coma and you are the son, well the second son, of God. You need some breakfast I expect, as you have things to do. Incidentally, we don't have a chariot of fire anymore"

"It caught fire." Brother Simon added helpfully.

"But," Brother Garry was looking with distaste at his shorter fellow acolyte, "We do have to go and do some dark satanic mills and actually with the weather as it is, the hills are quite cloudy. Err, well *clouded* I 'spose, so best not waste any time."

Christopher Sunday turned his head and looked around the room. He remembered last being surrounded by a white sterile space. He saw now a room of dark shadows, of piles, of books and magazines. Boxes stacked to the ceiling and old computer parts leant against the wall. Where those walls were not obscured by the debris of religious fervour there were posters, a pinboard had newspaper cuttings, post-it notes and a postcard of a rubbly desert scene. There was a crude altar made from a 1960s school desk with candles and a wooden cross. It was surrounded by crystals and old stones. There were old wooden carvings, feathers and a plastic doll's head. There was a stuffed otter sitting up on its haunches with its paws together like a supplicant looking for communion and brass Indian dancing animal headed gods enjoying the party. It was an altar of pagan offerings, religious eclecticism, new age nonsense and dubious taste. Over the window an old and faded set of nylon curtains allowed a little light to break through from outside, it barely lit the chaos and disorder surrounding him.

Looking at Christopher Sunday an expectant Brother

Garry, a serene Brother Matthew and the still smiling-broadly-at-not-having-killed-the-saviour, smallest holy warrior, an exultant Brother Simon. Staring closely at him was a mix of fervent eyes and beards and body odour and expectation. Christopher opened, closed, and then held open his mouth.

"Behold the Lord... from his lips shall cometh forth," announced Brother Matthew and the brothers sensed a moment.

Christopher retched. It was dark, thick, brown bile, which wasn't quite the moment anyone expected, but a gift from God is a gift from God so the viscous residue was carefully scraped off the sofa put in a small corked bottle and labelled *holy vomit of god*. Always forward thinking, it was dated and saved as a relic for the founding of a church at some point in the future.

"I guess breakfast would be good?" said Brother Garry, after the bottle of vomit of God was added to the altar display and placed in between the otters legs. "Don't suppose we can divine the countenance on an empty stomach. We got rice crispies or some Bakewell Tart. It's a bit old but it's not mouldy."

*

Jude's phone rang, he looked at the caller display, it was Martine. "Hi, he answered".

"Jude!! We won."

"Won?"

"The healthcare lottery."

"Oh" Jude said.

"Not how much? Are you ok?"

"I have got something on my mind, how much?"

"£150! We can go out for dinner."

"Good, ok."

"Shall I come round?" Martine was worried, Jude didn't sound himself. He frequently sounded lost and confused, but he really didn't sound like he was there at all and she was concerned, especially as she had expected him to be overexcited at winning one hundred and fifty pounds on the lottery ticket. She picked up her bag, checked everything was off and charged off to his flat as fast as she could.

*

Ian Piggot-Smith was on the internet, he has just been click baited into commenting on homosexuality, women's rights, transgender issues, immigration, state support, drink and drug dependency and single mothers. One little thing led to another. It was by his own admission his broad mind and broader experience that allowed him such an ability in educating people on how to better live their lives. Having helped the global community of internet users just a little, by comparing and judging everyone's unique experience to his own, 'a self-made unfashionably white and straight middle-class man who enjoys a drink but knows when to stop, who doesn't have a problem with anyone's rights but!' He was closing the computer down when he thought, *oh...*

lottery ticket. You never know and he grabbed his wallet off the side and typed the numbers in. Then he looked at the screen for a couple of seconds. Then he put the ticket in a plastic sleeve, rebooted the computer and typed the numbers in again.

"Blinkin' heck" he said. It was only ten thirty-two in the morning and it wasn't Christmas Day any more, but he went over to his drinks cabinet, poured himself a large glass of whiskey, walked into his lounge, whiskey in one hand and plastic sleeve containing lottery ticket in the other and sat down.

"Ian... Ian... where are you?" Katie Piggot-Smith was calling out to no response. Several minutes later she found Ian Piggot-Smith in the lounge on the sofa with a not quite as big whiskey in his hand and a plastic sleeve in the other. "Ian, why didn't you answer?" she asked.

In reply, he just lifted up his arm and handed her the plastic encased lottery ticket.

"What's wrong?" She said, thinking now that he may have had a stroke.

"Eight." He managed to get out, before he had to take a breath and another sip of the whiskey.

"We have won?" Said Katie.

"Eight." He said again.

"Eight pounds?" Katie Piggot-Smith asked her husband, confused at his blank expression and inability to finish his sentence. "Have you had a stroke dear, I think you have been drinking too much wine recently."

"No, millions." he replied.

"Eight Million?" Said Katie Piggot-Smith, suddenly engaged with the conversation.

"More." said Ian.

"Eighty?" Said Katie.

"No, eight hundred and seventy-three million, two hundred and thirty-two pounds."

"Oh." She turned around, walked into the dining room and to the drinks cabinet, poured herself a large glass of gin, walked back into the lounge and sat down next to her husband to look at the change of fortune on the coffee table.

There they sat, for a full twenty-seven minutes until the phone rang. Ian picked up the phone and clicked the button to answer. "Yes."

A foreign sounding voice at the other end said "Hello Mr Pidgotty-Smith, this is Steven calling from your network provider, we have a report that your computer has been infected and…"

"Clear off you thieving little monkey" snapped back the newly multi-millionaired but previously self-made man, "and its Piggot-Smythe" he spat down the phone, before hanging up.

It was a crank call but it shook him out of his trance. "Well wife" he turned to Katie, "lets go and get our money, this is what I worked so hard for. I deserve a new car, maybe a Roller and new clubs. I can join the Regent Golf club. Oh actually, I could get a Porsche as well," he added an affected 'a' to the end of Porsche, as though he actually gave a flying fiddle how it was pronounced in Germany. "I wonder if there is room for clubs in one of those little sporty ones, I guess there is. You'll want dresses, and a house. We can go on holiday, don't fancy abroad don't like having to speak to those people…" and in his head he spent approximately two million pounds, which left eight hundred and seventy-one million, two hundred and thirty-two pounds to fritter away, before interest. He could not wait to pay the cheque in, "those damn wastes of space on the bank counter, I'll demand the manager and an office and a cup of coffee, they will call me sir... oh yes, now they will."

He picked up the ticket and read the small print on the back, there was a winner's helpline. He took a final swig of his whiskey, put the glass down, picked the phone back up and dialled.

"Hello! Healthcare Lottery hotline this is…"

"Ian Piggot-Smith, that's Smythe not Smith." Interrupted the 8/10ths billionaire.

"Angelina." Fought back Angelina Poppleberry, Hotline Service Manager and recent winner of the annual award for winning service. "Angelina Poppleberry, how may I help?"

"Popple what?" Said Ian-Piggot-Smith.

"Berry," growled Angelina, its "Poppleberry, How may I

help?"

"I am a winner." Piggot-Smith said.

"We are all winners hehehe," said the ever-cheerful Angelina, "can I take some details please?"

"What do you need?"

"Can I take your name please?"

Again! thought Piggot-Smith, but for eight hundred and seventy-three million, two hundred and thirty two pounds it was worth it. "Ian Piggot-Smith, pronounced Smythe, that is P.I.G.G.O.T. HYPHEN S.M.I.T.H." He confirmed. He heard Angelina banging away at her keyboard.

"Ok Mr Smith," the winner of Winners Hotline Service Manager and recent winner of the annual award for winning service said, completely ruining her chances of winning for two years running.

"SMYTHE." Hissed Piggot-Smith.

"I am sorry Mr Smythe."

"NO ITS PIGGOT-SMYTHE." Piggot-Smith shouted down the phone.

"Oh, hehehehe" bounced jolly Angelina, "what an easy mistake to make, I bet you get that all the time?"

Silence. The unstoppable voice had just met the immovable temperament and the laws of social physics had just approached an event horizon and were staring into the abyss of an invisible singularity.

"Mr Piggot-Smythe, are you still there please?" Angelina negotiated the moment back down to Defcon3.

"YES, I am."

"Now, do you have a number on the ticket please"

"Yes, its: 1835-48263"

"No."

"No?"

"Not that one."

"Oh, well there is 8888875374894?"

"No again! We get this all the time, it begins AA, it's under the barcode."

"Right," Piggot-Smith had not expected to have to earn the eight hundred million by ordeal, "AA295404296."

"Perfecto! Ok, just a moment." Angelina hammered away at her keyboard.

"Oh. Mr Piggot-Smythe, it's not a problem but please can you hold. I need to pass you to the Hotline Senior Service Manager, who, you will be pleased to know, has won the annual award for winning service, FIVE times! Four of them were in a row and he missed one year because of an incident with a badly placed word. He is called Algy Bertwhistle."

"He is called what?" Said Piggot-Smith, wondering where these people could have come from.

"Algy Bee, we call him" Said Angelina Poppleberry. We are known as Algy and Ange at work, like a couple. But we are not an actual couple. Only professionally," she added slightly flustered. Then, as an afterthought and to quickly change the subject, "there is a link online if you would like to provide some positive feedback for this service. Transferring you nowww…" and the line transferred to an engaged tone, overlayed with a message that told Ian Piggot-Smith that everyone knew he was waiting. After several minutes of wondering how much interest he would be earning for this, an even more cheerful Algy Bee answered the phone.

"Ahh Mr Piggot-SmYthe" he over emphasised, what a lucky man you are congratulations on your award, Algy Bertwhistle at your absolute service.

"Award?"

"Yes, yes. Your award, I have checked the computer and you have been awarded eight hundred and seventy-three million, two hundred and thirty two pounds. CONGRATULATIONS!"

"But it's a prize? Not an award."

"Weeellll," replied Algy, "a lot of people think that, but it's not really. You seeee, weeell… that is to say 'the health service lottery' used to be registered under the Lotteries and Gaming Act but there was some rumpety-pumpety hoo haa over money, isn't there always?" He barely took a breath "…and after a little lobbying, the law was changed that allowed us to save a little of the tax. On the basis that eight percent of gross pops back into the health service to save lives, we were able to re-register as a charity. As such, there are no such things as prizes, just charitable awards. You have qualified for the biggest charitable award in history, congratulations! I think we have jolly well saved your life, what? By the way, thank you for your donation as well. Without your donations we could not award so much to worthy causes like... well like yourself and those poor people in hospital, it's all on the tickets on the back, the old proverbial small print."

"Bu...but... charity?" said Piggot-Smith, humiliated to the sum of eight hundred and seventy-three million, two hundred and thirty two pounds. "Charity? I worked for this, I speculated, I picked the numbers, I ticked the random box and I...I... charity?"

"Nothing to be embarrassed about we all need money. It begins at home Mr Piggot-Smith, it begins at home it's not greedy to be needy, it's your award, no one can take it away from you. Now, if Angy and I can poppity pop round to see the ticket and perhaps take a few snaps of the lucky charitable cause, or is it causes? Do you have a partner Mr Piggot-SmYthe," he said Smith in such a supercilious way, "is there Mrs a Ms or Mr… or a They or Them? Anyone else in need, we can split the award you know we are inclusive in more ways than one."

"Yes, er no, er yes. Mrs Katie, er Katherine Piggot-Smith. She is a woman you know… only one of her, not plural just one woman… we are married, in church." Piggot-Smith fumbled with his words, completely lost in a modern world where he was confused about treating strangers with respect.

"Good good, causes of the highest order. I have no doubt it's well deserved. We'll see you at oh nine hundred, we'll bring some champagne, not too early for a celebratory bubbly is it? What address? Have a nice suit for the photos or a dress, I don't want to make assumptions. Hmmm look at the time, STOP THE BUS Mr PS, there's time a plenty. I have seen your address, we can rustle up a snap happy chappie to take some pics, put your best togs on we can be there in an hour. This is charity we don't want to leave you in need any longer do we!" and the formalities were duly booked in with great haste.

*

Martine knocked on Jude's door. He answered. She had only known him a few weeks but she thought she knew him fairly well. His expression made him look ten years older. It was odd, he was normally so confused, he looked earnest and serious and perhaps a little scared and pale.

"Come in, come in" he said, "sit down, I need to tell you what I do. What I need to do." He added.

*

"So how was the Bakewell Tart?" Said Brother Garry.

Christopher retched again, but this time with lumps and possibly a cherry.

"Nice," said Brother Simon, "I was only going to found one church, but the more relics the better I 'spose. Perhaps I could found a couple of churches?" he mused, and he wandered off to find another small jar and a biro.

Chapter 10

Maryam

"Martine" Jude said. He stopped. "What I do, it's necessary for you to know what happened."

"Shall I make us a coffee?" Martine asked.

"Yes, yes." Jude replied impatiently. He paced the room as Martine went to the kitchenette. "I am sorry," he added, "I have something on my mind and I need to tell you." He speculated whether he should add, *because you are my best friend or because you are my girlfriend,* but he didn't because he wasn't sure if either were right, or both were wrong and there was some third friendship status. Perhaps the third zone was that she was his only friend? But he pushed that idea from his mind just as Martine came back into the room, she put a coffee on the table next to the sofa and sat on the other side holding her cup. It forced Jude to sit down next to her but it still took her by surprise when he turned urgently, to face her.

"Right, its complicated." He began then he paused and took a deep breath. Martine smiled and said nothing. "My job, what I do…" he paused again and for so long Martine had to help.

"You inspect waste, that's fine." Martine started to think that he was going to be embarrassed about it and waited, for him to speak again.

"What I do, people don't know. It's secret, it's a government job, not like the council not even really the government, but the security services."

Martine replied, far too quickly in fact and she immediately hated herself for saying it. "Double O Dustbin, licenced to spill." She then added "I am sorry I didn't mean that"

"No no, its fine; it is a bit like that actually. I do work for the security services, through some outsourced partner agency. They... well you know that there is a DNA database, most people signed up to it..."

"Yes," said Martine, "The government was encouraging people to register a few years ago, I think a lot of people didn't care and signed up."

"Well," Jude interrupted, the people who didn't register and provide a sample for the database, my job, I, er... well I get sent their names and I have to go and collect their rubbish and then I go through it and find things with their DNA on and it goes off and gets analysed and they get added to the database. But they don't know." He stopped talking, to let Martine think on that.

"That's outrageous, so people don't consent? They just get their DNA profile stored on a database without knowing."

"Yes," said Jude, "I am sorry"

"Well," it was Martine's turn, "there are worse, I mean more immoral jobs." She sought to reassure Jude on principal, although she was shocked. But then, she thought *I worked for Autonomous Accumulations? That was hardly the most right-on company in the world, even if she didn't get paid for it.*

"No, that's not it, I mean that's part of it, but not all of it, there is more." He took a deep breath. "I was called into an office the other day, by these men, well two agents I guess. They were like, well I don't really know. They were scary they demanded I tell them about Maryam White, you know the girl we…"

"Yes, I remember" Martine said, "beautiful, dark hair, floaty dress, well sort of floaty all over really, did she speak to us, it's a bit vague and it was all a bit weird?"

"Yes, Maryam, not sure what she said but well they wanted to know about her and they sort of interrogated me, they actually threatened me, they said they could…" He tried to think of the words "I think they threatened to kill me."

"Kill?" Martine was prepared to accept Double O Dustbins dubious career choices and that he may have been interviewed, but death threats seemed to be a little bit out there.

"I know and…" Jude was starting to gabble now. "They had her address on a form, they said she was wrong, not wrong, her DNA was wrong, or different or something and they could impound her, not impound her what were the words… um, um, err… that they could INCARCERATE her, that was it and terminate her, it said it on the form… and she had done nothing wrong, it said that and and… and they said they were from MIDI5."

"MIDI5?" Martine replied.

"Yes. You won't have heard of MIDI5 no one has, they are top secret."

"They are," replied Martine, "unless you process their agent's expenses. I don't know exactly what they do, but I know who they work for. They are a government approved partner agency, they do a lot of work for the security services. Their contractors are all ex-military types and they work for a company called MID Enterprises, which is an affiliate of Autonomous Accumulations, it's a rather complex relationship. I had the file once, because I had to do some work for the Chairman at AA. I read through how it's all set up, but it's very confidential and he didn't even want me to discuss it with the other Directors. They all have these really weird names like Mr Axe and Mr Angry and stuff like that. They are so ridiculous they can't be real names. There is a lot of office gossip about them, but nobody really knows that much and all their addresses are PO Box numbers. It's pretty secret even within AA. Their expenses get routed through AA's head office, we check receipts and when we input the amount, we have to change any weird stuff to something bland like consumables or stationery. MIDI5 claim for some really mad things, some of it's a bit creepy. I had to process an expense claim for two rubber sex suits and a sword once… same receipt! And another time for five dachshunds, you know dogs? I remember putting it through the invoice system as 'stationery.' I asked my manager about it because it seemed a bit odd and she just said, 'we don't ask, just clean the description and process it.' They also have massive order with "Electrogun" which is another AA company." It's mad, they get boxes and boxes of stun guns. You know, like tazers and 'stun collars," have you even heard of those, what the hell even is a stun collar? They all get sent to a warehouse somewhere called Greenfield every month. Oh, and blue suits. You would not believe how many suits get purchased. All the claims get sent on to Guernsey, it's almost like legal money laundering. AA have a subsidiary in Guernsey as well. Probably they own an awful lot, you should see the lists of companies in their portfolio, I used to work in the confidential ops finance department and we got reports of them all. A lot of it is government approved or partner agencies and services and consultants. They work for the army, police, the roads network, train services. Oh the health service as well, they have contracts to run all of that and news and media and lots of advisors hired out to government departments." Martine stopped. *"Schtukt."* She swore. "I think I have just broken my non-disclosure agreement."

"I can trump that," said Jude, "I think I have just broken the Official Secrets Act."

"Oh my god we are like Bonnie and Clyde."

"Who? Sorry I don't listen to Country and Western."

"Er… Princess Leia and Han Solo". She suggested, looking at the ceiling.

"Ah" said Jude, "yes a rebel alliance, very good."

"But even so," Martine added, "they can't kill you or Maryam, that would be against the law."

"You didn't meet them, they were like um, Darth Vadar and er… Darth Maul" Jude said, thinking that perhaps comparing state sponsored cut throats and gangsters to Sci-Fi villains perhaps didn't really make for a good comparison even if it did follow Martine's theme. He carried on regardless; "but the important thing is, they are after Maryam White and even on their own paperwork it says she has done nothing wrong. It just doesn't seem fair."

"There is nothing you can do about it." Martine was almost guessing where this was going.

"I can, well we can, we can at least warn her?"

"I suppose we can…" Martine responded quietly and rather more thoughtfully. She was humouring him a little but also weighing up the fact that it couldn't lead to much because she was sure Jude was exaggerating. He was a little over excited. "She is quite odd though, isn't she? You have to admit, maybe there is something in her DNA…"

"Doesn't matter, it's not a crime" Jude said, suddenly realising what his dull job had initiated and feeling a sense of responsibility. "But there definitely is something weird about her, I can't quite put my finger on it."

"Would you want to put your finger on it?" Martine didn't know why she said it. Perhaps jealousy, perhaps in fun. She felt she had been a bit spiteful as soon as she said it and Jude immediately went bright red and started gabbling again.

"No…no... what do you mean, of course not I well, no… not... I wouldn't… put my finger on what? It's an expression, I…I…" then he took a breath and said quite unnecessarily, "I told you before, she touched my arm, it was weird, it was like an electric shock, not like a tingle, like really horrid," and he looked up a blushed again and added "sorry!" for good measure. Then something clicked, his brain catching up with buffered conversation, "Oh. You have heard of MIDI5? when you worked for Autonomous Accumulations. Dachshunds?"

Martine laughed, as much in relief that her crossing the line comment had not done any more than fluster Jude. "Oh thank the Lord. You have gone red and apologised and are confused, it is still you. I thought someone had gone and stolen my..." she paused lost for the right word and then just leant forward and pecked him on the cheek without finishing her sentence. Then, as an afterthought "Come on then Double O Dustbin, let's go and save Maryam White."

*

Ian and Katie Piggot-Smith were standing by the door not expecting a circus, but it arrived in the dark, in a silver Jaguar. Angelina Poppleberry, Algy Bertwhistle and a cameraman called Dingo, "He went to Australia once, hence the nickname. Didn't you Dingo old chap?" were deposited by a driver. The silver car had large stickers on the side, 'Charity begins with health, are you a LUCKY case?' along with some coloured stars and a large pound sign. The unnamed driver didn't get out of the car and he looked unhealthy, unlucky, thoroughly miserable and spat out of the car window in between cigarettes.

"Hello…hello...hello... where are the lucky Piggy-SmYthes? My goodness me, open up we have come to make a donation or we will blow the house down HOHO." Algy Bee shouted at the top of his voice, trying as hard as he could to generate a little excitement. Mrs Babcock, from number twenty three stopped briefly to watch, her dog relieved itself on the silver cars tyre and almost got spat on. She left, it was dark and not as exciting for spectators as Algy and Angelina thought. Nobody could see much anyway, even under the streetlights. Algy Bee was fighting a losing excitement battle as far as the non-existent audience were concerned.

Katie Piggot-Smith opened the door. "Come in, come in quickly," she said. "Ian's in the lounge, we were expecting you." She surreptitiously looked up and down the street before closing the door behind everyone, as they were shuffled into the suburban semi. They wandered in unguided to a small square hallway, passed some stairs on the left and through a door, also on the left. Ian Piggot-Smith was sitting on his own in a brown leather armchair looking like someone had insulted his mother.

"Have you got the cheque?" Was all he said.

"Not so fast IPG and Mrs IPG, or should I say Mrs KPG? we do need to see the ticket and take a few snaps, CHAM-PAG-NAAY I think. Ange, pop the cork, There's a dear. Photos…photos, come along Dingo, wag that tail. Mrs IPG perhaps you could stand there next to the joyous…" He looked at 'the joyous IPG' who was still seething at being referred to as the biggest charity case in the world, "well, when we say joyous, we mean lucky don't we? Ange… Ange… the cheque, the cardboard cheque."

Angelina Popplebury pulled out a large cardboard cheque made out to 'Mr and Mrs I Piggot-SmYth' which she thrust at the P-Gs for a photo opportunity.

Dingo snapped away, he really was a snap happy chappy. He looked at Ian Piggot-Smiths puce and bloated face, perfectly matching his puce and bloated cotton shirt. *Might have to do something in the edit.* At least Katie Piggot-Smith managed to smile for the camera. *Close your mouth dear, you don't want those crooked teeth all over the front pages.*

"Right, is that over... is that my cheque?" grumbled the aforementioned puce and bloated IPG. Then, "Why is my name spelt like THAT? It's a silent 'Y', it's S.M.I.T.H. the bank will not accept that spelling, will they?"

"Oh don't you worry your golden socks IPG." Algy replied, unbeaten by the fierce look he was getting, "that's only for the photo op."

"Oh, have you got a normal cheque then, is that spelt correctly?" He was disappointed that he couldn't lord it into the bank with an oversized cheque, so that everyone could see the eight hundred and thirty-two million pounds he had won or been damn awarded, or whatever.

"Ahhh. No." Angelina thought she'd help Ian with this embarrassing problem. "We don't do cheques these days it's all electronic, we'll take you bank details and it will go in via bank transfer, far more discrete we don't want to make a fuss do we?"

"Oh" Said IPG, "OH!"

*

Jude and Martine got the bus, they could have walked to High Road. It was a quicker less dramatic and more mundane transport for saving someone's life (or freedom?) but more practical. It was late in the day, the sun was down and it was dark, which made it feel colder than it actually was. Double 0 Dustbin had a car but it wasn't an Aston Martin and actually the bus was quite convenient, it also didn't have the guilty reminder of a Martine size dent in it.

Subject1: Female, 28. Name Maryam (NONAME) White. Status: (UNKNOWN). 2a, High Road. Comments: Subject NGS, NBD, NCR, NVT. Pretty bog standard, except it's probably a flat. He hated flats, it was always a fight to identify the correct bins. He remembered exactly what it said on his EWP and exactly what he thought at the time.

Martine was thinking as well. *Why was she going along with this? Because this crazy slightly confused but quite lovable boy thought it was important.* She didn't think it was important but he did and at this time that was enough. She caught a glance of herself in the reflection of the bus window, she still looked like a car crash, which was unsurprising. She had been the soft, squidgy, bouncy, vulnerable, bleeding and painful fifty percent of a car crash. While she didn't hurt quite so much it was only a week after the crash and it would take white clown make up to cover up the yellow bruising migrating across her face. At least the swelling had gone down, a Georgian silhouette painting of her would look acceptable. In technicolour or any later technology, she would look overexposed. She also thought, *he likes me, I know he likes me when will he? He will its ok. Go along with it. Its only been a short time and he seems fairly serious. I doubt he runs over many people, that shows commitment.* And she laughed to herself.

"What?" Jude was worrying about MIDI5. He didn't know

why but he was having ominous thoughts. He was also worrying that ominous was too big and far too serious a word to describe his thoughts but ominous they were. He wondered if getting ominous thoughts were the next stage of adulthood and then worried he was aging too quickly.

"Nothing, we are almost there." He was snapped out of his worrying by Martine's voice.

The bus stopped in High Road, they got off and started the short twenty minute walk to Maryam's flat. "What are you going to say?" Martine asked.

"Not sure," swapping infringement of an NDA for infringement of the Official Secrets Act with someone he trusted was one thing. Telling Maryam was a step further. This was an action that crossed the line, not the official line that was already crossed, but the line in Jude's head that was a fuzzy grey, quite wide line. He was crossing a no-fly zone, a demarcation between official secrets and unofficial actions. He was coming out the other side of a vague area that he could almost justify but he would be out of the grey and definitely in the black area, or the white area. He wasn't sure which, but it was definitely the polar opposite are of where Mr Gun and Mr Savage were. It was a matter of perspective and he did not know which angle he was looking from. He was also not sure why he was doing this. *It was not for Maryam, he found her a little scary. Was it for him or perhaps for Martine? That would be a weird one, trying to impress Martine by saving Maryam. Or, was it just to do what was the right thing? The white thing even.* He had talked himself around and he was coming out in the right zone, the white zone with the uncannily, accurately, named Maryam White.

They were there, flat 2a was just ahead of them, nice bins he thought, almost new. He checked himself... *you idiot!*

"That's her flat" he said, and he stopped, unsure what to do next.

"Right then, let's go do it. Got your gun?"

"What, gun, no, I… oh! you are teasing me."

"Duh uh!" They walked up the steps, flat 2a was on the upper floor. Jude tentatively rang the bell.

The door was answered quickly, Maryam White opened it and stood there dressed as usual and to type, in white. The hall light illuminated her, giving her an ethereal glow. *Of course, it damn well did.*

"Hey Jude! and how exciting... Jude's beautiful girlfriend, oh do come in." As though them turning up was the most normal thing in the world. She reached out to touch Jude, but he nervously took a step back and trod on Martine's foot.

"Ow!"

"Sorry."

"No worries, go in" Martine pushed him.

"It's a bit dark in this hall let me turn on the light." Maryam said as she clicked the hall light on, illuminating her from behind with an ethereal glow which confused Jude. *Of course, it damn well did.*

Jude looked around, everything was white. The walls were

painted white, the curtains were white, the lampshades were white. It was a warm white, it didn't feel cold. There were books, ornaments, furniture that all added small elements of colour but they were minor distractions, the flat was overwhelmingly white.

"Er, nice colour scheme, it really er works." Jude said awkwardly. He was sure he heard Martine snort behind him when he said that.

"Thank you Jude, what a lovely thing. Come in sit down, I don't have many friends so it's nice of you to visit." The oddness of them both turning up didn't even seem to register. Martine sat down, she wanted to say something intelligent but all she could do was look at Maryam, who seemed to move in a timeframe just slightly out of synch with the world in which she existed. "Would you like some tea, is it too late for tea? No it isn't it's never too late for tea, how do you have it?"

"Err white?"

"Yes, white please," Martine followed Jude's lead.

"Please." added Jude.

"Ok." Said Maryam White and she wafted off.

Martine looked at Jude, who looked back confused. She nodded at him as if to say a whole string of questions. *What are you going to say and when and how? And, how do you think it will go? Will she believe you and what will happen?* Jude saw her nod and smiled awkwardly as if to say, *'why are you nodding?'* Martine pulled a face which given her still bruised visage, wasn't one hundred percent comfortable so her next 'five-question look', was a little pained. If he had even the slightest clue what was going through her mind, her painful expression could have been his excuse for still not getting the subtle visual conversation. Martine gave up the dark art of feminine eye communication, it didn't work, Jude couldn't read it. Maryam came back into the room, she had three delicate bone china cups on a silver tray. Jude looked nervous, it all looked a bit fragile and he wondered whether refusing a cup or dropping it would be the worst scenario. As Maryam put the tray down, there were three heavy knocks at the door.

"Oh" said Maryam, "more friends" and she turned and walked back into the hall.

"I am not sure about that." Jude said out loud, giving up all pretence of subterfuge. Martine was just startled by the loudness. They both listened intently, Jude now hoping that it was a parcel being delivered but having an uncomfortable feeling about the timing.

"MARYAM WHITE?"

'Oh nooo!" Martine read Jude's expression as though he had said it out loud.

"What?"

"That's Savage."

"It was a hard knock, yes."

"No no… Mr Savage, MIDI5" Jude hissed.

"Oh!" She replied and craned her neck towards the door.

"STAND BACK MARYAM WHITE" They heard, from the hallway.

"Oh, hello, why are you pointing that at me?" Martine heard Maryam say. She didn't sound upset, just a little confused.

"MY NAME IS MR SAVAGE, THIS IS MR GUN, WE ARE REPRESENTATIVES OF THE GOVERNMENT. WE DO NOT WANT TO HURT YOU BUT YOU SHOULD BE WARNED THAT WE WILL IF YOU DO NOT COMPLY WITH OUR REQUEST. TAKE A STEP BACK NOW."

"Oh" they heard Maryam say, "you call your gun 'Mr Gun'? That's very funny"

Martine and Jude looked at each other, they would have been amused by Maryam if they were not instantly confused and frightened because at the mention of a gun. The game had suddenly gone up a gear.

"NO MARYAM WHITE, THIS IS A ELECTRICAL STUN GUN. I WILL DISCHARGE IT TO DISABLE YOU IF YOU TRY AND MOVE, THIS IS MR GUN TO MY RIGHT"

"Oh" said Maryam again, "It's very confusing, hello Mr Gun," as though this was no less normal than the two virtual strangers turning up for tea.

"What the hell's going on Jude?" said Martine, do something. He did, he scrunched up his eyes as an ostrich might plunge its head into the sand.

"ahhh miss white mr gun isss my name now we must be quick k k" Jude heard the rattlesnake clicking of the hard consonant and it put a shiver down his spine. He opened his eyes and stood up. Martine looked shocked at his sudden movement, she had been inclined to follow his lead and close her eyes but stood as well. Jude walked out of the door into the hall.

"AH DRAZKOWSKI. I THINK YOU ARE NOW ACTIVELY AND WITH MALICIOUS AFORETHOUGHT, INTERFERRING IN OFFICIAL BUSINESS. STAND BACK NOW."

But Jude didn't stand back, he looked around him and had a moment of clarity, well a moment of adrenalin. It allowed him to assess the situation, consider all the possible options, run an internal risk review and act with expedience. Except from that list he got to ass' dumped the 'ess and went straight to act which meant reaching out and grabbing the first weapon he could. He now stood there holding a cordless steam-iron. He felt his hand around the handle rolled his thumb over the power swich, flicked it to the on position and the click gave him the confidence that he was now armed and ready for anything.

"STAND DOWN DRAZKOWSKI, STAND DOWN. YOU'VE DONE NO DAMAGE YET." Savage hollered at him in his most sensitive and encouraging voice. Jude stood still, he flicked his eyes between all the actors in the developing scene. He was standing to the side of Maryam, who was impassive, maybe even smiling? Savage was at the door braced and holding a yellow plastic tazer pistol out in front of him, a streetlight behind him giving him a light halo, which just added to the dramatic effect. Jude had a strange thought given the circumstances, *it looked like a toy*. Savage slowly moved the tazer pistol from Maryam to Jude. Jude revised his view. It now looked a little less child friendly. Gun (Mr, not tazer) was standing just inside the doorway in front of Savage, but not blocking his line of sight, or aim. In his hand he held what looked like a broken plastic hoop, it was the same colour as the tazer. Jude noticed it was hinged and had red writing on the side.

"What's that?" he asked, shaking his iron in what he felt was an intimidating manner.

'itss a stun collar mr drazkowski we are going to clip it onto miss whites neck and iff she does not do as we say I will click k k a button on a remote control and it will give her some encouragement if she tries to escape I will hold the button down and it will discharge fifty thousand volts and will immobilise her it is a humane method of control I doubt very much she will be harmed"

"Whaatt?" he felt a bead of sweat run down his forehead as he contemplated the most surreal Mexican standoff ever.

"DRAZKOWSKI, PUT THE DAMN IRON DOWN, ITS NOT EVEN ON, THE ORANGE LIGHT INDICATES IT NEEDS CHARGING." Savage showed a surprisingly detailed understanding of domesticity. Under different circumstances, Jude and Martine would have been impressed, though it may well be that Mr Savage's knowledge came from ironing faces, not shirts.

Martine's rather reluctant, but now fully committed, hero

contemplated his uncharged and therefore cold iron. He was standing off against a fully charged state sponsored psychopath with a tazer, supported by a slippery nutjob sidekick with a 'thing' and he did what anyone might do in the circumstances, he panicked. He threw the iron as hard as he could. Martine watched as it all appeared to happen in slow motion.

Jude's arm flew forward and she saw the muscles in his hand as his fingers opened, he looked like he was shouting but she was so intently focussing on the movement everything was silence. Savage shouted something and she saw him discharge the tazer just a split second before the iron left Jude's hand. Gun took a step forward and started to lift the stun collar up. Martine saw a spiders web line streak from the tazer, ricochet off the airborne iron and hit Gun on the cheek, his eyes opened wide in shock. Savage's eyes flicked between Gun as he initially jerked and then back to an iron sized chunk of steam iron which promptly hit him straight between the eyes, pointy end first. Savage stepped back in shock, missed his footing stood on the side of his foot which failed to take his weight and he fell backwards. Falling in reverse he cracked his head on the floor and stopped moving. Throughout this split-second sequence of actions, Maryam White barely moved or reacted. She just smiled as though somebody was throwing a surprise party in her honour, which everyone, in their own way, was.

Gun fell to the floor and twitched briefly.

"Jude, Maryam… run." Martine screamed, snapping everyone out of the moment and as she started towards the door she looked at Gun on the floor. He had the stun collar in one hand, a remote control in the other. He had stopped twitching and was now groaning. She didn't know why she did it but she grabbed the collar out of his hand and clamped it round his neck. It made a satisfying click when it closed shut. She grabbed the remote from his other hand just in time to hear him say "don t move nowww you have transgressed children" and she made up her mind. She pressed the button and held it and Gun responded by saying "nnhhgghhggg" She smiled to herself and quietly said "one nil." She then grabbed Jude's arm, beckoned Maryam who was now moving, albeit delicately and in slow motion like she was in a ballet, not a life and death situation and they all piled out of the door.

"Go.Go. Now." Martine shouted and they started running, leaving the mess of Gun and Savage writhing on the floor.

"What the hell just happened?" Jude shouted, mid-flight.

"No idea Double 0 Dustbin?" Martine hollered back, "but well done with your secret weapon. You are quite a cute secret agent and also a domestic goddess it seems?"

Jude felt himself blushing as he ran. They all ran, one after the other into the dark.

Chapter 11

Keystone

The Police Commissionaire was slumped in a worn velvet covered, padded seat, beaten. He was compromised, not yet financially, he could fight off that temptation if it ever arose, but he was morally beaten.

Walking into Diemos, the private club in James Street, behind Marquis Square had left a dirty stain on his soul. He should never have come, but he had come. The rug that you were met with as you entered was red and to him, as you trod on it and then trod off it onto the worn wooden flooring, it represented a red line that you crossed. When you went out, you crossed it again. Every time you crossed it in any direction, you crossed that red line for another time. It was cumulative, there was no going back, just forward, further into darkness.

He had agreed to meet with the Chief Constable and the businessman in advance of the public speech. It was barely a meeting it was a summoning. He had expected it to be at the station, at Peel Circus, but he was given the address of this club and in attending, he got a sense of where he was. Conspiracy, collusion, coercion, compromise. He had thought that having a lager shandy, watered down the poison he was ingesting. That the barman just looked at him when he said, "a shandy please," made the situation just that little more humiliating.

"I understand Sir", he had said, "something weak. We are not used to that here, but I am sure we can open a bottle of, something for you." Something weak, that was exactly how he felt. Not even some*body* weak. He was derided, even by the bar staff.

He looked at the businessman who he had been told was just called Number Five. It sounded like a rather sinister introduction for a business meeting.

"He is a director at Autonomous Accumulations, you will of course have heard of them" the chief constable had said. The commissioner had heard of them, of course he had. One of their subsidiary's provided the HR Services, management framework, strategic planning and manpower for his contract police force. His recruits. He'd met with business consultants, legal teams, sales and support leads during negotiations but not anyone at AA. It was not necessary, they were not doing the work they were the money behind the scenes, not the technical expertise. He had heard of them though. Smooth operators, money men. They were hoarding the money behind the scenes and now, calling the shots as well.

His contract force, he reflected on it. His recruits, not the nations. The nation wanted it, but he was accountable for them. Bob's hobby bobbies, that was how they were known, that was why he was here. His job had been to represent the people to fulfil their wishes. In his first term of office he had given the people what they wanted. A cheaper, more representative police force. A more diverse police force, a friendlier, accountable, approachable, less intimidating police force. He had lobbied to expand the force with real people, not paramilitaries and he had managed to do it through the financial benefits of contracting it out.

This had suited Autonomous Accumulations, they had primed their consultancies with some very generous discounts, barbed loss leaders that went in so smoothly you felt no pain until you tried to pull out. More consultancy, recruitment, revenue. For every new recruit a finder's fee. No one had anticipated the turnover and inexperience of the recruits, except perhaps the market analysts at Automated Accumulations and they were not going to tell anyone outside the twenty seventh floor of that revenue stream. More importantly for AA, it was yet another tentacle slithering around Government and the civil service. More soft influence, more power, more control. Another dependent department secured and they also now owned the bricks and mortar of Peel Circus, leasing it back to the police force under favourable terms.

Contracts were written under the AA subsidiary and supplied to the police service nationally. Despite regionalisation, the contract was mandated to all the national forces but financed centrally by government. On paper it represented a cost saving. For every member of the police force AA supplied, their subsidiary raised a fixed monthly charge. It was all off that back of a loss leader, but it was very good business.

There was a large publicity drive to increase the contract force, to get more feet on the ground. *'More plod to plod'*, the papers had said. There was a queue to join this new expanding force, even on a voluntary basis. The job was sold as exciting old-fashioned feet on the floor policing. Then, fast cars and a Friday night rumble, flexible hours, comradery and the chance to do something positive with your life. The alternative promotion was for friendly neighbourhood policing by human beings. It was made to appeal as both charity work, public service and an extreme sport and every combination in-between. Who would not want to give up their time for a national service that could be so rewarding?

It looked cheap for the government, but it came at a cost. Professionalism and an unaccountable force that was highly visible, but mostly ineffective. The regulars used them as cannon fodder - they were contractors, unpaid contractors that were signed up under disclaimers, they were expendable. The recruits came and went. With little in the way of salary and expenses only, life assurance cover was the only tangible benefit. It became a steppingstone job like bar or restaurant work. The commissioners special force haunted him. He had done everything that was asked of him and when it came to implementation, it was handed over to the lawyers and the accountants to strip the benefits out as margin and leave the husk of the idea to start big and die slowly. It wasn't long before the cracks showed. In the police force and in the Commissioner himself.

Three years, almost to the day. It was a lifetime ago and the Commissioner had felt that he was winning. He had worked hard through his entire career in public service, political campaigning and held management contracts in the charities sector. The reward had been long hours and modest remuneration, but a strong sense of purpose. His election as Police Commissioner for the country's largest metropolitan force had been his crowning glory. He had bold new ideas for a tired regime and the public stood behind him. Unusually for a police commissioner of a force this size, he had never been in the service and he had felt that was what gave him his edge. He was one of the people, it was why he fought for their ambitions and supported their demands. Often at odds with the establishment and incumbent management he thought that he had fought for changes for the better.

But in a day, it all turned. The public changed with the wind, they had wanted a representative and friendly force but when that didn't create enough drama, demanded authoritarianism and action. He had put in place a large but weak agency, fronting a shrunken regular professional force. The police were not solving serious crime, they were picking easy targets and administering the soft end of criminal justice system, not fighting villainy. Most of this work could and was, being done by cameras and computers. Autonomous Accumulations counted the profit. They sold and managed the cameras and computers. There were more administrators for petty money-making crime, creating revenue to buy more cameras and computers.

And then his wife decided that she cared about her family just a little more than she cared for everyone else. There were another twenty million people in their relationship and she could no longer compete. She had apologised, told him he was a good man, but she needed a husband and their son needed a father. He had said "ok." He has just said "ok" when what he wanted to do was to scream and cry and shout and explain, he wanted to tell her he loved her and express everything inside as it was; anger, upset, frustration and a lack of control. He wanted to melt down and he wanted to be looked after and held. He wanted to admit that he had been a bad husband and a poor father and to try and get some balance back in his life for all of them. But in the end, all he could do was just say "ok" and he let her walk out of the house.

The Commissioner had given everything for everyone. He was exhausted by it and no one was happy. His anger was amplified by his frustration and the inadequacy of failure. Within three years, everyone now wanted the diametric opposite of everything they had previously demanded.

In his anger and his resentment, he was warming to the old-fashioned 'stamp on their feet' attitude of the Chief Constable who got things done in a calm, conscienceless way. The Chief Constable didn't suffer foolishness or genius any differently and neither gladly. Everyone was, as he often misquoted Paton, *'In front leading him, behind following or otherwise in his damn way and feet to be stamped on.'* He always knew where he was going and he had thick leather on the soles of his shoes, just in case there were toes in his way. Commissioner and constable had not got on at first and for obvious reasons. They were personally opposite and professionally polar, including the ice. But over time, things changed. The Commissioner had never had time to make friends but after his divorce he had gravitated towards the Chief Constable, who was always there and as solid as a rock had a calm answer for everything and a zen like attitude to the violent world they lived in.

Between the nagging dissatisfaction and the soul wrenching sense of failure, there also developing venomous hatred for the people that voted for him. He started to have moments where he despised them and their fickle and chaotic behaviour and for the impossible job they had given him to do. He blamed them for the stress that he was struggling to cope with. It all started with them, they were the perpetrators as well as the victims. A report he had read recently was about a court case where an officer had beaten a protester with a baton. The policeman had been shouted at, he had been spat at, he had lost control. The Chief Constable had been pragmatic, "Shouldn't have done it on camera Bob, probably deserved it but I can't have my constables getting caught out like that. Trained 'em better. Don't need people like that in my force."

The Commissioner read the report transcribed from camera footage describing blow by blow, how the attack unfolded. A crime had been committed, but it didn't start with the policeman. The Commissioner swung between reading the report as a description of despicable and unprofessional behaviour by a member of the force and then despicable behaviour by the people he was supposed to represent. He read about the pure animal response and the uncompromised violence that stopped the spitting and it thrilled him, it was real life but he read it like a novel. The talking, the writing, the argument the words, the money that was spent in a court. Pointless. It was simply and efficiently resolved by the baton. The Commissioner fantasised occasionally that instead of just shouting at a mostly deaf world, he could launch himself across the meeting room table and beat his opponent to a pulp. God, he wanted to hit something, someone, anyone and had cried himself to sleep when he had those violent thoughts, because he was getting less able to control them.

All he had then was his job and he had been coerced by the Chief Constable into lobbying for a comprehensive database. A DNA database was what the force wanted for proactive policing and to investigate crime by numbers. To scrape samples and identify suspects, without gaps. To get a head start in any investigation by casting a narrow net in a very targeted direction. Guilty by association, let the lawyers argue them out of the crime scene. Now he was embedded in conspiracy to immorally steal genes from the general public. He was in a room with the businessman, managing the corporation who owned the company, that were building the tool, that the government had approved (secretly), to achieve what the state wanted. It was not what the citizens of a benign liberal democracy had voted, for or even knew was happening. He spent every moment of his life in a mixture of denial and terror. Terror of what he had become and denial, that it was ever really anything to do with him. It wasn't, he couldn't stop this monster growing, he no longer had the strength. His head was spinning again.

In just under three years, he had become what he despised, a complicit part of the machine, working for state control, vested interests and drinking in a club that stank of evil. He no longer felt he had the strength of character to even despise himself.

The Commissioner slunk a little lower in the seat.

"You ok Bob? That shandy taking it out of you, you want to slow down lad." The Chief Constable said, knocking back a double brandy.

"Yes, I am fine" came the weak reply. "It's quiet, are we the only people here?" He asked hopefully, he had not seen a single person except the barman.

"No" said the businessman, Number Five. "It's busy tonight, but the club manages to find places for people to do business, it absorbs them all." It was said with no sense of irony. The Commissioner just looked around not sure whether to believe him, or worry that someone might see him.

He didn't fully understand how he and the Chief Constable had become friendly. Their relationship for four years had been one of animosity and argument. If one said black, the other said white. Shortly before his new force went live, he had gone on a business trip with the Chief Constable to Stockholm. That was ironic, that the visit started to change his perspective and persuade him that a hard line was sometimes necessary. It was a syndrome for a reason. They had been to see the new Sweolandia shock troop police force as a fact-finding exercise.

Sweolandia spent generations as one of the most civilised and inclusive cultures on the planet. It was not completely without problems. Organised crime was creeping up alongside the rises in disposable income, lifestyle and the liberal attitude towards personal freedom of a successful first world nation.

The answer had not been more militarised service, that did not interact well with an affluent educated liberal democracy, but the popularity and romance of Norse mythology did. If you need a tough and violent assault force to kick in doors and break skulls, make them beautiful and let the internet do the rest. New recruits had to be tall and strong, they had to fit a photographic convention, they had to be hard as nails but still smile at any cameras. It was a sensation. Sweolandia's new Thor modelled shock troops could evade all harsh criticism and managed to plough a trail of testosterone through the crime statistics, wearing just slightly too tight clothing and with batons that would loosely be described as axes. Loosely, as the steel cored rubber batons had a weighted head that although it was more of a club than an axe, continued a Viking tradition that the most civilised nation in the world could feel a little bit sentimental about. These men could listen to Nordic pop, pose for photos, cuddle babies and fight like wolves. It was all anyone had ever wanted, crime fighting as a spectator sport. Nobody cared about due process anymore and the Police Force became the best-looking gang in town. Television programs were made about them, toy dolls were made of them and small children learnt that if you were big and good looking you could knock down anything that got in your way. Ultimately though, most people felt safe or were entertained, some felt both. A few were derided for being un-Viking.

The Commissioner of Police enjoyed the trip, he was seduced by the media friendly Sweolandia police force like everyone else. It was an exciting three days spent with the Chief Constable, an old-fashioned no-nonsense policeman. A man who said things like "I call a spade a spade" and "You can't make an omelette without breaking a few eggs." He said other things that the Commissioner of Police could never repeat. Three days in a black and white world of skull cracking, door kicking machismo and the Commissioner briefly felt less like a lost child and thought the Chief Constable was his friend. And then, like the holiday was over, he was back answering to them. They were shouting about unfairness, about bullying, about a weak police force about costs, about parking tickets, speeding fines and stop and search, odd looks and unsolved crime and badly run investigations and stats and numbers and… and… *WHY COULD THEY NOT JUST LEAVE HIM ALONE!*

He had another three years of this sentence and every day when he woke, he just wanted to solve it all the good old-fashioned way by stamping on everyone's toes. But he wasn't brave enough.

He looked around, at the businessman, a devious dark eyed man. A man who saw no value in you except as prey. But he wouldn't murder you in a dark alley because that was a waste when you could be used. He was a predator, but he would bite a piece off and leave you living and take another bite when the first had healed. He'd keep going until all that was left was scar tissue. He looked at his friend, the Chief Constable. Bullet headed straight talking, a rolled-up shirt sleeve, let's get stuck in, sort of guy. He wondered why he was here, but he knew. The crowds at the gates were shouting, complaining, fighting. The three of them were now in a coven of conspiracy. The businessman wanted to keep his business running smoothly. The policeman saw this meeting as pragmatism, as a means justifying the end and the commissioner was the patsy, the fall guy. He had to toe the line and stop the people before they rioted. He had to speak untruth to the mob, to tell them to put their pitchforks down and let the police do their job. There wasn't even a justifiable reason for a riot, not that anyone knew. There were plenty of reasons that they didn't know about, not least of all their genetics being stolen by the government and the government being stolen by big business. Ironically, it was mostly boredom, opportunity and mass hysteria that had everybody fired up and looking for a fight.

There was riot in the air, that's what AA's analysts had told the police. 'There was a bridge that was going to be attacked, they had heard of trouble brewing at Tuckers Mill and the fire at the hospital.' It was all a sign of something, of dissatisfaction, of itchy feet, of a season of discontent. 'And, by the way... the DNA database, when that gets through parliament then we can solve everything without investigation, keep the public onside Commissioner yes?'

Everyone in the room knew that the database was already implemented; albeit with tacit agreement by the public who didn't know that voting for a government that would make difficult decisions meant that decisions no longer needed to be discussed publicly, just made for the publics benefit, behind closed doors. The Commissioner still thought it was all down to him, to salvage the reputation of the police force, keep the public onside and get support for the database. It was a plan as great as a profit driven health service. He was still serving them; trying to convince them that it was all a good idea, before lobbying a government that would bite of his hand, after damning his reputation for authoritarianism.

The government were never going to publicly support a DNA database at this point of the argument, they needed the public to want it enough first and that was the Commissioner's job now. The government needed to be the last people to support such an infringement of civil liberties, but once their hands were tied, they could at least make it the quickest most efficient implementation ever. Everyone was a winner. Except the Commissioner.

He looked around again, furtively and nervously and he saw the dark wooden walls, the velvet of the curtains, the pile of the carpet on the floor. The sick glass and the faded brass. He saw verdigris on the candle sticks and wax dripping like melted dreams distorting and misshaping the chandeliers. He looked at the darkened silvering in the mirrors which reflected back everything but tainted by unnatural shadows. He felt he could have been in a room that existed outside of time. He didn't know that he was he was. He was in a room that set the time, in cubicles and quiet rooms in and amongst the ghosts of ten thousand secret conversations. Diemos was the place where the clocks were wound up and where time was synchronised, where alarms were set and other alarms were stopped. Behind the white portico and the black walls of the building; across the red carpet, the faded grandeur just soaked up another dark secret or two and as it did, a piece of plaster dust dropped from the ceiling and landed in the Commissioner's shandy.

"Oh!" he looked up at the ceiling, shaken out of reflection and realising that his shandy was ruined. He was too embarrassed to ask for another. "Where were we?" He asked.

"We were just saying Bob," that the police need your support, well the people need your support. They don't know what's good for them so we'll tell 'em what we know they really want. Your speech tomorrow Bob, you need to wind back their anger. We can't have riots, we can't have trouble. Your boys," he paused, "and girls," he added with a cynical smile. "Well, not sure they are up to it. We can't fight riots with the Hobby-bobbies, you need to defuse the bomb fella. You can do that can't you Bob?"

"You'll do it. Bob." the businessman added, it wasn't a request, it was a threat with unknown consequences.

The Commissioner picked up his glass, got it almost to his mouth, remembered the flaked plaster and put it down, with an uncomfortably dry mouth he croaked "yes, I can do it. I'll tell them."

The businessman just got up and left, not a thank you or even a goodbye.

"Efficient lad that isn't he Bob, no messing? Wish we could get our policing done like that, eh? Like those Sweolandia chaps. Gotta break a few eggs now and then Bob, gotta break a few eggs."

Bob nodded and slumped even lower in his chair, he was like a barometer measuring the pressure of the worlds responsibilities and they were crushing him.

*

The following day, In Jerusalem House, Christopher was also suffocating, not just because of the attention he was receiving, nor from the pile of blankets that had been dumped on him, but from the cloying dark atmosphere. He had been in the dark for eighteen years, he knew the light was not far away. His saviours, or disciples as they kept referring to themselves, were arguing in the kitchen.

"You can't just give him bread and wine and fish."

"What about sausages? I don't like fish."

"Well. The original one wouldn't have had sausages, its pork"

"Would this one?"

"Dunno, probably not, we could ask"

"Or look?"

I am not asking and I am definitely not looking."

"Well ok, but you should cook the fish first"

"But in the bible…"

And on it went.

Christopher could move, he had enough strength now so he pushed the blankets and the parka off, tried to stand up and he found he could. Unsteady at first and a little off balance, but he could stand, so he put one foot in front of the other. He stumbled slightly but those muscle memories were strong. He was slow, and it hurt, but he could move, so he did. Slowly, reassuring himself as he went, with an arm out here and a hand on a wall there, he stepped over the debris. He navigated the chaos and artifacts (which included a half-eaten pizza) and he walked, in a manner, to the door. He reached out to the handle, turned it and pulled it towards him and whilst you could hardly describe the corridor outside flat 13b as light, it was certainly less dark than flat 13b. You could not describe the air as clean, but it was cleaner and it was easy to find the way out, even for someone who had spent the last eighteen years in a coma because there was a convenient trail of rubbish and an occasional dried patch of vomit. Christopher just followed the yellow sick road and he made it eventually into the street. He looked out onto the majesty of everything that the world had to offer and saw a derelict garage, complete with buddleia and dog mess but it was a definite improvement, so he kept walking and as he did, his movements became easier and his balance became better. After a few minutes he was overawed by wonder instead of by the smell of Jerusalem house. He looked around and he walked and he smiled and he smelled the air and he touched things and he felt alive, truly alive.

Back at 13b Jerusalem House, pandemonium had followed a debate about the menu. Brother Simon had been nominated to go and tactfully ask whether sausages would be ok and had noticed the front door was wide open. "Who left the door open?"

"Not me"

"Nor me"

"Oh no, the Saviour's just gone and naffed off, whoops! Sorry lord the devil had my tongue. He's gone, he's gone, HE'S GONE."

*

The crowds were gathered outside the Police Station. They had been building for hours, there was a pedestal, with microphones. Everyone knew that the police were going to make a statement. There was a national mood and it was tense and it was still only early afternoon. There had been a number of small flare ups of trouble, signs that the people were unhappy. There was talk about threats of terrorism and that the police were ineffective in reducing crime. There were protests at Tuckers Mill, by people who threw stones at the workers to save the animals. There was the Radical Automobile Consortium threating the privatised road network, apparently. The roads used to be free. Under the new funding model, you paid by the mile, clocked by cams, deducted at source. Instead of a car tax you added your bank details to a monthly direct debit. On bridges you paid by mile, or portion thereof rounded up, with a multiplier for height. Bridges were the current focus of the crowd's unhappiness. At least until something else caught the mood.

Nothing had happened yet, but it was a tense time all round. The police needed to do something, to declare a position, to draw a line on the ground. There was going to be a public statement, so the protest groups were there, mixed in with a curious crowd; drunks and minor criminals, families and children all just hanging out to see what was going on or get stuck in. People had come to take photos of themselves in the melee, because that was what a life well lived was; being photographed and hoping you looked hot in front of the chaos and disorder of everyone else.

The press were milling around. Buster Onions, from 'the Daily Heart Online', had barged his way to the front. He was expecting another waffling speech from the police but he was sure he could turn it into a story, so he determined to be at the front to help liven it up with a little heckling. At least, he thought, he would be heard from there. He looked behind him and was surprised to see so many people. *They are bored, they'll come out on the streets for anything these days,* he thought to himself and he popped off a couple of pictures as the crowds grew and the jostling started. It was like the hospital all over again, camera phones were up and everyone was taking pictures. *Why don't they leave it to the professionals* he thought and snapped a picture of an attractive young woman, who was taking a photo of herself. He then also noticed that most people were doing the same.

A door opened at the front of the Police Station and out walked the Commissioner and Chief Constable together. One, a tall man. Upright, tough looking, wiry but smartly dressed. He carried his hat under his arm and his shaven head gave him a slightly militaristic bearing. The other, a shuffling middle-aged man, shapeless; a hang-dog sagging face that looked like it had given up with both life and gravity.

The unlikely friends moved to the lectern. The Chief Constable nodded to the crowd, a sharp nod of acknowledgement only, because he didn't intend to speak today. He adjusted the microphone for the commissioner turned to him and said "You ready Bob."

But it wasn't a question, it was a statement. Bob didn't answer. He just shuffled up to the lectern.

"Ladies, Gentlemen, I am speaking to you today, as the Commissioner of the Police, your representative in the police force and as your voice. I am, however going to challenge you." He stopped, the adrenalin was now rising and he stood a little higher. "You wanted a cheaper force and a more approachable force and that is what you have got. The police force however is more than that. We cannot honestly and with credibility say that we are the rock that society is built on, but I do feel we can say with some confidence that we are the stone, that stops the arch of society collapsing in on itself'. He paused for dramatic effect, proud of his inspired metaphor. It was an opportunity leaped on by Buster Onions, from the Daily Heart Online, who hollered out at this pause.

"That's a good one, I am sure if you searched all the way back to silent movies of the 1920's, you could find a name for your style of policing."

The crowd laughed. Somebody shouted out "Keystone cops" and the crowd roared again and surged forward, pushing and shoving each other. Buster Onions smiled smugly to himself for creating the news he was reporting. Again. He took a few photos of the flustered speaker.

The Commissioner's short burst of adrenalin was faltering now, "I, I… you... you..."

"Keystone cops, Keystone cops, Keystone cops" the crowd sang back, miraculously synchronising and coming together under a simple chant. It got louder "KEYSTONE COPS, KEYSTONE COPS."

The commissioner saw the faces of the people. He had spent his life trying to serve them as a union representative, a councillor as a lobbyist and more recently as Commissioner of Police and he cracked. The stone fell out of the arch and something changed forever… "STOP… STOP. He shouted at the microphone, "it's your fault, it's all your fault, it always is your fault, you fools you ignorant whining fools." His speech was off-piste now, flying down the slope out of control, an avalanche behind him and a cliff edge in front of him. "I have been trying to protect you with kindness but all you want to do is argue and complain, fight… and riot," and he felt his eyes well up in anger and emotion.

He had just waved a red rag. *Hmm… riot?* thought the crowd, *we hadn't considered that, but it's not a bad idea.* Someone threw a bottle and then there was shout, a surge and a punch was thrown, a window was broken and someone lit a smoke bomb. People started running towards it and away from it, around it in circles and took photos of themselves posing in the smoke.

"Oh dear" said the Chief Constable, "that didn't go well Bob, think you need a holiday son. Oh dear oh dear," and he calmly clicked the radio mike attached to his chest dropped his head down to the left and quietly said, hand in front of his mouth and the microphone. "Right boys, it's gone to hell, send in the cavalry but try not to hurt too many people, the press are all over this. Standard form, defensive in front, contain the sides, squeeze 'em in, don't give 'em room to breathe. We'll see how this develops, hold that line until the next order."

From the back of the building a small force of shielded officers in riot gear marched out. Paramilitary samurai with batons held out in front and their bodies protected by round plexiglass shields. Faces masked; these were not Bobs boys and girls, this was the real deal. Just the boys this time. These were the Chief Constable's private army. They moved into an aggressive defensive position before the lectern. Sirens sounded from all directions and black vans with steel meshed windows and bull bars pulled in from the sides, screeching sirens cranked up to eleven and blue flashing lights appeared out of nowhere, suddenly spilling out more police to re-enforce the area. The jostling crowd were stunned by the speed of the action, they were easily restricted and contained, then compressed. The shouting started, crying. From out of nowhere horsemen arrived, the horses resembling heavy battle horses from the Napoleonic wars, cavalry but with extended nightsticks instead of sabres. These were not the horses that trotted around the park carrying young officers, happy to allow the horses noses to be scratched and photos to be taken. No. The Chief Constable held something back because you never knew when you would need force and you couldn't show your hand too soon. He was waging a war on crime and Bobs democratic approach was given a chance but found wanting. "Good old-fashioned policing" The Chief Constable said to himself, "Takes me back to Orgreave, now that was a day." And he smiled.

Somewhere in the crowd, Christopher Sunday was being pressed by people and he was terrified. He had wandered into the group and was entranced by the bodies. He was fascinated by the variety the honesty the anger, humanity, clothing, hair styles, the smells of perfume and body odour, the language and the accents. Humanity at its best and worst and most varied, but most importantly he was surrounded by human beings, then, suddenly the atmosphere had changed. He had heard the man at the front talking and seen his mood change, he heard him shout and he heard the crowd jeer and then the pushing and shoving started and then there was a wall of soldiers, dressed in black. They had shields and they were banging the back of those plastic shields with black sticks in a repetitive rhythm. They were faceless and it stirred something deep in Christopher's mind, they were like soldiers. Christopher tried to get out, he was pushed against a shield and then he felt a jab of an elbow from behind. Then, the movement of the crowd caused him to sway to the right and he was pushed back again and then he heard his name,

"Christopher... Christopher it's me, Doctor Golding, your doctor Christopher..." and an arm briefly reached from between the soldiers with a small box. "Call me, call me when you can..." and Christopher took the box, which was a mobile phone, but he did not know what it was or what to do with it. The arm was dragged back and though Christopher did not realise it, Ernesto Golding had been there and had been cut off from the majority of the crowd but had just caught sight of the confused Christopher. The only thing he could think to do was to give him a means of contacting him. Although the police were looking out for him, they were not looking in the crowd and they were not listening to a doctor trying to shout above the noise. Golding did the first thing he thought of and the only thing he could, he passed his phone through a gap between the police wall. Christopher took it and put it in his pocket without even knowing what it was.

Bob took a step backwards, to the steps in front of the Police Station door. He felt the back of his foot hit the first step and allowed himself to collapse backwards onto it. His head dropped into his hands. He had intended to quell the riot before it started, to pacify an excitable crowd. All he had done was to light the match and the bomb had gone off. He hunched his arms tightly into his chest pulling himself tightly into a ball like a lost child, trying to protect himself from the disorder around him. In the chaos and the smoke, amongst the shouting and the drama, no one could see him. He cried and cried and cried.

Chapter 12

The litter tray, Temptation

Mabel Boggit had been absolutely sure, when she spoke to the nice reporter Mr Onions, "Very nice man that Mr Onions, he was very polite, not like all those other reporters. You could tell he was honest. He called me Mrs Boggit, not Mabel like the others did. He showed some respect, like in the old days." She had said to the lady in the next bed. "Oh yes, I am quite sure. I didn't meet Christopher Sunday but he did cure my gangrene. It was in my foot. Yes, the foot the hospital cut off. You can tell that Christopher cured it because it hasn't spread. It's obvious, anyone can see that. He was on the same floor in the hospital, I was quite close. Those strange hairy doctors sat me on a seat outside his room. Well I don't know, it must have been waves, or maybe his aura, not magic, that's not real. They said he was a Christmas miracle, and it was, I don't have gangrene any more the doctors have said its gone"

"I think Mable, they said it has been removed. Amputated not cured?" The lady in the bed next to her said.

"Oh, I know dear, they always say things like that, those doctors. They just don't believe in miracles, they think you can cure everything with science. But when you think about it, that doesn't make sense does it? I mean science can't do everything so it must mean miracles exist, you know, like in the old days. I haven't got it anymore and that Christopher was across the corridor so answer me that?"

"Answer me what Mable? You have not actually asked me a question."

"Exactly, it's a mystery isn't it?" Said Mable. "A miracle. I was cured by him being nearby, just like I told nice Mr Onions."

"How is your leg, Mable?"

"Can't feel it dear, they keep giving me those pills to stop it hurting, but actually I don't think they work, I think it was that miracle and that's why it doesn't hurt."

"Did you tell Mr Onions that Mable?"

"Of course I did, well he suggested it was probably the miracle, but it sounds right, doesn't it?"

CHRISTMAS MIRACLE! PENSIONER CURED BY HAND OF GOD! The report in the Daily Heart read. It had a lot of hits. In the absence of anything else more uplifting, a ridiculous story of an improbable situation, reported by a heavily medicated old lady who had also forgotten that her cat died 4 years previously; and was worrying about who was feeding it while she was in hospital, was enough to go viral. The cat section of the interview was dropped in the edit as it didn't add anything to the story.

Eduardo Goldman looked to the stars when he heard about the report and had looked it up. "Jesus blinking Christ," he said, sitting back in his chair. "Sweet Jesus," he said again. With no sense of irony.

*

Jude Drazkowski was also saying "Jesus blinking Christ" as he paced around in Martine's maisonette. They had not known what to do but Martine pointed out that MIDI5 knew about Jude so his place was not an option. They had seen Martine but didn't know who she was. They assumed that MIDI5 would have some surveillance capability but they would at least have a short time to regroup at Martine's. The three of them had been there now overnight and for most of the day of the twenty-eighth and mostly pacing. They had crashed out on sofas. Woken five minutes later. Slept a little, drunk coffee. Well, Martine and Jude had and they were totally wired. Maryam had tidied the flat, done some vacuuming, rewashed some dishes because she thought they were not clean enough and generally, seemed to have no need for sleep.

"It's so much fun having an adventure with friends." She said to herself because no one else was listening.

"Oh my god. Oh my god. Oh my god." Jude, following a variation on a theme repeated, as he turned and paced in the opposite direction.

Maryam looked wistfully out of the window, until Martine shut the curtains, pointing out that they were being hunted. "Oh" tinkled Maryam in her piano voice, "I thought they were friends, are they not?"

"Mother of God!" Said Jude, subconsciously determined to exhaust every possible blasphemy in his repertoire. "Is she on the spectrum?!" He said it to himself, possibly to Martine, but rather too loud and Maryam sang back.

"Spectrum, hmm… I am light, all colours of light, so I am

white, I am Maryam White." And she stood up and said to Martine "You have a nice flat, can I clean upstairs as well?" and off she went, not waiting for a reply.

Martine and Jude just looked at each other. Martine was holding it together, but even she said, "Jude, what have we done?" She said "we," she was originally going to say "you," but she subconsciously changed that to "we." This was a subtlety that Jude was unaware of, which was a shame. He heard "you," even though Martine had said "we" and while he didn't feel accused, he suddenly felt that everything was his fault.

"Look" Martine said, taking the initiative because someone had to. Jude had dropped the initiative somewhere on their escape from Gun and Savage. "My Aunt has this flat, it's sort of like a family resource for holidays and things in the city. Well, the thing is, she is mostly out of the country, so are my parents, but she is my mum's sister and it's owned by her company, so it's really not connected with me very directly, it's in a different name totally. We can go there and hide-out."

"You have an Aunt that has a spare flat?" Said Jude. "She has a few" said Martine, "she is quite well off."

"Oh," said Jude. He hadn't come across Aunts with lots of money and a spare flat before. "What does she do?"

"Oh, this and that" said Martine vaguely. She didn't mean to be evasive, but she was conscious that she hadn't really said much about her background to Jude. She knew Jude's mother was a single parent and had bought Jude up in a small flat, before moving to Dun Eideann, to yet another small flat. Actually, she didn't really care about that at all, but she was slightly self-conscious that her wealthy parents, who had bought her a two bedroomed maisonette, had several houses and had the additional advantage of an even richer Aunts house in a very nice part of the city as another occasional bolt hole. It was not something she really wanted to say to Jude at this point in their... friendship... relationship? COURTSHIP! That was it. Well, it would do. It was going to be a slow courtship with the dipsy Maryam White in tow. She realised she had blown any chance of impropriety by committing an act of criminality and being on the run from a secret government organisation, who she had also, incidentally, assaulted with their own containment device. *Oh dear* she thought, *it was all going so well. Well, apart from the car crash and being sacked and electrocuting a psychopathic government agent and the weird girl.*

*

Mr Savage was feeling very damn savage, even a day later. He had a v shaped cut and bruise ironed onto his forehead that furrowed his brow even more than his natural scowl did. "SCAN THE POLICE CHANNELS" he said to Mr Gun.

Gun had seen him like this before, not often. Savage was rarely disadvantaged in a straight fight, but he did not like losing. Their contract was deniable, they were off the books, which meant that any trouble they caused was quietly brushed under a carpet. The carpet was rolled up and stored in a dark room that no one had a key to and the dark room was in a building that not many people knew about. They were not unaccountable, but they had some latitude.

"near where we aree post office robbery in progress request armed response"

"THAT WILL DO, GET ME THERE, NOW."

Gun got into the Range Rover driving seat, Savage got into the passenger seat, opened the glovebox and emptied his pockets, removing two tazers, a flicknife a set of brass knuckles, a small spray canister and a stainless-steel cylindered ballpoint pen. "HURRY UP GUN, BEAT THE POLICE."

Gun gunned the engine, ignored the red lights and did his absolute best to save his colleague's temper from boiling over. If they managed to save some people in the process, then all well and good. Collateral compensation wasn't the prime directive, they wouldn't be thanked anyway. In fact, they would probably get into trouble. Not with the law, they were above that. Or below it, certainly around and in-between it. But Mr Savage needed therapy, it kept him focussed and he needed some therapy now.

They arrived at the post office to see a crowd outside, craning their neck into the danger zone to get a sight of the armed robbers. Cameras were all out to get a shot of the shot if it happened. Savage jumped out of the car, bellowed at everyone to "PUT THE CAMERAS AWAY NOW" and they did. It was strange, the effect Mr Savage had on people who would normally photograph everything, including their dinner. He had an authority that his size and slightly psychotic expression only assisted. The cut on his head added a further element of danger to the look. Gun watched from the car, he kept the engine running, it wouldn't take long and crime fighting sometimes needed a quick getaway, especially when Mr Savage went into hero mode.

Savage stomped inside and assessed the situation as he moved, it wasn't great tradecraft, but he preferred the element of surprise, direct action over subtlety. There were three targets. *One had a shotgun (double, 2 shots, sawn down, wide spray) one had a large knife (Sabatier, a chef's knife, nonce) and one was just standing by the door, looking shifty.* Savage walked over and headbutted shifty, before anyone could respond. He collapsed like an unset jelly. Savage kept moving, scanning between Knife and Shotgun as he cleared the floor. Shotgun shouted… "hey man, what djou fink your doin'? man I gotta gun."

"YOU NEED A DAMN TANK SON." Savage didn't even ask him to put the gun down. He looked at the people on the floor. *RUDDY HELL* he thought, but he stepped over, them. There may be collateral damage but it wouldn't be from his size 12s. Treading on old ladies never felt good, he didn't like eating whitebait for the same reason, little bones. Savage did have a grandmother who he quite liked because she refused to call him by his ridiculous first name, which he appreciated.

"YOU WAIT THERE." he pointed a finger at knife without even looking at him. Knife had frozen, he thought that with a gun and a knife and the three of them, they were invincible and a post office full of old dears didn't stand a chance. But then this man just ignored the gun the knife the three of them and the old dears and was banging around like a bull in a lightly armed china shop. Shotgun was waving his weapon now,

"Don't come near me… don't come near me… Am gonna

shoot ya maan!"

"NOT WITH THAT YOU WON'T" Savage said, took three steps and snatched the end of the twin barrels in his right hand. He directed it up and away and yanked hard, pulling the weapon quickly against its owner's tense trigger finger; KABOOM!! there was smoke and fire and noise and everyone was covered liberally in ceiling tile dust and plaster fragments. The room filled quickly with smoke and the smell of cordite.

Outside there was another collective gasp, everyone took a step back and still no one got out their phones.

With the discharged gun, Shotgun dropped his arm releasing the weapon in shock. Savage flipped it in a smooth movement, pressed the barrel release on the stock, ejected a still smoking cartridge along with the unused cartridge, cracked the stock back into place with one hand then heaved the now unloaded shotgun like a battle-axe, so hard at its owner that the sound it made when it connected with his head made the crowd outside gasp again. Shotgun's owner spilled across the floor like a dropped drink, the kinetic energy transferred by the bad-tempered agent was brutal.

"RIGHT, YOU NOW." Knife wasn't moving, but he did drop his weapon, which clinked pathetically on the floor. "TOO DAMN LATE ZORRO," Snarled Savage, still wielding the gun like a medieval hand weapon and he jabbed the end of the stock hard into Knifes face with an unpleasant crunching sound, rendering him unconscious and inverting his nose in the process.

Savage didn't bother to do or say anything else, he turned around and walked out of the post office door. The crowd seeing him with the shotgun gasped, which he acknowledged by lifting his knee and breaking the weapon in half over it. "RUDDY GUNS." He added and threw the pieces on the floor and stomped off toward his colleague in the Range Rover. Just as he was about to get in, a black police van screeched to a stop outside the post office discharging armed police who moved methodically and quickly to cordon off the area, weapons out and aggressively shouting at the crowd to move out of the way. "TOO LATE NONCES." Savage muttered under his breath as he twisted and stretched his shoulders making a light clicking noise as the synovial joints relinquished air bubbles and a little tension was released in the process. If you had just seen Mr Savage in action, you might have described the stretch as dramatic effect, an affectation. He got into the car, opened the glovebox and started to fill his pockets back up with weaponry, looking as calm as ever Mr Savage could. Gun drove off at speed, running through the gears as the vehicle growled its way up the road.

The police would clock the registration, but they would be more focussed on the robbery, their investigations into the gunmetal grey Range Rover with smoked glass would not get far, it was flagged on systems as Security Services, do not impede.

"are you better mr savage" Gun had a surprising caring side to his personality, especially where Mr Savage's pent up anger was concerned. He cared that it found an escape route or Mr Savage was not fun to be around.

"THANK YOU MR GUN, MUCH BETTER YES. THIS ANGER MANAGEMENT WORKS. FIND AN OUTLET MY THERAPIST SAID. MUCH BETTER, TOTALLY AT PEACE. NOW WHERE ARE THOSE RUDDY KIDS AND THAT NUTJOB WHITE?"

*

Christopher stumbled from the riot that wasn't a riot, it didn't have a chance. The police had given peace a slight chance, but civil disobedience no chance at all.

The public, after being kettled for four hours were well and truly suppressed, they were angry, but too tired to fight. A few tried to aggravate the situation, those few were dragged away from the cameras and dealt with discretely. Social media had lots of unverifiable stories, but no good photographs. The Press had been sectioned off quickly, the police had carved up the protest like a pizza and as people tired, they were allowed out in dribs and drabs and with the fight gone from them, they wondered what had happened. The selfies showed sad and miserable faces, no one had stuck it to the man, the man had stuck them in a pressure pot and let them boil dry. They were out of steam and they wanted to go home.

For Christopher's awakening into the lives and passions of man, this was an experience that did not start well, but he was approaching it with wonder. It was intense, but better than eighteen years of darkness. He wandered lost but entranced by the world around him and explored the city he had woken in. He looked at the buildings, at once tall, majestic pillars of marble and stone, like palaces from his dreams. Then, glass and steel and between them boarded up homes and shops. The wood faded, with flaking pasted pictures and adverts and layers of rotting board and corrugated zinc-covered steel, like shanties lost in his memories of childhood books. Parkland that stretched green forever with trees, leafless in winter but with limbs stretching into the sky, fingers reaching out and trying to catch air and water with finer exploratory tendrils trying to find space. People of every shape and size and colour. There was white hair, black hair, green and blue hair, hats, shuffling old people and crying children. Dogs and cats, birds pottering around on the ground, looking for worms and seeds, ever expectant and hopeful. Vehicles; lorries and cars and trains and motorbikes and bicycles, pumping out smoke and noise and horns and light and ringing. People were speaking and behind the sound of a hundred different types of music, there was shouting and screaming and cheering. There was dirt and dust and leaves, paper and plastic. There was banging noises and clanking noises, squealing and ringing. There were smells of food and perfume, of smoke and dirt. There was no longer darkness, there was colour and movement. There was no longer silence there was a cacophony of sound. There was no longer nothing. He could smell and he could touch. There was life in all its glory, its embarrassment, its ambition and its seediness. It was everywhere and he was living it, he was alive. Christopher kept wandering, soaking it up. He walked the streets for several hours, just looking and listening and smelling and touching as the light fell and everything was changed and lit by lamps. He was in a darkness that was not so all consuming and it was different to the one he had experienced for so many years.

A car went past, it had a siren and a flashing blue light and

Christopher remembered the crush of bodies, the faceless soldiers banging their clear plastic shields with nightsticks, the smell of fear in the people around him. The anger, short bursts of anger and shouting and those people being dragged by gloved armoured hands from the mass, kicking and shouting as they were roughly dragged away by the black masked soldiers. Disappearing into the distance into the dark. The darkness. It was now about seven forty-five in the evening and cooling off significantly. The siren triggered an instinctive response in Christopher and he ran. He stumbled, he wasn't fast but he ran as much as he was able, tripping and falling and standing again until he saw a gap, a wooden board had been pulled aside from a wall of overlapping wooden panels. There was barbed wire at the top and a 'danger – no entry to site' sign, just above where an entry had been forced. The fence was stickered and posted with advertisements for long forgotten gigs and over sprayed with badly spelled criticisms about the police force. He forced himself through. When he got through to the other side he saw a pile, a mountain a pyramidal peak of stones. Hardcore from the previous building, the derelict mid-century modernist Church of The Archangel Gabriel which had been crushed. It had been ground, dug and ploughed into a pile of stone that would become the hardcore base for a new building. It was a temporary monument to destruction and regeneration. He scrambled up the pile, it was the only direction he could go, his feet digging into the stones as they slipped and fell away under him. Hands scratched and bleeding he made it to the top and collapsed, tired and scared and as he did so he heard sound and felt movement in his pocket. The box, the plastic thing he was given was moving and ringing, he put his hand in his pocket and pulled it out. Slide left to answer, he touched the screen, it was all he could do as the ringing and vibrating stopped and he looked at it.

Faintly "Christopher...Christopher... are you there?" He lifted it closer to his ear. "Christopher... answer me, are you there?"

"Yes", he said out loud, the first time he had heard his own voice in eighteen years, he was surprised how it sounded, deeper than he expected, it did not feel like him. "Who is it?"

"Ahh, call me Uncle Max, yes, Uncle Max, I am also a friend of Doctor Goldman, he said you had his phone, he was going to call but I told him I would. I am your benefactor Christopher, I will be. Did you know you had one? No. Probably not. We have been helping each other Christopher for the past fifteen years. You will want for nothing, but I do need you back. To come back, can you do that Christopher?"

Christopher said nothing, he just let the night seep quietly into the phone. But it was darkness that spoke next.

"We need each other Christopher, you need somewhere to live, you have nowhere, no one. I can provide a house, a large house, gardens, a swimming pool, do you know what that is Christopher? Everything you ask for if you come back, its already waiting for you. We can make you a star Christopher, all you want we can bring to you, because we need you. We need to know where you will be. You will have everything you want at that house, money, entertainment, friends. I will provide you with friends

Christopher, do you know what friends are, have you ever had any?"

"I am free now" he answered, it was all he could think to say.

"No you are not, nobody is, don't be such a fool." The voice changed, no longer friendly and persuasive, it was urgent, angry even. "You need me and I need you Christopher. I need your blood, not all of it, but just a little a month, its special, it has proteins that normal blood does not. Do you understand that Christopher, you are special, but I need you. Dr Goldman has been helping me for fifteen years, since we found out about you but now you have woken up, we need you to be with us, we thought if we gave you everything you would stay you would help us. You would help me, we can live forever if you come back Christopher... listen to me." He was sounding desperate, now. Anger was overtaking urgency as his voice started its crescendo, provoked by an old pain, the pain in his head, which was throbbing.

"But I am free?" Christopher said it again as a question.

"Damn you no, I want your blood, I'll have your blood I'll take your blood, I'll suck it out of your damn veins if I have to." The storm broke, his head was splitting and the Chairman's temper was out there, he had lost it again. "Damn you to hell" he screamed down the phone, seething both with himself for his loss of temper and at Christopher for provoking it. He hung up and as he did, he looked at his left hand, he was clutching a white king chess piece so tightly, it had left the imprint of the cross in its crown in his hand. He dropped it on the floor, his hand painful from gripping it with such intensity.

Christopher just dropped the phone and it slid down the pile of rubble and broken bricks to join everything else that had been crushed and left and seemingly forgotten about.

Chapter 13

Goths, Vandals, Huns

Christopher sat on the pile of stone for a full twenty-four hours and during that time, he looked out. He was cold, the weather was changing but despite that he sat and looked at the stars out in the dark sky and it took him back to those long eighteen years. He looked at the city below him. He had time to look and reflect on the towers of light and glass. He watched planes and helicopters on night flights, the stream of endless headlights on the arteries and veins of the city. There were occasional sirens that caused him to panic briefly, before he realised that where he was, he could not be seen from the street. Then the man, Uncle Max. Initially persuasive and kind, then screaming from the small box at him, threatening him, demanding his blood. He tried to process the soldiers [police] with shields, the shouting from the angry crowds and the man on the stand, who fell apart and cried at the crowd. They mocked him and the tide of emotion had turned. He contemplated it all, cold and alone for the first time in this new world. For everything that the world had to offer him, a lot seemed wrong. Christopher lost himself inside his mind, he drifted back into a place that was familiar. A place where he had spent eighteen dark and cold years and he did not feel his temperature dropping. His body slowed down and his mind travelled back to a place where time and people did not exist. He sat on top of a pile of broken brick and concrete, in a trancelike state locked back inside himself, where he was safe.

*

Brothers Matthew, Garry and Simon, had been pacing the rooms of flat 13b, for a day.

"How can you lose the Messiah?"

"I didn't, he has gone walkabout"

"I know, but without his disciples?"

"You know why they are called disciples?"

"No?"

"Discipline, same root word, you have none."

The shortest warrior monk and most undisciplined disciple made a noise, something like a camel sneezing. He stomped over to the television, switched it on and went back to the sofa, kicking it for good measure and allowing a small amount of its sad history to form a little cloud. Then he sat down, allowing that historic dustcloud to settle back to where it felt safe. The shortest warrior monk had a look on his face like the pout of a camels rear end. No one said a word, there was nothing to say.

Until. "Jesus! That's him."

Brother Garry responded, "Christopher, not Jesus, different Messiah," missing the point completely that they were looking at their lost prophet on the news. He was surrounded by police, kettling the crowd at the failed police speech. The report was sufficient detailed for them to know when the people were released from police constraint and it was clearly at Peel Circus. The footage showed "the tired crowd, walking slowly back to whence they came... dissolving back into the city like water into the drainage system" the rather over eager reporter said.

"He can't have got far," an excited Brother Simon shouted, "it's not like he's got the chariot of Fire."

"He wouldn't have got far in the Chariot of Fire, even before you set fire to it. Now no one has a Chariot of Fire." Brother Garry sarcastically commented.

But they had a chance, a lead, they grabbed the scruffy green parka off the sofa and a beret from a pile of clothes and charged out of the door. They barrelled down the street, heading to the location of yesterday's riot, protest, speech disaster.

*

Reverend Roger Rogers should have had a speech impediment for comic effect, to fulfil his stereotypical vicarness, but his diction and enunciation was perfect. Despite his oral advantages, he did have an unfortunate habit of over embellishing his ideas and putting his over embellished foot right in the proverbial. Apart from a slight nervous laugh he had perfected the art of RP'ing his way beautifully, through every pratfall. "The occasional misplaced postulation does not take away from illustrating life with colour and comprehension and it helps the flock," he would say, to himself, while trying to extricate himself again from another inappropriate comment. He brought kindness and decency to the world and delivered it with accidental comic effect.

The flock, ironically, were being assembled to protest against an errant shepherd. Reverend Roger was pacing the church hall waiting for them to arrive. He was organising a protest against Tucker. "That brutal capitalist shepherd, turning God's gentlest animals into violent creatures, for profit." Tucker was all of those things, but the protest was also a little to do with Reverend Rogers online humiliation, which Tucker knew little about.

The news had got the Reverend's gander up. "Golly gosh It gets my gander going," Reverend Roger Rogers announced, on his Sunday Sermon. Everyone present was shocked by the amount of alliteration that he managed to squeeze into a single sentence. The gander was at a high bar.

"I saw the news this morning. A shepherd who should be guiding his flock has been breeding them to fight. To fight people, for money." *Tuckers Mill Tours* had caught the headlines again, with Tucker touring his prize wrestling sheep at a series of exhibition fights. And there it could have rested, if Roger had not said the same thing on a radio interview later that day, following it up with a criticism that Tucker was abusing sheep. A line picked up by Buster Onions, who joyfully played with the punctuation and some devious comma placing in the Daily Heart Online and made his own headline: ***Reverend Roger, rogers SHEEP!*** causing national hilarity and giving Roger a greater impetus to battle Tucker head on. It was corrected the following day to ***Reverend Roger Rogers, SHEEP!*** but the damage was done and the accompanying apology was so discretely hidden, that even a computer virus could not have infected it.

So here he was, on his crusade against immorality. He had run a few sessions already to get the flock mobilised, they should be arriving soon. The protest was in several days' time and the final planning about the wording of placards needed agreeing and some hearty songs would need to be chosen. He was hoping for a few more people to join the group. The flock was more of a smallholding to date and the regular members were more fringe protestors than religious zealots. He could do with some zealots. His first members were Gavain and Stevo, who had heard the radio interview and had found Reverend Rogers so hilarious they had attended his protest session for pure entertainment purposes. They were now committed to protesting. Roger told them; "what could be more dramatic than your leather clad muscles in action against the cad Tucker." It was awkward and a pure Rogerism, but he meant well and it had the boys choking on their coffee trying to supress their laughter.

It only ever got better than that in following meetings as the Reverend had a habit of putting his foot in it and then doubling down with his other foot. Grrrlstorm were always up for a fight about anything and would send a couple of members that varied week to week. There was also Ezzie and Bronwen the Wiccans, who were genuinely distraught at Tucker's despicable corruption of nature. All in, the flock rarely topped five. Roger rearranged the teacups and biscuits for a second time and checked his watch nervously.

*

Sometimes, in every story fate and coincidence is the only plotline required. It was under those unlikely circumstances that Christopher had come down from his moment of reflection on the deconsecrated remains of the Church of the Archangel Gabriel. He had climbed back though the gap in the fence and was wandering lost, lonely and hungry through the city streets, when the bickering, arguing brothers of the sleeping sword caught sight of him.

"It's a miracle." The proclamation was from Brother Matthew.

"Praise the Lord," praised Brother Simon, secretly thinking that he had just escaped crucifixion, but having the discretion not to say it out loud. His holy vows were being well and truly tested of late.

"Well, it may well be a miracle," argued Brother Garry, "but equally, it's not such a coincidence. We know where he was, we know he was tired, how far is he likely to have got since yesterday? We have been walking around a small area now for two hours, so yes, it might be a little divine intervention but it's also statistically quite a likely possibility."

"Naysaying fig witherer," muttered Brother Matthew, whose faith was also being put under pressure with the task they were undertaking to create a green and pleasant land. The Messiah was not a very together Messiah and had barely said anything to them, let alone a parable or anything vaguely messianic. A Messiah who had spent a week on the sofa then disappeared. Not to mention the burning of the chariot of fire. It wasn't quite the moment in Christendom he had imagined, although arguably a Chariot of Fire actually on fire, felt a bit prophetic. Or rather it would have been, if it wasn't for Brother Simon being a bit pathetic. It was, all in all, very challenging.

They ran over, grabbed the confused Christopher, bundled him into the parka and hat, which was thoughtful as he had been out all night in only a rather saggy red jumper and a t-shirt and shuffled him back in the direction they had come from, with the intention of taking him home to regroup.

As they were returning, Christopher who continued to be silent as were the brothers. They were exhausted by twenty-four hours of arguing and two hours of running around. In that lull of attention, no-one noticed Special Police Constable (David) *Johnny* Johnson recognise Christopher's face as he drove past in a squad car. They would not have known SPC Johnson called in the description and got confirmation that Christopher Sunday was still a missing person assumed kidnapped. They definitely wouldn't know that SPC Johnson, was planning a commendation, by successfully rescuing the already twice rescued Christopher Sunday. *Best drive around the block and see where they go,* he thought and the car drove on, to take the first of a series of left turns that allowed him to come back around the same route.

"SPC JohnnyJ calling in, possible misper sighting"

"Johnson, use your damn number, you are not an American truck driver you are supposed to be a police officer."

"Sorry Command my bad. Possible sighting of missing person, Christopher Sunday. He doesn't look like he is being held against his will. Accompanied by three white males, mid, late forties, two five, ten to six, one. The other... err... hobbit? All bearded. No perceived threat. Church Street, request permission to intervene and apprehend. Katz and I can handle this."

"Withheld officer. Monitor only, wait for the big boys... Hobbit?"

But SPC JohnnyJ, Special Police Constable and DJ superstar (to-be), was having none of that nonsense. He could handle this, gangster stylee and he wasn't going to let the regular heavies get the glory, like they always did. SPC Johnson was going to score a point for commissioner Bobs special force. This was his arrest, even if it wasn't technically an arrest. SPC JohnnyJ DJ extraordinaire, almost believed it himself. He could see everything playing out in slo-mo like a film scene. He'd dreamed of a moment like this ever since dropping out of his Geography degree, when he discovered that he had to write essays and get up in the morning for lectures. It was hard work when he was also spinning the decks and partying all night. In the absence of a louche lifestyle and too few bookings for his DJ set, he swapped to an all-action lifestyle and *Commissioner Bob's Special Forces*. Well, special constables anyway. It didn't turn out to be quite as rock and roll as the advert promised, but on the plus side, he more often got the evening shift so didn't have to get up early, too often. His side kick; SPC Zachary (scaredy) Katz, was hyperventilating.

"Are you going in Johnny, are you going in?" He panted.

"Affirmative pardner." This would be his moment. "I am going in, back me up."

SPC Zachary Katz closed his eyes and carried on breathing deeply, trying to get more oxygen into his blood.

Inside the hall people were arriving. "Hello. Hello" Reverend Roger greeted Ezzie and Bronwen, they nodded. They found it was best not to give Reverend Roger any further opportunity to say anything. "Cup of tea?" He asked.

"Yes" replied Bronwen, "No milk" She added suspiciously.

"Oh yes, milk. Of course, *God's* creatures. I almost forgot" Reverend Roger replied, winking patronisingly.

"Creatures," growled Bronwyn "Just creatures and yes, we are vegans as well as Wiccans. As you well know".

Saving the world, made for some uncomfortable alliances.

"Well, I daresay your bones were a poor creature once." The Reverend added snootily. He was referring to the velvet bag containing small bones that Bronwen frequently referred to, when she wanted to practically cross reference life's theoretical choices.

"They didn't belong to a poor creature" replied the witch, they are carpal bones and they belonged to my Uncle Andrew, he was not a poor creature at all."

"Oh," said an initially flummoxed Reverend Roger, then added "um, Uncle handy Andy eh?" which was the first quip that came to mind.

"You are not the first person to call him that. The last died from leptospirosis, from a rat bite"

"They were bitten by a rat?"

"No no. *Biting* the rat, it was Uncle Andrew. He died shortly afterwards and left me his hand bones in his will." Luckily, the escalation of hostilities was interrupted by the door opening again. Two young men came in, nervous initially. They saw the two witches dressed in long black frocks and the first, a rather awkward male, in his late teens asked,

"Oh is this the right place, are we sticking it to the man, bringing down that fascist Tucker?" He looked at the two witches, then the vicar, hoping for a response and some assurance.

"Well, I would not go as far as fascist," replied Reverend Roger diplomatically, "but he is a very unpleasant man."

"He is an animal Nazi" added Ezzie provocatively, "I think he is a fascist. Commit yourself Roger."

"Right on Sister," the other young man said, waving a fist in the air.

"Uhhh, well young men, young men," interrupted Reverend Roger, causing young man number two to protest indignantly.

"We're not young men, we are anarchists."

"You can be a young man and an anarchist." Bronwen added helpfully.

"Well we're not young, we are just anarchists, right."

"Oh," Said Ezzie, "how old are you?"

"I am twenty, Dunc is nineteen, he is twenty next month. We are studying philosophy."

Quite young then, thought Bronwen, but discretion now being better than furthering the conversation, she nodded and said, "Mmm, anarchists, of course you are dear."

Reverend Roger decided to intervene again, the last thing he wanted was his new recruits to be put off. "Well boys, I am Reverend Roger, what are your names and would you like a drink?"

"Black coffee" said Gnat "It's Gnat with a silent G, like the insect, I am the irritant of the ruling classes."

"I am Dunc" Said the other, slightly quieter.

"Is that Dunc with a silent E" said Ezzie, and both she and Bronwen giggled.

"Dunc, ha...hmm, Nat" Roger quickly tried to get in before the witches hijacked the situation further… but he wasn't quick enough.

"Isn't coffee a little bourgeoisie dear, tea is more a drink of the working people" Bronwen, provocatively suggested.

"HA, no." replied the defiant young Gnat. "Déjacque wouldn't drink tea."

Reverend Roger jumped in and instantly regretted it, "well no, he was a Gaul, you are right he probably wouldn't."

"Nor Pilnyak" Dunc argued, triumphantly sticking it to the most unstickworthy 'man' this side of Jerusalem House.

"Well… no" said the good reverend casually, "he's Ruscian so he would probably have drunk vodka."

"Aha!" said Gnat, sensing victory, "with orange?"

"Hmmm... maybe, yes." Replied a now mentally exhausted Reverend Roger.

"Right then," Gnat, conspiratorially demanded; "two vodka and oranges."

"We, ah… don't actually have any vodka." Said Roger.

"Oh" Dunc took over the revolutionary negotiations, "Please can we have two oranges then?"

"Squash?" Said the man of God, who had just been stuck to, but who had also deviously managed to extricate himself from the anarchist pincer movement.

"Yes please." both Dunc and Gnat nodded together. Both were convinced they had won a small victory against the establishment.

Bronwen and Ezzie were both stuffing their hands in their mouths, almost in hysterics and trying not to cry. Gavain and Stevo arrived next, accompanied by a tall young woman, with a sharp dark bobbed haircut and a pair of black wayfairers which she did not take off, even in the low light of the church hall.

"Hi Gavain, StevO" Reverend Roger said in his deepest voice, awkwardly emphasizing the O, as an afterthought.

"Hi Rev, hows the rogerin'?" Stevo asked, knowing full well it would trigger Gav, who almost choked trying not to laugh.

"I…I...I... very, very good, very good." Roger answered him in a strangely high-pitched voice. "Er um, hello young lady" he quickly swapped to the other new face in the room.

"Salome," Stevo gave a general introductory wave, "this is our friend Salome."

"Oh." Roger held out his hand, limply and added "yes, yes, like the er um… granddaughter of er... well... never mind, hello." she just brushed past and stood waiting for the world to catch up with her. While the world sorted itself out, she expected at least, that Gavain and Stevo would get there. Inwardly she was fuming at having been coerced into attending the meeting. She had planned to meet the boys for a drink later that evening and had been encouraged to join them early. They then told her that she was coming to the session. "It's so funny, I think he fancies Gav, it's hilarious." Stevo joked, but Salome was just not in the mood. She had suffered a day of idiots at work. Her PA was off sick and she had had to spend most of her afternoon trying to get a flight to Lutetia. She'd fought with an airline, a hotel, a hire car company and frankly, all she wanted to do was to vent with her friends. Mostly vent at her friends. They were idiots too, but they were at her idiots.

"She's not that scary really" whispered Gavain to the vicar, which wasn't one hundred percent true.

Next to arrive were Ali and Barb from Grrrlstorm, they nodded at the vicar on arrival but that was their only concession to politeness. Ali and Barb were in it for bigger fish than Reverend Roger. He was the tiddler that would be used to bait Tucker.

So, there it was, the good Reverend Roger's group of loyal social reformers. The witches thought he was an idiot, to Grrrlstorm he represented middle-aged white patriarchy, Gnat and Dunc had already decided he was *the man*, the establishment. The most charitable were Gav and Stevo, who thought that the worst thing about him was that he was the most awkward person they had ever met. Salome most definitely was not thinking of him, but if she did, she would be the least charitable and say, 'all of the above.'

Nervously the vicar went to the front of the room, while the crowd of nine took the front row of seats. "It's like the beginning of the sack of Rome" announced the vicar, with a subtle eye towards the Catholics. "Here we are together, Goths." He glanced at the witches' "Vandals." a nod to the junior anarchists "and the Huns" he smiled sweetly at Grrrlstorm convinced they would appreciate the wordplay, but before any of them could call him an prat. Salome spoke.

"You haven't included the LGBTQ+ crowd in your ridiculous inane insults, buffoon. You're not even inclusive in your offensiveness." This surprised everyone present, as no-one thought she was even listening.

Ali from Grrrlstorm, not wanting to be left behind in protesting at the protest organiser, followed that roundhouse with a jab from the left "Huns, HUNS? what the hell are you thinking?" Bronwen also indignant, added, in a rather frustrated manner but not quite so aggressively as she was after all, more in touch with her inner earth mother,

"And how many times do I have to tell you I am NOT a goth, I am a witch, wiccan or pagan but I am not a ruddy goth. I like dubstep actually."

To which the good Reverend tried to apologise badly.

"oh… err I am sorry ladies, ladies I also like a little dubstep now and again." (which nobody believed)

"Ladies!" Screamed the now fully fired up Barb, "I ain't no lady, I am a woman, not that you would know anything about that!" and she glared at the Vicar.

Only Gav and Stevo thought everything was going well and were glad Roger had left out team LGBTQ+. It had brought Salome into the ring.

Salome looked at her fingernails as if it would make the next hour move a little faster. Gav and Stevo sniggered and only Gnat and Dunc were pleased with the insults they had received. "Vandals man, sweet, yeah." Gnat beamed from ear to ear.

"Oh Gav, this is better than the TV, Sal's just getting fired up now! Hahaha." 'Sal' heard that and looked daggers at her friend through her Raybans. This would have stopped him ever calling her Sal again if he could have seen her eyes.

Outside, while the protesters inside were finding plenty to protest about and none of it relating to Tucker, Christopher and the Brothers Grimy were shuffling down Church Street on their way back to the unwelcoming and non-biodegradable Jerusalem House.

SPC JJ DJ had his custodian helmet on ready for action. It was for dramatic effect mostly, he wasn't expecting agro. The leather chinstrap was loosely fastened and it was worn at an inappropriately cavalier angle for a serving police officer. Like the gangster cop, the hunted turned hunter, the poacher turned gamekeeper, the failed Geography student turned special police constable and DJ, SPC Johnny Johnson, stalked his target. He patted his nightstick and almost sensed the air changing around him. That could have been because he was downwind of the Warrior Brothers of the Sleeping Sword and a Messiah who had spent a night on a rockpile.

"Oh Lord, the rozzers!" Brother Simon saw the car.

"The Lord is actually with us," Brother Matthew, calmingly responded.

"They *think* we have kidnapped the Lord," pointed out Brother Garry, overlooking the fact that they *had* kidnapped Christopher, albeit he was so unused to the conventions of the world where he now lived, he did not know he had been kidnapped.

"And they may have mistaken us for the Radical Automobile Collective," blurted out Brother Simon, feeling like confession was the first step on the stairway to heaven.

"Why would they do that?"

"I might have felt a secret sect of warrior monks needed a… er... well, a cover story. I have been establishing some bona fides, some relations with other underground organisations"

"Like whom?"

"Would rather not say?"

"Why?"

"No reason," *hope he doesn't find my Grrrlstorm login*, thought Brother Simon.

"We'll come back to this." Said Brother Garry, "In the meantime, Why have you decided to go undercover as a terrorist organisation to draw attention AWAY from us?"

"Er... the Radicals are not really a terrorist organisation," said Brother short and slightly awkward.

"It's all over the papers, they have been threatening to attack a bridge."

"No they are not"

"And you would know this because?"

"Would rather not say?"

"Why?"

"No reason." *I hope he doesn't find out I was trying to impress Grrrlstorm* thought Brother Simon.

"Oh dear," said Brother Matthew, finding understatement a better solution than out and out hysteria. "In there, quick" and they bundled themselves and the messiah through the nearest open door, into a church hall. Inside, unbeknownst to everyone, a secret warrior sect disguised as terrorists, trying to impress Grrrlstorm, witnessed by anarchists, witches and a small group from the not be overlooked LGBTQ+ community, along with the said Grrrlstorm, all managed to partly achieve Brother Simon's poorly thought-out plan of bringing together a supportive network of underground organisations to overthrow the new world order. Only Reverend Roger was surplus to the plan, which was ironic as it was his meeting. On the plus side he now had some religious zealots as part of his flock, which sadly he did not know.

"That's interesting" Bronwen stood up, walked towards Christopher and put her hand on his cheek. She looked into his eyes, cocked her head, smiled and turned to no one in particular and said again "very interesting." She turned to see Brother Simon standing expectantly by the side of her so she reached into her bag, pulled out a flat silver tin, flipped the engraved metallic lid and dabbed a finger into the red paste that was inside it. She next daubed a cross on Brother Simon's head, put the small container away and walked back to her chair.

Ezzie leaned over and prodded Bronwen. "Why did you put lipstick on the little ones head?:

"Because it was funny, did you see his face when I did it?" Both witches giggled, "but," Bronwen added, "the other one, the one who doesn't look like a bag lady with bristles, there is something very well… very, about him."

"Hmm" Ezzie squinted and looked more closely at Christopher. "Yes, very very indeed"

Reverend Roger could see his meeting, spiralling out of control before it had even started. "Um.. everyone, everyone, so nice to see so many new faces, can we talk about how Tuckers Mill is blighting our land."

Something triggered in Brother Matthews mind on that comment. "Is it a dark and Satanic Mill?" he called out.

The Reverend at this point was prepared to agree with anything vaguely supportive, "Yes," he answered, "very dark and satanic."

"I think God has sent us" said brother Matthew. The vicar looked confused. Everyone else looked to the stars, only Ezzie said anything. She leaned over to her friend and said,

"Maybe not a god, but something has."

Brother Matthew, who had not heard that, smiled the warm smile that told the world that a prophesy was playing out.

"OK, enough of this circus." Salome stood up and took a step towards the door. "Idiots galore and now tramps as well. Boys, I'll be one drink in, I have had as much as I can take." She walked another two steps forward, almost treading on Brother Simon who looked up and his jaw dropped.

"Back in the hole hamster-thing." She hissed, not looking at him. This covered at least part of what Brother Simon was thinking, albeit the other half wasn't his vow of chastity. "And don't you dare think it, incel." She added to an equally jaw-dropped Brother Garry who, confused as to why thinking of how to beat a level three wizard, with a shape changing potion and his new d-twelve dice, was anything to stop thinking about shut his mouth sharply, just in case. Leaving the idiots in her wake she was stopped next, by the heavy oak door flying open just six feet before she got to it.

"Everybody freeze." Shouted SPC Johnny J, waving his nightstick more like a vulgar weapon rather than an offensive one.

Salome paused mid-step, not something she would ever normally do. Officer Johnson stopped, something he frequently did. Time froze. Johnson slowly raised his nightstick in front of him and nodded towards it. He raised his eyebrows and, then in an act of lemming like suicidal stupidity, looked Salome up and down. Twice. He licked his lips before saying "Calm down darling" and he winked at her.

Time restarted, at a much greater speed than it was moving before it stopped.

"For the love of god," muttered Salome and in rather a faster motion than officer Johnsons licentious truncheon waving, swung her handbag with such speed and accuracy that three pounds of leather and crystal, including its contents, hit the officer on the side of his head. It was not at quite the speed of a cannon ball, but with rather enough power to breach the blue battlements of the law. The loosely fixed strap snapped and his helmet flew off, spinning into the air. SPC JJ and wannabee clubland darling's head jerked hard to one side. Almost instantly, the muscles tightened in his neck in response to the trauma, but the floppy jelly mess that was his brain, had already hit critical velocity and came to an immediate standstill on the other side of his skull. He crumpled like the sack of sad and stupid that he was and crashed out even before his spinning helmet landed beside him. His feet pointed towards the door in a subconscious statement of intent, to escape.

Outside SPC Katz was standing by the car, he had on three occasions taken a step forward, before stepping back and he was hovering on one leg in the same spot he had been on for the last ten minutes. Only when Johnson had gone through the door did he say, almost in a whisper "shout if you need me Johnny." Glimpsing the action through the gap in the door he had caught a flash of a silver aimed at his colleagues head and then Johnsons helmet somersaulting in the air before hitting the floor and spinning to a stop with its shiny top décor pointing outwards towards the terrified Katz. All he could see of his colleague was his feet. Putting two and two and terrified together, he got five and was sure that he saw SPO JJ DJ poleaxed by an assassin with a viciously shiny weapon. Katz, earning his nickname twice over, dived back into the car, buried himself deeply in the footwell and grabbed his radio for dear life. "Send reinforcements, they have beheaded Johnny J," he bawled down the phone, before ducking deeper into the well with his hand over his head, almost in tears. He didn't see an elegant young lady with a silver crystal Louboutin handbag walk out of the door and stroll down the street as though nothing had happened."

"Oh god, hurry up, hurry up" he said to himself and kept saying it even after SPC Johnny J had woken up confused, and staggered into the street.

"That's gone and done it," Gav whispered to Stevo.

"Oh dear, we best be off, is there a back door?" Brother Matthew looked around but none of the boys were waiting to find out the answer and had started running through the kitchen, where luckily a back door opened out into the graveyard. It was dark and suitably atmospheric outside.

Bronwen emptied the knuckles from the velvet pouch in her bag and had rolled them gently on the floor. She studied them for a moment before leaning over to Ezzie, "that is definitely interesting, I think we may have something to do dear."

Half an hour later and the police reinforcements had still not turned up. Ali and Barb were staying on to say they had seen nothing but they were up for a fight with the police regardless. Reverend Roger was contemplating deeply how his protest was going to work out.

Gav and Stevo had decided to sneak off straight away and were only fifteen minutes behind Salome, who had got to the bar already. She was sitting on a table on her own and had an open bottle of Merlot and a large glass. She was halfway through her first drink when Gav and Stevo caught up with her. They found her rummaging through her bag checking for damage, "make up- ok. glasses– ok, condoms– hmm fat chance, Dior – thank goodness... pens, coins, notepad and… there." she breathed a sigh of relief, picked up her wine glass and took a large sip.

It was a small hardback copy of 'Winnie the Pooh' by AA Milne, with a note on the inside front cover that read "Dearest Solomon, you can be everything and anything you want to be. We love you to the moon and back. Happy first Birthday darling. Mummy and Daddy XXX"

Chapter 14

Hotel 'Schwein-Schmidt'

Savage was in the Range Rover, hammering the keyboard that extended on a cable from a slot built into the glove compartment. He was ham fistedly punching the keyboard, which he thought ought to produce the result that he wanted, but it was producing an error message.

"may ii mr savage" said Gun, whose hands were not quite so well equipped as Savage's for smacking the hell out of a wild bull should it ever be necessary, but were far better designed for typing.

"ALL YOURS GUN." Savage threw the keyboard as his partner, who noted that Savage was in a much better mood today. He spent a moment typing in some parameters and pressed enter.

"nothing still nothing I have generated a facial matrix and left it running if he is picked up on any camera it will alert usss" They only had a photograph of Jude from his work records and could only run a search on his face, not Martine's or Maryam's. Jude wasn't cleverly keeping out of sight, his limited security training did not include evasion. It did include a little evasive talk about dustbin bags, but mostly, he had been lucky so far. Martine had shrewdly suggested switching their phones off and removing the batteries. They were not completely off grid but it would take Savage and Gun a while longer to track them down.

"ANYTHING ELSE ON THERE GUN?"

"no mr savage an all eyes alert for the other one who disappeared from the hospital but at the moment they are leaving that one with the police"

"DAMN IT." Muttered Savage, as Gun fired up the Range Rover engine. He put his foot on the pedal, and they roared off up the road, heading back to their office in Pimlington to await further orders or a new clue.

*

Ezzie and Bronwen were excited. The pathetic protest group had thrown up a very unexpected event. In Ezzie's small house, they had lit candles and incense. Bronwen was studying Uncle Andrew's bones and Ezzie had a set of cards laid out on the carpet. She was currently sprawled very inelegantly and very un-mystically on the floor looking at them. "It's not going to end well you know," she said. "But, we do have to help"

"Yes dear" Bronwen answered but her mind was elseware for a moment. Pop! She was back. "Yes, a little soft influence, just a little nudge I think."

"And you will meet your little man again Bron" Ezzie giggled.

"I'll bring my lipstick dear, yes."

*

"I have been chosen by witches. Like Hamlet!"

"Macbeth," corrected Brother Matthew, "and that didn't go well"

"Well, it wasn't actually real, it was a film." Said a grumpy Brother Garry.

"But anyway, witches. They have marked me with blood I am special"

"You are that." acknowledged Brother Garry, who then looked to Christopher. "So are you. Dark Satanic Mills, we can nail that tomorrow, we've got to start building a Jerusalem here, or it's all been a waste of time."

Building a Jerusalem? Christopher was reflecting on his life surrounded by these people, they meant well he felt, but they were lost. They were looking for something that only existed in their imagination. He did not know why, just that they were and that they thought he was a part of it. But he had no one else. There had been screaming crowds, crumbling oratory, crazed vampires screaming at him for his blood whilst promising him the world. Sirens, soldiers; he had seen women knock down men, men knock down women, witches arguing with vicars and in it all, the least confusing and the least threatening, were the self-Styled Warriors of the Sleeping Sword. They had a simple non sensical quest that he was seemingly part of, but he didn't really understand. And actually, there was no one else. He did not want to go back to hospital and he did enjoy just wandering and taking in the simplicity and complexity of the world around him. If all he could do was to walk around, to just live and to absorb everything that bombarded his senses, that would be enough. He had a roof over his head, he was given food and he was clothed. He had company that cared for him (in a rather strange manner admittedly) and when he thought it through, he really wanted for nothing more. There was no more to need. Food, clothing, shelter and friendship and the opportunity to exist, that was all he had wanted in eighteen years and he now had everything. He could see, hear, touch, taste, smell and feel the world around him, it came in waves that poured out of all of life. It had been confusing and overwhelming at first, but he was coming to terms with that other sense. The shapes that he felt in the air around everything that initially conflicted with what he saw and touched. The shapes that moved with sound and that changed colour with taste and smell. Everything was more than he had imagined or remembered, but it was intense, and was beginning to learn to process it. In fact, he could not get enough of it, he wanted to gorge himself on the world outside his head. He realised why he had sat on the pile in the cold for so long now, it was because of that symphony playing out around him as the world spun. Building a Jerusalem, wherever he happened to be? This was his Jerusalem, the centre of wonderment. Jerusalem was everywhere he was.

The boys, however needed something a little less metaphysical and a bit more tangible. They appeared sure he would help create it though they, or he, had no idea how. But… and the best plans are dynamic, flexible and started incomplete, they were throwing themselves into every and any opportunity. They were allowing fate, prophesy and forward momentum to fill in all the gaps.

"This Tuckers Mill," Brother Garry asked, "what is it? Apart from being a satanic kind of mill."

"Well," said a smugly up to date with all the info, Brother Simon, "Tuckers Mill is the promotional organisation set up to develop Sheep Wrestling tours, along with regional and international competitions and includes media and merchandising. There is a league you know. Grrrlstorm hate Tucker and describe him as a perfect example of retro chauvinism and toxic masculinity."

"And... how do you know all that?" Brother Garry asked, suspiciously.

"Erm... rather not say" *said the recent member of Grrrlstorms online community, login: lilcutebits72*. "Just, err... general research... you know... know your enemy and all that"

"Hmm" mumbled a deeply sceptical Brother Garry.

"Where is Tuckers Mill?" Brother Matthew joined the conversation.

"It's on a farm near Glastonburgh, but he is doing a tour and is at the House of Grenville department store, on the Brampton Road. There's going to be fighting sheep, t-shirts, photo opportunities talks and all the stuff apparently" and then, before he could quite stop himself "It sounds like fun."

"Fun?" said Brother Matthew. "FUN. Hmm, Brampton Road, that sounds more dark and satanic than fun, we'll take the good fight there, it sounds like a pit of sin."

Lilcutebits72, chosen by God and marked by witches, felt that discretion was the better part of valour and said nothing, but he did think, *hmm witches, Grrrlstorm... nice...*

that'll be a good fight.

*

Ian and Katie Piggot Smith were prisoners of their own success. The press had gone mad and the general public followed close behind and also in front. Ian Piggot-Smith was irritated by it all and was whining at his wife again. "We are just your average, self-made billionaires. No idea why everyone wants to interfere in our lives." But interfere they were and they had also helped add another one hundred and thirty million onto Ian's eight hundred and seventy-three million win. He had sat back and watched the money go up before his eyes. A lot happened in a very short amount of time, almost as though the media plan was there waiting. It was.

During the last three days, film rights, book write rights, rights to a television series and three documentaries were already lined up. News interviews and advertising deals we also bolstering his out-of-control finances. So far, he would be promoting golf clubs, tweed suits, hangover cures and health insurance for the over sixties. Katie had been a little more selective and had focussed on high street clothing brands for women of a certain age, holidays and gin. The gin paid the least, but they promised her a case of their finest when she asked for one.

Ian could barely keep up with how successful they had become. "Don't know why we didn't do this before?" he commented, overlooking the fact that it was just good luck that made him a person of interest and a gullible and desperate public that gave any intrinsic value to people of interest. Those very same people who massed outside his self-made semi in suburbia hounding him at his door for a selfie and treading on his dahlias. Where, despite over eight hundred million pounds in the bank and the balance of their billion in a pile of contracts, waiting to be signed, they could no longer live.

Ian and Katie Piggot-Smith were holed up in an executive suite at the Royal Barchester Hotel with the largest television they had ever seen and a stream of delivery men turning up with Katie's online shopping. She wasn't holding back, why would she, it was almost a challenge to spend money faster than it was accumulating. Autonomous Accumulations had a similar problem and spent it on government departments. Katie was a little less focussed, but no less ambitious.

Ian, for his part had never seen a million pounds in cash so had a small suitcase delivered with fifty-pound notes in two and a half thousand-pound bundles. He had initially looked at it, then taken it out of the case and then tried to stack it up into a single tower. He almost managed to get it to his height but it kept falling over. He then ruffled a bundle through his fingers for about ten minutes before smelling it. He put a bundle in every pocket and did a quick sum, "twenty-two thousand, five hundred." It was not comfortable, nor discrete so he took it all out again. He amused himself for a day with a million pounds in cash, like a child with building blocks. He laid all the bundles out on the floor and walked along them in his socks, which turned out to be surprisingly difficult for the overweight middle-aged man. He then took a bundle and placed one on every surface in the suite. He walked around for several hours looking at the money. Everywhere he looked was a bundle of money wrapped in a paper gummed strip. Once he had done that and bored himself with the repetitiveness of endless money, he decided to stack it like bricks in the doorway of the main bedroom. What he discovered was that one million pounds doesn't go quite far enough in a Royal Barchester bedroom door. From the inside, with a wall built only up to his middle, he called out, "Katie, Katie look, come here woman." Katie left her laptop for the first time that day and came towards the bedroom door, she saw her husband standing behind a wall of fifty-pound notes. She looked at him for a minute, switching between the money-wall obscuring half of him and the look of annoyance and frustration on his face. "It's not enough" he complained, "it's just not enough it only goes halfway up" and he stepped forward kicking out with his right leg and distributing the inadequate million-pound wall of money everywhere. In the process, one of the bands split and notes spread over the floor. "Oh my god woman, look what you made me do." He dived on the floor, reaching with his hands to try and get all the money back into a pile.

Katie left him to it. She walked back through to the other room, the main state room of the suite. It was an early Victorian room that had its history toned down. The walls were white, corniced and skirted but the wood and plaster of the frills were just a little too perfect. The walls, too finished. There was no build-up of paint to soften the edges, no cracks from time, no sense that a woodworm may have ever been hungry and visited the wood there. The ceilings were high, at least fifteen feet, the chandeliers glistened and the fabric of the curtains had a heavy draped lushness, but you could put them in a washing machine. The curtains and possibly even the chandeliers. The furniture looked like antique furniture but closer inspection revealed it as veneer on compressed fibreboard. It was good quality and it looked the part, there was no doubt about that. But expensive as it all was, like the nouveau'est of the nouveaux-riche in the room, it had everything but authenticity. Where a building of its period should have a slightly decayed splendour and should have had the scars, stains and stories of one and a half (and a little bit more) of a hundred years of love and lust, modesty and bad behaviour; of decadence, deceit and joy, excitement spilt drinks, dropped food, dropped underwear and lived lives, it had none. All of the life had been scraped and ripped out from the heart and fabric of the building. The paper and then the plaster had been peeled from the walls and replaced with clean lines and modern paint over central heating air conditioning, soundproofing, triple glazing, wi-fi, hi-fi, filtered water directly from the taps and a built-in cinema screen above a mini bar. It was *period+*. Absolute luxury, a perfect temporary home for the newly billionaire'd Piggot-Smiths.

The Piggot-Smiths had been there for almost three days now and Ian was bored, frustrated and ungrateful. He was almost beyond being pompous to people, which he had revelled in for the first few days. On their first evening he had demanded, not asked, although asking would have achieved the same end, for champagne by room service. When it arrived, he was annoyed that he struggled to understand Milosz the waiter who clearly didn't have a sense of humour. Despite the fact that the young man had served him perfectly well, he hadn't fully understood Ian's "reds in the bed Ruskies" joke. Milosz, had smiled politely but slightly confused, asked if he should check the bed for him. Well, why would Milosz understand crass 1980's cold war jokes? He was born 8 years into the following decade and was from a small town on the Germania/Czechia Border. He spoke Czechian, Slavic, Germanian, Britannic and was fairly proficient in Gaul. He didn't speak the global language of stupid though, he was wholly unqualified there. Milosz was quite happy being admonished for his treatment of the 'Schwein-Schmidts' as the Piggot-Smiths had become known in the corridors, backrooms, kitchens and desk areas. He was also rather glad that he didn't have to serve the executive suite again. Ian wasn't having any of this nonsense for what he was paying, he had a hotline to the manager and made his unreasonable complaints quite clear.

"I have nothing against foreigners Mr Defarge" he said, "you know that. I mean, we get on well and you being a Roman and all."

"Gaul" replied Monsieur Defarge.

"Well, yes...yes... Gaul, Rome...same accents. Anyway, anyway, I am sure he is very good at what he does in Ukrania or wherever he comes from, but I am an easy man to get on with and he didn't laugh at my banter. I made a few friendly jokes to put him at ease and he looked at me like I was speaking a foreign Language. This is Britannia Mr Defarge. Britannia, not, you know, one of those other places. Don't you value communication when you recruit these people Mr Defarge?"

"Oui" replied Defarge on mute then, "I am sure we can find someone who meets your exacting requirements Mr Piggot-SmYth."

"I don't mind continental you know, just as long as they

can speak. How about one of the girls, they will be more you know, better at that sort of stuff if they are continental, because well..." luckily he didn't finish his sentence and no one had to find out what he was implying.

"Sacre Bleu!" breathed Defarge on mute. Then again, "I am very sure we can find someone who meets your exacting requirements Mr Piggot-SmYth."

The Piggot-Smiths were served initially by Mathilde, who despite being perfect in almost every way had the wrong colour hair, it clashed with the curtains. Anieska who was not tall enough and Pierre who had a devious look in his eye. Eventually, once a bored Ian Piggot-Smith had found that fifteen thousand pounds a week, bought absolute compliance and he could demand whatever, whoever and whenever, he said that he wanted room service from someone with one leg, because "you have to help those people with disablements." By this point the 'Schwein-Schmidts' were the most despised people in Knightsgate. Given the disparity of the localities wealth compared with the service industries poor pay and long hours as a whole, this was quite an achievement.

Monsieur Defarge however was a consummate professional and managed to recruit the one-legged David, who annoyed Piggot-Smith intensely by proving that it was barely any disability at all to the capable, likable and proactive young man. After demanding to check his prosthetic, Piggot-Smith lost interest in being awkward and down-graded his behaviour to just average arrogant, haughty, selfish and basic level unpleasant.

Katie Piggot-Smith, was frankly not interested in her

husband's bad temper, his rolling around grasping at his money and baiting the hotel staff. She had greater priorities, an online shopping business to deal with. She could buy anything she wanted, she thought. Then she realised she could buy everything she wanted. After that, she started buying anything and everything that she didn't want. The second bedroom was full of boxes, packets and bags. She had even stopped opening the parcels. "I can do that later". Then later came and she demanded a member of staff be allocated to help her open all the deliveries. Then they were gainfully employed repacking many of them to send back. Not that Katie really needed the refunds, but she did need the space. There were only so many dresses, shoes, kitchenwares, soft furnishings, ornaments and healthcare products, you could fit in Five Star hotel suite. She didn't mind who assisted, both Mathilde and Anieska did shifts and did their absolute best to avoid Ian.

The Piggot-Smiths, taken out of their small, predictable lives, were bored.

"I want to go out" said Katie, "I want to go to a proper shop."

"I want a curry", said Ian, "I am ruddy fed up of oysters and caviar and haughty cuisine I want a proper Britannic curry" which he said in his most haute of voices. "Damnit Katie, look I have got all this money I can do anything I want."

"*We have* dear, *we want*"

"Yeah... yeah... we, we, we. We want a curry, don't we? The people in this hotel, they are not going to stop us, they are not going to stop this Britannic bulldog when he wants classic Britannic cooking."

"I don't think they ever were going to stop us Ian."

"Hmm… that Pierre one would, ruddy shifty he was, did you see his eyes? Certainly not leaving my money behind. Wouldn't trust any of them."

*

Maryam was in the lead, almost skipping down the road without a clue where she was going. Martine was steering her verbally and Jude was surreptitiously following. He was sheepish, nervous and frequently hid behind lamp posts, more so than usual. He had read spy thrillers, he knew he was being spied on. Like everyone else in the small band of outlaws, he had sensibly put on a hat (one of Martine's, it was orange, with flowers) dark glasses and he was wearing a scarf, as were Maryam and Martine. The scarf was around his neck but pulled up to cover his face. He walked in a ridiculous gait, which he explained to Martine was to disguise his movements, "as they can track that sort of thing you know." Martine, who had not read any spy thrillers, thought hats and scarves were a sensible precaution but she thought that Jude walking like he had just had an embarrassing accident, was a little over the top. They had worked their way across town and had just crossed Cannon Street, towards Corinium Square. Jude could not believe the houses. Six story, red brick town houses, that seemed to go on forever. Remarkably, or perhaps not so, he had not spent much, if any, time in this part of the city. It was a different "waste zone" so professionally off territory. He was, despite the dark glasses wide eyed, "people own these?" He asked

Martine.

"Well, yes," said Martine "They are houses, of course people own them and live in them" She thought it was a silly question and didn't give much thought to her reply.

Jude looked at the pillared facades, the porticos and the arches of the windows in terracotta and sandstone. "Wow," then, "is your Aunt's like this?"

"A bit" said Martine, "we are almost there, but its white stucco, not brick, she only has two floors not a whole house." She added that, as if that made it somehow less extravagant as a crash pad.

"White stucco, ah!" Jude muttered, wondering what the heck stucco was. "I see," said a highly undercover Double 0 Dustbin. It had been a highly stressful forty-eight hours and he hadn't fully processed what was happening. He was in freefall at the moment, just following the only option open to him, gravity… but he needed to stop and think about it all. He had found this girl, found another random girl, assaulted a lunatic member of the intelligence services. He had almost certainly lost his job, probably lost his freedom, potentially lost his life and he didn't know what stucco was. *Right*, he thought, *we need a plan. I need to know what stucco is before I die.*

"It's like icing on houses, think of it that way," Martine called out, apparently reading his mind but actually noticing the expression on the little of his face that she could see. Every little bit of him managed to look confused. He looked back at her. She winked. Under the scarf he smiled and relaxed a little. *Ok*, he thought. *I can probably die now* and he followed her.

*

Not half a mile away, Number Five was back at Diemos, doing what came naturally. Scheming, subverting, undermining and doing what he would explain quite reasonably as succession planning. He was looking at what would happen when it was time for a change of chair and he had an idea that this would be sooner, rather than later. Within two years he estimated, if plans were playing out just as they should.

Niklaus Kloeven-Hoef was not a guest at Diemos, he was a member. He was known to and by Number Five, but by reputations only and they had some mutual acquaintances. He was Managing Director of one of the largest Banking organisations in Europa and he was a very established member of Diemos. You rarely toyed with money at that level, unless you had been to a few of the right schools and had been ingratiated into Diemos by close friends and family. Kloeven-Hoef had both.

"Number Five. Of Seven I believe? Pleasure." He offered a cold white hand to Number Five. "It amuses me that Autonomous Accumulations have dispensed with names." Number Five took it, it looked small and weak but even though Kloeven-Hoef only squeezed back gently, politely, Number Five sensed that he could perhaps crush his hand if he chose. He immediately took to Kloeven-Hoef, he had a charisma, that was at odds with his cold white hands.

"Niklaus. I assume we are dispensing with formalities, your name, Dutch, South African?"

"Older than that, I am told." Said the tall, blond man with the white hands and green eyes. His explanation explaining nothing, only that he didn't want to discuss it.

"You wanted to see me, a proposition?"

"I thought I was the only person who knew I had a proposition?"

"You would be surprised what I know Number Five, you may also be surprised that I might be interested."

"You know what I have to offer?"

"You have only one thing that I might be interested in, we both know that. Now you are playing games, cut to it Number Five." Kloeven-Hoef knocked back a large brandy and laid the glass on the table, with such speed that Number Five was surprised that there was no sound when it hit the table. Kloeven-Hoef smiled, his eyes twinkled and burnt with copper sulphate fire.

"Indeed, the chair. I suspect it may become available within a year or two. I have my own plans for Autonomous Accumulations. I, we, are going to nationalise it."

The blonde man looked at his empty glass and before he had looked up, the waiter was walking his way with a decanter. "Ok, now that does surprise me, the chair. Yes, I am interested. AA almost runs the country, it's big enough to be of interest. I am sure I can keep a foot in Banking as it were. But, you are going to nationalise AA. The Chairman?"

"He doesn't know. Nationalisation, it's more a merger of

interests. AA are planning on moving into politics. We have a lot of influence, the hard edge of soft power. But frankly, the government are just sand in the machinery. We own most of the country's human assets, we run most of what we do not own. We supply almost everything and can switch it on and off as we like. In short, we are already the biggest state within the nation. The politicians have sold it to us, bit by bit because they have not got the guts to take any risks, so we have taken the risks and they, for the most part do what we tell them. The monarch as you know does what the monarch is told by the Prime Minister, who is a fool and the only loose cog in all of it. It just all runs too slowly, inefficiently. The people, well the people are the problem, because they keep voting in one idiot Prime Minister after another. They are allowed too much by this political system and vote for fools who just want to talk and that is what we need to change."

"And you have. a plan to change it?"

"Autonomous Accumulations, becomes the government."

"Bold, Number Five, also curious, you need to be voted in?"

"Twenty six percent of the population is all we need. A few rotten boroughs would do it and the whole country is a rotten borough. You can buy votes with stupid news and large prizes. The country is full of gaping mouthed fish, we throw maggots and they come swimming. But the plan, the model? It's more economics. A capital merger, Autonomous Accumulations and The Bank of Britannia. Cost take out, we rewrite the political system to replace the cabinet with a Board of Directors. We look to squeeze a little more margin out of the department budgets, I think we ought to be more speculative in how they are spent. There is a lot of resource there, if we own it we can profit from it. If there is profit then, well everyone is wealthier. Everyone benefits if they are shareholders. We create a nation of shareholders.

"It almost sounds like socialism Number Five." Kloeven-Hoef smiled at his own joke.

"It almost is Niklaus, it almost is," replied Number Five, not seeing the irony. "The people will of course benefit, but they will need to do what they are told, if they are to be shareholders. We will make decisions on their behalf. Sometimes difficult decisions, always difficult decisions, there may be some tiering in the distribution of shares."

"A land of milk and honey Number Five?"

"A powerful nation again Niklaus. At the top. One nation, a global economic power. When we have Britannia, we may need to clear out a little dead wood but then we look for 'offshore' opportunities"

"Expeditionary wars are a little last century, no?"

"Ha! The odd small war may be an amusing distraction. Father would like that, good for the family firm, but no. Offshore business opportunities. Initially. We have a business model, it will work nationally, it can work internationally so in time we will expand the model internationally a country at a time. But home front first, don't you think?"

"Yes, the home front. The job you have offered me…"

"Have I?"

"Not yet but you will"

"You are right. I will, *we* will. The Chair of Autonomous Accumulations will be vacant soon. The Chairman has, how do we put it… misplaced his medicine. You have only another year on your contract and you want a chair but there is not a vacancy at Interbanck. We need someone aligned to our business philosophy who wants to lead but will allow his executive team, what might you say? Latitude. We need someone to front our national 'execution', become Prime Minister, you are, how might we say it? *Palatable and charismatic*, to the great unwashed. I am not, my father sells guns, as did my grandfather. You are a banker, who could be more trustworthy than the man holding the money? The Executive will keep the organisations motivated. You will enjoy working this way Niklaus, we have a very specific approach to doing business."

"Latitude Number Five. I suspect you know the answer already, or we would not even be having the conversation and, this ah… cabal you are forming?"

"The chancellor can see the writing on the wall, he is protecting himself by building a coalition of political support for us, from within. They will not want to lose their influence, oh I mispronounced that, their *effluence*. It's all they will have, but it will allow them to stay in the top tier. They will damn well do some work for it though, proper work, making money not spending it. The police are ours already, we as good as own the health service, the roads, the press. Education, the only other policy that anyone gets excited about? We do not have to do anything about that, it's easier to allow the public to get stupider. While people are excited about idiots winning millions and photos of people falling over in the street and arguing with each other about whether something is blue or black, or big or small, we'll maintain stronger more cohesive control. They do not understand, they do not really care. Short attention spans. We can mostly execute for their benefit.

"The judiciary?"

"Judges, like Doctors and the Church, ha! the public do not believe a word they say. It's like education, if people do not understand it in five words they think there is a conspiracy."

"Number Five. There is a conspiracy. Tell me about the police?"

"We have two forces. One larger, cheaper public facing, it has the numbers, and it spends most of its time scraping data from cameras. There is another more focussed paramilitary force for when its needed. We own the first outright, we control the latter. Ultimately, we have a plan for crime control. A database. A rather thorough one in fact. Work in progress, but we will be able to cut through crime like a swathe within a few years. Our friendly police force is looking for the Chairman's medicine as it happens, I suspect they are incapable of finding it. Hence my confidence of a position in the not-too-distant future."

"Very good Number Five. This has been an interesting conversation, do keep me posted."

No money or salary or benefits were mentioned. Number Five and Niklaus Kloeven-Hoef no longer worked for personal wealth, it had no longer had value. It was simple arithmetic in the end. Number Five worked for an organisation with forty-eight million dependents, some might consider them customers or clients. Niklaus Kloeven-Hoef had thirty-two million customers and clients who were not quite dependent enough. Kloeven-Hoef could cause financial waves in seven countries, Autonomous Accumulations could switch an economy on or off, which would cause waves in the very same seven countries. Both gentlemen measured success in the number of lives they controlled and the balance sheet that they toyed with. They worked for nothing so dirty as cash, it was power alone. The seductive energy of absolute power, over enormous numbers of lives and businesses.

The dust of deceit and collusion, of deals, schemes and much worse caught the breeze very slightly as the door opened for Kloven-Hoef to leave the club. He stopped for a moment in the doorway and breathed in deeply, taking the filth of generations down into his lungs. His eyes flashed again as he smiled to himself. *Succession*, he thought. *Prophetic really* and the door of Diemos closed silently behind him as he stepped out into the street and walked to his limousine. The door opened, he got in, it closed, and the car drove away, with barely a noise.

*

Jude's mouth had spent the last ten minutes in a dropped position, it wasn't that he was walking around Westgravia surrounded by generations of wealth that had dislodged his jaw. It was that he was with Martine, who was unphased by both the wealth embedded in the streets and the fact they were on the run. He wasn't quite sure where she got her confidence from, but it made him feel safe, when really he was a million miles from safe. It also made him feel a little inadequate. Oh, the other reason his jaw was dangling from his skull was because they had just overtaken Maryam who had stopped to talk to a magpie. It tweeted, she spoke in that tinkly bell-like voice and the magpie croaked, chirped, clucked and made noises that Jude didn't even realise a Magpie could make. Weirdly, it seemed to be a conversation, but in two different languages. Jude shook his head. "Martine, why did we do this? She is off her head. I just thought we were doing the right thing, but I don't know. Maybe we are not?"

"We are doing the right thing Jude," Martine was absolutely sure, "we must do the right thing, we have started this, it will work out but we need a plan. We'll get to my Aunt's flat, it's only a few doors away now and we'll think." Jude looked up. The house did look like it was iced *stucco*, he thought as he looked first at the railings then the floors, five including the basement. The whiteness of the paintwork, barely any dirt on the walls, or the street, no litter, no rubbish, no bins. *Wow*, he thought, *a different world*. Martine brushed past him.

"You ok?"

"No, not really" he replied, "I feel a bit sick. I am not going to be sick, but I feel a bit sick."

"Let's get inside," she got a key out of her pocket. "It's the middle two floors, it has its own door. Maryam!" she called back as Maryam floated up. Clearly, she had exhausted all conversation with the magpie.

Chapter 15

Green and pleasant land

"WHERE ARE THEY GUN?"

"you meean codename ironman"

"HA RUDDY HA GUN, WHEN DID YOU GET A SENSE OF HUMOUR?"

Gun and Savage had been sitting at the computer for five hours, trawling through camera footage. They had set up a trace on Jude's phone and voicemail, but all they had for the past two days was a message from his mother, asking if he had any cabbage left. Had he eaten it all because she had some recipes for left overs? She had mentioned "a girlfriend", but frustratingly had not mentioned her name. They had set a trace on her phone as well, but there was nothing to date.

The office in Pimlington was, to say the least, utilitarian. The main office space had three desk-style tables, the drawers had nothing in them but basic stationary. Each desk had a computer terminal, with a retinal scanner built in. There was a coffee machine, a small kitchenette and a locked cabinet. The cabinet did not need opening, it contained spare blue suits and a rack with tasers and stun collars, they had already replaced the ones that had been used on them and didn't need any more.

Savage looked around the room. There was also the "fish

tank," another secure room with a glass panel in the wall so they could see in, it was one way glass. It was a hermetically sealed room, with stainless-steel shelving and a stainless-steel bench. There was also a sink and a chest freezer.

Savage looked at his desk and on it was a picture of the bag, containing the DNA sample from Maryam White. In its curled and foetid form, it looked revolting, the latest photos showed that it had stopped growing and had collapsed in on itself. It gave Savage the creeps, he didn't like it. He looked at his lunch, chicken and bacon mayonnaise sandwich. Savage wasn't especially squeamish, but he suddenly didn't feel hungry.

"savage the girl the other girl her name drazkowsky said it martina I think can you remember"

"NOPE, I HIT THINGS, YOU GOT THE BRAINS."

"he said it when we asked him about white"

"WELL RUN IT THEN, HOW MANY MARTINAS CAN THERE BE? RUDDY WELL WISH THEY HAD GENCHECK UP AND RUNNING."

"gentech mr savage it is going to be called gentech"

"RUDDY STUPID. THAT'S WHAT HAPPENS WHEN YOU GET STUFF DESIGNED BY RUDDY COMPUTER HEADS. IT SHOULD BE GEN-CHECK, NOT RUDDY GEN-TECH. MAKES NO SENSE. IT'S FOR CHECKING THINGS NOT TECHING THINGS. IDIOTS."

Gun left Savage to stew on his product design and

marketing issue. He'd risked having his arm ripped off by mentioning 'Ironman.' He wasn't going to push his luck any further. Savage was never happy when he was stuck in the office. Savage actually, was never happy.

*

Tucker was pacing the floor in the House of Grenville. It was one of Brampton Roads oldest and most distinguished department stores, founded in 1788 By Mr Granville but named Grenvilles to take advantage of the, then Prime Ministers name, which lent it just a little more commercial prestige. It was early evening, the action was tomorrow. His assistant would bring in the sheep then, they needed to be brought in close to the action, as they got a little feisty in their fenced off cages.

Tucker had been amazed that he had been able to organise a publicity appearance in Grenvilles. It had been building enthusiasm in the media, since it had been announced, over a month ago. On the street, the excitement of seeing a man go head-to-head with a sheep was palpable, little could be better to fill the dull gap between Christmas and New Year. Sheep wrestling in Brampton Road. It turned out that all it would take was a financial sweetener for them to clear the floor, in ironically the lady's knitwear department, to create a gladiatorial ring for sheep and men with mid-life crises. There were plenty of them Tucker had discovered and they were mostly middle class, had expendable income, had sat behind desks for too long and were longing to find their inner alpha male. They kidded themselves they'd found the capital A in alpha. Tucker could never get over the looks of triumph on the faces of sweaty, dirty, bruised overweight forty somethings. That look, after rolling around in sheep droppings for half an hour and managing to get a sheep in the sort of wrestling move that an average shepherd would do in his sleep, during shearing season. He remembered the times he had done that, tired and in his sleep as he fought through hundreds of sheep for wool, that would barely even make back the money it cost to feed them. It had been a chance documentary opportunity, five minutes on a television magazine show, watching a morning television presenter struggle to try and shear a sheep. The look of joy on his face when he had got the sheep into almost the correct position, had made Tucker realise, that it was difficult to tell which was the less intelligent, the sheep or the man. He realised the man was a lamb to the slaughter and the shepherd, for the first time in his life, heard the sound of money being made by his flock. Sixteen years of selective breeding and extra supplements of his own design had given him a flock of "fighters" who would take on a wolf if it fancied its chances. He knew there would be a protest, there always was. He could not understand the logic. *Damn sheep live and 'ave a fightin' chance at a long life, ain't slaughtering them to stew no more.* And yet, people didn't like the idea of one of gods most gentle creatures being corrupted for profit. He had developed their temperament from 'run in circles and head to the high ground' to 'stand and take the battle to the enemy.' "Them buggers ain't been kicked in the knackers by a bad-tempered ewe, 'ave they!" And he chuckled to himself. "Ah well Tucker. Shows on, there 'aint no stoppin' the circus now." Here it was, in Grenvilles. Something for everyone, the men could fight, the women could shop, it was life affirming, as long as no one was looking for ladies knitware.

*

"Right, I am one of the richest men in Britannia." Announced Ian Piggot-Smyth, which was nowhere near true, but he was now exceedingly rich, so why split hairs. "And, if I damn well want to get out of this prison" *[one of the most exclusive and fashionable hotels in Britannia]* "away from these damn Changi prison guards," *[adding offence and ungratefulness to inaccuracy]* "and live like a normal billionaire" *[which was, in a manner almost accurate, though emphasizing the moronic in oxy-moronic]* "I will."

"Can you take me shopping Ian, somewhere nice, there is only so much online shopping you can do. It's not the same, I want people fussing over me, bringing me prosecco while I shop and I'll need one of those assistants carrying my bags. Can we go to one of those up market shops? I don't know… Brampton Road, somewhere fashionable, there are nice shops there."

"Damnit woman, we'll go to Grenvilles tomorrow, its two streets away, get the hotel to sort out one of their Rollers and make sure the driver speaks Britannic. Don't they teach it in their schools? And, and, tell them I want a nice coloured Roller, something that looks sophisticated, in fact tell them I want a gold one. Then, we are going for a proper Britannic curry, none of this nonsense foreign stuff they keep trying to feed us here. Proper Britannic curry, made by Indians. That's what I want. I want to get back to my roots. Now where's my money? where's that case? got it. Don't take your eyes off it. They want to steal it, all of them do, 'specially that dodgy Pierre one." Ian opened his suitcase full of money and checked it. He ruffled through the notes, he counted the wrapped bundles, he secured the elasticated retainers, he bent over to smell it, before closing the lid. "It's all there, they haven't got it yet."

"No dear, they haven't, I'll order the car." Katie Piggot-Smith picked up the phone and managed to annoy the hotel again.

*

Martine had turned on all the lights in the flat and drawn the curtains, she had slumped into a chair and watched while Maryam skipped around saying how lovely everything was. Jude, in slow motion walked around the flat as though he was walking on the moon. Martine was not unaware that she came from an affluent family but she had not expected Jude to be so distracted by it.

"These ceilings?" He was looking at the flowered cornicing and the ceiling rose, which relative to his flat and which he always thought was quite impressive, was palatial.

"They are a beautiful colour, look at the light" Added Maryam, who had also noticed that the ceilings were… white.

"They are about fifteen feet high, this is a drawing room, it's pretty standard for a Georgian townhouse." Martine answered, she was getting a little bored now of dumb and dumber's reaction to the flat.

"And your Aunt owns this?" Jude asked. For about the fourth time.

"It's like being on holiday" added Maryam, "I have never

been on holiday, I'd like to go on holiday, maybe with friends, to enjoy it with me."

Martine had been holding it together, but the emotional pressure that had been building since their run in with Gun and Savage was peaking, it wouldn't take much.

"I'll just go out and get some cakes…" Maryam, in the strange parallel world of Maryam White, had what she thought was a brainwave.

"Noooo!" Martine snapped. She was sitting on a green velvet buttonback sofa and she banged her hands hard on either side of her, bringing the universe to an immediate stop. She looked up and as Jude watched her, her still slightly grazed lip quivered a little. Her eyes started to go watery and then the dam broke, she burst into tears. Jude looked at her for only a split second and instinctively just dropped everything. The wonderment of the flat, the bewildered wheels whizzing round in his brain. It all got immediately filed under *to do later* and he went across the room and threw his arms around her. It was awkward, because she was sitting and he was standing, she was soft, shaking and sobbing where he was slightly and crookedly bent over, being as instinctively sweet and awkward as only Jude could be. Time stopped for just a moment and Martine looked up, at the stupid boy (who wasn't stupid, he was anything but) and she allowed herself to fit into his inarticulate hug. She allowed him to relax and a little like at the car crash, except not in the middle of a road, they hugged which lasted a few moments before it was interrupted by Maryam, who said, "Or If you don't like cake, I could get a pineapple?" and Jude and Martine smiled, then they both laughed, because frankly; at that point, it was funny and they couldn't do anything else. They laughed for a minute or two and let the emotional tension drain, then more seriously. "What are we going to do Jude? This has got so out of hand."

"I don't know," now serious, "I really don't know how much danger we are in, a lot I guess, but Maryam, ok she's a fruitcake, but she really is in danger, she can't look after herself and I don't think we can look after her. I don't actually know that we have done her any good at all so far."

"You can't think like that Jude, you really can't. You do what is the right thing at the time and you stand by it, because it's all you can do. You did the right thing... we did the right thing, but we do need to do something else now."

"You are so sensible" They were still holding on to each other. Jude looked at Martine, still slightly bruised, a sort of pale greenish tint in places and he saw her mascara had run down her cheek and he reached up and wiped it with his thumb in a moment of unself-aware tenderness. Martine looked back at him, her mouth opened slightly... Jude lent slowly in towards her, his lips now tight together, Martine closed her eyes and her lips and...

"...Avocados?" Maryam was still trying to treat everyone to exotic fruit and vegetables. Pop went another moment of opportunity.

Jude and Martine, both sat back, looked awkward, half smiled. Jude blushed (obviously) and he said "Avocados?"

"If you like, or Pineapples?"

Maybe it was the sudden rush of blood to the head, the excitement of the almost-kiss but Jude had it, "I have got it, we turn ourselves in."

"Woah, Double O Dustbin? are you kidding... they will kill us. You brained the big one and I electrocuted the weaselly snake one."

"No, no. Not to Gun and Savage, look… they work for the security services, so do I actually. They don't work for the police. If we hand ourselves into the police, also the press, then we will be too visible to disappear. There may be a bit of trouble but Gun and Savage will be too worried about the gen collecting getting out, that really, really is seriously secret and they are not going to do anything bad to Maryam if she is all over the news. If we are documented in the police records and she is all over the news because she is, " he stopped, he was clearly looking for the right words and everything he thought of to say next, was most definitely wrong.

"Absolutely, mind-blowingly, stunningly, beautifully gorgeously photogenic?" Said Martine smirking (and adding under her breath, "and nuts")

"Yeah…er...no...No...NO, not that." Jude, slightly unconvincingly replied and he blushed again.

"Don't worry Romeo, I have noticed how pretty she is, and I actually don't think she's your type, she's not even in the same reality as you. But that is actually a really good idea. Or rather, it's the least bad of any possible option."

"And I know where we will get the police and the press

and loads of witnesses. Tuckers Mill, you know, the sheep bloke? He's doing a demo at Grenvilles tomorrow. There's already loads of media attention because of all the protests, which also means there will be crowds and police and press and everything, all together and its pretty close isn't it?"

"Brampton road! It's a ten-minute walk, Jude you are not just a pretty face." Martine stood up.

"I have got a pretty face?" Jude sat down, blushing some more, just in case no one had noticed.

"Grenvilles, we are going shopping? Oh good" Maryam joined the excitement, "have they got a food hall?" and she wandered off to explore the flat again, in case she had missed something the first time round.

With a plan, they could relax, just a little, until the morning.

*

A car backfired, serenading the morning exodus of the warrior monks and their trainee Messiah from Jerusalem House. The vehicular explosion caused paint to fall off the wall which exposed some sprayed graffiti, that had originally said REPENT, but somebody had adjusted it to REPEINT. It was a badly spelled joke that had subsequently been repainted, badly. Like a lot of bad jokes, it resurfaced again on New Year's Eve.

Christopher, again had no idea where he was going or what he was doing, he was following the madness wherever it went and there was plenty of it. Everything was a new experience. Everywhere, different hues of sound and flavours of colour. Everything he saw, smelt different and he wanted to be part of it all. So, he followed the deluded Warriors of the Sleeping Sword as they trudged towards Knightsgate. The weather was colder now than it had been, noticeably so. A cold wind blowing in from the north was bringing scarves and coats with it and people were starting to dress for winter. Christopher was wearing the scruffy parka that had been used as an extra blanket and the beret. The boys, the brothers, the warrior monks wore bobble hats. It was coincidence, or perhaps unintelligent design, but they all had bobble hats.

"It's a quest," Brother Garry had been lost in thought for about ten minutes.

"A quest?" Brother Simon was slightly confused, which wasn't unusual. "I thought knights had quests, not monks,"

"Hmm"

"Chivalry, knights are chivalrous" Brother Matthew threw that into the mix.

"Chivalry, that involves..."

"Oh. Women." Brother Garry, almost a little awkwardly was suddenly concerned about where this was going.

"Women... mm... what about witches?" said a rather speculative Brother Simon.

"Got nothing against them."

"Witches?"

"Women and witches, don't understand them though."

"I think that's why witches might be better, because you are not meant to understand them" said Brother Simon, Witchfinder General. "I quite like witches, I think".

"They quite like you, they see you as some sort of familiar, like a toad, or a gnome."

Christopher smiled, he had no idea what was going on, but he liked the colours that played around these conversations. It was argumentative, combative, chaotic and frequently confused, but the colours were of light and warmth and that was a contrast to the air around him. He pulled the coat tighter and shivered.

They had just passed the Gaulish Consulate. Christopher looked at the complex framework of scaffolding and plastic sheeting covering it and he shivered again. Wherever they were going, it was getting colder.

Chapter 16

The Dark Satanic Mills

The Witches had also got a head start on the day and had arrived at Grenvilles by mid-morning. They had set up camping stools and were sitting with a sign that read, 'the Goddess does not approve of Sheep Wrestling.' It wasn't snappy but it was nicely written in a runic script. It looked elegant, and the words were surrounded by esoteric symbols. "Spells dear" Bronwen had said to Reverend Roger when he looked suspiciously at the sign.

"I don't know, I don't think we should be casting spells should we, it's not the dark ages. We live in a more enlightened time." He muttered.

"Oh yes, sheep wrestling in Brampton Road" Ezzie snapped back sharply, it's just like the Renaissance, isn't it?"

"Science" he said, ignoring that the renaissance was as much about science as art and that science had less to do with religion than art did.

"Oh we believe in science, we are scientists mostly" Ezzie was off on one now.

"It's what we do really" added Bronwen. "We just give those little particles you don't bother to see, a little nudge in the right direction. We just take charge don't we dear?"

"Yes, someone's got to you know," she glared at Roger.

"But, spells, really... what nonsense" blustered the Reverend.

"A bit like your prayers really" Said Bronwen, "But with one big difference. We are not asking for help or hope. No. Spells dear, are statements of intent, a warning that we are getting things done." And she shut the conversation down with an expression that said, just you dare respond.

Reverend Roger decided at that point, that the best thing to do would be to think and not say a prayer. He whistled 'Colonel Bogey' as he walked off nonchalantly, only to bump into Buster Onions, phone camera in hand and notepad at the ready.

"Any comment for the Daily Heart Online Reverend Rogers, your feud with Tucker, will we see sparks today? Is the vicar going to fight the Shepherd, will it be flocking crazy eh, just a quote vic a couple of words?"

But Roger wasn't going to be lured into that trap, "I am not baring myself for your filthy website unless you donate a sum to the church fund." he said and instantly regretted saying it.

'Euphemistic Vicar improperly propositions the nations favourite journalist. Pervert busted by Buster! Click to hear the recording' But that would be tomorrow's headlines, unless there was anything better in the offing, which there most definitely was going to be.

*

Some several hours later, Samson and Delila had been led

through the loading bay on the ground floor, slightly red eyed and kicking their hind legs out as they walked. Jethro (Jet) Trelawne pulled on the thick nylon rope securing the two sheep. They were braced by a double wooden yoke that allowed them to walk side by side but would not let them turn. They prevented each other from a lack of disorder. If Samson pulled one way, Delila would fight back and pull the other. It was a delicate balance and not entirely consensual, but it was a balance that worked. Rubber matting had been put over the carpet and the route through the store had been fenced off, it prevented stains, though the smells still lingered in the air. Despite a couple of hours of "rest" neither sheep was in a good mood, even accounting for them being bred to be in a bad mood. Parading through Knightsgate shops when you would rather be bouncing around a field, butting fenceposts and chasing dogs, is going to set the mood for the day and Samson decided to leave his own feedback about his shopping trip to Brampton Road on the floor.

"They ain't gonna like thart in the perfume department, we'll leave it lingerin for'em', thart'll mature nicely like a fine cheese." Jet, chuckled as he push-pulled, encouraged and coerced the two sheep on.

In the ring, deep into the centre of the shop, Tucker was still pacing, it always made him nervous. It wasn't the crowds, the people he could deal with watching, just the anticipation of the action. There were always volunteers. Since the business had started, a queue of almost exclusively middle-aged white men, of which Tucker accepted with not a little irony, that he was one, queued up to prove themselves. It never ceased to amaze him how quickly they would sign the disclaimers to impress wives, mid-life-crisis girlfriends, children, and grandchildren. "Show 'em a little bit of Albion" had been Tucker's catch phrase and they had loved it. He had dropped that when he opened centres in Cambria, then Caledonia followed. "Strictly amateur, no Shepherds allowed," he would call, "present company excepted", he would add with a knowing wink. This always got a huge laugh as long as you left the pause for long enough. "Swig o' cider to get your strength up, before you go into battle." Everyone took a drink before they went in. It was expected and they all wanted to impress the audience as well as their significant others. Swigging cider from a glass demijohn was West Country juju to the crowds gathering round. "Hurrah, Go on, Kill 'em, show 'em what you are made of." Then, "mint sauce." Someone would always shout mint sauce. The sheep didn't care, they were as riled as they were going to be by being shut in a van for hours on end, tightly wound on Tucker's secret medicine. The clapping would pre-empt the madness. It seemed that cider was a rite of passage, before beating the sheep. It would be a five-minute competition, to those brave gladiators entering the ring. Tucker looked at his watch, he looked out to the sea of faces, anticipatory looks and expressions. It was like an amphitheatre in ancient Rome, only it was a luxury retailer in Knightsgate. The only togas were on floor two in the boutique evening wear department and came with a price tag that could get you an apartment in Milano for a week. It was getting on for three o'clock, not long to go now.

Jet arrived with Samson and Delila the fighting sheep. He led them into the ring that was set up, walked them around twice so everyone could see them before leading them off into a small, re-enforced enclosure, near where Tucker was pacing. The crowd that had gathered gasped, shouted and took photographs. There was pushing and shoving and flashing of camera lights. A small child cried at the front, as a middle-aged woman behind her, bustled forward to take a photo and squeezed her against a fence. "Oi, watch my daughter," a young man shouted.

"She shouldn't be there" the woman squarked back, without taking her eyes off the two sheep. And they were magnificent.

Slightly oversized, if you knew your average sheep, lower set, more muscle. Sheep with a centre of gravity a little lower to the ground, their gait was firmer on the boards and rubber mats, set up in the centre of Grenvilles. Fleeces trimmed short mainly, but Samson had a line down his back, mohican style. It was dyed red. The red line. Who would cross it? The red line matched his eyes, dark black pupils, thin amber iris and the white, a web of red veins pulsing with blood as they delivered images of war to his little sheep brain. Samson flicked his feet, kicked up a little straw, Delila shuffled her shoulders from side to side, she was dribbling foam.

The crowd were ecstatic. They were in Grenvilles, waiting for a fight. Man verses sheep. It was not even New Year's Day yet. Two weeks of shopping, then Christmas, sheep wrestling, New Year's Day, sales and more shopping. A whole month. One whole twelfth of the year, taken up with fun. This was what a first world economy was all about.

*

Reverend Roger hated Tucker with a vengeance measured against a standard set by God in the Old Testament. He wished sometimes, that he could be more evangelical and threaten the raining down of hail and fire and fury and God's wrath, but he wasn't that sort of unhinged preacher. Instead, he said a silent prayer to himself, which counter intuitively ended with sheep being happier roasted for Sunday lunch, than drunk punching it out in a department store. The sentiments were there though, this was ungodly and cruel and represented everything bad about the world. Bronwen and Ezzie, were also chanting, in a slightly more archaic tongue. Bronwen was fumbling Uncle Andrew's bones between her fingers as she whispered. They had plans as well, intervention. They needed a little something to add to the recipe, half the ingredients were but something would arrive, it always did. The particles moved a little like that. They only needed a modest nudge and guidance. They carried in their own solutions. It was a little like fate, you made your own fate. It would all happen, of course it would but only if you demonstrated a little intent and nudged things the right way.

Gnat and Dunc arrived, neither sure what they would do but there was the chance of some aggro, so there they were, with cameras. They wore protest badges; you could see they were revolutionaries but only if you looked closely enough. Dunc looked at the witches and the vicar both lost in chant, one in a mixture of Latin, nineteen-fifties BBC patois and the occasional apology spoken out loud. The others in a strange language of extended vowel sounds and glottal stops. One looking for help and guidance, the others warning of an intervention, intervening on the breeze... Dunc shivered, it was like something walked over his grave, in both directions.

'Witches, Reverends and Revolutionaries.' Buster got a shot in, before wandering over to talk to the two young lads. "Buster Onions, Daily Heart Online, morning boys, are you here with Reverend Roger?" This was it. The moment, Gnat had been waiting for a chance to make a statement to the world, to kick start the new world order with a charismatic and quotable statement, some rabble rousing. "Yes" he replied.

"And me," said Dunc.

Buster realised that the picture would say a thousand words that the interview would not, so he snapped another picture of the reverend and the witches and wandered on, leaving the boys ruminating on whether less was sometimes more with political statement. He managed to get a good shot of Samson, eyes on fire, tongue out and several children squashed tightly against the fence and crying. Life was good; rather, it wasn't good, but there was good money in bad. It was misery farming, but he wasn't the only one. Tucker was and doubtless Reverend Roger was as well, in his own spiritually misguided way with his flock. Probably.

Onions forgave himself and wandered to the next shot in his garden of earthly delights.

*

Jude, Martine and Maryam were keeping their heads down. It was about timing. They had made their way in through one of the smaller doors, at the back of the shop and walked through several corridors and a department full of really rather awful but very expensive art. Jude had been distracted by socks, Maryam by almost everything, but they had navigated their way to the "sheep arena" and were assessing the situation. There were no police inside, but that in itself was not a problem. The police would be hovering outside and once any protest started, which it would, the police would join the scuffle. Timing was everything, there were cameras dotted around the room, but the gang were keeping their hats and scarves and dark glasses on for the moment. They would reveal themselves at a time of maximum exposure. Jude nudged Martine, "That's Buster Onions, celebrity journo from the Daily Heart Online, we'll get millions of hits if we get a shot in the Heart."

"You may want to rephrase that. But worth knowing, keep near him" Martine mumbled, she was struggling to see how this was going to work. It worked in her head, but all the elements were not in the right place. "Particles not aligned, yet" the witches might have told her, but she was too sensible to believe in witches, so she would have smiled politely and ignored them.

On the other side of the arena, Christopher Sunday was also concealed in parka and beret combo and accompanied by the Warriors of the Sleeping Sword. They were in a clever disguise of undesirability. Like Jerusalem House they were hiding in plain sight by looking like the sort of people you wouldn't want to look at and definitely wouldn't want to catch the eyes of. "Right Christopher, get ready, you can do your stuff soon" Brother Garry prompted the saviour.

"Do what?" Christopher asked him.

"It's a dark satanic mill, you need to turn it into a green and pleasant land. Don't worry, it's not literal, you just need to make people feel like it's a green and pleasant land. Banish the darkness. What?" Brother Matthew felt a tugging on his jacket.

"Did you see the witches?" Anointed-by-lipstick whispered chivalrously. Brothers Garry and Matthew both rolled their eyes upwards.

"Anyway, Christopher; dramatic effect, wait until the mill is really dark and satanic, then do it."

Christopher still didn't know what he was supposed to do, but he nodded. There was light everywhere, colours and flashes and glowing, too much to comprehend, but as he looked around the room, he saw something that was more remarkable than anything he had seen before. A glow, white, a halo of white surrounding something, someone. Intense white but then it was gone, wherever or whoever shone like that, had been pushed back behind the crowd, it was only a flash. He looked around the room and smelt the air. Fear, anger, excitement, love, greed anticipation, he could smell it all there. Life, he could smell the living.

*

The Piggot-Smiths had been shopping now for an hour, Katie was trying on her seventeenth pair of jeans. "Does this pair make my bottom look big?" She had asked her husband.

"They all do" He had replied grumpily. He had thought that he would enjoy being out, but Katie was getting the attention and he was bored sick. She would have been better off asking one of the three shop assistants trailing behind her carrying bags, jeans and dresses for an opinion. They would have been less honest, but they would not have been rude. Katie Piggot-Smith wasn't really looking for the truth, she was buying more clothes than she would ever wear and all she wanted was servitude, attention, to be told she was important. Ian clutched his case of money and decided to wander round the shop, he was surprised how quiet it was. "Hey, you. Why is it so quiet?" He asked a cashier.

She looked at him for a moment, something triggered in her mind. "Do I know you, are you like someone famous?" She asked, then, "sorry I shouldn't say that, been told not to. Sorry sir."

Ian puffed up his chest, "don't you worry dear, you can ask me if I am famous, why not? I am as it happens yes. Piggot-Smith, Ian Piggot-Smith, there has been a lot about me in the news recently, I am a billionaire."

"Oh yeah," replied the cashier, "it wasn't quite a billion was it? eight hundred and something, biggest charity handout on record. Yeah, everyone's downstairs watching the Sheep Wrestling, that bloke Tucker you know, Tuckers Mills presents, all that stuff."

Ian Piggot-Smith had not been to Grenvilles before so he would not have realised how uncharacteristically unprofessional the cashier was. He was however, indignant at being referred to as *not* a billionaire and a charity case to boot, so he huffed off. He wandered towards the stairs and then down them out of curiosity, leaving the cashier to contemplate her fingernails. There was not much else to do in ladieswear because everyone was either avoiding Grenvilles like the plague or downstairs watching Tucker.

Both for exactly the same reason. Tuckers Mill presents... @Grenvilles.

*

Bong.Bong.Bong.Bong.. the decorative clock in the hall, now gladiatorial arena; at Grenvilles announced that it was four o'clock. The clock that had, until a few years ago, shown an intricate wooden articulated scene of a ships officer on the deck of a ship beating a small black boy with a stick in time with the hourly bongs. The little boys' arms flew wildly in the air and his head nodded. But now, the officer beat a ghost. It had been donated to the shop in 1798 as a sweetener to sell coffee. The beans had been imported from a plantation grown in Africa. The offensive part of the statue now was covered by a piece of white cloth to save offence. It had given the news the opportunity to report that Grenvilles' racist clock now beats out the time on the KuKlux Clan. Ian Piggot-Smith had read the news at the time, "political correctness gone mad, that's what it is." He had told as many people as possible. But he had forgotten about it now, that's how important the madness of political correctness was. However, for all of its dark history, the clock was very well made and did tell the time accurately.

"Good afternoon ladies and gentlemen." The rather starchy voice of Aldous Harpen-Pop, Grenvilles' General Manager, cut through the joy of anticipation like a cold south easterly on a hot summers day. The crowd went quiet, he'd killed it just like that. "May I introduce to you, Mr Tucker, who is a valued customer of Grenvilles and we at Grenvilles would also encourage you to investigate the special offers we have in homeware on lower ground two, ladiesware on floor four and enjoy a nice afternoon tea in Grenvilles garden cafe. Thank you." The crowd remained quiet, it didn't deserve a clap and no one wanted afternoon tea, they wanted afternoon sheep and action.

"Errrreee we arrree! Ladies an genelmen, Tucker's ere." Boomed the West country accent, thick as clotted cream as Tucker leapt onto the platform, brusquely nudging Harpen-Pop to one side. Harpen-Pop grinned politely, but no one saw, because Tucker, now on stage recovered his audience from the dire introduction.

The was a roar in reply, followed by flashes from camera's a few cheers and the inevitable "mint sauce... mint Sauce..."

"We are gathered here today! Ello there? Ar-er-noon Roger the Rogerer!" Tucker nodded at the vicar he had seen at the back of the room, the story had finally made it to him.

The Reverend riled at the reference, retorted "You Somerset Satan", which he thought was quite witty, but no one heard because the laughter from Tucker's comment drowned him out.

"What do we want?" Tucker fist pumped the air.

"Cider and Sheep"

"When do we wan' 'em?"

"Now!!" The crowd had heard it all before, they knew what to say.

"Ladies, genelmen, 'ere we arr, to watch some wrestlin'. Wrestlin' with sheep, do we have any victims 'ere today, eh?

Anyone brave enough to take on Samson or Delilah? Eh... any wolves in the 'ouse brave enough to give it a go, there is a prize if you can take em down in five minutes. Five hundre' pounds, eh, could anyone do with five big 'ens for five minutes in the hay?" There was tension in the air, everyone knew that it would go up to a thousand, the routine was as familiar to the audience as an encore at a rock concert after the lights went out.

Maryam intrigued, moved forward through the crowd. She had not seen anything like this before and the crowd did the usual bow wave, moving away as she approached and closing as she passed. It only took a glance at her eyes, which alone were enough. Everything else was hidden by hat and scarf, she moved through them, with Jude and Martine behind.

Ian Piggot-Smith was also hooked. The thought of more money was like a carrot on a string dangling in the face of an ass and he used his money case to barge people out of the way, his eyes focused on Tucker's fist in the air, as though it was clutching the cash.

"Ow," said a lady with a walking frame as Piggot-Smith stood on her foot.

"Shshh," as though she was an errant child interrupting an adult conversation. Tucker was still scanning the crowd. "Me…me... ME, ME!!" Ian shouted as he got to the front, louder with each step he took, looking at the hand with the promise of money, "I'll do it, I'll do it" and he got to the fence… "ME!" he shouted at loudly as he could. The crowd went silent. Nobody wrestled for five hundred, but the man with almost a billion in cash and the remainder in promises, could visualise nothing but the bundle of notes. Why wait for a thousand in the bush when you could have five hundred in the hand?

"Well well, congrats.. Mr?"

"Piggott-Smith, Ian."

"Is it now? Said Tucker, "now tha'll be a bonus if it's the Ian P-S?" He looked at him for a moment before leaning forward in recognition at the dumpy man, in ironed blue jeans, pink shirt and green tweed jacket. "Ian Piggot-Smith, looking to win another big prize this year," as he assured himself and the crowd that they were none of them mistaken. There were cheers, a roar from the audience... "Ian...Ian...Ian..." Piggot-Smith felt a foot taller as he heard his name called out by his new fans, he puffed himself up, he smiled at himself. God he felt like a winner, the money was his. Everything he did led to more money, he had a golden touch like Midas, could hold back the waves like Canute, could fly like Icarus to the sun. He could do everything, he pumped a fist and the crowd screamed at the top of their voices "IAN."

"Elp 'im over Jet lad, ladies and gents we got a winner already, just a rumble in the sheep pen and Tucker's 'ard earned cash is leavin' 'im like a runaway tractor out o' Glastonburgh, come on! For Ian now... what does he want?"

"CIDER...CIDER..."

Jet had a demijohn in his left hand, grabbed hold of Ian Piggot-Smith and half lifted, half hauled him over the fencing into the ring, over a circle of hay bales and towards Tucker.

"He can't wrestle with that case can 'e?" Shouted Tucker, Jet grabbed the case, he pulled it, Ian had a moment of realisation and he pulled back… "Don't worry, we'll look after your shopping." Tucker winked at the audience and laughed at his own joke, Jet yanked had on the case, pulling it from Ian's hands. Ian suddenly snapped into reality and looked around. There were hundreds of people in a ring around him calling his name, taking his picture. Buster Onions, also at the front of the crowd, was snapping like there was not a tomorrow. Piggot-Smith watched as his case, containing a million pounds, was pulled away from him. Tucker leant down and put an arm around him. "We just need you to sign a disclaimer." He smiled, like a benevolent farmer, after a badger shoot.

"What?" A pen was thrust into Ian's hand and a piece of paper followed. "My money…" but he signed, he scrawled a signature quickly to get to his money faster.

"Five hundre', yerp' all yours if you get one of me sheep down, an we'll reunite you with your shopping. In a minute, 'ere young lady," Tucker was drawn to Maryam, he couldn't help himself, it was her eyes. "you'll look after Ian's shoppin' won't yer moi darlin', eh?" and Jet passed the bag to Maryam, her scarf slipped down as she took hold of the case. Jude and Martine both froze, as they realised that the cameras were pointing at them. Their plan was enacting but without the police present, they were suddenly, briefly the centre of attention.

"Oh, no," said Martine.

"Oh, gawd," answerred Jude.

"What are they going to do?" Maryam asked.

"My money." Said Ian.

"CIDER, CIDER, CIDER" Screamed the crowd and before any of those conversations were resolved, Jet thrust the demi-John at Ian. Piggot-Smith looked at his money, the crowd, the demijohn and decided to fight for it, it was the only way. Like George and the Dragon, he would beat the sheep and win his money. Good old Brittanic pluck, damn it he was Ian Piggot-SMITH... pronounced SMYTH. He took a swig from the jar and put an arm in the air, took off his jacket and handed it back to Jet, along with the jar. "Bring it on." he shouted and the crowd were beside themselves.

Gee, thought Tucker to himself, *it never ceases to amaze me how many of them there are.* "Who are you gonna take on then Ian, Samson or Delilah?"

Ian considered himself a gentleman; "I am not fighting a woman sheep" he shouted out to the audience, most of whom questioned that briefly for so many reasons, before responding with

"SAMSON... SAMSON... SAMSON..."

"Samson it is!!" Bellowed Tucker in response. It was amazing that the crowd had a voice left, but they did.

"Hurrah, Samson, Mint sauce, Ian" came back a cacophony of sound and a thousand different voices.

"Remember Ian, no training, but money for the taking. Five minutes to wrestle Samson to the floor. Remember a shepherd, a bumpkin like me, can do it in three seconds, but an untrained man... a man such as yersel' a fine and fit man, you should be able to do it in five minutes, eh? Can you beat Samson Ian... can you claim your money?" Even Tucker had not realised how much money Ian was thinking of, because the case that Maryam was carrying, only Ian knew, contained a million pounds, in cash.

The crowd went quiet, you could hear a pin drop. It was a loud 'clunk, clang' as the pin holding Samson's cage door closed, was pulled out of its socket and dropped on a chain to bang against the steel fencing. Samson looked out at the audience and the first thing he did surprised everyone. He stepped backwards, so hard and fast that the cage shook and Jet almost fell off the straw bale he was on. The sheep's eyes were so bloodshot that he could only see for a short distance, instinct told him the fight was straight ahead and he twisted his neck, allowing his pupils to focus better. The round dark eyes narrowed to a slit as, head jerking from side to side, the sheep fired forward towards Ian Piggot-Smith. The crowd gasped in unison, as Samson crashed into Ian, knocking him backwards before jumping slightly in the air and kicking out as though there was something behind him. Ian had the wind knocked out of him, but adrenalin surged through his veins as he staggered to his feet to counter strike. His shirt was now untucked, a button had broken on his sleeve and his cuff flapped open, his normally flushed red face was now a beetroot red. It was difficult to tell which was more claret, Ian's face or Samson's eyes. Ian bent and charged forward, he grabbed the sheep's ear and pulled. Samson twisted his head and shook him off, his red wool mohican, now became Ian's target. He threw himself forward into the sheep, grabbing on to the wool and fighting to hold the animal into him. Samson shook, his feet braced into the ground as his shoulders fought to shake the man off, but Ian was gripping onto him like one million and five hundred pounds was at stake. He wasn't letting go. Samson pulled back dragging Ian across the ring, the rubber mat now spread with sheep dung and straw and for a moment there was a stand-off. A second of no action, where sheep and man were both able to contemplate the situation. The crowd held their breath.

"It's not natural said both the witches together, it can't end well." and for the first time Reverend Roger agreed with them.

"It's un-godly" he said, before "dear God, please end this soon."

He was interrupted by a shout from the crowd the little old lady with the walking frame… "Kill 'im Samson, stamp on 'is 'ed… Kill 'im" and almost in response Samson threw himself to his side, again knocking the wind out of Ian, who fell to the floor knocking his face and giving himself a nosebleed. Surging with adrenalin and testosterone Ian had heard the crowd yell and he had managed to hold on, so he pulled hard on the sheep's wool. Samson caught off balance staggered to correct his gait while Ian used the momentum to haul himself up and on top of the sheep. Ian kicked out with his legs and managed to knock Samson's balance out and the sheep fell, sideways to the floor with the weight of Ian on top of him. It was almost over. The sheep kicked, catching Ian's leg and tearing his jeans slightly, but he held on. As Samson, lying on his side struggled to get traction, the crowd shouted louder. They were screaming in ecstatic excitement "Ian... Ian…"

Ian held tighter to the sheep and he didn't hear Tucker in the background calling out, "Five, four, three, two, one..." and he rang a bell "IAN PIGGOT-SMITH IS A WINNER," and that was enough. Ian relaxed and as he did that, Samson kicked again and caught Ian right between the legs, Ian choked and the pain was immense and Samson struggled to his feet and walked shakily to the side of the ring where he slumped down exhausted, but a loser. The winner was doubled over on straw and sheep dung, with ripped clothes, a nose bleed and the pain of *'a kick in the knackers'* to contend with, but he had won. He had bettered the sheep.

"You gotta' watch that," smiked Tucker "never let go, even when you have won, but let's not take it away from Ian, he won fair an' square. Ian Piggot-Smith has beaten Samson and won five 'undred pounds, congratulations Ian."

The crowd clapped and cheered and screamed and took photos and as they did, Maryam White started moving towards the pen containing Delilah. "That wasn't very nice" she said to no one in particular, "poor sheep." Jude and Martine pushed and shoved and tried to keep up with the girl who could open and close a crowd of people, like a series of automatic doors.

Christopher had also been watching the show with the same sense of loss and despondency. He had seen the colours fade in the room. There was a darkness in the ring and an emotional silence that he had not felt since that moment on the rockpile where the mysterious 'Uncle Max' had screamed for his blood. It was wrong, all wrong, but he had also seen the light again, it came from a girl. It was almost the only light in the room, so bright that the colours already dulled by the angst the anger and the blood lust, faded into almost nothing by comparison and he followed that light. The Warriors of the Sleeping Sword, more attuned to the vices of the world and frankly, thinking it was good to start a collective epiphany from a low base, were following him and were trying to keep up. Buster Onions was getting it all. The Piggot-Smiths, Tucker, Reverend Roger, one of the prettiest girls he had ever seen holding Piggots case and then Christopher Sunday, he alone recognised him. He snapped shot after shot and realising that he could break the story with all of these elements, he uploaded the pictures, putting, a stake in the ground. **'BREAKING NEWS – REPORT TO FOLLOW.'**

*

Gun's computer made a noise, Gun flipped screens. "oh goodness mr ssavage we have a hit action stationsss and itss in brampton road"

"WHAT GUN?"

"white the girl the kidss"

At the same time, the officers outside Grenvilles picked up a similer alert from the station... "all available officers, missing person. Christopher Sunday, sighted in Grenvilles, ground floor, green parka, black beret. All available officers now."

*

Maryam got to the sheep pen with Delilah, all she felt was compassion, all she wanted to do was look after the sheep. But mammals didn't like Maryam White, they didn't. She spooked dogs and cats and rats and bats and squirrels and foxes and... sheep. Delila backed into the back of her cage. Her eyes now narrowing as well, but Delilah did not want to fight. When Samson saw Piggot-Smith, he saw red. When Delilah saw Maryam she only saw fear and she backed up and up and then forward and hammered herself against the cage doors again and again and again.

"Oh dear" Maryam said "I didn't mean to scare you," and she backed off, but Delilah now was in a passion and kicking at the fence to get out. Maryam backed off some more but as she did, the gate twisted under Delilah's pounding and she got a foot in the rungs and leapt out and over. She careered into the crowd and then into the ring. She ran backwards and forwards before seeing an opportunity. She ran at the now rising shape of Ian Piggot-Smith and kicked off him, to launch herself up and over the straw bales. She managed to scramble over the metal fence, knocking it down as she went, her weight twisting the metal out of shape as it had the gate. The crowd broke into groups and ran as though the sheep was rabid, knocking over stands, and clothing. What seemed to happen in a split second had actually taken ten and as the chaos of a sheep fight turned into a human stampede just as the police made it into the room.

"Stop" shouted an officer, but it was too late. The old lady, blood lust up swung and hit him with her walking frame.

"Kill 'em all" she shouted, like a medieval berserker. Sheep wrestling could have that effect. Tucker looked out from his small stage.

"Oh dear, that weren't sposed to 'appen Jet." His assistant nodded. "Still, tha' idiot was five undred nicker, well spent," and he looked at the prone and bleeding Piggot-Smith slowly coming to on the floor below. "Very well spent, I'd 'ave spent the thousand, to see him get that kicking."

The police saw Christopher, who had almost got to Maryam, "There he is, grab him, Christopher Sunday, this is the police, stop."

Somebody heard and shouted, "It's Christopher Sunday, look" and suddenly the crowd was split again, between running from rabid sheep, from old ladies fighting policemen or to crying children, because there were always crying children. Or should they chase after the recently awakened, disappearing, and now reappearing Christopher Sunday. Christopher froze as cameras flashed in his eyes. The parka and beret lending him an accidental revolutionary look. And just as things could not get more chaotic, Gun and Savage tore into the room.

"MARYAM WHITE, DRAZKOWSKY, OTHER GIRL – FREEZE." Savage barged past a police officer, who indignantly said, "Oi" and put a hand on Savages arm. Savage did not like hands on his arm, especially the long arm of the law, so instinctively he shortened it, with an excruciatingly nasty snapping sound.

"Argghh!!! Officer down, officer down," the policeman managed to shout before Savage punched him in the side of the head, still trying to push his way through people to get to Maryam. Gun pulled a taser, which was indiscrete and impolite, especially in Londinium's foremost department store. The police responded accordingly. "Gun, everyone down"

"how did they know my name" gun muttered before a nightstick caught him on the neck.

"ow damnit" turning to his left to block the next attack, incoming from the third officer in the fray.

"DAMN POLICE." Said Savage and decided that a slash and burn approach was best to level the land. He turned to face the distraction.

Buster Onions was having possibly the best day of his life, he hoped there was enough memory in his phone to capture all of this.

Christopher, the crowd following him and entranced by him appearing out of nowhere, got to Maryam. He put up his hand and she looked at him, she lifted her hand and put it on his. It was instinctive, they touched palms. Buster got the moment.

Jude and Martine, Brothers Matthew, Garry and Simon watched the strange sight unfold. Even after the last forty minutes of strange sights it was difficult to imagine things getting stranger, then the lights in Grenvilles flickered on and off for a split second, until Maryam took her hand away and smiled. Christopher smiled back and everyone looked at each other, but no one said a word, immediately.

But immediately doesn't mean forever, "oh my god," both Jude and Martine said in synchronisation and then they shouted to Maryam, who was still holding Ian Piggot-Smith's case and staring at Christopher. He was as entranced, looking back at her, and so Martine shouted louder, "run." Jude and Martine, the brothers, Maryam and Christopher ran, all together because Martine had said run and not one of them, at that point disagreed with the suggestion. They were caught at the door by Onions, who grabbed Christopher's arm. "Christopher Sunday... it's you, what are you doing here, where have you been, tell me, tell the world?" and he thrust his phone camera in Christopher's face.

Christopher stopped, he looked at the camera that was pointing at him and Maryam. He was confused for a moment, but he gathered his senses. "These people, these people who watch men fight animals for fun. The people who make this happen, I cannot understand it, it is wrong, it is evil it is sick, I dreamt for eighteen years alone and not once did I dream anything like this. These people, there is no light in their hearts. There is just darkness, they are jumping into the abyss." Then he turned and he ran, with everyone else, because hell was likely after them.

Buster had got everything on film and a final quote from the now living Christopher Sunday, dressed like a revolutionary and with a beautiful girl on his arm. *What a photo op. God, life was good.* He did not hear Bronwen, who turned to a dumbstruck Reverend Roger.

"Now, you didn't pray for that did you dear? No you didn't; because that dear, was science." And Ezzie laughed, because who didn't believe in science?

*

The last thing Buster Onions remembered from Grenvilles was that he had the story of his lifetime. Photos, film, recordings, everything, including the pretty girl with Piggot-Smiths suitcase. When he opened his eyes, he didn't have a story at all, he didn't even have his clothes.

He woke with a jolt, blinked, tried to move, found his hands were secured and he wobbled, with little control over his balance, he jerked instinctively into an upright seated position and re-found his centre. He looked around. He was in a room, it looked like a laboratory or a small surgical theatre, it had a stainless-steel table, refrigerator, shelves and cupboards. It also had a large black glass wall panel. He recognised it as one way glass. Presumably he was being watched.

He started to get his bearings. He was naked, secured to a plastic chair by both his wrists and ankles and had something around his neck, it was a collar of some description, it wasn't tight, but it weighed enough to make itself felt. He was off the floor and it took him a moment to realise that he was seated on a plastic chair in a sink. That was ominous. *Oh my god*, he thought. *Blood, they don't want blood on the floor.* The door opened.

Six foot four of bull necked and bad-tempered Mr Savage walked in. "I'M SAVAGE" he said, stating the obvious. He was followed by Gun who slunk into the room, closed the door and added, "gun". He didn't use Mr, it helped to get the imagination whirring away.

"Who are you? Where am I? Why am I in this sink?" Onions blurted out questions, he was terrified. He felt vulnerable enough being tied naked to a chair, but he was in a sink as well. No one wanted to be sitting in a sink.

"WE ASK.YOU TALK." Savage kept it short and sweet.

"you are tied to a chair do you read bond" asked Gun.

"Bond?"

"VODKA MARTINI. THAT BOND."

"Yeah…yes"

"good so you know that in the nineteen-fifties interrogation was completed by knocking the bottom out of a chair kicking it over then giving your underside a good going over with a knotted rope"

The blood drained from Onions face, "I… I… is that what you are going to do?" he asked.

"no" Said Gun, "because mr savage is not that nice"

Onions was speechless.

"NAME. JOB."

"Buster Onions, Daily Heart Online."

"NO IT'S NOT." Onion's didn't reply. "YOU ARE CALLED FARQUAR, GORDON FARQUAR"

"Yeah…yes."

"YOU ARE NOT EVEN A COCKNEY, YOU ARE A MOCKNEY. AREN'T YOU GORDON FARQUAR?"

"Yeah…yes."

"oh dear" said Gun.

"I HATE COCKNEYS, I EAT 'EM FOR BREAKFAST, BUT AT LEAST THEY TASTE LIKE PIE AND MASH AND JELLIED EELS. WHEREAS MOCKNEYS, THEY DON'T EVEN TASTE NICE, DO THEY MR GUN"

"no mr savage they do not"

Gordon Buster Farquar Onions gulped. He didn't realise that he had lost control of his bladder, the wetness welled up in the plastic seat of the chair.

"MOCKNEYS TASTE LIKE A PARTICULARLY BAD FOOD ADDITIVE CALLED M101."

"There isn't M101. I…I…I… did a piece on food additives." It was all Onions could think to say.

"SHOWS HOW LITTLE THE MEDIA GETS RIGHT. YES THERE IS. YOU MAKE IT BY GETTING A MOCKNEY, YOU BEAT IT TO A PULP, BOIL IT FOR TWENTY MINUTES THEN YOU DRY IT OUT, CHOP IT INTO BITS AND GRIND IT INTO DUST. THAT'S HOW YOU MAKE M101."

"mr savage sprinkles m101 on his breakfast cockneys to make them taste bad"

"THAT'S WHAT KEEPS ME IN A BAD ENOUGH MOOD TO DO MY JOB. ONIONS FARQUAR, ARE YOU COLD?"

"Yes."

"WE BETTER WARM YOU UP THEN. GUN?"

Gun lifted his hand and squeezed the little plastic box that he held. The pain was instant, the collar felt like it was frying his brain, every muscle in Onion's body locked into a ridged spasm, he could feel his wrists and ankles straining against their bindings. He wanted to scream but his jaw was locked. He managed "Gnnnnghhh" that was all. Gun dropped his arm releasing the button and a wave of nausea hit after the slump in his body that followed the shock, everything hurt, he thought his heart had stopped.

"PAVLOVS DOG, SORT OF. GOT IT?"

Onions Farquar felt wetness running down his leg. He glanced down.

"AND THAT'S WHY YOU ARE IN THE SINK, STUPID." Savage was proud of that, it always worked.

Onions Farquar was crying as well.

"GOOD, YOU ARE DOING WELL GORDON. GUNNA THROW YOU A LIFELINE"

"Yeah...yeah… please?" Farquar blubbed.

"WE ARE GOING TO GIVE YOU YOUR PHONE BACK. BECAUSE NOW YOU WORK FOR US."

Gun took a polyethene bag out of his pocket, it contained a mix of broken glass, plastic metal, resin, some bits of sticker. He dumped it on Gordons wet lap.

"MR GUN HAS A COPY OF EVERYTHING ON HIS COMPUTER, HE IS CLEVER LIKE THAT. AREN'T YOU MR GUN?"

"very nice of you to say so mr savage"

Onions looked up, face to face and back again from the unfunniest double act in the world.

"INTERESTING STUFF THERE ONIONS. SO, NOW YOU WORK FOR US. TELL HIM WHAT WE PAY GUN."

"we pay back k k everytime you do not tell us anything we want to know gordon anything"

"HEH, HEH. PAYBACK, I LIKE THAT. YOU DON'T WANT TO BE SPRINKLED ON MY BREAKFAST DO YOU MOCKNEY GORDON?"

"No sir" he was sweating, crying, shaking.

"GOOD. EVERYTHING ABOUT EVERYTHING, MRSAVAGE@GUN&SAVAGE.NET. BEFORE YOU PUBLISH ANYTHING, WE WANT TO SEE IT. GOT IT?"

"Yes sir."

"GET HIM OUT GUN."

"NO!" Cried Gordon Farquar in a surprisingly middle-class accent, as he saw Gun approach him with a hypodermic needle but he passed out, even before the syringe was sunk into the flesh of his leg.

He would wake up at three o'clock in the morning, in a muddy ditch, with his clothes dumped next to him. It would be freezing cold, dark and he would have no idea where he was. His wallet and a packet of ground up telephone was dumped on top of his clothes. He started crying again, he was no longer an independent journalist. The Daily Heart Online had lost editorial control.

Chapter 17

Ass

Martine, Jude, Christopher, Maryam and the Brothers had run, all at once. None of them really knowing which way they were going except for Martine, who ran back to the closest and for her, safest place she could think of, her Aunt's flat. Somewhere along the way she had grabbed Jude's hand and they had run together hand in hand, but when they arrived, she realised that she had a whole new problem to deal with. Maryam and Christopher stood next to each other, staring and smiling at each other. Both following the herd that had carried them safely here but in a world of their own. The Brothers, confused, scruffy and slightly unhygienic were, by default, hanging around Christopher, that was also obvious. They were all a nuisance in a nice area, just by existing in a group and that was before anyone looked more closely at the Brothers. Or smelt them.

"Oh my god, everyone inside, I need to think." Martine panicking and pulling the key from her jeans pocket, she opened the door. Jude looked at her and shrugged.

"How did that happen" he said to no one in particular, he was still pondering on what, "that" (which had just happened) was, when Brother Matthew announced, arms crossed on the doorstep and looking suspiciously at the grandiose porch,

"It is easier for a rich man to pass through an eye of a

needle"

"Than what baldy?" Martine challenged him.

"Um... I don't know." He'd messed up the metaphor and couldn't really finish it with camels going to heaven.

"Then get inside, because the rich men in the houses next door will pass you through the eye of a needle if they see you all on the street. We can work out what to do inside."

Brother Matthew harrumphed, he should have known what the expression was. This religious order was failing at the seams, but at least he wasn't chasing witches. It seemed Brother Garry was the only one left with a bucket full of piety but he was erring towards Christianic Jihad, which Brother Matthew felt was rather fundamentally mixing your major world religions. It threw the balance rather too far towards warrior than monk. Life was very confusing, it always had been and religion had initially seemed like a way of making sense of the world. Once dungeons and dragons had let your fate be decided too frequently by an icosahedron, he had looked for order and answers. He uncrossed his arms and wandered into a very expensive piece of architecture which, despite its postcode and that fact that there was no dog mess in the street outside, he really didn't like as much as he liked Jerusalem House.

Maryam and Christopher sat down next to each other on the Chesterfield, the case of money unopened at their feet. Martine nervously looked at the Brothers.

"Take your shoes off" then she glanced at Brother Simon's (almost) socked feet. "No, I mean put your shoes on, please keep your shoes on, don't take them off ever again. Oh my God, don't tread on anything." She looked at brother Garry "and don't touch anything" and then she glanced at Brother Matthew who seemed to be tempting the pictures to fall off the wall, "just... I don't know... just don't even look at anything. Jude, what now?"

"Beer" Jude said the only thing he could think of. "I want a beer and I have given up. We are at least all over the news and I just want a beer, it's all I can think of. Let's go and have a drink, how much worse can it get if I get attacked by the MIDI-idiots? I think I just want to have just had an evening on my terms before... We have been running for almost four days. I am tired, I am frightened, I am and... I don't know... it's just all gone to hell. We'll hand ourselves in after. We'll get a journo to meet us at the police station, the others can take their chances. Now we have Christopher it will be a bigger story. Same plan, but a drink first." Martine agreed, it would at least get the tramps out of the flat. It was difficult to see an alternative and she thought of how simple Christmas Day had been, with turkey curry, rice and a centrepiece of red cabbage.

"Where can you get drink around here, it is a bit posh?" but Martine didn't acknowledge Jude because she was thinking of the Christmas walk to the hospital and the alleged kidnapping of Christopher.

"Just what the hell is going on" she commented, to no one in particular.

Jude was wondering at that point whether he was deranged, it seemed to be the common factor in everything relating to Maryam White. It was only about six o'clock in the evening. Maryam had managed to destroy a department store that had been one of the country's finest, in less than an hour of arriving by trying to make friends with a sheep. A deranged sheep. She was being chased by deranged secret agents, she had also managed to attract deranged tramps. He looked at Martine. "You ok?" he asked.

"Not really," she answered, "you?"

"Not really, it even feels a bit odd in here. Can you feel it? it's like it feels before a thunderstorm, all sort of dense and still and ozoney, it that just me?" He loosened his clothes a bit, he felt hot.

"No, you are right, it wasn't like that outside, the weather was cold, not all weird like this. I'll check the heating." Martine turned, to walk towards the kitchen and the thermostat just as Christopher and Maryam kissed. The lightbulb in the drawing room blew, showering glass on the coffee table in front of them, a fuse then blew somewhere, because the whole flat was suddenly plunged into darkness. Martine glanced towards the only light she could see, which was the streetlights outside. Through the still undrawn curtains she saw the streetlights flickering and then almost as soon as it started it stopped. A car alarm went off and over the noise of the car blasting out PAARRRP.. PAARRRP... PAARRRP... PAARRRP... PAARRRP... Jude and Martine saw the silhouette of Christopher and Maryam parting and they could just make out Maryam say, "My love".

"Blimey Double o Dustbin!" Martine was whispering, "It looks like you have a love rival..." She couldn't see Jude blushing in the dark, but she heard him reply, "no, I, you,

I... oh dear." She smiled and to herself, "just say it Jude?" but with the PAARRRP... PAARRRP... PAARRRP... from the street and Brother Garry accusing Brother Simon of 'messing with witchcraft' any reply was lost in the chaos. "RIGHT, ENOUGH" She shouted, someone had to do something, "WE ARE LEAVING NOW," She upped and walked towards the door. Only fifteen minutes after arriving and they were leaving for a drink. Perhaps the last they would have, but it was better than standing still and doing nothing.

*

Where, two hundred years previously, would have been only a short sedan ride away, Ernesto Goldman was standing at the door of Diemos. He had been invited. He wasn't a member, but he had hung around some of these people long enough to have heard whispered rumours of the club. He knew enough, that if he had been invited it was a summoning and it wasn't a choice. He needn't reply, but he would attend, so here he was. He was surprised by who had summoned him. Niklaus Kloeven-Hoef had asked him to arrive at seven sharp, no earlier and no later. The banker, why the hell would a banker demand his attendance? He knocked nervously on the door. So nervously, that it was amazing that anyone heard, but the door opened before he made contact with it for a third time.

"Mr Goldman" a liveried attendant invited him in. "Mr Kloeven-Hoef said to expect you, he has his own room, he will see you there, would you like a drink, of course you would we'll get you a.." the attendant looked him up a down... "large one." He left Goldman in the corridor.

Goldman looked around, he had been in plenty of large houses like this, they all had broad entrance halls, but most had been redecorated and brought up to date. Diemos carried its history in every part of its décor. He glanced at the door to his immediate left, a dark room, there were lights on, but it was low lit. He could see flickering lights and shadows. It was a bar by the look of it. He could just about make enough shapes out through the narrow gap, but he was excluded, he had been left in the hallway. The door opened and the attendant was back, he had a silver tray with a glass of brown liquid, brandy, whiskey, rum, it was difficult to tell but it was large, it was a tumbler almost full of the spirit. The attendant pulled the bar door shut with a loud click, a noise that clearly said to Ernesto Goldman that the bar was not available to him. He followed the braid and silk along a corridor to a dark red painted door, the paint so thick and heavy and worn that it looked like it was covered in leather and then down some stairs. "Private lounges Mr Goldman, some of our members have their own rooms." Goldman noticed he had been called Mr, nor Dr. He felt that it was the opposite of respect. He was a Mr not because he was a consultant, but because he did not matter. Convention would dictate he should be addressed by a title and Mr was the lowest in the titular pantheon.

"Goldman", not even a common title. Ernesto followed the voice through another door, this one open. He walked into a room and stopped. The silk and braid overtook him, nodded his head at the man in the armchair and turned the tray to Goldman who took the drink and stood where he was. The attendant may have left. To Ernesto he just evaporated and the door shut with a gentle scrape and a click. The silence was broken only by the crackling of a roaring fire, the flames licked the chimney breast and their reflection flickered around the polished brass, silver and various mirrored surfaces of the room. The heat was unbearable, Goldman put his finger in his collar and loosened the fabric from around his neck.

"Goldman," again, "nice of you to visit, I hope the rum is to your liking. It's a rather special one. It was from a case that was recovered from a ship that sank on its way back from Cuba, it had been delivering, ah... goods. The captain's own supply. Eighteen-thirty-two. It may have lost a little of its strength in the intervening years, but it will have picked up some more complex flavours no?"

"Cuba?"

"Your mother, from the Caribe no? Ernesto, your name."

"A ship, in eighteen-thirty-two to Cuba, was it a slave ship?"

"Yes, yes... but does that taint the spirit Ernesto?"

It was joke, a clever play on words and a challenge. It was a clear demonstration of hierarchy.

Goldman took a sip, he was too weak not to. It was a complex flavour, but he had taken a drink from the slaver's personal drinks cabinet, recovered from the bottom of the sea at who knew what cost. He put the glass down without saying a word.

"Hmm" Kloeven-Hoef said. "I would have thought you would appreciate it, but never mind. I need some help. I have half a story. You can fill in the missing parts, you have some interesting history. The Chairman, Autonomous Accumulations?"

"How do you know about me and the Chairman?"

"Ha! I know every black heart in this city." Which did not answer the question. "Let me help you Goldman. Ernesto, maybe that is better. Yes, Ernesto, I'll frame my question. The Chairman of Autonomous Accumulations is in decline, I know this. I know that he is pursuing Christopher Sunday, the unconscious boy. Number Five, I know he is on the ascendent, he has his agents after a girl, for what I believe are the same reasons."

"A girl, for the same reasons?"

"Ah, so there is a missing part you do not know. Between us we have a few pieces to put together and perhaps a few still missing. Yes, Number Five has an Autonomous Accumulations agency chasing a girl, for the same reasons the Chairman is chasing the boy."

"Huh, how do you know this?" Goldman was confused.

"I told you Ernesto, I know every black heart in this city" Kloeven-Hoef shuffled slightly in his chair, Goldman looked at him, the light of the fire created contrast in his face, it was dark and darker still, somehow the highlighted areas had no light in them, his hair brushed back and silver grey. His eyes though, the green eyes, looked deeply into Ernesto Goldman, not inquisitively, but like clutching claws, he wasn't asking questions, he was dragging the dark secrets from him. " So... The boy turns up, eighteen years ago, the good people turn him into some sort of novelty and he defies everybody, by not only surviving but flourishing. He has been in your care all this time until you, ah... lose him, a week ago. The Chairman is bereft, this I know. We have not seen or heard from him in this time and yet, for twelve of these eighteen years he has been very involved, he has an almost unhealthy interest in the boy and an arrangement with you. You have wealth Ernesto, not as much as you want, but you have wealth. It can be doubled or taken away and I believe you will soon need a new sponsor. How close am I to the truth?"

"The Chairman has... is..." Goldman paused, he was not sure whether to go on.

Kloeven-Hoef softened slightly, he lent forward and looked deep into Ernesto Goldman's being. "You have made a Faustian pact with the old man. Well... Ernesto, I can buy you out of that pact, tell me everything. You will feel better for it, I promise you." Goldman looked at him for a second and double or quits, he made his choice.

"I was a research student, I had been doing a thesis on genetic anomalies before I qualified as a doctor and surgeon. I had been studying a woman called Mary McDonald, who barely seemed to age. It was curious but she was both older in years and younger looking than everyone who knew her. I interviewed neighbours who had grown old around her and they all swore blind that she had not aged in fifty years. She was fascinating, she lived in a small cottage, had no obvious relationships and lived an uncomplicated life. She was… Superficially she presented like she was on the autism spectrum and yet, she was also very capable of complex and emotionally connected thought and relationships. She was unique, I thought she was unique anyway. I managed to get a blood sample from her which changed everything but she... she disappeared shortly after that. I have no idea where or what happened to her. One day I visited and she was gone. The flat had been emptied, no one had seen a thing. But in her blood, she had proteins in it that we had just never seen before. There were additional cells as well as the usual red and white blood cells like, well like free-range stem cells is the only way I can describe them. Everything degraded before I could study it in detail, but her biology was beyond anything I had seen before. I wanted to find some scientific explanation, but I couldn't. I had written up my studies and filed them but the samples and files disappeared as mysteriously as Mary McDonald. It was odd, very strange but around the time of the Grand Plan and there was a lot of movement, and chaos. I, well... it had made me curious but there was nothing left to study. Without case studies and my notes, I had to start again. I wrote my doctorate on traumatic brain injury, I won an award. I became a junior doctor, specialised in Neurology and then Christopher Sunday came into my care and he had the very same proteins in his blood as Mary McDonald. We were able to study him a bit more. There were other physical anomalies, he had senses that you would be more likely to see on animals, his retina for instance had additional sensory cells and his body reacted to infra-red light and electricity, you could see the hairs on his arm respond with some of the equipment we used in a way that you or I would not. Essentially, he looked like a normal person, but his biology was subtly different, more developed. You might even say an evolutionary step different. The Chairman approached me, he funded private research based on my original paper and,"

"And?"

"I had speculated that Mary Mcdonald had a unique biology and if we could identify what prevented her ageing, we could develop treatments that would allow people to live far in excess of their normal lifespans, we could develop treatments for illnesses such as cancer and degenerative diseases like dementia. We could treat male pattern baldness, re-grow limbs, organs, we could control life, quite literally if we could isolate what was going on we could cure everything." Goldman stopped.

"Then?" Kloeven-Hoef said it like he already knew the answer, but this was a confessional. He wanted to hear it first-hand.,

"We were able to extract these same proteins from Christopher Sunday's blood that, after treatment, after a process that I, we... the Chairman's funding and my research developed, could treat cancer. We tested it... we had a test subject."

"The Chairman?" It was an educated guess.

"Yes, yes, the Chairman. He has a brain tumour. He has had a very aggressive brain tumour for a number of years. We are not yet able to destroy it but we have stabilised it with the treatment we have developed from the proteins in Christopher Sunday's blood. We cannot yet synthesise them and they degrade quickly, but we can use them to treat the Chairman and it works. The tumour, with Christopher's blood, we can stop it growing. We have even shrunk it a little, the cancer cells are restricted by the treatment. The additional cells, I described them as free-range stem cells, they act very strangely, they absorb any new cancer cells and seem to reprogram them, you can see it happening but it's difficult to explain without more study. Even in the twelve years, we have so many more questions. The tumour growth is suspended, the body cells around them grow normally. With weekly injections he is a normal healthy person. But without Christopher Sundays blood he has maybe a few months, he will deteriorate very quickly. It's at a point where even a few days will affect him, he already has headaches."

"Ha!" Kloeven-Hoef laughed! Goldman looked at him, shocked. "You don't get it do you? the old vampire really does need blood. Hahaha… and now his supply has been cut off, how much have you been taking?"

"Five hundred millilitres a week, that is all. We could take more, but the nurses may have questioned it and we wanted to be discrete."

"Is that all? Well, now, Ernesto, let me tell you what you do not yet know. There is another one, a girl. She is being pursued by Number Five's agents. Number Five you see, has spotted this market opportunity. He is looking to further the research once the Chairman's grip is relinquished and he has more commercial ideas, he is also hoping that the Chairman does not find Christopher Sunday first. There is a change of leadership in the planning stages, so you see, you want to be in the right place to continue your research. Do you not? I would suggest that there is further investment for your research and perhaps more opportunity to experiment, but you do want to be working for the right people, don't you?"

Goldman was confused. He said nothing initially then, "How do you know all this?"

"I told you Ernesto, every black heart in this damned city. Doing business is motivating don't you find?"

Goldman thought of the oath he took, the hippocratic oath. He thought of how much of what he had said, he had now broken in the pursuit of wealth and yet beyond all of that, it was the rum that had left a greater bitterness in his mouth. He had no faith, but he had fallen. He was not sure who he would be judged by beyond himself but he was judging himself now. He asked, "this is all just business to you?"

"You have no god, do you?"

"No" Goldman replied, confused again, the statement was not what he expected.

"Then who else is there to believe in Goldman, to judge you, to measure yourself by? It is all business. Everything is business. Your life is measured in gold not by steps to heaven when you have no god. But, you now have more gold. Don't let it weigh you down Goldman. Goodbye.

Chapter 18

Beer

The phone rang on Gun's desk, he picked it up. "yes" was all he said. "its for you" he handed the phone to Savage.

Savage looked at the caller ID 'MID_OPS_CONTROL'. "SIR" he said, then he heard the voice at the other end. He gulped and urgently added "I MEAN MA'AM, SORRY MA'AM DIDN'T KNOW IT WAS YOU, MR GUN, HE..." but he did not get a chance to finish because it wasn't MID_OPS_CONTROL' on the phone it was MID_OPS_EXEC.

"SAVAGE YOU DAMN IDIOT, YOU OVERBEARING OAF. YOU OUT OF CONTROL BUFFOON. YOU ARE A DAMN ELEPHANT IN THE CHINA SHOP"

"BULL" He instantly regretted his instinctive correction and closed his eyes.

"DON'T YOU BULL ME, SAVAGE I'LL COME ROUND THERE AND TEAR YOUR DAMN WEZAND OUT WITH MY BARE HANDS. STRANGLE YOU WITH IT AND THEN EAT IT WASHED DOWN WITH PORTWINE."

It flashed through Savage's mind that when Ma'am started threatening him in Elizabethan, he probably had overstepped the mark somewhere. He was hoping he would be told where? Nothing sprang immediately to mind.

"YOU CANNOT GO ROUND KNOCKING OUT POLICE OFFICERS, THEY ARE AS USEFUL AS TITS ON A TOAD, BUT THEY DO REPRESENT THE DAMN LAW THAT YOU WORK AROUND"

"MA'AM." *Ah, that was where.*

"AND I HOPE THAT DAMN LITTLE FERRET GUN CAN HEAR ME"

Gun was doing his best not to hear but struggling. Ma'am was off on one at both four hundred decibels and miles per hour.

"BECAUSE YOU ARE SUPPOSED TO WORK AROUND THE DAMN LAW, NOT KICK IT TO BITS WITH YOUR DAMN SIZE TWELVES."

"SORRY MA'AM"

"AND DON'T YOU DAMN SORRY ME SAVAGE, YOU APE. YOU HAVE TO BE SELF AWARE TO BE SORRY."

"MA'AM."

"NOW, WHATEVER YOU ARE DOING FORGET IT UNTIL THE MORNING. THERE'S A REPORT THAT THE BRIDGE NEXT TO SIX IS UNDER THREAT FROM THE RADICAL AUTOMOBILE COLLECTIVE. THE TOAD TITS ARE GOING TO BE ALL OVER THE BRIDGE BUT I WANT MID AGENTS CLOSE BY. DAMN GOVERNMENT

SPOOKS DONT HAVE THE MANPOWER AND HAVE REQUESTED EXTRA CONTRACT RESOURCE. CAN YOU DO THAT WITHOUT HITTING ANYONE?"

"YES MA'AM."

"GOOD AND IF YOU DO NEED TO HIT ANYONE, HIT THAT WEASEL GUN."

"AFFIRMATIVE MA'AM"

"AND DON'T USE BIG WORDS SAVAGE, IT DOESN'T SUIT YOU" and she hung up so heavily that she broke her telephone in the process, but Savage did not know that. He just heard the line go dead and felt able to breathe again. He said nothing, he just shrugged at Gun, who picked up the keys to the Range Rover and they headed across the river, to try and be discrete.

*

Jude and Martine were sloping down the road, shoulders down, contemplating the future and how short it may be. Best case, they were arrested. They didn't feel they had done much wrong on a moral level but knew they had committed crimes against the state. Jude had broken the Official Secrets Act. They had prevented the law, presumably the law, though Gun and Savage seemed to respect and follow the law rather less that the Radical Automobile Collective. The worst case was unthinkable. In their minds, the safest possibility was a highly publicised arrest and at least trust the legal system. But before that, they were going on a date. Well, they were having a drink. Jude was trying to remember what he said. He was hoping he had asked Martine out, though it would be the worst date ever. Apart from Gun and Savage potentially around the next corner, the full weight of the law, their parents, who currently had no idea what was happening and both of them jobless, they were being chaperoned by three mad, arguing hobos and a loved-up couple of fruitcakes. Worst date ever, but it was a date, or was it? Did he actually ask her out? Were they going out? they had almost kissed once, maybe twice, but there had been distractions. It was lack of opportunity not a lack of commitment. *And...and... she had called him her boyfriend, Maryam thought she was his girlfriend, Maryam the perfect judge. Oh god what is going on?* he thought.

Martine was thinking along similar lines. She didn't say anything but she grabbed his arm and pulled him closer, she held onto him for security and reassurance, not affection. "Did you ask me out?" She blurted out without thinking.

"Yes" Jude replied, also without thinking. "Sorry." He looked behind him at the crowd of chaos following them.

"Good" Martine tightened her grip on Judes arm. "It will be fine, it has to be" and they kept walking.

"Are we there yet?" Brother Simon, like the others, had followed Jude and Martine, without really thinking. Thinking had turned out to be a mistake, not thinking had to be a better approach now, by default.

"Almost." Martine responded, they were walking through St Andrews Park, keeping to the back streets and under the shadows of the trees. Martine knew of a nice backstreet pub, an old inn in New Minsterville, not so far from the Police

Headquarters at Peel Circus, which would make sense for a drink. A drink, just a few hours they had decided. They would have to look at a phone and would use Martine's as she was still the most likely unknown, of all of them.

"Who do we contact?" she had said, as much to herself as to anyone else.

"It has to be the Daily Heart Online" Jude replied, they are one of the only independents now. "That man, Onions, his name is all over it, he is always asking people to contact him if they have a story. He must have a contact number on there. It's got to be him." Jude didn't know that Onions was already on the story, with new executive editors. They would meet him at the police station and then face the music.

Martine saw the pub. "There it is, my dad told me about it, he was doing some work nearby, he said it was really quiet, quaint, very old you could lose yourself there.

"The Black Cap?" Jude saw the sign.

"My dad really liked it"

"What does your dad do?"

"University lecturer, he also writes and does bits of consultancy."

"Not a lawyer then... shame." Jude looked at the pub sign, with a picture of a bewigged old man with a black square of fabric on his head. It was dark, it was cold, he was being chased by mad people, surrounded and followed by mad people. He wanted to be generous and say eccentric people, but he looked at his and Martine's entourage and not for the first time did he question what he had been thinking of. He looked back at the sign, 'the black cap,' if anything could be more ominous at this point he didn't know what. "I just hope they have beer" he said.

"And gin" replied Martine.

"And lemonade" Brother Simon called out.

"Lemonade?"

"We stopped drinking and smoking and all earthy sins when we formed our order," added Brother Matthew.

"And washing?"

"Not sure they stood much chance of earthy sins." Jude replied to Martine's comment. She sniggered and pushed the door open, she and Jude shuffled through. They didn't see Bronwen and Ezzie, each with a pint glass of cloudy cider, sitting at the back of the pub and mostly obscured behind a wooden panel.

"Told you they'd be here." Bronwen beamed at the other half of her coven, "late though, typical Uncle Andrew, he always was over optimistic. You know he bet a week's salary on a horse with one eye? He reckoned it was an advantage because it wasn't distracted by what was happening on its left side and the odds paid better because it had a disability."

"And?" Ezzie asked.

"Ran into a fence, didn't take the left-hand bend wide enough."

"Oh, inconvenient. A week's salary, I didn't think Uncle Andrew worked?"

"That was the problem, it was someone else's salary, it all ended up very tricky."

"Life is Bron, life is. What are they doing now?"

Jude and Martine were at the bar, the Brothers were looking shifty, even by their own standards. Maryam and Christopher were just like star-crossed lovers, fulfilling a destiny of sorts perhaps.

Jude asked for a beer, the landlord, a typically landlordy person, eyed him up suspiciously. "You all right son? You look guilty of something."

Martine interrupted, worried that Jude would say something regrettable, "he has just found out his dog's ill." She said, thinking on the spot.

"Huh, he looks like he made it ill" the Landlord replied, demonstrating exactly the sort of customer service skills that could deconstruct an entire industry. "What about... them?"

"They are only drinking lemonade."

"Cola."

"Orange juice."

"Not sure he is tall enough." Pointing at anointed-by-witches, who bristled at the indignity, pulled himself up to a full five foot five and a half inches and decided to say nothing.

"Jude grabbed his wallet, A pint of erm?" he looked at the pumps.

"Only got one on. Undertaker, 6.2%"

"Undertaker, ok. Gin and tonic, orange, lemonade, cola and..." He looked at Christopher and Maryam.

"Water" they both said in synchronisation, neither taking their eyes of the other.

"Water? What, there are seven of you and only two drinks, hardly worth me opening. Not like the old days."

Jude felt awkward, "We'll have a bottle of mineral water please." He added to try and soften the shock of people going into a pub and actually drinking something they wanted and as though cola, lemonade and orange were not drinks. He looked at his wallet, he had enough in there, but not much.

"I'll pay Jude, you have been so kind." Maryam produced a fifty-pound note and Jude almost choked when he saw it.

"Ok." he looked shiftily at Martine.

She shrugged her shoulders "You sure know how to treat a girl Double O Dustbin... thank you Maryam."

"I would have paid" Jude protested. Martine winked at him. "You are teasing me again, aren't you?"

"Yup!" and she leant forward just a little, towards him near to his face, he responded and then, "ow" she jerked back suddenly. Brother Simon had trod on her foot. *Worst date ever.*

"Oh, just getting my drink, your feet were there," he looked, up at her and grinned. He didn't look any more hygienic with a smile, perhaps even a little less so now she could see his teeth.

"I expect my feet underneath me, I do not expect you underneath me, move. Now."

"Do you want to take your people over to that corner, I'll get Maggie to bring over the remaining drinks. Just, can you go now?" The landlord, like Jude and Martine seemed to want the Warriors of the Sleeping Sword, anywhere but at his bar. Martine was sympathetic, they were here so the warriors were not in her Aunt's flat.

Jude and Martine coerced everyone into a wooden booth in the corner and that was where Jude first, properly looked at the remarkable old building. Superficially it was just an old pub, the sort of pub that you remember from a brief visit but never see again. It was how you imagine all old pubs, but they rarely were like this. The wood, there was a lot of it, was ancient. It had the scars of worm, of fire, of hacking swords and chips that looked like bits had been shot off it. Wood was everywhere except on the heavy stone floor. The walls were wooden panels, the ceiling was beams, the whole was supported on wooden pillars and braced with angled joists. It was carved up into nooks and crannies, small wooden booths separated by wooden rails and lit by light that could have been candles but wasn't. Everything was pegged. On the roasted coffee colour of the old oak, there were horse brasses, swords, old paintings of people long dead and in one of them, dead and on a dissection slab in a Victorian theatre. There was a wooden police truncheon and clanking old cuffs. Stuffed animal heads gazed down on the pub guests and on one wall a thick heavy piece of old rope, tied into a noose and nailed to one of the old beams. Not hanging but pinned through its entire length to the old wood. There was a tattered old paper label tied to it by yellowing string and though Jude couldn't read it, he had a suspicion it documented a previous patron of the rope. He shivered as they walked to the table. The table had a deep cut carving of a cross in it, and approaching, Jude thought was inverted. As he squeezed round to the wall side he thought again and it was a cross facing the seat, though he also reflected that inversion was only a matter of positioning, of perspective. He sat down. Martine sat to his left, Maryam to his right then Christopher and the boys squeezed in around on the other side. Jude had his beer, Martine had her gin but everyone else was waiting expectantly. Christopher and Maryam sat quietly in the middle, the suitcase was now between them on the floor. After a short wait, a youngish woman, early twenties, wearing black leggings and a top cut rather too low came over with a tray. Brother Matthews jaw dropped, Brother Garry crossed himself and Brother Simon smiled at her with his biggest witchfinder grin.

"Eww?" she said, squinting at Brother Simon and she put the tray she was carrying in front of Jude. He smiled awkwardly as if to say, they may be with me but they are nothing to do with me, I barely know them. But he didn't manage to convey the message because she said. "Lemonade, Orange Cola and a bottle of red, how many glasses do you want?" Jude looked at the tray and the bottle of red wine.

"We err, we didn't want wine, we wanted a bottle of water"

"You sure duck?" Maggie replied, "Dave said to grab a bottle off the top rack, its only wine that's racked, not water, you don't have to rack water you know."

"Well yeah I know that"

"Its only, sometimes people think they have ordered one thing and they have ordered something else, you know after they have been drinking." She said it accusingly.

"This is my first drink" Jude said, slightly annoyed that he was having to defend his sobriety.

"I brought some crisps as well, its Christmas week you know, happy Christmas" and she flounced off, determined that nobody wanted water.

The dark claret wine sat on the table in front of Jude. 'Rosso Toscana - Castillo di Sangue Santo', but it wasn't water and they wanted water not wine. Nobody took a drink and with the sombre mood, nobody wanted the crisps either.

"Well," Brother Garry, "not exactly a new Jerusalem yet is it? But I think we sorted out the dark Satanic Mill, those Sheep were possessed I reckon, definitely satanic."

"The route to heaven is paved by single steps" Brother Matthew added. "Unless you only have short legs." He looked in the obvious direction.

Christopher surprised everyone by speaking. "I have never had friends before, you are my friends, you are mine and

Maryam's friends, friendship is everything. It is the only thing we have to give, that costs nothing. Love. We can give it freely and it does not cost, and by giving love, we grow."

Brother Matthew smiled, a deep and contented smile. Brother Simon thought immediately of witches, Brother Garry, shifted in his seat awkwardly; Jude leant over to Martine and whispered, "where did that come from?!" and as she turned to look at him a voice interrupted.

"Hi, Bronwen and Ezzie, sorry, bad timing, came to say hello. Met your friends before. Red wine, not touched? Good job you don't want to get muddled up with all that symbolism and mixing it with beer, never good. Hello dear, you are pretty, gin, hmm, you should drink cider, much better for your complexion, not that you need to worry. Except those bruises, he did that? No wonder you are playing it shy, hold these dear and budge up, we need a seat." Martine took a velvet pouch off Bronwen, who used both hands and all of her body to bustle, fuss, squeeze and wedge herself into the seat next to her. Ezzie found it a little easier, for reasons no gentlemen would document. "Empty them out dear go on, that's right tip the bag up" and Martine did as she was told.

"Oh my god, are those bones?" Martine dropped the bag.

"It's ok dear, they are Uncle Andrew, he won't bite. Not anymore. Now, ooh that's interesting" She leant across, squeezing Martine back into the chair by some not insignificant witch bosom. Martine held her breath, in part because she was being crushed and couldn't breath, but mostly because the smell of patchouli was as equally overbearing and also in plural. Like bosom, twice as much but still described in the singular. Bronwen eyeballed Jude "You dear, need to pull your socks up, she won't wait for ever." He cringed. Bronwen was being helpful, just like Jude's mother would have been, whispering discretely at the top of her voice. He looked at Martine and grinned awkwardly. Martine was unable to respond because she was still holding her breath.

"Are you witches?" It was difficult not to jump to that conclusion, given the black frocks, hats with feathers, esoteric jewellery, beads, outlandish over confidence and a bag full of human bones.

"Yes dear, good guess."

"I don't believe in magic." Jude said. He didn't. There was no point dropping bones on him and life had been weird enough without witches.

"Nor us dear, we are mostly scientists. We study, we make predictions, it's all calculation and measurement."

"We sometimes nudge the particles" Ezzie added in, "just for a little balance."

"We do, yes, but we are a weak force, a little like gravity. And anyway, even at Cerne, those hadrons don't collide without being pointed in the right direction do they dear. No, so there you go, now stop interrupting there are things to say." She waved at Brother Simon, who gulped.

"Right, now, those two, Hansel and Gretel just there, it looks like they don't have a braincell between them, but they are in danger."

"Hansel and Gretel?" Martine was confused.

"You know the story, two innocent children in the woods, they come across a man in a suit, in a tower made of concrete and glass and he is eating all the animals and burning all the trees and he tries to tempt them with money but they chop him into six bits and feed him to the wolves and then blow up his tower. That Hansel and Gretel."

"They have probably heard the other version Bron, you know... that one"

"Oh, huh! Anyway the beautiful two, those loved up little birds, as I was saying they are in danger and they haven't got enough sense to do anything but sit there and be happy, they are special, you need to get them out of here, send them abroad where they will be safe."

"But. I am confused." Jude was scratching his head, he looked at his drink, it was almost gone and he really wanted another one. He glanced briefly at the wine.

"Don't drink it" Ezzie said. "You'll have a headache in the morning"

"I have got a headache now."

"Ok, you, little man, run and get a drink for captain not-a-clue here."

"Double O Dustbin" Martine volunteered and then looked in amazement as Maryam pulled out another fifty-pound note.

"Very good dear, yes. Now these two, get them away, send

them abroad. They would be happy living in a tree, it's in their nature, they are sweet like that, pretty as well aren't they?"

"Hadn't noticed" Jude lied, just a little too quickly to the mischievous witch.

"Why" Martine asked, "what's special about them? I mean they are a bit odd."

"Oh, they are children, innocents, they will be happy anywhere doing anything. They need nothing, enjoy everything and, well they see things you don't. They shouldn't be turned into money and that is what will happen. They need to be sent somewhere where they can just live and be themselves."

"Why are you helping them?" Martine was curious.

"Because its right, same as you" Bronwen replied, "Some people do right things, others,"

"Wrestle sheep?" Jude answered, despondently.

"Exactly" Bronwen added, she reached deeply into the handbag thrown over her shoulder and pulled out another fabric bag which she opened and got out a wallet, she opened that and took out a small plastic bag which she popped open and took out a small piece of paper, "here we are dear, a name, a pub, the captain of a boat. Find McIntire, you'll get those two to somewhere safe."

Jude looked at the torn off piece of paper 'McIntire, The Broken Arms.'

"What the hell, the Broken Arms, why is every pub called something weird?"

"Do I look like I do business at Witherspoons dear? No, you go and find a sailor at the local wine bar and see if they will smuggle Pinky and Perky to the back of beyond, all you will get is a white van and your plumbing sorted for cash. That's them. Now her." She pointed at Martine "Get on with it or she'll run off with one of those three," and she waved in the other direction. Martine and the three Brothers froze in various expressions of horror, embarrassment and awkwardness. No one saw in the low light.

Ezzie got up, she grabbed her friend's hand and hauled her out from behind the table, almost capsizing it in the process and spilling Jude's beer. As they toddled and waddled off and just before they lost sight of the table, Bronwen turned round put her arm on her hip, then on her shoulder and then pointed at brother Simon, whose eyes opened wide at the mystical gesture.

"Wasn't that the Macarena?" Ezzie asked when they got to the door.

"I think so dear, so long since I have danced that I can't remember, but did you see his face?" And both witches sniggered as they disappeared into the night.

The weight of responsibility was again on Jude. The idea of trudging across town to meet some sailor in a dodgy pub to smuggle Christopher and Maryam out of the country, seemed ridiculous. That he had been told by witches to do this just flew in the face of all common sense. His average and slightly lonely life had gone off on a trajectory that only a spinner of tall yarns might have predicted. But he was there in the middle of it, with real people. Really strange people, but living, breathing, speaking, not speaking sense, but at least mostly sentient people. The alternative and what seemed to be the most sensible option, was to stick to the plan. Approach the police, they upheld civilian law. The press was free and the people must see that Jude, Martine and Maryam had done nothing wrong. Or, if they did it was justifiable, because of the extraordinary situation they had been placed in by some shadow organisation of state sponsored out-sourced thugs. Christopher had been saved by the people. His life was testament to the good people can do. It was a long time ago, but eighteen years previously a campaign had saved him, had protected him and had allowed him to live. No, he had to do the sensible thing, he looked at Martine.

"This is us, not you Jude. We do this." Martine was nodding her head.

"But, you don't know what I am thinking" Jude's heart was racing.

"Yes I do, I can see it all over your face. Witches or Plan A? We both know that Plan A is the most sensible, anything else is madness. Is the world really so crazy that we have to take advice from witches? I am switching on my phone. We do this, yes?"

"Yes" It was all he wanted, Martine to agree, to do this together, to not be alone.

Chapter 19

Fall

Martine and Jude had been offline and off-grid or trying to be, for four days now. Martine wouldn't look at anything else, she didn't need distractions at this point. She thought it probable that MIDI5 could access their location from the phone, so she had to be as quick as possible. She wanted to find a number, switch off the phone, use a public phone and then put some distance between themselves and this location. The police could track them in the same way, but not until the press were with them, photographing them, making them too public to disappear. Martine didn't want the police yet.

'Dailyheartonline – the independent news channel' Buster Onions, slow signal. "Come on…quickly… quickly please?" The page loaded and was it was loaded, the headlines, **'ECO TERRORIST STEALS NATIONAL TREASURES, HARD EARNT TREASURE.'** There was a picture of Christopher, beret and parka, next to Maryam, smiling like a goddess. **'CUT-PRICE CHE GUEVARRA!'** An interview with Ian Piggot-Smith, **'BRITANNIA'S NEW SHEEP WRESTLING BILLIONAIRE SUPERSTAR.' 'BRIDGE BOMB SUSPECT SHUTS DOWN LONDINIUM.' 'KIDNAPPED CHRISTOPHER SUNDAY'S PLOT TO OVERTHROW GOVERNMENT'**, she scrolled. It was endless. It was all about Christopher and Maryam, **'MYSTERY GIRL STEALS HEART OF DARKNESS.'**

"What the hell?" She read the text, in the box below.

Interview with Ian Piggot-Smith, recovering bravely from his Grenvilles adventure. He told us,

"You probably can't blame the girl, too pretty to be a terrorist, but look at him, camouflage coat, black hat, paramilitary, he probably has a gun. He must have put the girl up to it, did you see his comments? he had the audacity to call me evil. I am offering a reward, one thousand pounds of my hard earnt money to anyone who can get my er... money back. That's not the act of an evil man is it?" Below that an advert with a beaming, red faced Piggot-Smith, still with a bruised face, advertising cashmere scarves. No photos of her or Jude, or the three Brothers, that was something. **'PIGGOT SMITH LOBBYING THE POLICE.'** "People are scared to go out of the house, we don't even know where he is from. Eighteen years ago, he could have dropped off a plane, you hear about that you know, they hide in the undercarriage. They, them, those... those people. I am contacting the Commissioner of police personally. If my recent success affords me anything, it's to be the voice of the people, good honest hard-working people, the people of Britannia. People who cannot cross the bridge. People who pay taxes, who buy health lottery tickets to benefit the country. Has he worked in eighteen years? Well, it didn't used to be like this, these people coming here sponging off the health service, using up our police force's valuable time. I shall be speaking to the Commissioner to make my thoughts known." And the public was fired up, barely a dissenting voice, they all sounded like Piggot-Smith in the comments. "Bring back hanging, soft on crime, It's the judges, the teachers, put him in a pen with Samson and

Delilah! Hahahahahaha" and on it went. The same people who a week ago were excited by the long-lost Christopher Sunday waking from his eighteen-year sleep, were now baying for his blood.

"Oh god Jude, read this, it's bad." Jude did.

"We need to tell Onions the truth Martine, we need him to know." Where's the number? 'GOT A STORY - CALL BUSTER DIRECT ON' and Jude memorised the number and went to the payphone in the doorway of the bar.

Onion's hotline number rang. *Landline? Unusual.* he answered, "Buster Onions, Daily Heart Online, yes?"

"Mr Onions, I'd rather not give my name yet. I am, I guess I am a whistle-blower, I... I... I am with Christopher Sunday, everything you have been told about him is wrong, its untrue. We, I want to tell you the truth, but... I... we are being chased. We haven't done anything, there is this secret agency... MIDI5."

Buster sweated when he heard that word, "and?"

"And we want to turn ourselves in to the police, to tell our story, we need photos, we need people to hear the truth so they know we haven't done anything, can you meet us?"

"Where?"

"Peel Circus, the police station, we are quite close."

"I'll be there, thank you." Buster hung up, he ran the telephone number through his internet reverse search, "the Black Cap pub, close" and sent a quick email. A reply came back almost immediately. In caps it read,

"WE ARE ON OUR WAY, PUBLISH WHAT YOU WANT. KEEP US OUT OF IT. NO PHOTOS." There was no thanks. Thanks was avoiding the sink. He didn't want to be back there.

Buster Onions thought his mystery caller had a good idea, particularly as he was also somewhat engaged in a transaction with MIDI5, who until this week, he had never heard of and now could not forget. It was a very good idea. Just like whistle-blowers, investigative journalists could not disappear if they were involved in the story so very publicly. He picked up the phone again, dialled a different number and spoke briefly to the voice at the other end.

*

The old man was wandering the streets, it was unusual for him to be out without his car and his driver. He had left the chess game abandoned. His head was hurting. It had been over a week since his last injection and the pain was coming back, the pressure was building and his anger with it. He had seen the report online, Christopher Sunday was nearby. He was in the city, he was walking the streets, he was with a girl... the White Queen, that was who he was with. She was dressed in white, he saw that on the reports. His head, the pain shearing through it, like a meat slicer in waves that made him nauseous. And angry. He needed Sunday, he needed the medicine, he leant against a wall. He was weak and when he thought, he thought pain. When he fought through that, he thought that he could find him. He must find him, he had his blood already in his veins, not literally, but there was a connection. He could find him, damnit he would smell him out. He was almost animal now, feral. He stopped and vomited, spat, wiped his mouth, winced in agony and kept going. Through the streets, through the dark, he didn't know where, but he sensed it. He knew he would find him. He'd get him. Goldman, they could complete the procedure quickly. He walked slower because of the pain, but he walked. The pain in his head fighting with his thoughts, confusing his intelligence which was now just playing second fiddle to what? To blood lust. He needed that blood.

*

There were police everywhere, on high alert because of the bridge, because of the terrorist, because of public demand. Jude, Martine and the outlaw group were in an alley, they watched a police car go past, Jude saw Christopher squeeze Maryam's hand and he visibly shook, just briefly at the sound of the sirens. They waited. Jude didn't know why it occurred to him, perhaps seeing Maryam with the case in one hand and Christopher in the other, sparked a latent thought. Maybe it was the news that he had read about Piggot-Smith. "Maryam, where did those fifty-pound notes come from?"

"Oh, dear Jude, look I have lots, they gave them to me, they took it off that horrible man who was fighting the sheep." She put the case on the floor and popped it open. Jude looked, he didn't take his eyes off it, he just reached out and pulled at Martine's arm, she looked, she couldn't take her eyes off it.

"Oh no," Jude said to everyone and no one, "Now it's even worse".

"Not necessarily" Martine said, "There is a thousand-pound reward for returning it."

"Nine hundred actually." he replied glumly.

"Eh?"

"We spent a hundred of it on drinks."

"Don't worry," said a slightly pompous Brother Matthew, "I kept hold of the change".

"Were you going to tell us?"

"I am doing God's work."

"Not very well. Why am I even arguing about this?" The Brothers had this effect on Jude and everyone except Christopher, who saw light around them. Everyone else just got dragged, kicking and screaming, into their black hole of chaos.

The sprawl and drama of the city on New Year's Eve was counter intuitively, an aid to anonymity. There were people on the streets and the outlaws did their best to avoid them, but apart from the police sirens, it wasn't difficult. Revellers were staggering around drunkenly in groups and expected to see other groups. The lynch mobs with their cameras looking for a video were travelling in packs looking for Christopher and Maryam, ignoring the potential danger that didn't exist. They were looking for a photograph that showed they were there, as it happened. As Christopher and Maryam were in a group of seven, everyone assumed they were a stray pack of party people, amateur journalists, rival thrill seekers and risking it all for the money shot. Because of the constant intimidation by police sirens, even the short walk to the police station was indirect. The group walked past a thousand windows and no one looked out. There were lights and sirens in the distance, the glow of flood lamps and streetlights, neon and headlamps, Christmas tree lights and blue flashes. It was the pulse of a city on the edge and yet, if you looked in on those thousand windows, people were glued to the windows on their laps and in the corners of their rooms, because that was where the action was. Not outside where it was *distant* and only a couple of streets away. The action was beamed in, from different angles and different streets and different perspectives, to be there and present on a thousand LCD screens, through those thousand windows.

A report was made, eighty-seven miles away in 'Little Litterler-on-the-Sea', where Marjory "I'd rather not give my last name, because you know... them" was being interviewed. Returning from the local shop with a bottle of sherry she told the nation how she was too frightened to even stand in her back garden because of what was going on. The nation sighed, in sympathy. Poor Marjory, luckily, she could console herself with cheap sherry and a warming sense of smug self-righteousness. In Londinium there were police cars going backwards and forwards, people shouting about terrorism blighting their lives. The anger was irrational, everyone was out on the streets to complain that they couldn't cross a bridge that barely anyone needed to cross on this cold and breezy winter night. It was also threatening to drizzle. Happy New Year. Almost.

*

The Commissioner of the police was pacing his office. He had three telephones and all of them were ringing. He had taken call after call and every call he took he could barely hear because of the ringing of the remaining two phones. The last one had been from the palace, even the monarch was ensuring their officers had made the palaces displeasure known. "One expects this sort of civil unrest to be dealt with, showing commitment and competence"

The Chancellor had been on the phone before that. "The police have the numbers, they have the powers and they have to use them. We cannot have our streets overrun by terrorists. Even people in Little Littler-on-the-Sea were scared to leave their home and no, this is not a political matter it is a criminal matter that the police needed to take some responsibility for." He passed on a comment from the currently holidaying Prime Minister who had been disturbed in a villa in Benidorm. He had been singing the Britannic National Anthem to the music of a famous Euro pop song, as a challenge by a Spanish industrialist. It was an important party that was being hosted for close friends and young women in bikinis, secretaries probably. It didn't seem necessary for the prime minister to ask. He had been interrupted in the middle of verse two and had shouted down the phone to the Chancellor "Why the hell are you calling me to sort out this tomfoolery, haven't I left you a Police Force to work with over there?"

"Tomfoolery," repeated the Chancellor to the Police Commissioner"

"Tomfoolery" The Commissioner had said out loud to himself when he put the phone down. And now they were all ringing again.

The last official report he had received had been that all roads in the area surrounding the bridge had been shut. There was still no intel on how the attack would unfold. Yes, it was credible Intel, it had been lifted from a subversive website. Six was on high alert, they had supplemented their already overstretched agents with MID contractors. *OH NO, not those thugs.* He had already dealt with two incidents in the last week where MID had overstepped their official brief. He didn't know what the brief was, but he was pretty sure it didn't involve breaking his officers' arms. Although, knowing the government's attitude to the police force, it might do. Streets were closed, roads were closed, officers were trying to keep people away from the scene. In other parts of town, the concentration of the police in the West, had allowed looting in the East, illegal raves in the North and nothing interesting at all in the South, which was at least a relief. Law and order was going to hell on a handcart and the phone. Phones! All ruddy three of them were still ringing. "eeny meany miney mo catch a rapist by the..." he picked phone number three for entirely random reasons.

"Commissioner speaking".

"Ah, Commissioner, it's Ian Piggot-Smith, spelt with an 'i' pronounced with a 'y', as in crime. You'll have heard about me I am sure, I have had some success recently, its elevated my status somewhat. I feel I represent the good people of this city and have the resources to do just that. I am sure you have. A plan?"

"Piggot... Smythe... yes...yes, I have read the papers" *It's the sheep wrestling lottery winner,* he thought, who he also held at least partially accountable, if not responsible for the mess at Grenvilles and his injured officers. He was four men down, due to their operational engagement with the MID team. He knew that Piggot-Smith-Smyth-Smith was barely responsible, but he had seen his stupid sweaty gloating face on the news almost every day in the last week and wanted to hit him. His temper was rising already, he could not believe this man had called, but the Commissioner was accountable to the people and even Piggot-Smith was a person.

"Well, I don't want to tell you how to do your job commissioner, but this terrorist. Who! I should add, we do not know where he came from. And, incidentally, this charlatan scrounger has, we suspect been asleep for eighteen years, planning this robbery."

"Robbery?"

"He has stolen a case of money, there is a reward, your 'people' have not taken the crime report seriously. Typical of the service since you took over. Feet on the ground you said and you have recruited children. Plastic policemen. They talk to people now, not arrest them, its political correctness gone mad, the people deserve more. I deserve more, criminals everywhere. Have you seen that man? with his beret his army coat, his wild eyes? The photos of him show what he is capable of. Robbery, theft, terrorism. He is probably armed you know and your force of amateurs will deal with that? Eh, will they? I am speaking to the Heart Online next and I'll give them a piece of my mind."

"Did you say armed?"

"Yes." screamed Pig down the phone. He had worked himself up into a beetroot faced frenzy now and believed it himself. The man, the illegal, the loafer the tramp the radical beret wearing terrorist must have been armed, he must have had a gun to go with the camouflage jacket. It all made sense. HE was Ian Piggot-Smith, billionaire, sheep wrestler, entrepreneur, how would a loser steal his money if he wasn't armed. "Guns, grenades have you seen him, he has probably got my money to further his terror plot." Piggot-Smith bawled down the line, he was foaming at the mouth now... "The good law-abiding people of this city deserve better," he shouted "what are you doing about it, what are you doing?" Piggot-Smith banged down the phone and immediately went viral again. Onions was next to him, recording every word. **'MAN OF THE PEOPLE REPRESENTS US ALL, A MESSAGE TO THE POLICE FROM BILLIONAIRE'** It was uploaded as quickly as it was said and there was a collective scream from the public. Guns, grenades, terrorism, enough money for a private army. RUN, grab your camera and RUN!!! To the action or from the action and if neither appealed, run around in circles creating even more confusion and drama.

As soon as the commissioner put the phone down, it started ringing again. He looked up. The Chief Constable had come into the office. "Hear all that Bob, guns and grenades and money to start a war, not looking good, what you going to do?" he asked, you want me to give the word to Viper team2, they are on stand-by, just need the order, Bob?"

The Commissioner barely had time to think. *Viper team2.* They did not report to the commissioner, they reported to the chief constable. Viper team scared the Commissioner.

"Good lads they are Bob, use 'em wisely," the Chief Constable had said. "Clean cut policing, zero re-offending, the prison service can't say that can they Bob?" But Bob didn't use them, he had to hand over operational control to the Chief Constable. The chief constable didn't really use them, he programmed them, set them loose, put them out on the streets. They were the next level up, the ultimate force from his private army. Stealthy, brutally efficient, deadly. The Prime Minister had handed control to the Chancellor who had reminded the Commissioner that this was a matter for the police, not politics. He had to hand over executive control to the Chief Constable. Situation command was anything but. It was chaos and handed over ultimately to a gunner, who was looking for the kill, because by that point it was who had the bigger gun, subtlety was history. It was always chaos, everyone expected it ran like a slick well managed plan, but you lived in the shadow of what could happen. Not what had happened when you could review your choices. You acted on the worst-case scenario and it was already pretty bad.

"Mobilise Viper team2 Chief Constable, you have command. Suspect is a clear and present danger to the public."

"Gloves off it is then Bob, I'll give the order."

Savage saw the Viper Team Helicopter as he was crossing town. He had crossed the bridge after an argument with the police. Gun had shown his credentials, Savage had threatened to throw the sergeant in charge over the side. Gun had apologised, there had been a series of phone calls, radio calls some awkward standoffs, waving fists and the honking of car horns. But, after five minutes and no physical injuries the barriers had been moved aside.

"MA'AM AIN'T GONNA LIKE IT, BUT WE CAN GUARD PROACTIVELY. THAT PRETTY NUT JOB'S WITH THE CRUSTY NUT JOB AND WE CAN GET EM ALL AT ONCE."

And then, as they had crossed and were leaving the bridge, heading along the road to where Onions had tipped them off the group were heading, Savage saw the Viper Helicopter. Spotting offensive vehicles was something of a day job for Gun and Savage and the Viper Team Heli was not so undercover. It wasn't marked but Savage spotted the model, the lack of marking, that fact that the midnight blue bird made barely any noise as it cut low level through the city skyline. You looked out for the things that didn't want to be seen or heard, when you worked for MID Enterprises and it was a vehicle that shared its identity openly, by its lack of markings. Savage did not like Viper Team, "THEY AIN'T RIGHT YOU KNOW GUN. NO SOULS. KILL SQUAD, DON'T CARE. DON'T FEEL, SEEN EM IN ACTION. SEEN WHO THEY PICK." Savage would never have been picked for Viper Team, he was a straight up one-man force multiplier, a door kicker. He would kick in a gate, a door, a room full of people and if needed he would kick down any dubious looking trees in the garden, but he didn't really like killing people and he didn't like the efficient emotionless killers of viper squad. "AIN'T POLICING GUN, AIN'T INVESTIGATING. ITS DELIVERING A SENTENCE, EXTRAJUDICIAL, NO TRIAL, DON'T LIKE IT. LEAST EVERYONE I GO

FOR'S GOT A FAIR FIGHTING CHANCE." He was kidding himself a little, but Savage sometimes didn't like his own job. He liked fairness generally, which mostly meant Savage verses three-plus offensive anyones or anythings. He'd squeeze the odd singleton journo if he had to, but he didn't like it as much as he pretended. He wondered how long he would do it. Not even Gun knew that Savage was looking forward to a day when it was all over. He wanted to buy a little cage fighting business by the sea. Fair fights, anyone in. Men, women, anyone self-identifying as either, neither or both. Savage didn't mind. Anything but sheep. Savage had a liberal view on fairness in a fight and that was you just strap down anything wobbly or dangly and the only categories you needed to get right were size/weight/muscle mass and motivation. That's all you needed for a fair fight and that's how all sport should be. He was intrigued to meet a woman in the same category as him, it would be a pretty niche category but ultimately all that mattered was that warrior spirit. Anyone could have that. Variety could only add to the fun. One day. But, Viper Team, no fairness there. He didn't like them at all. "WHEN YOU GOT RESOURCES LIKE THAT GUN, YOU GOTTA USE 'EM TO JUSTIFY 'EM. GOTTA HAVE KILLS OR THE MONEY GETS CUT." Gun shivered. Savage was mostly right. They were agents outside the law, for people outside the law. Just once in a while, they saw how the law was applied, they preferred the hinterlands of lawlessness. They were outnumbered and outgunned but they felt safer, because they were the apex predators; but only there, in the dirty unregulated world of deniable assets. Compared to the streamlined regulated efficiency of the law's assassination squad, they were fresh meat, like everyone else.

Chapter 20

Collision

Jude was contemplating their position in the alley, just a few streets away now. Buster Onions, police, probable arrest, but that was fine, because the law would deal with Jude and the rest of them fairly. MIDI5 were on the outside of the law, off-piste, Jude was ski-ing between the avalanche and the cliff edge, unaccountability. It would be difficult, but they would be all over the news, they couldn't disappear. They could return the money, that was a misunderstanding. They could return Christopher, he probably needed help, he had, after all, been in a coma. Maryam would at least be safer in police custody and the others... too many questions, the plan didn't have to fit every scenario, just keep them within the systems of the state and not between the cracks. Jude's head was like an unset jelly, it was all too much to contemplate. He just had to act or remain frozen.

Christopher was the first out of the alley, he didn't wait. He saw in the street, in the distance, a dark cloud, an absence of light that was coalescing from two directions. A smaller darkness coming down the street and in the centre of it a stooped, hunched man, half walking and half running, dragging tired feet through a cold dark city street in winter, shirt half untucked. He was old, Christopher could see that, in his eyes he could see something else, a lust a gluttonous greed for something, there was despair and anger, loss of pride in his broken appearance and a slowness and weakness in his gait, yet there was something envious deeper inside and a want, for…what? It was all there, in his face and the cloud around him. The old man caught sight of him, and he regained something, was it the energy of anger and adrenalin that launched him balefully across the road? "Sunday, Sunday, Christopher, Christopher you are mine now, it's meant to be"

At the same time there was a larger darkness, a cloud in the sky. Almost silent, no anger, just a cold operational efficiency. Outcome focussed, a single order to follow. Terminate the threat. The five members of Viper Team2 exited the helicopter on thin nylon ropes. Hovering thirty feet above the street, they spun down like dark spiders on webs, five lines from the humming and hovering craft. Wraiths, black combat fatigues, light body armour and a single cyclopean night-sight strapped to their helmets. Then the weaponry; knives, pistol, grenades, strapped to their bodies in elasticated webbing, tightly so the equipment made no noise and the guns and knives were blended in as part of their musculature. Already spreading into an attack position, a vee shape, arcs of fire covering each other and the street. Muscle memory and instinct from training now presiding over emotional judgment. Swarming in like bleach in a drain, cleansing, unjudgmentally scrubbing the bacteria from where it had lodged. It could have been described as elegant if it wasn't a smooth, murderous motion. And, murder was never elegant.

Savage and Gun had pulled into the street when they saw the five bodies dropping, "SCHTUKT" Savage swore "MUST'VE BEEN MONITORRING US YOU CAN'T TRUST ANYONE." They had kept back, they had a clear view, as did Jude and Martine, but it was safely distant. Maryam and the boys also held back in the alleyway and they saw it like a film playing out, a film that would have been entertaining, exciting, pure Hollywood, if it wasn't real, threatening, terrifying and had them at the centre of it. Christopher walked out of the alley, the old man saw him and lurched into a staggering run from the nearer end of the street. Five black shadows, human shapes almost, but enhanced by machinery, half machines, broke out from the shadow of the heli from the opposite end, spilling out from the dark as half beings in the vee formation, cruelly parodying their own call sign, Viper team, fangs bared, poison ready.

Viper one, "target sighted, viperteam, radios dark. Respond."

Viper team two to five, "roger, over." A flip of a switch ensured that any radio contact was now encrypted and restricted to the five-man viper team. No one else mattered now. There were just five vipers and a target. No one could veto their action, no one could second judge the tactical decisions they now made. Absolute authority and control had been handed over.

Viper one, "viper team, target? copy back"

Viper three, "target confirmed, clean shot, copy back?" Viper three had the shot, it was viper one's command decision now.

Viper one, "viper three, target two approaching, three o'clock, hold fire copy back"

Viper three, "hold three" the radio crackled.

The old man half ran, half staggered to Christopher, from the side, obscuring briefly the shot that viper three had lined up. Christopher, who perceived the threat, just opened his arms out. It was a naïve counter to the situation. Showing he was no threat.

A small crowd had gathered in the other end of the street, a camera was raised. Viper five broke out of formation, running submachine gun up, laser on, held up and out, targeting between the members of the crowd, assessing threats. "DOWN, DOWN, DOWN, ARMED OFFICER." He shouted as he ran across the street, leaving vipers one to four on the primary mission. The crowd panicked and dropped to the floor, 'ARMS OUT, LEGS OUT, DOWN... DOWN... DOWN... ARMED OFFICER." he saw the young man who had the phone out, took his left hand away from his weapon and grabbed a small yellow box from his belt. He kicked the phone from the young man's hand and keeping his gun on the group, put the box near the phone and flipped a switch. There was a loud buzzing noise and a small pop, the group looked up as viper five returned the yellow box to a magnetic clip on his belt, leaving the phone where it was, useless. Electronically wiped and non-functional.

"STAY DOWN." They didn't move. "Viper five, off cam. Viper team are back dark. Mission on, copy back."

"Copy Viper five, maintain perimeter." No one was likely to film what was happening now, everyone had seen what would happen. Viper five dropped into a braced crouched position, his gun searching between targets for threats.

There wasn't anyone or anything that could threaten the viper team nearby. Single optic, enhanced vision night-sight, making him a terrifying cyclopean monster in the dark.

Savage and Gun watched, they had seen events like this before. *Too often*, thought Savage. They kept their hands where they could be seen, they were too far back to be considered a threat to the viper team and their blue suits probably gave them away to that secret underworld of sub-law, but they didn't want to take any chances. There would always be witnesses, it was impossible for there not to be an audience in the city. As long as it wasn't filmed it was opaque enough for the salient facts to be shared, but the detail to be deniable.

It started to spit with rain. Even the weather wanted to wash away what was happening, into the river and out to sea where it could be forgotten about.

The old man made it to Christopher, whose arms were held out at his side, "Uncle Max, are you my Uncle Max?"

"I want your blood Christopher I need your blood," the man grabbed Christopher's green coat and pulled himself in to smell Christopher, animal instinct now taking over from any humanity he ever had. His brain was exploding and he needed to smell the blood beneath Christopher's skin for reassurance.

"Viper three, target lost, risk of collateral damage obscured by T2. T2 no perceived threat, retargetting."

Christopher said nothing. His hands were out, he moved them towards the old man's twitching head which was smelling him, licking the air around him and moving in and then out of Viper threes line of sight.

"Viper two: clear shot, confirmed, copy back."

"Viper one: Viper two, take shot."

Crack.. k.. the shot was off, faster than sound, ripping air as it spun towards Christopher's head, a slight echo returning from the walls around... It hit him in the forehead, in and out skimming off into the ground behind him, disappearing into the dirt of the city. It might be found but the reports would present the facts in line with the official story, that the public was under threat. The threat had been removed.

Martine opened her mouth but like Jude could say nothing, as they watched from the alley. Christopher's head jerked back and his body folded into the ground like a marionette, all its strings cut at once. He seemed to collapse as slowly, as his head had snapped back fast.

"JESUS" said Savage, "THEY COULD SEE HE WASN'T ARMED. HE WAS NO THREAT, THEY COULD HAVE PUNCHED HIM OUT, TASERED HIM, CHRIST HE COULD HAVE BEEN TALKED DOWN, I PROBABLY WOULDN'T HAVE TALKED, PROBABLY WOULD'A PUNCHED HIM."

"ahh but we are door kickers savage as you say door kickers they are killers we all do what we do we do not do anything else they do what they do" Gun replied quietly, but Savage wasn't listening. It was a simple philosophy, we all do what we do.

The Chairman took a moment, it didn't immediately register, he didn't know what had happened and he smelt it first, iron in the air, warm intoxicating... "NOOOO...NO...NO...NOOOOO..." he screamed and like the animal he had now become he threw himself onto Christopher's broken body, even as the echo was still bouncing back from the hard walls of the street.

Threat neutralised, Viper team broke into a sprint towards the old man who had collapsed onto the body, alternately squealing and shouting, licking the spilt blood from his face and trying to mop it up from the dirty ground with his hands. Trying to push the liquid back into Christopher's body while alternately licking it off his hands, in his madness and his pain.

"Viper one, "open channels, off dark, get the regulars in to clean up this mess. Viper two, three do something with... that..." even Viper one was lost for words "That ghoul, copy. Get that ghoul restrained." The Chairman was raging now, blood smeared over his face and Viper two and Viper three pulled him from the body of Christopher Sunday, dragged him fighting backwards and tried to hold him down, but he fought and he raged and he had a strength that was unbelievable. He was angry and frightened and greedy and pumped full of adrenalin and he fought with everything he had. It took the two viper team members to hold him down, to cuff his arms and legs and still he fought. They backed away to let him burn it off. They were an assault team, not a response team. The event was already written up, it didn't matter what happened to him. The regulars could clean this mess up. Viper Team's mission was complete.

"Viper one, air support, close in ready for ex-fill once handoff complete."

"GOD ALIVE" said Savage, the most unlikely of consciences, but before he could say another word everything was stopped. It was a scream of anger, rage, revenge, despair; of life lived and love lost, as Maryam White screamed and as she did, the lights flickered and a car alarm went off, an electricity cable running overhead made a sizzling sound and sparks arced off it. The rain, now heavier, snaked around Maryam as she shrieked and no one near her moved, because the sound was the music of terror and it poured out of her like a discordant orchestra, playing an agonising symphony describing the emptying of a pit of lost souls. Everyone froze, it was primeval. Nothing, nothing could escape that noise and there was no point trying. Only if you heard it, could you understand.

Viper one. "Viper four, respond, respond" But viper four could not hear because the radio network was out. All any of the viper team could hear through the comms link, was white noise, static crackling in their ears as Maryam White screamed a sound that caused everyone to hold their breath. It was the sound of a banshee, but it had not foretold coming death, it had responded to death and that somehow, made it more painful to listen to. The sound didn't just enter your body through your ears but through the ground, though your skin, you could feel it in the air and almost see it as it changed the atmosphere, just briefly, but perceptibly. Jude squeezed Martine's hand and she squeezed back, she was crying but it was the noise not what she had witnessed that had brought the tears to her eyes. They were both frozen to the spot. As the scream receded, it was replaced by a vacuum that felt to Jude and Martine like a door had suddenly been opened and as air rushed in to fill this new space, it hit them both like a punch in the chest and then the return of all normal sound brought the alarms; shouting, there were smaller screams from the crowd prone on the floor and footsteps, sirens in the distance and a humming of the viper copter monitoring from above. There were searchlights now panning left and right across the road, reflecting from the rain soaked darkness and making the evening a contemporary interpretation of Bosche's vison of hell, incarnated in the street of a large cosmopolitan city of humans. The viper team shouted "DOWN, DOWN EVERYBODY DOWN." to regain control and the only person who had managed not to be shocked by the punch to the chest was Savage who grabbed Gun by the arm and pulled him forward shouting, "IGNORE IT GUN, IT'S LIKE A FLASHBANG, YOU DONE THE TRAINING, FIGHT THROUGH IT KEEP MOVING IT WILL CLEAR," and he dragged his partner forward. "MISSION'S STILL ON GUN, WE STILL GRAB THE GIRL, THAT ALLEY, GET TO THE ALLEY."

"We need to go, I want to go, I need to protect them." The words surprised Martine. Maryam had spoken clearly, with clarity and urgency and had just caused an extreme weather condition in her agony. But them? Martine looked at the only them, there were. The slightly fidgety monastic order of tramps. The Brothers of the stupid sword, she needed to protect them?

"Them?" She pointed.

"Hi," said Brother Matthew.

"Difficult shot, quite impressive, doesn't make it right or fair but it was a good shot" Brother Matthew looked at Brother Garry with an expression that was slightly effete, but definitely disapproving.

"I am just commenting on the technical side, it's not good. If we were the Brothers of the Sleeping Gun, we could have evened the odds."

"Not if it was sleeping." Jude helpfully added, he needed the conversation to move on. Fast.

"Not them, my twins, my darling twins, my babies."

Jude looked at Martine, who opened her mouth and said nothing. Jude looked back at Maryam and said "Who...whaaa... what?"

"Well it wasn't me" Brother Simon helpfully commented.

"Shut up!" Both Martine and Jude snapped together at the little man, looked at each other, evaluated the situation and both said, again in synchronisation, "RUN."

As they broke out of the alley, the scene across the road was rapidly changing, not least of all because the slippery weasel and out and out ape shadows of the MIDI5 team were caught in the rain and the spotlights. They were splashing through puddles towards the group. Police cars had swerved into the scene with a crackling of tires on wet ground and there was a whole blaze of lights and a squall of sirens and shouting. An incident tent was already going up and the viper team made their exit allowing the uniformed police to pick up the pieces, the chaos. They would ensure that everyone was documented, in readiness for their witness statements to be taken, but their witness statements were already taken and no one had seen anything. Despite what they might protest and what the news may say, no one would listen anyway. There was no longer an independent press, just an online lynch mob, saying whatever they thought, which helped with the establishment code of silence. Nobody would ever believe the outlandish stories of state sponsored assassination teams. Cranks and crazies all, and how was Ian Piggot-Smith? and had he got his money back? The terrorist was killed. The bridge was intact and now it was only Ian's money that was missing. The conspiracy theorists would blame the police, the police were happy with that. It wasn't the crime they wanted kept out of the news, so it was a perfect distraction. Everyone would be talking about the conspiracy theory that nobody really believed, and the death squad would fade back into the night like the shadow wraiths that they were.

Savage had spotted them now, dragging a still dazed Gun he broke into a sprint, he had power and momentum but a gazelle, Savage was not.

Jude and Martine saw him heading their way, it was like being charged by a rhinoceros, they ran, they kept running it was all they seemed to be doing, running from one chaotic scene of madness to another. Through puddles, down the street, past the shouting and the sirens. Jude could see Martine in his periphery vision, she had Maryam to her right, who seemed to be flying not running, or was that just his imagination? Everything Maryam did, including screaming, didn't quite follow the normal laws of physics, but that was likely Jude's imagination, which at this point was overactive. Run run...run... Jude hoped the brothers grim and grimmer and grimy were behind him. He didn't know and if he was going to leave anything to slow Gun and Savage down, he was be happy if it was the chaotic Warriors of the Sleeping Sword. They turned the corner, at the lights, "Oh My God, yesss, it's one of the trucks, a rear loader, it will be empty... going from the depot to the east. In, get in the back, everyone in the back... it will be cleaned, mostly!" A dustbin truck, Christmas and New Year, double shifts, they started late at night. The truck would get them where they needed to be. Almost. Jude had a burst of energy, the truck was at the lights, if they could get there in time. "Martine, run... the truck, the back... run," and they ran. The lights changed, Jude saw the brake lights go off, heard the air brake release air and a slight movement... he clocked the indicator... "they're turning, turning... cut the corner," and he pulled, hauled Martine by the hand, urging her on, trusting the others would follow to get to the truck. It was turning, still slow, it paused briefly "run...run..." Martine chanced a glance over her shoulder, they were in the clear. Gun and Savage were not there yet, though they were fast approaching the turn of the street which would give them a view of the escape. But not yet. Gun was now back in action, he ran, long legged like a comic book character, but he kept up with Savages rampaging rhino.

Run, Jude Run... he was thinking it to motivate himself. A push, he got a hand on the metal of the truck and pulled hard on Martine's hand. She was there, he was there, they were still moving as the truck was on the corner, and they ran and jumped and scrambled and he and Martine fell into the back of the lorry. Martine landed on top of him, face to face and they shared a moment, just a split second, but that was all as she turned and he pulled himself up to see Maryam next, with the case of money and the three Brothers collapse into the back of the truck. They had made it just in time as it started to pick up speed. They felt a rumble and a bounce and they collapsed and held themselves flat on the metal base and only then did they breathe properly. Breathlessly, Martine managed to say,

"Blimey, you really are Double 0 Dustbin, how did you manage that?" and Jude laughed. Maryam, was silent and still and a tear slid from her left eye, but she said nothing and then, Brother Simon said,

"It smells a bit?" and everyone replied "so do you, shut up." so he did. They breathed and for a moment at least, despite sitting in a dirty metal box beneath a hydraulic crusher, bouncing through the bumpy streets of Londinium in the cold and the rain, they felt safe.

"WHERE THE HELL GUN" Savage had breached the corner, just as the dustbin lorry, had turned the next corner and had left Gun and Savage not knowing which direction to take. "DAMNIT GUN WHICH WAY" But Gun didn't have time to respond, because his phone rang. He answered..

"sir I mean ma am"

"GUN YOU DAMN LITTLE FREAK, I AM CALLING YOU BECAUSE THAT OAF SAVAGE DOESN'T UNDERSTAND ANYTHING BUT A HAMMER ON HIS HEAD. WHATEVER YOU ARE DOING NOW, YOU ARE REASSIGNED. WHERE ARE YOU?"

"outside six" Gun stretched the truth, he could still see Six across the river if he walked back two streets.

"WHAT ARE YOU DOING THERE YOU IDIOT, THE ACTION'S OVER THE RIVER. THAT BOY WHO WOKE FROM THE COMA. POLICE THINK HE'S THE TERRORIST, THEY HAVE SHOT HIM. THEY WILL TAKE HIS BODY TO PEREGRINE MATTHEWS, GET IT."

"ma am the body?"

"YES THE BODY, DON'T YOU LISTEN? GET A BAG, AND ICE, AS MUCH ICE AS YOU CAN. DON'T SEAL THE BAG. WE WANT THE BODY TAKEN TO GREENFIELD. SITE 2. THEY WILL EXPECT YOU THERE BY 0300. LET SAVAGE DEAL WITH THE DIPLOMACY AT THE HOSPITAL. JUST GET IT DONE."

Gun looked at Savage "the boy they shot they want his body on ice at greenfield." Savage shrugged. It had been an odd twenty-four hours, even by his standards. Bodysnatching was just par for the course, based on his experiences of the day.

"BETTA GET GOING THEN, SUPERMARKET TWO STREETS AWAY, WE CAN GRAB SOME ICE" he replied, and they turned to walk back to the car.

Reverend Rogers was at the hospital as duty Chaplain when Christopher's body arrived. It was only an hour later, a remarkably short time for an investigation into a shooting, but it was a Viper Team shooting, so it was processed at speed. Everyone knew that there would be no questions asked and no answers given. He had not realised that he had seen Christopher at the department store, that the chaos had followed his arrival, that the sequence of events started with a sheep and a metaphoric lamb. Now slaughtered. He prayed that Christopher would be taken to a better place.

Later that night, Christopher was taken on ice, by Gun and Savage, to Greenfield 2. MID Enterprise's bio-technology laboratory. Government Partners. Nobody knew which government departments did business there, policing, defense, healthcare or pharmaceuticals. Perhaps all of them, perhaps none. It was a dark site. Government funded, privately managed and even the government didn't know exactly what was done there. Plausible deniability, it's what the government wanted and had. The Prime Minister was in Benidorm, he was staggering back to his bedroom and had forgotten his shoes, he could plausibly deny everything tonight as he would have forgotten it all by the morning and he could start the day with a bad head and a clear conscience. The best condition to plausibly deny everything.

Another MIDI team collected the screaming, kicking, spitting Chairman from the police station later that night. Once his identity became known, events moved very fast. Number Five had taken the call, the police had no record of family, dependents or any next of kin. "He lives alone, we'll ensure he is taken to hospital, he'll get the treatment he needs, we will look after him, thank you officer, yes I will sign the forms." An ambulance arrived at the police station at the same time Savage was staring down a doctor at the hospital. The Chairman was sedated, bound, loaded onto a medical trolley and taken with great care from the police station. He arrived by private ambulance at Greenfield 2, where he would remain sedated until such time as he left his sins behind.

Now that changes things, thought Number Five and he called the number for Niklaus Kloeven-Hoef.

Chapter 21

Nailed

The truck sped up and slowed down, bouncing everyone uncomfortably against the cold metal. Its suspension had been designed for moving slowly around the streets and its daily trip across the city from the depot was never going to be smooth. In truth the driver Ned quite liked the late-night drive, pushing it just a little bit harder than it should driven. Neither was it designed to carry people, it turned, throwing the runaways around in the steel container beneath the hydraulic compressor, which still looked less intimidating than Mr Savage. Everyone was filthy and tired. Everyone but Maryam White who had developed a strange aura of serenity. In the twenty-four hours where she had fallen in love and seen love lost, not just emotionally but physically. Love spilt in pints across a wet street on a cold violent night in a large and ambivalent city. Where she should have been shocked, or upset or angry as everyone else was, she was apparently at peace. It was impossible to say why, but there was a calmness in her demeanour that was tangible. She had a quietness and self-assuredness at odds even with her usual transcendent otherworldliness. The Brothers were also at odds with their normal state of chaos, they now had to digest the fact that Britannia, may not become the home of a new Jerusalem. They were now outlaws, revolutionaries, potentially criminals and about as saintly to the general public as Rasputin was to everyone but Alix of Hesse. They were also visible, they had never been before. Now, in the hunt for a new Jerusalem they have left the anonymity of their old Jerusalem, Jerusalem House. Jude and Martine had apparently left their predictably dull lives (car crashes aside) and were on the run from an agency that worked, apparently for the state, but outside the law. Life was complex. They were all now following the advice of witches, looking for a sailor to smuggle their friends. No not even friends, but smuggle these people out of the country. It was beyond complex, it was a parallel universe running within their normal lives. One of many allegedly, but somehow Maryam White had pulled them through it, like the opposite of the existential darkness of a black hole, the styxian torrent between worlds. Maryam White seemed to be a conduit, where the chaos of splitting light coalesced back into something clearer. Maybe. But they had all been dragged through the anomaly and were yet to reform as something shining. *Now* Jude thought, they were sore and bruised and smelled of old cabbage and that was when the breeze did them a favour. He grabbed Martine's hand, this had become an undiscussed instinct in the last few days. He opened his mouth to speak to her but did not get a chance.

"I know", Martine pre-empted his question. She looked at Maryam who even in a dustbin lorry surrounded by lunatics, looked like she was ready for a magazine shoot. "Maryam, you said you were having babies, er, should we tell the father?" She had spent just twenty-four hours with 'her love' and apart from messing up the electricity in the flat, there hadn't been an opportunity for any other sparks to fly, so to speak. Logically there was someone else.

"He has gone, he has been taken from us, but he has done what he needed to do. We need to go, leave this place protect my children."

BOOM… They hit a pothole in the road and the jarring sound resonated in the echo chamber of steel they were in, they were bounced six inches in the air before awkwardly hitting the base of the truck, as it re-levelled itself on the road surface. The case of money made a loud thump, reminding a neurotic Jude that he was also complicit in the theft of one million pounds, or nine hundred thousand nine hundred and whatever the hell it was. No, it was a million that had been stolen, it just would not be a million that was returned. Jude still assumed that honesty was the best policy, even in a hopelessly dishonest situation.

"Maryam, it's been… it's been traumatic, I think. Well, I think you may have been confused, Christopher. Well, you were not… er, how do I put this?" Martine started, she looked at Jude who was about to say something helpful, but when he saw her expression, he closed his mouth. BOOM… another pothole and as they all came down to land. Maryam's position had shifted slightly. She had turned and was looking at both Martine and Jude, which confused them when they discussed it later. They couldn't work out how she could look them both so deeply in the eyes at the same time. "I have twins, Christopher's twins but he is gone and I have to go too, for them, they are in danger here."

Martine and Jude looked at each other. It appeared conclusive but made no sense. "B…but?" Jude looked back between Maryam and Martine. Martine shook her head. Maryam was like a marble statue, unmoveable. She was going. Jude leant over to Martine and whispered, "But how?" Martine shrugged, now wasn't the time and there was undoubtably something slightly strange with Maryam's biology. That was the given, if there wasn't, they may have been walking back from the cinema. Not, on a wild chase across town in a dustbin lorry with the nutjob and fruitcake gang... which was a little unfair, but currently life and circumstance seemed to be.

The lorry lurched to an abrupt stop and everyone slid into the back with a bump against the hard metal. Jude snuck forward and peaked his head above the rear and saw the old tower with its commanding view, as medieval guardian of the river entrance to the city and he thought of its opening into the water, the traitor's gate. He had broken the Official Secrets Act, was that treason? He didn't understand the technicalities, but probably. No time to think now though. "We are almost there, everyone out now."

Out of the truck in the dark, drizzling rain, Jude looked for a spot to regroup, he made a beeline for a bus shelter by a tree. It was around two o'clock in the morning and it was dark, very dark. There was no one around but it was an unsleeping city and the six of them would stand out to anyone who did see them. The Brothers of the Sleeping Sword had been very quiet, which was a relief, they were along for the ride. Jude wasn't quite sure what, why, where or anything about them. How had they ended up in his crisis? In fairness to Jude, the Brothers themselves had all the same questions. Their purpose, the mission, the shining light that had given them hope and purpose had gone. The green and pleasant land had never taken seed, it was a dark satanic blood spilled mess in the street. "Are you coming on holiday, away from here, to somewhere safe?" The question was to everyone.

"No" said Jude, he looked at Martine who nodded in agreement. "If we find the witches sailor, you must go, but we stay. I want my life back, or as much of it as I can salvage." He again looked at Martine who was nodding, tiredly. He smiled, she smiled back. Neither was happy but they wanted to reassure each other that they could salvage something, surely?

"Well." Brother Garry spoke, it broke the brothers unvowed silence and confused Brother Simon who replied. "No not really, I have got a stomach-ache"

"I bumped my head in the lorry." protested Brother Matthew, now the conversation was in freefall. But nobody cared.

"I wasn't asking, what I was going to say was that, well actually, this might be a sign a symbol, our calling, to protect the maiden?"

"Technically, she is not a maiden." Brother Matthew pointed out.

"Why?" asked Brother Simon.

"Because she has, well... she... er... it's complicated" Brother Mathew was now on dangerously awkward ground.

"I am not sure she has?" questioned Jude and immediately wondered how he had been dragged into this conversation. He shuffled his feet and blushed as Martine gave him a glaring look. "But, um... go on," he decided to back out of the conversation now, before he was in too deep.

"I always saw myself as more a chivalric knight" quoth, *Sir* Garry.

"Chivalric? But it's peeing down, it's not a chivalric night" Brother Simon added.

"Knight as in medieval-knight. Friar Tuck." Sir Garry retorted.

"I think you are mixing up your legends, Robin Hood and King Arthur" Martine pointed out, like Jude, wondering why on earth she could not help herself comment.

"It is not legend, its rhyming slang. We are, in *the East* now," Sir Garry quothed again, narrowing his eyes to a knowing look and turning his head slightly to one side and ginning. His knightly language had a little more scope than his parsimonious vow of monkish moral propriety and he managed to make the run down overbuilt post-industrial part of historic Londinium shine with the exotic majesty of the orient. For a split second…

"Um, quick question" Brother Simon interrupted quoth with counter quoth, "Knights and witches are sort of ok aren't they, I mean. Well, I was just thinking that..." Sir Simon felt that he had just had a career change, but that was ok. Warrior monks, guardian knights the only real difference was a little manoeuvring room in the witchy department. Brother Garry was thinking along similar lines, but more on the potential for a crusading holy war, than fraternising with eccentric women holding herbs and spouting strange words. Brother Matthew had a philosophical crisis that lasted all of five seconds,

"You need me to look after you both." He said, which wasn't true, but neither were they monks, knights or even fully formed adults, so no-one was going to split hairs. "We follow the maiden, to lands afar, to new worlds, to spread the word, to protect the children." Said the noble Sir Matthew, quothing to anyone who would listen to his monumental new calling.

"My knight protectors, I feel safer already." Maryam White smiled, as the Brothers glowed with the sense of purpose that their new life mission heralded. Maryam believed it as well, which made everything sixty-six percent better.

But you believe whichever statistic you liked and Jude and Martine had used and been measured by them. Jude looked at Martine, who just shrugged as she said, "I don't even know where they came from, any of them… I mean what planet have we crash landed on?" Jude was thinking about the jettisoning of sixty-six percent of his headache. They just needed a sailor, to get this lot out to sea and over the horizon damn fast. As far as he could make out, they were four hours late for the boat. The starting point was the pub. Open or closed they needed to find 'The Broken Arms.'

On the Isle, outside the Broken Arms, Macintire checked her watch again. "Och, damn witches and their plans, thee never run to time." Macintire was born on the sabbath fifty-three years previously and as a child was bonny and blithe and good and gay. Years on the sea and under the sun, face full of salty air and far too much brandy, had given her a ruddiness that matched her wiriness. It also gave her demeanour a wryness that matched her canniness and dealing her whole adult and most of her adolescent life with sailors, dockers, dealers and dubious men of all descriptions, had given her a right hook that matched her left parry. All in all, it made for a cantankerous but capable captain of a forty-seven year old trawler. The boat had been converted for light freight, passenger charter and occasional smuggling between Northern Europe and the Mediterranean, which she knew like every 'ruddy crag' on her brow. The trawler could still catch the odd fish, but from a rod for Macintire's dinner. Macintire as an adult was still categorically born on the sabbath but was now grumpy and blithe and bad and gay. Some things were now just a little more cemented in her personality, by a life most interestingly lived. She was wearing a thick heavy woollen fireman's coat with dulled brass buttons, secured with a thick leather belt and a black sow-wester. She had a red woollen scarf thrown surprisingly jauntily over her bony shoulders and with her brown sailing boots, a cranky attitude and a sheathed heavy divers-knife stuffed in her belt she looked like a pirate, which is what most people who knew her suspected anyway but were too afraid to ask. "A'hm leaving at eight, wi' or wir'oot ye" she said out loud and turned to walk back to the dock, where her unnamed boat was moored. "I dinnae give it a name, so Davy Jones does'na reet it in his wee boook, what's he going to reet? Blue booot!" she'd tell anyone that asked. It disadvantaged more than just Davy Jones's record keeping and that also suited Macintire just fine.

"How the hell are we going to find this pub?" Jude was panicking a little, already four hours late, it was likely that there was no longer a boat.

"I could switch my phone on again" Martine replied. It was a risk, a big risk, but perhaps at this point a risk worth taking.

"Yeah, do it, fingers crossed and do it quickly, we haven't any choice." Martine pressed the power button and her phone flashed and bleeped into life. She couldn't help a brief look at the news, which was depressing; **'POLICE SAY THEY EXPECT A DE-ESCALATION BY MORNING.' 'SHOOTOUT IN THE CITY.' 'TERRORIST GETS SUMMARY JUSTICE.' 'BRITANNIC BULLDOG IAN PIGGOT-SMITH TELLS HOW HE CONVINCED THE POLICE TO ACT.' 'SEXY WITNESS IN WHITE DRESS SOUGHT BY POLICE.'** The police statement appeared to say that they had their only suspect. Maryam had apparently dropped off the radar except as a witness, the police would still be looking but not with guns. Martine hit the search engine, centring on their current location. "BROKEN ARMS" PUB... search...

"Got it Jude, we are really close, it's just around the corner, just off the docks. If Macintire is there, the boat must be too."

"Good, now switch it off, everyone, let's go."

The conversation mirrored Gun and Savage's, as the alarm went off in the Range Rover. Savage, who had nodded off after almost twenty-four hours of chasing around the city, kidnapping a dead body and dropping it off with a group of "WHITE COATED LUNATICS GUN, THEY OUGHT TO GET A PROPER JOB, NOT HIDE UNDERGROUND DOING WEIRD STUFF WITH DEAD BODIES AND CHEMICALS, AIN'T GOT NO MORE PERSONALITY THAN THE VIPER TEAM, THEY HAVEN'T," was jerked to consciousness by his partner. Gun had no need for sleep and was enjoying an hours peace and quiet after the action of yesterday.

"found them mr savage out east by the docks"

"WHAA?".

"maryam white drazkowski and the girl." That was the adrenalin shot Savage needed.

"GOOD, THEN STEP ON IT GUN, WE'LL 'AVE 'EM FOR BREAKFAST." and the wheels span, spitting gravel, as they accelerated away from the steel and concrete bunker village of the secret Greenfield site, for the three-hour journey back towards the metropolis. Back through the glare of the city lights, to the backstreets and brickwork of the old east and towards the docks.

"WHAT ARE THEY DOING DO YOU RECKON?" Savage was slowly putting two and two together, but he was helped by Gun, "they have a million pounds mr savage that would buy them a boat and a new life"

"WHAT I WAS THINKING." Savage stretched the truth a little, but he would have got there eventually. "HOW LONG GUN? SPEED UP, HOW LONG?"

"oh four hundred now mr savage should be there by seven."

The Pub was surprisingly unromantic. Jude had expected something old and wooden and, well he didn't know what, but he didn't expect a non-descript red brick Victorian building. It did have a frosted window and the sign was surprisingly, a picture of a broken china vase. It was an anti-climax, because he was also hoping that something would say, *'Macintire this way* --*>'* Nothing did. The building was standalone, detached, with a fenced yard to its left and an alley on its right. There were no lights on. There were some old beer barrels, a plastic dustbin full of glass bottles and a couple of styrofoam burger trays. There was some dried sick on the wall outside and some rubbish bags and boxes on the street waiting probably, for the lorry that provided the gang's escape vehicle. Jude looked over at the three *Knights* of the Sleeping Sword, who had developed more of a sense of swagger and braggadocio than their former monastic lives allowed and were fussing around an oblivious Maryam. She was still holding tightly to the case as her prized possession.

She's not that stupid thought Jude *she's sussed the money… but it has to go back.* He hoped.

"Jude, look" Martine was halfway down the alley, orange lit, by an old sodium streetlamp, that was so out of the way it had never been upgraded. If it went out, it would probably be off for ever. "It leads onto the docks." If the sailor wasn't at the pub, it made sense they would be with their boat and that probably wouldn't be sitting in a car park. Though with Jude's luck over the last few weeks, that was still a distinct possibility.

"Psst, all of you, this way." He followed Martine through the alley which did, as she'd spotted, open out into the dock area.

The pub did back almost onto the docks, beyond a warehouse behind it, they walked out onto the cobbled quay of one of the inland river docks. It was hardly a busy port, now mostly the warehouses had been converted into expensive flats. There were some house boats, a couple of riverboats a row of canal boats, homes and a single seagoing vessel. "I think that's it, that's the only boat it can be?" Martine pointed to a tatty blue trawler, rust washed and dripping down the side, its name and markings overpainted with a different colour blue.

"How do you know?" Jude asked.

"Can you imagine any of the other boats going out to sea? They are barges and houses. If it's moored near the pub, it has to be that one. And, it's got a light on deck."

"I guess" Jude replied, worried that it was too easy. Also worried generally, he couldn't actually imagine that boat out at sea. The bottom of the sea yes, but not out at sea. Jude shrugged and checking around, walked across the wide cobbled area towards the boat with no name.

Macintire saw them coming. She was used to watching out for strangers, she also had an inkling there was a human cargo that may just find her. The six shadows, with the lights of the quay behind them, were clearly neither police, money collectors, revenue men or harbour master. "Och, thee witches pick some funny friends thee do." But better safe than sorry, she took her knife out of its sheath and put it on a box near the side, close enough to grab it if necessary.

"Excuse me" Martine spoke. *'the wee lassie's polite a' least'* thought Macintire, no less suspicious. "We are looking for someone called Macintire?"

"Why Lassie?"

"We, we need help. We were sent by, well um, two ladies." Martine couldn't quite bring herself to say witches, it sounded like some ridiculous fantasy story, not real life.

"Och, dress in black do thee, wi beads and trinkets and silly bones in bags?" Macintire was warming to Martine, who was politer than anyone she had ever dealt with. Politer than anyone not disadvantaged by being in an armlock and advanced negotiations.

"Um, yes. You know the witches?"

"Ha, lassie, there you said it and you han'a turned into a tood. Well doon, aye they mad ol' bats."

Martine, breathed deeply. "Are you Macintire?"

"Aye, lassie, ah'm Macintire"

"But you are a woman?" Sir Garry couldn't help himself.

"Aye, what are you?" Macintire snapped back at him.

"I am on a quest" He answered, rather awkwardly.

"Well, laddie, assuming you could prove ye are a laddie! I am Sharon Macintire, Captain o' this boot, ye negotiations o' price ha jus taken a tumble eh?" She winked at Martine.

"Sharon?" Sir Simon said rather ignobly, "that's a funny name for a boatman"

"We'll ye didnae get a first in classics did ye?" The mini knight looked confused. "in fact, ah think ye got a second to last, at the University o' Life and hard knocks did ye not?"

"Second to last, why not last?" The shortest knight asked, missing the point completely.

"b'cus, ye rotton rudder o' a friend came last, didnae he?" and Macintire laughed a loud lingering cackling laugh, that resonated around the echoey dock, like electricity crackling through the air, leaving the knightly numbskull's wholly intellectually outmanoeuvred.

"Lassie, ye talk sense t'me, they two can jump in the sea. Tell me what ye want, come aboard. Wi ye wee good lookin' friend."

"Me" Sir Matthew smiled, his sweetest proudest good looking friend smile.

"No him, the other one that looks like he has a breen in hees head." Jude blushed, or perhaps it was just the cold as Captain Sharon Macintire's bony finger pointed at him.

Macintire picked up the knife and secured it back into the sheath on her belt, a move that Jude caught sight of and it made him nervous, though nothing he had done had not made him nervous in the last week. Now, he was just running on fumes… just running and running some more. He took Martine's hand which, like it had done a lot in the last few days, held back onto his instinctively and tightly and they walked to the side of the boat and a ladder, that they rather awkwardly had to jump on to climb.

"Reet youse two, dinnae start by telling me tales, I see ye are runnin' and I ah'm goon te judge ye on hard cash, not ye moral sensibilities. Ye may get the witches discount if ye story amuses me enough, I owe they mad 'ol birds a bit."

And somehow, Martine and Jude instantly trusted the bad tempered, rough around the edges, knife carrying, piratical Captain of a dubiously unnamed rust bucket. They spilled out everything. The whole of it, in a twenty-minute therapy session that left them exhausted, but also purged of the emotional baggage they had been carrying.

"Och aye, ne tha' is amusing enough for the witches discount, twenty-five thousand and I'll take ye friends away to safety"

"Twenty-five thousand pounds!" The bottom fell out of Jude's world. "Where will I get that?"

"fifteen" Maryam walked out of the shadow of the brothers. Svelte, like a sharp blade from an unexpected angle. She had the suitcase. "Cash."

"Whaa?" Jude didn't realise he could be bamboozled by life any further. Maryam was negotiating, he hadn't credited her with even understanding what was going on.

"Blimey, where did that come from," Martine was equally as surprised.

Macintire smiled, she looked at the girl on the dock, she had never seen anyone quite like it on land or at sea. "Aye, she's special alreet, ah'll give ye that," she said to Martine, out of the corner of her mouth.

"Ye've been sent to taunt me by the Gods havnae ye, eh? Twenty t.."

"Eighteen, take it or leave it" Maryam cut her off before she'd finished. Jude and Martine just looked at each other bewildered.

"Twenty", Macintire narrowed her eyes, waiting... pensively.

"Done, wonderful, help me aboard my dear protectors" and the old Maryam was back, where she had been was anyone's guess, but the planets were back out of line and the awkwardly shuffling Brothers all argued about helping her up the steps, while she jumped, case in hand and climbed the ladder on her own. She stepped on the boat and the deck light flickered and dulled. MacIntire looked at her. "Our deal, aye t'was good and fair lassie, wasnae it, we are good?"

"Maryam looked up at her, dark eyes looked deep into Macintire's twinkling blueys, under weathered scaly eye lids and brows, surprisingly plucked into an elegant arch yet narrowed and furrowed in suspicion. She looked through the eyes, deep into Macintires soul and she saw it all, darkness and light. But the light was lighter than the darkness was dark and she smiled at Macintire and simply replied "yes, thank you Captain," and as she smiled the icy moment melted and the light in the cabin brightened and Macintire thought she would check the wattage, because it damn well looked brighter than it did before and she didn't want to waste power on unnecessarily bright light bulbs.

And then Jude clicked, but the money… it's not hers, she can't, we've got to return it."

Macintire looked at him. "Nay, its hers alreet, ye seen thee news, was tha' lump Piggot that shootin his mooth of about her laddie stealing it. Its compensation fair enough. Wi'oot it she's na goon anywhere." Then to Martine, "Lassie, go to tha' cabin, I have some advice for you about MID enterprises, sticky buggers, they. I've had my run ins wi' them. Last one o' they who tried it on wi me got hees arm broken, but they got no influence outside this island. They work for the government and they selves, but neither speaks much t' the other nor the police. Off to my cabin, I have the starter of a plan for ye." A confused Martine wandered through to the cabin, to wait for Macintire. Once Martine was out of earshot Macintire leant close to Jude and whispered, "and you laddie, I dinnae wannae gi' you advice aboot girlies, but the lassie could do wi' a kiss and if you dinnae wannae do it, I'd offer. Pretty little thing she is, ye could do worse, pull ye damned socks up there." She winked at Jude, who felt that his mother had spies everywhere and in the most unlikely of places. He didn't feel like arguing about the money. Macintire was right, though he couldn't believe that anyone of authority would agree. It, along with everything else was giving him indigestion. He was sitting, pondering the meaning of life and how long it might realistically last, when Maryam White floated over.

"Thank you Jude the Bin Inspector" she said, sounding again like bells; it reminded Jude of how dumbstruck he was when he first met her and it brought him full circle to the moment his life changed for ever and the decisions he'd made since then. He wasn't sure that any of them were good decisions, but sometimes you did what was right, not good. Right and good were not mutually exclusive concepts.

"For what? I am not sure it's all worked out well" he replied.

"It has, it's all worked out. Not perfectly but life happens and you live it. You live with the consequences of the best decisions you can make at any one time and life is linear, that's the only way you can live it, imperfectly but well."

Jude was more than surprised with Maryam's response. He'd not heard Maryam speak so much as she had in the last thirty minutes. "But" he started to say, but he didn't finish, because Maryam White leant over and gave him a kiss on the cheek and it felt like an electric shock again, but not like before, it left him tingling and speechless. "Thank Jude's lovely girlfriend as well." said Maryam White. She took a step back and the world went a little misty. Jude's trance was broken by flapping and he was amazed to see a magpie crash land into Maryam shoulder, flap madly, scrabble desperately, its legs like a couple of hysterical stick insects before it managed to drag its self onto her shoulder. "Oh! hello Sorrow" she said, "are you coming?"

"Chukkachukkachuck" replied Sorrow.

"He's called Sorrow? after the rhyme, 'one for'…"

"No, replied Maryam, it's a joke, because he is always so happy. His real name is" and she made a "clackclack" noise from the back of her throat, smiled and turned away. "Bye bye kind and lovely Jude."

Jude watched her walk off towards the other end of the ship and he looked at his watch. Five o'clock, he was tired and cold. He put his hand on his cheek, it felt warm and still tingled a little bit.

"You ok?" Martine was back.

"Er yeah, fine; what have you been doing?"

"Writing my will, I have left you everything!"

"What?"

"I am joking, I'll tell you later, Macintire wants to catch the tide as soon as its high enough, she thinks they can leave at eight."

"Where are they going?"

"She wouldn't say, said we were safer not knowing, that they would be safe and away from here and they had enough money to be alright. She actually said alreeet." Martine laughed at her joke.

"What about us?"

"What about us?"

"I am tired."

"And me"

"Lets get some sleep, Macintire's boat is warm inside, I need to crash, there are a few hours before they leave."

"Yeah..."

Chapter 22

Revelations

Jude woke first, the engines were grinding and gurgling away like a phlegmy old man coughing his lungs up, as he woke and tried to motivate himself to move. The diesel engines spluttered and stalled, belted out an explosion of dirt black smoke then stopped, started, eventually caught, then shaking the whole boat and everyone in it to life, started running in a way that someone optimistic might describe as regular. Jude was slumped on a comfy chair, Martine next to him, her head on his shoulder. He looked at her for a second and nudged her, he was amazed she didn't wake with the boats noise and vibration. She must be tired, he still was. He looked at his watch, three hours sleep was better than nothing, it was almost eight o'clock.

"Och, peak a boo.. sleepy heed." Macintire squeezed past them both. "yon wee bunch a stupides are makin' the'sels useful. Scrubbing the decks, got they convinced they're crew not passengers" and she laughed her cackling laugh that provided a godawful accompaniment to the thumping, growling rhythm section of the engine. "No discount, but I may increase rations, especially for that wee little one, he may grow a bit." She bustled off, hitting pipes and kicking bits of the boat that looked functional and didn't look like they should be kicked, she was cursing her craft into life, whilst intermittently laughing at her own joke.

"We need to go" Jude said, "Martine, are you awake?"

"Yeah..." Martine was groggy but awake. "I'm good, let's go." They got up and walked towards the deck, the three Brothers bizarrely scrubbing the wooden walkways, fixed to the steel decks. The wood was not original, but the mahogany boards added a softer touch to the finish for passengers, than the steel of the deck. They also allowed Macintire to walk around comfortably barefoot on her deck. An eccentricity she enjoyed and allowed her a closer physical bond with her boat. She'd kick the damn thing with heavy boots to wake it up, but on a warm evening she'd walk barefoot around the deck, running her hands along the rolled steel of the side, touching the metal cables and occasional bits of wood, picking the odd fleck of flaking paint from the structure of the boat and making a mental note to touch it up. It reminded her that she was free and answerable to no one and nothing but the sky and the sea. She spent her life between the devil and the deep blue. One she feared and respected, but the other? She wasn't scared of gods and monsters, only the briny deep itself and the secrets in it. Secrets that would scare angels.

Jude helped Martine over the side of the deck, she climbed down the ladder, he followed her and they jumped one after the other to the cobbled dockside, which was still quiet. A couple of boats had lights on and there were some lights in the flats of the converted buildings, but they were the only people on the wharf. They watched as Macintire hauled in ropes, tying them off, it wasn't an end, far from it, but a moment of transition and it felt important.

"I saw Maryam briefly" said Martine, "she said the darkest thing, I am not sure I liked it."

"What did she say?"

"She said Sorrow liked you and would keep an eye on you. Just weird"

Jude laughed. She looked at him "Don't you think that's a weird thing to say?"

"Oh, it's a weird thing to say but its Maryam who said it. Sorrow is her Magpie and apparently, he is very happy. I spoke to her briefly yesterday, she thanked us"

"Oh," Martine commented, non-committal. She was still a little jealous of the mysterious, elegant, beautiful, out and out fruitcake, Maryam White. Even though any thought of her and Jude, was totally ridiculous. Then, "I am glad we helped, I hope we did, do you really think she is pregnant?"

"We did" Jude replied, "and yes. I don't know how, and I don't know why I am sure, but I think she is." He rubbed his cheek, which was no longer tingling and they watched the boat rock and push into the water as it drove its prop at full power kicking up white foam as it pulled itself out into the basin of the dock and towards the river gate.

"GOT EM, TWO OF EM ANYWAY, THERE GUN, THE BOAT, I'LL GRAB THE KIDS YOU GET THE BOAT." Gun had no idea how he would stop a boat, but he put his foot down, spinning the wheels in and down the Wharf, toward Jude and Martine, who heard the noise, spun around, saw the Range Rover with the dark windows heading towards them. Both of them had the same thought at the same time. *Here it ends.*

"SIDEWAYS GUN, BLOCK EM OFF, DON'T WANT ANYONE SEEING US EITHER." Gun spun the wheel, floored the accelerator and hit the electronic rear brake at the same time, swerving the large car into a sideways slide on the wet cobbles and bringing it onto the wharf with a shake and rock of the suspension. There was a gap at each side, but it only left a choice of rat runs, with Gun out of the door on the far side of them and heading between the bonnet and the nearby wall and Savage's bulky body, exploding out of the car door, blue suit stretching at the seams and still looking at risk of exposing far more of Mr Savage than anyone needed to see. Jude and Martine were cornered, the high wall to their left, the freezing cold water of the dock to their right, the Range Rover blocking their escape either to the alley that they had come in through and the main road, where the MID agents had driven in. Gun had a yellow pistol in one hand and unbelievably ran straight past them. Savage, realising that he had his prey cornered stopped running and smiled. "MORNING DRAZKOWSKI, GIRL." He still wasn't completely sure of Martine's name and he decided, gentleman that he was, rudeness was still politer than getting it wrong. Martine was slightly in front and Savage reached out a big hairy mitt towards her.

"Nooo," Jude shouted and charged forward, barrelling into Savage and having no effect whatsoever.

"BRAVE, DRAZKOWSKI", Savage was genuinely impressed at Jude's bravura. "BUT POINTLESS." He grabbed him by the scruff of the neck and almost lifted him off the ground. He grabbed Martine by the arm and pulled her in, she kicked out as hard as she could, catching Savage with a hard blow on the shin and having no effect whatsoever. "COUPLE OF LITTLE FIGHTERS YOU TO ARE." It was two kittens fighting a gorilla. Over in seconds. Jude just hung from Savage's grip, beaten. Martine tensed, waiting for what came next and it was the most surprising distraction. Gun had run in a chaotic long legged jangly sprint to the edge of the quay, where Macintire's boat was entering the lock to the river. Charged with stopping the boat, he did the only thing he could at that distance and shot off his taser, which spiralled out through the air, losing height over distance and falling pointlessly in the water. Sir Garry, the noble, who had heard the commotion on shore watched as Gun lifted and then pointed the yellow plastic gun at the ship and fired. He watched with interest as nothing happened, except Gun, hopping on the spot in frustrated anger. He glanced over to what he had seen earlier. An old brass very pistol, clipped to the back of the door of the cabin, which had been left open as Macintre negotiated with the gate keeper.

Hmmmm Sir Garry thought to himself. *Nobody shoots at me* and he grabbed the large bored gun and pointed it at Gun, whispered, "Make my day punk" and pulled the trigger, startling himself when the thing went off with a loud thump. Gun ducked, slipped and keeled headfirst into the freezing water and the flare (purchased in a box twelve years previously and dangerously out of date) chose its own random path across the quay in an irregular streak, past Savage's head and in through the open door of the Range Rover, embedding itself between the leather seats and plastic centre console. It exploded with a bright red flash that continued to burn at a temperature that immediately split the leather and started flames in the foam seat lining. The temperature of the burning flare was so hot that even the fire retardant foam burnt with the plastic and wooden panelling of the central box. The flare kept spitting fire, throwing out a vigorous red glow and lots of smoke.

"SHTUKT." Savage swore, conflicted on whether to drop his two prisoners to deal with the car which was slowly becoming a smoking bomb waiting to go off. It looked like it would soon match the long-departed Chariot of Fire.

On deck, Macintire watched with a wry smile. "Good shot laddie, I'd say take another, but yeed shoot yersel in the foot, and youse, " to Sir Simon, ye can stand back up now, thee dangers over"

"I am standing up" Sir Simon protested, to Macintire's cackling joy.

"Good luck youse two, remember what I said girlie, I've got ye letter safe" she said out loud. Knowing that all she could do now to help, was to fulfil the deal and get Maryam and the boys out to sea and gone. The outer gate was opening, and the blue unnamed boat was almost out onto the river and safe, or at least in the hands of the river and sea gods. Macintire thought that with Maryam on board, somehow; she would have those gods on side.

A bedraggled Gun crawled, dragged and hauled himself uncomfortably out of the cold water, dripping misery and curses. There was a piece of weed over his shoulder and he was already shivering when he saw what he had left on land while he was not enjoying his swim. The first thought that ran through his mind was self-preservation and the warmth the burning car would provide but his professionalism quick took over and he lolloped soggily over to his colleague and the two young prisoners.

"AINT GOT COLLARS GUN, GUNNA HAVE TO GO OLD SCHOOL ON EM." The collars, along with everything else, were in the back of the now furiously burning car. They were gone, it would have to be old school Savagery, which in credit to Savage, he wasn't looking forward to. He had rarely in his professional and unprofessional life been out manoeuvred in a fight and yet, the two twenty somethings, had beaten him fair and square with a household iron. Out run them twice, managed to dump Gun in the water, which while tactically inconvenient, amused Savage immensely, even if he couldn't let it show. Oh, and they wrecked the car. All hugely awkward and yet, Savage did appreciate spirit. But not as much as his salary, so he lifted Jude up, one handed by the scruff of his neck, carried him limply over to the car and held him face first close to the flames. Jude could feel the heat as the fire was spreading through the car, igniting the plastics and belching out dirty black smoke. "IT AINT HIT THE TANK YET, BUT ITS GETTING HOT AINT IT?" Savage sneered. "WHERE THEY GOING DRAZKOWSKI?"

"Don't know" Jude's initial reply was that of a surly teenager, at this point he could feel the heat but not the pain of the fire.

"We don't know, we really don't know." Martine protested from behind Savage, his grip increasing on her arm and causing her more discomfort than Jude was in.

"NOT GOOD ENOUGH." Savage leant forward, pushing Jude's face much closer to the fire and Jude really felt that. He could smell the toxic heavy sweet carbon smell of burning plastic, the gagging smell of burning leather and he imagined he could hear the bubbling oil from the cars parts rapidly being consumed by the flames as the fire crept towards an inevitable explosion.

"I don't know, I really don't know... I...I...I..."

"She wouldn't tell us where they were going, just away, away from here." Martine screamed. Savage was determined, he took a step forward and waved Jude's face close enough for him to feel the flames on his skin and the pain as the wispy unshaven hairs on his face sizzled in response to ignition.

"OWWW, SHUTKT NO. I DON'T KNOW, I DON'T KNOW" he screamed. Martine was angry, crying shouting and hitting Savage with her free arm, but not enough for him to notice.

A crowd was building on the far side of the Range Rover, well back, standing far enough away to take photos and film without getting burnt. No one thought to help with the fire, but they were at least recording the event though the smoke. Flames and the bulk of the vehicle prevented them from seeing the interrogation behind.

A horn sounded, Gun looked up, the sudden noise shook Savage out of his compulsive torture game. At the far side of the dock where the road joined the wharf, a gunmetal gray Daimler had swerved into the dock area, it slowed suddenly and honked as it avoided the building crowd. Or rather, it slowed enough for the crowd to avoid being carved into pieces by its aggressive driver. The audience of fools separated in a wave of panic as the car accelerated and spun, as Gun had done, sideways across the cobbles, providing a further barrier to the crowd getting closer, or seeing what was happening on the far side of the inferno.

"SHTUKT" said Savage, he recognised the vehicle.

"shtukt" acknowledged a dripping, shivering Gun, as he did too.

The door opened and a woman got out, dressed in an orange trouser suit, fox fur coat that she had won from a Siberian gangster in a poker game, oversized sunglasses and her red hair cropped short. She was chewing on a smoking

Cuban cigar the size of a courgette. She slammed the door shut behind her and walked in the gap between the flaming Range Rover and the wall, as though she was strolling through a perfumery, the fire seemed nervous of her and rolled itself back a little as she passed, or did it... who knows?

"YOU, YOU, THEM. NOW. FOLLOW ME." and she walked past both Savage and Gun, beyond the car, further down the wharf. Savage dragged his two prisoners with him as he and Gun did as they were told.

"THREE, TWO, ONE...AND..." WHOOF. BOOOM! On cue, the car erupted in a fireball, as the flames reached the tank. They all felt the heat of the expanding air and the stink of burning fuel as a flaming stream of burning petrol ran from the underside of the car and into the water. They were now far enough away to avoid any injury, but the scene and the smell and the flames and the isolation of their position felt to Jude like a vision of hell. Another one.

"PUT THEM DOWN NOW" snarled the woman, who hadn't even winced as the Range Rover exploded, almost at her command. She took the cigar briefly from her mouth and spat into the water. Savage dropped Jude and Martine and they flopped to the ground, finding each other and grabbing one another into a terrified hug. Martine's arm hurt where it had been gripped, Jude's face was dry, sore and red from exposure to the flames and his eyes stung. They watched as the woman pulled out her phone, clicked a button and shouted **"I NEED A CLEANER TEAM HERE NOW. GUN AND SAVAGE HAVE TOTALLED ANOTHER VEHICLE. SEND FOUR AGENTS AS WELL, GOVERMENT ID. I WANT THE CROWD HERE COOLED. FIFTEEN MINUTES? DAMN YOU. TEN."** She put the phone back in her handbag and looked first at Jude. **"RIGHT. DRAZKOWSKI SPEAK."** She pinned Jude to the floor with a look, whilst rolling the cigar from one side of her mouth to the other.

"I, er, um, sorry Miss, I mean Ms, Mrs.." he was lost, he looked at Savage surprisingly. Savage shrugged and mouthed, "MA'AM."

"Ma'am" Jude added, "I er... I haven't done anything wrong."

"OFFICIAL SECRETS ACT? THAT'S TREASON. YOU CAN GO AWAY FOREVER FOR THAT." She was toying with him, like a tigress, just playing with her prey, softening him up and tenderising the meat before the kill.

Martine was passing from fright to fight. "LEAVE HIM ALONE!" She shouted, which snapped Jude out of his paralysis.

"Smoking is bad for your health" he said lamely, not even knowing why he said it but just scrabbling for something obtuse to say to this terrifying woman. She looked back from Martine to Jude, always behind the sunglasses and took the cigar from her mouth. She blew on the end of it until it glowed, then looked back at Jude,

"ONE OF US HAS A RISK OF DEVELOPING A LIFESTYLE RELATED MEDICAL CONDITION DRAZKOWSKI. THE OTHER ONE OF US IS GOING TO STUB THIS CIGAR OUT IN YOUR EYE." Jude, considering discretion to be the better part of valour, kept his mouth shut, feeling perhaps she should have the last word.

"WHAT DO THEY KNOW SAVAGE, WHERES THE WHITE GIRL GOING."

"DUNNO MA'AM, ER INTEROGATION WAS UM...INTERUPTED, WOULD YOU LIKE ME TO FINISH"

"GOOD GOD SAVAGE, IF YOU FINISHED THE INTEROGATION WE WOULD BE INTERVIEWING AN OVERCOOKED STEAK NOW, SUBTLETY MAN, FOR GODS' SAKE." She reached into her handbag and pulled out a small tube pulled the top off, revealing a spray nozzle, she lifted it towards Jude's face. In terror he backed off crawling back into the wall, assuming that it was some sort of toxin, some torture spray. **"MEN HA, PULL YOURSELF TOGETHER DRAZKOWSKI. ITS JUST GOING TO MAKE YOU TELL ME THE TRUTH. IT WILL ONLY HURT IF I GET CROSS AND STUFF THE DAMN BOTTLE DOWN YOUR THROAT. WHICH IS POSSIBLE."** and before he had a chance to comment, she sprayed him full in the face. Nose and mouth, he didn't even have the chance to hold his breath, he just took in air, in shock and the chemical was drawn into his lungs. He looked stunned, he was. It tasted disgusting on his tongue and slightly stung his nose, he started to feel woozy and his eyes went in and out of focus. He lost sight of what he was looking at and his face broke into the strangest smile that Martine had ever seen. He looked like he had just had eight pints of beer and it happened in a split second. Ma'am took the cigar briefly out of her mouth and again spat into the water. Holding the cigar in her right hand, she looked at Jude. **"RIGHT BOY, QUESTIONS, DO YOU UNDERSTAND ME?"**

"Yes"

"WHATS YOUR NAME"

"Judek Draskowski Ma'am"

"GOOD, HOW DO YOU KNOW MARYAM WHITE?"

"I had to do a scrape of her rubbish Ma'am"

"AND?"

"I did a scrape of her rubbish Ma'am"

"SCRAPE?"

"I had to collect samples and send them off."

"WHY ARE YOU FRIENDS?"

"We are not friends Ma'am."

"BUT YOU TOLD HER THAT SAVAGE AND GUN WERE AFTER HER."

"It didn't seem fair, the paper said that they could impound her because she was different."

Ma'am glanced at Gun and Savage, who both gulped, it had been their carelessness that allowed Jude to see the collection form.

"WHERE HAS SHE GONE?"

"I don't know, with Macintire, away. Abroad. I don't know"

"MACINTIRE, SKINNY MIDDLE-AGED BAD-TEMPERED SAILOR MACINTIRE?"

"Yes Ma'am"

"DAMNIT, WHY DIDN'T ANYONE TELL ME SHE WAS BACK?"

"I didn't know you Ma'am." Jude responded as though it was a question to him.

"FOR CRYING OUT LOUD, IS THERE ANYTHING ELSE IMPORTANT YOU NEED TO TELL ME?"

"Yes Ma'am, I am in love with Martine, she is the most beautiful person I have ever met, I love her." Martine's jaw dropped, and she blushed, but the blood flow to her face came with a sudden rush of adrenalin, and the hairs went up on the back of her neck. She was going to fight now... "I love you too, silly." She thought she said in her head, but it was out loud.

"WHAT THE HELL. SAVAGE, HAVE YOU TURNED THIS DAMN ESCAPADE INTO A LOVE STORY?" Ma'am turned, baring her fangs to Martine, **"AND YOU, I KNOW ABOUT YOU AND YOUR FANCY AUNT AND RICH PARENTS"** and that was all that Martine needed to bring her into the fight, because there was no option for flight. Fight it was and all she had was her wits and a few scraps of knowledge that she had left Autonomous Accumulations with, but possibly they were enough. A tacit threat to her family, brought out the lioness. She stood at the covered eyes of the MIDI Exec, faces locked onto each other, studying every small movement. Martine was the lioness who had walked into the land of tigers, but she wasn't going to go down without a fight.

"You cannot do anything to me, or Jude. You have no jurisdiction" On paper, this was true, but MID Enterprises did a lot the government didn't want to know about, to get the things done, that the government needed. It was the outsourcing of embarrassing and dirty business.

"I THINK YOU WILL FIND THERE IS LITTLE WE DO NOT DO."

"But you don't want it found out about?"

"IF YOU DISAPPEAR, NO ONE WILL"

"Except the note that Macintire is getting to my Aunt's lawyers in Lutetia which says everything. Which tells them about the gen collecting, kidnapping, Greenfield, the Chairman drinking blood in the street, of MIDI5, of everything" Martine was burning brighter than the Range Rover now.

"MID ENTERPRISES ARE PART OF ONE OF THE BIGGEST ORGANISATIONS IN THIS COUNTRY, I THINK OUR LEGAL TEAMS CAN SUPPRESS THAT."

"You could if the lawyers were in Britannia, but you have no influence abroad. Autonomous Accumulations have given up any influence abroad, for absolute power in Britannia. You can't suppress the lawyers in Gaul. That is AA's weakness, they have no influence anywhere except Britannia. My Aunt is a global celebrity, she has a massive following and influence," Martine was gambling now on international celebrity. Hoping that Florentine Waverly, writer of the 'Montparnasse detective novels' would trump national intelligence agents.

"I HAVE READ HER BOOKS. I WOULD HAVE THOUGHT THERE WOULD HAVE BEEN MORE SEX AND VIOLENCE IN EIGHTEENTH CENTURY GAUL." Ma'am was smirking, but she was buying time because she was on the ropes.

"…and MID enterprises is owned one hundred percent by the Chairman, its run through AA, it pays AA for services as a supplier. It's not part of Autonomous Accumulations. If the Chairman is unfit or dies, it will be intestate he has no family. Which means that MID Enterprises goes to the government, which in the least will have to audit it but may then choose to break it up. I know the Chairman, I worked for him and I saw him scraping blood from the street after a murder, was that you too?"

"NO, THAT WAS THE POLICE" Ma'am spat out, she was caught out, she did not know about MIDs ownership, she bit her lip for showing that concession.

"AND YOU KNOW THAT BECAUSE?"

"I worked there, I have seen his files, he needed help with the paperwork, I have been through it all. Mid Enterprises is NOT an AA business, the Chairman is old, he was foaming at the mouth and screaming like a dog in the street. How long will he last? how long will it be before someone finds out and MID is investigated? If the Chairman dies and anyone finds out, MID dies with him." Martine could tell, just by the look on her foes face, that something clicked. There was a pause, the battle line had changed, it was looking suddenly like a demilitarised zone. Martine was panting now she was so angry. For a moment the pause lasted…

"YOU SNEAKY LITTLE BITCH" Ma'am laughed **"HAHAHA… I DON'T KNOW WHETHER TO STRANGLE YOU WITH MY BARE HANDS OR GIVE YOU A JOB."** Martine bristled, the red headed woman thought for a moment.

"CONGRATULATIONS. STALEMATE. I THINK YOU WILL STAY QUIET BECAUSE OF THE POTENTIAL ESCALATION OF HOSTILITIES. YOU ARE RIGHT, AA IS BRITANNIC, BUT DON'T FOR A MOMENT THINK I CAN'T GET BUSINESS DONE ABROAD. ONE WAY OR ANOTHER, PROBABLY ANOTHER. AND DON'T FORGET HOW MUCH OF YOUR LIFE AND

FAMILY ARE HERE." She looked dismissively at Jude, **"HE'LL STAY QUIET BECAUSE YOU WILL TELL HIM TO."** She turned, she looked at her agents, who shrunk, perceptibly and resembled just briefly a gross parody of a comical silent era double act. Then it was gone, they were back, Savage at least looked as dangerous as before.

"SAVAGE, GET OVER THERE AND HELP THE CLEANING TEAM. GUN?" She looked at the wet and shivering Gun, **"YOU CAN FREEZE TO DEATH YOU IDIOT, AND THAT'S AN ORDER."** She stormed off, passing the still blazing car, again ignoring the furnace and seemingly scaring the flames back, in her wake.

Martine went to Jude, who was still looking a little confused and leant towards him. He lifted himself a little leant into her and kissed her fully on the lips. She jumped back surprised, looked at him briefly then moved back and kissed him in return. Then they slumped again; tired, confused, relieved and silent, because there was nothing to do but watch MIDI5 clean up the mess that they had made; remove the blazing Range Rover, corral, interview and convince the gathering crowd that they had seen nothing at all. In less than an hour, it was over. They watched the vehicle get towed away, the crowd disperse and all that was left on the wharf was a large wet patch and a pile of sand, which may have smelt of burnt oil. There was only a slight reminder of where the car had been extinguished and spilt fuel mopped up. It really was over.

"What now Jude?"

Jude replied by putting his arm around her and he held her tightly. She did the same and together they cried, because that was what was needed, a good hug and an emotional release.

A thought flashed through Jude's head and he hated himself for it. In the end, what saved them? Wealthy and influential connections that he didn't even know he had. Life seemed imbalanced and very unfair, even if he had just won.

The date occurred to him next, "Happy New Year Martine," He hugged her just a little bit more tightly, just in case she might escape. She smiled back at him. It was at least, a new year.

*

The Board Meeting at Autonomous Accumulations had not gone exactly as planned. Number Five had by default, his own default, taken charge. No one had made him the Chairman's deputy but no one wanted to cross him.

He had introduced Niklaus Kloeven-Hoef to the other directors and taken Niklaus through their roles. "We have an effective directorate, he had explained again, that focusses on motivations. Number One is our Director of Corporate Promotions, Number Two our Director of Speculative Acquisitions. Three, Director of Social Exploitation. Four, Director of Excess Capitalisation & Liquidity. Number Six the Director of Oppositional Asset Assessment and Seven the Director of Leisure Investments. Of course, you know me, Number Five, Director of Aggressive Takeovers."

The banker had nodded at each, impassively and not saying a lot. He was sizing them up. Perhaps as an undertaker may mentally take note of everyone he meets, for coffin size. "Thank you, Number Five".

Five continued, "The Chair, well, we need to consider succession and I, we felt, given our broader plans and ambitions, a more public facing Chair may help promote the brand."

He was interrupted by Number One, "I'd been thinking about our rebranding exercise, especially with the plans for national takeover, I mean the merger of interests. Perhaps gentlemen, we could consider a slight change to the logo? The letters AA could stand out a little more on our logo, perhaps. If I could volunteer a suggestion, the black letters would be more front and forward on a white circle, it would help them, ah... project?"

"Indeed Number One, but we have another more pressing issue regarding the jewel in the crown. MID Enterprises, which also, I might remind you all, includes Greenfield..." There was murmuring in the room. "Before we can move to phase two, there is a small legal challenge to overcome. We need to purchase Mid Enterprises, from the Chairman before he... well as we know, he is, ahem... indisposed. Time is short."

Epilogue

Flat number 7 at Jerusalem house was very different to flat 13, as was its occupant. Once through the debris, the rubbish, the animal mess and cigarette ends of the corridors and walkways. The inside of flat 7, though small, was painted in shades of pastel pink and buttercup yellow. It had china ornaments on display, embroidered tapestries on the wall, flowers in a vase and there were puffed up cushions, prim little chairs with lace, a comfy sofa with cake crumbs on it and a very well used coffee table, that had never seen coffee but had seen plenty of tea and cakes. It was warm and cosy, maybe a little twee for some, but the only thing you could really criticise was that it smelt of cats. It would smell of cats. The little old lady who lived there had five of them and that was a lot of cats for a small flat.

The couple who owned the local shop knew her as Gloria. "Call me Gloria that's what my friends call me, my surname, oh, its Hibernian, you know." That's as far as they had ever got, nor had they ever seen any of her friends, but she was kind and sweet and spent a lot on tea and cakes and cat food, so they smiled, made small talk and didn't wonder too much more about her.

"I am an accountant" Gloria had once told them, "you know, charities, that sort of thing. I help out where I can." They didn't know and didn't get a chance to ask what sort of thing. Gloria grabbed her cakes, smiled sweetly and bustled off back to flat number 7 Jerusalem House.

Gloria looked at the chess set. She'd finished playing the game with herself, months and months ago. It had sat there ever since while she pondered the outcome. It had come close to stalemate but white had won, the queen was sacrificed but the game had been saved by knights and pawns. *Unusual outcome, what an odd game,* Gloria had thought and still did. *Games, oh, dear, oh dear I am forgetting the accounts* and she pottered over to her computer and switched it on. The light on the front flickered orange, then green and the disk on the old machine hummed loudly. The computer made far more beeps than it should as it powered up. Eventually she logged in and opened up her spreadsheets and the accounting program. She browsed the figures on the screen. "Hmm, Mysterio, what do you think?" The black cat purred. It had been fed, or it would have meowed. Mysterio only ever did one or the other, based only on whether he was hungry or not and he was hungry more often than not. "I think I should transfer the money over you know, its sat there long enough. I am now the only trustee and the money should end up where it belongs. When you donate, you can't demand a refund can you Mysterio?" She completed the transfer to her client account before weighing up the next dilemma. "Now flat 13 and New Road, what shall we do with them? Cleaner in downstairs for sure, especially after all this time but I think we should keep them on. We'll keep paying the bills Mysterio. No one leaves anywhere forever, do they?" She pressed a few more buttons, transferred some money between accounts and felt, quite rightly as it was now almost twelve o'clock, that it was time for a nice little cake.

*

Brother, Sir Matthew had gone out for a walk with a heavily pregnant Maryam. She had waved for some company and he had come running, "I really do not deserve you all," she told him and he beamed.

"Tis our noble sacrifice, to protect the maiden." He summoned the knightliest statement of affected gibberish, to the heavily pregnant *maiden*.

She stood on the stone embankment of Giudecca, looking out onto the hazy city of Venicia. The warm late summer sun was rising, illuminating the domes of the city with light and heat, the tourists would arrive and go and Maryam watched the city. The shallow sea of the lagoon slapped against the side of the embankment and she thought of her lost love, only briefly. He lived on, she knew that. One way or another, and another? Or perhaps all three ways. Venicia wasn't forever.

Sorrow was on her shoulder. "Chukkachukkachukka" The black and white bird squarked into her ear.

"I know," she replied wistfully, "one day."

Brothers Sir Simon and Garry were in their church. It wasn't quite yet as glorious as Brother Simon had imagined. It was a dirty room, hanging off the side of a canal which flooded twice a year and sometimes more, but they had not been there long enough to know that. The congregation was small. Antonio the gondolier and a little dark-skinned lady in rags who brought a dirty cardboard coffee cup in and sat in the corner cross legged and facing the floor. It was cooler than begging for money in the street, and she was given sandwiches and coffee by the boys.

"The problem is the name of our Church. That's why no one comes in to worship"

The GRANd ChuRch of St ChristoPHer the Messiah and The Bakewell Vomit of the LOrd'

It was carved beautifully, sort of. Occasionally capitalised in jagged spidery letters with only one spelling mistake and a slightly crooked cross on a piece of old driftwood. It was clear, the carved letters were emphasized with black paint. Except for the last two words where the paint had run out and the thumbprint which made the word mesiah (sic) a little indistinct. It was rustic and propped against the wooden door for passing pilgrims to see. The smallest of priestly, monkish, knightly, witch toys was confused by Sir Garry's comments. It was a fantastic name for a church, full of glory and majesty and it fully described his vision. They had 'relics' as well, two jars full of relics and that surely the cherry added gravitas. "What's wrong with it?"

"It should be written in Venetian, no one knows what it says."

Antonio, the gondolier, interrupted. Thankfully, for everyone. "My gondola has sunk again, I donna understand it boys, it keeps a happening?" The slightly overweight, balding Venetian with the prominent nose, looked at his friends. "They fixing it badly. But, I tella you, it isna naturale, damned water beasts eating a hole in my bottom." They must have been eating the end of his oar. The last three times he had holed his hull by steering into the same bent metal pole, in the water by 'Osteria Diavoli Polpo.' Too coincidental. Same pole, same time, just after closing. It must be a conspiracy.

But who knew what beasts really lay beneath? Mcintire had suspicions, but she was suspicious by nature and too suspicious to tell anyone. She was long gone. She had dropped off the refugees, pointed them at lodgings and told the boys that they "hadnae done a bad job, but it isnae good enou' fer ye wages." She had left on a high tide with four mysterious boxes, sealed very tightly in brown paper, black ribbon and shrink wrap. That was a long time ago, now.

On the other side of the canal, opposite the new chapel, there was a small pier with two ancient wooden poles that rocked in the slapping green water. The ancient heavy wooden door had a small brass plaque above a bell to the left side. It had a line drawing picture of a face in clouds, lightening radiating outwards. It was as you might see in the clouds of an ancient sea map. The back door of the club had no obvious name and it unknown to anyone uninvited to join, which was almost everybody. It was called 'Phobos.'

*

In Londinium, Jude and Martine were eating breakfast at Martine's flat when the letter box clapped and two envelopes landed on the floor. Martine went through to the hall and picked them up. She opened the first, it was addressed to her. "Oh my god Jude, I have got an interview!" She squealed excitedly.

"What?"

"An interview, at Salome Somniferum"

"Who?"

"Oh my god Jude, the designer, Salome Somniferum. She was looking for a… well the advert said, 'Business Manager and Dogsbody,' but I applied, I have an interview." Martine was over the moon. She remembered the other letter. "Oh, this one, it's for you." She handed it over. Surprised, Jude took the envelope, looked at it briefly and none the wiser, ripped it open.

"Weird. It's my driving license, I wondered what happened to that. How did they know to deliver it here?"

Finis

Quia Nunc.

About the author.

Anthony Brown (not the childrens author, who has an 'e') was born at the tail end of the summer of love, in 1967. He disliked school mostly, with a few exceptions. He did disappointingly in the majority of his exams which he is still rather proud of. After school he failed (with some style) in retail and then banking so went to art college. Here he succeeded a little bit and also met the most wonderful person in the world; Jo, wife and mother of his two children. All are the greatest achievements of his life to-date and unlikely to be eclipsed. Failing then to make a career in graphic design, he also luckily failed to be a singer in rock and roll band and along the way, failed to ride a horse. The necessary consequence of all this failure is a sensible job which he has done for rather a long time and not failed yet. And backache. If he was honest, he would say that all his great failures were the most fun, except retail and banking which is less fun than backache. This is his first book. It includes a pirate and some witches just in case it is his last. It may not be.

Printed in Great Britain
by Amazon